THE THIRTEENTH
APOSTLE

ALMA BOOKS LTD
London House
243–253 Lower Mortlake Road
Richmond
Surrey TW9 2LL
United Kingdom
www.almabooks.com

The Thirteenth Apostle first published in French as *Le secret du treizième apôtre* by
Albin Michel in 2006

First published in English by Alma Books Ltd by in 2007

Reprinted five times in 2007

This revised and expanded edition first published by Alma Books Ltd in 2008

Copyright © Michel Benoît, 2006

English translation © Andrew Brown, 2007

This book is supported by the French Ministry of Foreign Affairs, as part of the
Burgess Programme run by the Cultural Department of the French Embassy in London.

Liberté · Égalité · Fraternité
RÉPUBLIQUE FRANÇAISE

*Ouvrage publié avec le concours du Ministère français chargé de la culture –
Centre National du Livre*

Printed in Great Britain by Cox & Wyman Ltd, Reading, Berkshire

ISBN: 978-1-84688-062-9

THE THIRTEENTH APOSTLE

MICHEL BENOÎT

ALMA BOOKS

To David,
the son I would like to have had

Prologue

The narrow path, clinging to the steep mountainside, looked out over a valley. Down in the far distance, you could sense a rushing spring that collected the mountain rains. I had left my camper van at the end of the forest road – it couldn't go any further than that. In the Italy of tourists and everyday toil, the mountain range of the Abruzzi seemed as wild and deserted as in the earliest days of humankind.

As I emerged from a grove of pine trees, the bottom of the coomb came into view: a sharp slope rising to a fringe of trees that hid the incline facing the Adriatic. Birds of prey were soaring lazily above, and the solitude was absolute; I was tens of miles away from the busy roads filled with holidaymakers, none of whom would venture here.

It was then that I met him: he was dressed in a sort of smock, with a sickle in his hand, leaning over a clump of gentians. The white hair floating around his shoulders brought out his fragility. When he straightened up, I noticed an unkempt beard and two clear, almost aquatic eyes – the eyes of a child, as naive and tender as they were as piercing and alert. His gaze stripped me to my very soul.

"So here you are… I heard you arriving. Sounds carry a long way here, and nobody ever comes to this valley."

"You speak French?"

He straightened up, slipped the handle of his sickle into the belt around his smock and said, without offering me his hand:

"Father Nil. I am – or rather, was – a monk in a French abbey. That was before."

His smooth face was furrowed by a malicious smile. Without asking me who I was, or how I had managed to reach this remote spot, he added:

"You need a drink, it's a hot summer. Some herbal tea. I'll mix this gentian with mint and rosemary – it'll taste bitter but refreshing. Come along."

It was a command, but given in an almost affectionate tone of voice. I followed him. He was slender and erect, and his steps were light. At times the sunshine filtering through the spruce trees cast bright patterns on his gleaming silvery hair.

The path narrowed, then suddenly broadened out into a tiny terrace overlooking the sheer cliff. Barely emerging from the mountainside was a façade of dry stones, a low door and a window.

"You'll need to lower your head going in: this hermitage is a converted cave, as those in Qumran must have been."

Was I supposed to be familiar with Qumran? Father Nil asked no questions and gave no explanations. His mere presence created an order in things that was simple and obvious. The appearance of a goblin or a fairy at his side would have seemed perfectly natural to me.

I spent the whole day with him. When the sun reached its zenith, we sat on the parapet overlooking the abyss and shared a meal of bread, goat's cheese and exquisite sweet-smelling herbs. When the shadows on the opposite slope just started to fall on the hermitage, he said to me:

"I'll walk you back to the forest path. The water running in the stream there is pure, you can drink it."

Everything seemed pure after contact with him. I told him of my desire to camp for a few days in these mountains.

"You won't need to lock your vehicle," he said. "Nobody comes here, and the wild animals respect everything. Come along tomorrow morning, I'll have some fresh cheese."

I lost count of the time. The following day, his goats made their appearance on the terrace, and came to eat the crumbs from our hands.

"They were observing you yesterday, though you didn't see them. If they are prepared to show themselves in your presence, I can tell you my story. You will be the first to hear it."

And Father Nil told me his story. In this adventure, he was the main protagonist: yet he did not tell me about himself, but about a man whose traces in history he had uncovered – a Judaean of the first century. And behind that man, I perceived the luminous shadow of yet another man, of whom he spoke little, but who explained the clarity of his limpid gaze.

On the last day my whole world – that of a Westerner brought up in the Christian world – had been up-ended. I left just as the first stars were coming out. Father Nil remained on his natural terrace, a small shadow giving meaning to the whole valley. His goats came with me part of the way. But when I switched on my torch, they turned back.

Part One

1

The train plunged onwards into the November night. He glanced at his watch: as usual, the Rome "express" was two hours behind schedule on the Italian stretch. He sighed: they wouldn't be in Paris until nine in the evening...

He tried to settle down more comfortably, poking his index finger under his celluloid collar. Father Andrei was not used to this uncomfortable clerical garb, which he wore only on those rare occasions when he left the abbey. And these Italian carriages – they obviously dated back to Mussolini's days! The leather-imitation seats as hard as the benches in a monastery, the windows that could be pulled right down to the very low safety rail, the lack of air conditioning...

Anyway, there was only another hour to go. The lights of the station of Lamotte-Beuvron had just whisked by: it was always on the long straight stretches of the Sologne that the express reached its maximum speed.

Seeing the priest fidgeting, the thickset passenger sitting opposite him raised his brown eyes from his newspaper. The smile he gave Andrei did not light up the rest of his olive-complexioned face.

"He's just smiling with his lips," thought Andrei. "His eyes are as cold as pebbles on the banks of the Loire..."

The Rome express often carried clerical passengers; sometimes it resembled a branch of the Vatican. But in his compartment there was just himself and these two silent men: the other seats, although they had been reserved, had remained empty ever since their departure. He glanced at the second passenger wedged into the corner seat next to the corridor: a bit older, elegant, with hair as fair as a field of wheat. He seemed to be asleep – his eyes were closed – but every now and then the fingers of his right hand drummed on his knee as if playing the piano, while his left hand struck chords on his thigh. Since their departure, he and Andrei had exchanged nothing more than a few polite words in Italian, and Andrei had noticed his strong foreign accent without being able to place it. Somewhere in Eastern Europe? He had a boyish face, in spite of the scar that stretched from his left ear and vanished into the gold of his hair.

This habit of Andrei's, observing every little detail... He had doubtless picked it up from spending his whole life poring over the most obscure manuscripts.

He leant his head against the window and gazed out absent-mindedly at the road that ran parallel to the railway.

Two months had already elapsed since he should have sent to Rome a translation and analysis of the Coptic manuscript of Nag Hammadi. He had quickly completed the translation – but as for the analysis that was supposed to accompany it... he had been unable to write it. It was impossible to *say everything*, especially in writing.

Too dangerous.

So they had summoned him to Rome. In the offices of the Congregation for the Doctrine of the Faith – or the Inquisition, as it was known in former days – he had not been able to evade the questions of his interrogators. He would have preferred not to talk of his hypotheses, and take refuge instead in the technical problems of translation. But the Cardinal, and in particular the formidable *minutante*, had forced him into a corner and compelled him to say more than he wanted to. Then they had cross-questioned him about the stone slab of Germigny – that's when their faces had become even more unfriendly.

After that uncomfortable experience, he had gone to the book stacks of the Vatican Library. It was there that the painful history of his family had brutally caught up with him – this was perhaps the price he had to pay for setting eyes at last on the material proof of what he had suspected for so long. Then he had had to leave San Girolamo in a hurry and catch the train back to the abbey: he was in danger. Peace was what he desired – nothing but peace. All these machinations were not for him – he didn't feel at home. But could he call anywhere home these days? Entering the abbey, he had changed his homeland for the second time, and solitude had invaded him.

Now the riddle was solved. What would he say to Father Nil on his return? Nil, who was so reserved, and who had already travelled part of the path alone… He would put him on the right road. What he himself had discovered in the course of a whole lifetime of research, Nil would have to discover by himself.

And if anything happened to him… Nil would be worthy to pass on the secret in his turn.

Father Andrei opened his travel bag and rummaged around in it under the impassive gaze of the passenger opposite. After all, it was rather agreeable to have just three people in a compartment meant for six. He took off his stiff new clerical jacket and placed it, without crumpling it, on the empty seat to his right. Back in his travel bag he eventually found what he was looking for: a pencil and a small sheet of paper. He jotted down a few words, holding the paper in the hollow of his left hand, then he mechanically folded his fingers across it and threw his head backwards.

The noise of the train, echoed back by the trees bordering the road, made him feel drowsy. He sensed himself dozing off...

Everything happened extremely quickly. The passenger opposite him calmly put down his newspaper and stood up. At the same moment, in the corner seat, the expression of the fair-haired man became resolute. He got up and came over, as if to take something down from the luggage rack above him. Andrei looked up mechanically: the luggage rack was empty.

He had no time to think: the golden head of hair was leaning over him, and he saw the man's hand stretching out towards his jacket lying on the seat.

Suddenly everything went black: the jacket had been flung over his head. He felt two strong arms encircling him, pinning the garment against his torso and lifting him up. His cry of stupefaction was muffled by the fabric. He promptly found himself face downwards, heard the squeal of the window being lowered, and felt the metal of the safety rail against his hips. He struggled, but his whole upper body was already suspended in the void outside the train, and the wind slammed into him without blowing away the tails of the jacket still being held firmly against his face.

He was suffocating. "Who are they? I should have expected it, after so many others over the last two thousand years. But why now, and why here?"

His left hand, trapped between the safety rail and his stomach, continued to clutch the piece of paper.

He felt himself being tipped out of the window.

2

Mgr Alessandro Calfo was satisfied. Before leaving the great rectangular room near the Vatican, the eleven other members of the Society of St Pius V had given him carte blanche to act as he saw fit. The society couldn't afford to take any risks. For four centuries, it alone had watched over the most momentous secret of the Catholic, Apostolic and Roman Church. Those who got too close to that secret needed to be neutralized.

He had of course abstained from telling the Cardinal everything. Would they be able to keep the secret for long? But if it were to be divulged, it would mean the end of the Church, the end of Christianity as a whole. And it would be a mortal blow to a West already faltering in the face of Islam. It was a huge responsibility that rested on the shoulders of the twelve: the Society of St Pius V had been created with the sole aim of protecting this secret, and Calfo was its rector.

He had revealed to the Cardinal that there were, as yet, no more than scattered clues that only a few scholars, spread across the world, were able to understand and interpret. But he had concealed the most important thing: if these clues were all put together and presented to the public, they might lead to absolute and indisputable *proof*. This was why it was important for the existing trails to remain scattered. Anyone malevolent enough – or merely perspicacious enough – to put them together would be able to discover the truth.

He got up, walked round the table, and stood right in front of the bleeding figure on the crucifix.

"Master! Your twelve apostles are keeping watch over you."

He mechanically twisted the ring that encircled the annular finger on his right hand. The precious stone, a dark green jasper with glinting red highlights, was abnormally thick – even for

Rome, where prelates are fond of the ostentatious signs of their dignity. At every moment, this venerable jewel reminded him of the exact nature of his mission.

Anyone who penetrates the secret must be consumed by it, and disappear!

3

At its maximum speed, the train plunged across the plain of Sologne like a glowing snake. His body still bent double, his torso lashed by the wind, Father Andrei arched his back against the pressure of the two firm hands pushing him towards the abyss. Suddenly, he relaxed all his muscles.

"God, I have sought you ever since the daybreak of my life: now it has come to its end."

With a *hrumpf!* the thickset passenger pushed Andrei into the void, while his companion, standing motionless behind him, stood gazing on.

Like a dead leaf, the body whirled down and crashed onto the railway track.

The Rome express was obviously trying to make up for lost time: in less than a minute, the only thing left by the side of the railway was a broken puppet lying in the icy breeze. The jacket had flown far away. Curiously, Andrei's left elbow had got caught between two sleepers: his fist, still clutching the piece of paper he had been writing on only minutes before, was now pointing up at the black, silent sky in which the clouds slowly sailed eastwards.

A little later, a doe emerged from the forest and came to sniff at this shapeless mass with its smell of man. It knew the sour odour that humans give off when they are very afraid. The doe sniffed for a while at Andrei's closed fist raised grotesquely raised heavenwards.

The animal suddenly looked up, then bounded to one side and darted into the shelter of the trees. A car had caught it in its headlights, braking abruptly on the road down below. Two men came out, climbed up the slope and leant over the shapeless body. The doe froze: soon the men went back down the slope and stood next to the car, talking animatedly.

When the doe saw the reflection of the flashing lights of the police car speeding along the road, it took another bound and fled away into the dark, silent forest.

4

Gospels according to Mark and John

On this Thursday evening, 6th April in the year 30, the son of Joseph, whom everyone in Palestine called Jesus the Nazorean, was preparing to have his last meal, surrounded by the group of his twelve apostles.

With a grimace, Peter pulled up the cushion that kept slipping away from under his hip. Only the rich were in the habit of eating like this, Roman-style, reclining on a divan: poor Jews like themselves took their meals squatting on the groud. It seemed that their prestigious host, the Judaean, had wanted to confer a certain solemnity on this dinner, and had made a real effort for them – but the Twelve, lying around the table in a U shape, felt a bit lost in this large room.

They had cast aside all the other disciples to form a tight bodyguard limited just to the Twelve of them: a highly symbolic figure that recalled the twelve tribes of Israel. When the time came to launch their assault on the Temple – and that time was now near – the people would understand. There would then be twelve of them to govern Israel, in the name of the God who had given twelve sons to Jacob. On this they were all agreed. But at the right hand of Jesus – when he came into his reign – there would be only one place: and they were already locked in a violent struggle as to who among them would be the first of the Twelve.

But first there was the riot that they were to instigate in two days' time, taking advantage of the hubbub of Passover.

When they had left their homeland, Galilee, and moved to the capital, they had first met with their host for this evening, the Judaean who owned the fine house in the western district of Jerusalem. He was a rich man, educated and even cultivated – while the horizon of the Twelve did not extend beyond their fishing nets.

While his servants were bringing the dishes, the Judaean remained silent. He felt that Jesus was running a considerable risk, surrounded by these twelve fanatics: their assault on the Temple would of course end in failure. He had to shelter Jesus from their ambitions – even if, for this purpose, he had been obliged to forge a temporary alliance with Peter.

He had met Jesus two years earlier, on the banks of the Jordan. He had been an Essene and had turned Nazorean – one of the Jewish sects attached to the Baptist movement. Jesus was one too, though he never spoke of it. Between the two of them a bond of understanding and mutual esteem had soon been established. He would sometimes assert that he was the only one who had really understood *who* Jesus was. Neither a kind of God, as some members of the populace had hymned him after a spectacular cure, nor the Messiah, as Peter would have liked, nor the new King David, as the Zealots dreamt.

No, he was *something else*, which the Twelve, obsessed by their dreams of power, had not even glimpsed.

So he considered himself to be superior to them, and said to anyone who would listen that he was the *beloved disciple* of the Master – while Jesus, for the past few months, had found it more and more difficult to put up with his gang of ignorant Galileans, greedy to get their hands on power.

The Twelve were furious at the sight of another pretender moving in, just like that, to a position they had never managed to reach, furious that he had gained the confidence of the Nazorean.

So the enemy within this group was this beloved disciple. He, who never left his native Judaea, said that he had understood Jesus better than all of them, even though it was they who had constantly followed Jesus in Galilee.

An impostor…

He was reclining at the right hand of Jesus – the host's place. Peter never took his eyes off him. Was he about to betray the terrible secret that had only recently bound them together – would he make Jesus realize that he had been betrayed? Was he now regretting having introduced Judas to Caiaphas, to set up the trap that was to close on the Master this very evening?

Suddenly Jesus stretched out his hand and took hold of a morsel that he held for a moment over the dish, so that the sauce would drip off it: he was going to offer it to one of the guests, as a token of ritual friendship. Silence abruptly fell. Peter turned pale, and his jaw was set. "If it is to that impostor that the morsel is offered," he thought, "everything is ruined: it will mean he has just betrayed our alliance. If so, I'll kill him, and then make my escape…"

With a broad sweep of his hand, Jesus held the morsel out to Judas, who remained motionless at the end of the table, as if transfixed.

"Well, my friend… Go on, take it!"

15

Without a word, Judas leant forwards, took the morsel and placed it between his lips. A few drops of sauce trickled onto his short beard.

The conversations resumed, while Judas chewed slowly, his eyes riveted on those of his Master. Then he got up and moved to the exit. As he passed behind them, their host saw Jesus turn his head slightly. And he was the only one who heard Jesus say:

"My friend… What you have to do, do it quickly!"

Slowly, Judas opened the door. Outside, the Passover moon had not yet risen: the night was dark.

There were now only eleven of them around Jesus.

Eleven, and the beloved disciple.

5

The bell rang out for a second time. In the uncertain light of dawn, St Martin's Abbey was the only place in the village with its lights on. On winter nights such as this, the wind whistles between the desolate banks of the river and makes the Val-de-Loire seem more like Siberia than France.

The bell was still echoing in the cloister when Father Nil entered, having taken off his ample choir robe: the office of lauds had just finished. People knew that the monks maintained a complete silence until terce, and so nobody ever called before eight o'clock.

The doorbell rang for the third time, imperiously.

"The brother porter won't answer it, he has his orders. Too bad, I'll go myself."

Ever since he had brought to light the hidden circumstances of Jesus's death, Nil had been suffering from a hazy sense of unease. He did not like it when Father Andrei went off on one of his infrequent trips: the librarian had become his sole confidant after God. Monks live in common, but they do not communicate, and Nil needed to talk to someone about his research. Instead of returning to his cell, where his ongoing study of the events surrounding the capture of Jesus awaited him, he went into the gatehouse and opened the heavy door that separates every monastery from the external world.

In the gleam of the car's headlights, an officer from the gendarmerie snapped to attention and saluted.

"Excuse me, Father, but does this person reside here?"

He held out an identity card. Without a word, Nil took the laminated piece of paper and read the name: Andrei Sokolwski. Age: 67. Address: St Martin's Abbey...

Father Andrei!

The blood drained from his cheeks.

"Yes... of course, he's the Abbey librarian. What?..."

The gendarme was used to these disagreeable duties.

"Yesterday evening, two farm labourers informed us that, going home late, they had discovered his body on the side of the railway track, between Lamotte-Beuvron and La Ferté-Saint-Aubin. Dead. I'm sorry, but one of you will have to come and identify the body... For the inquiry, you understand."

"Dead? Father Andrei?"

Nil wavered in dismay.

"But... it must be the Reverend Father Abbot who..."

Behind them, they heard footsteps, muffled by the swish of a monk's habit. It was the Father Abbot himself. Alerted by the doorbell? Or impelled by some mysterious presentiment?

The gendarme bowed. In the Orleans brigade, everyone knows that, at the Abbey, the man who wears a ring and a pectoral cross has the same rank as a bishop. The Republic respects these things.

"Reverend Father, one of your monks, Father Andrei, was discovered yesterday next to the Rome express railway line, not far from here. It was a heavy fall, and he didn't have a chance: his neck bones were broken, he must have been killed instantly. We won't take the body to Paris for autopsy until we've identified it: could you come along in my car and carry out this formality, please? It's painful but necessary."

Ever since he had been elected to this prestigious post, the Father Abbot of St Martin's had never allowed a single feeling to show. True enough, he had been elected by the monks, in accordance with the Monastic Rule. But, contrary to that Rule, there had been several telephone calls between Val-de-Loire and Rome. And then, a high-ranking prelate had come to make his annual retreat in the cloister just before the election, in order to put discreet pressure on any waverers and convince them that Dom Gérard was the right man for the situation.

Only a reliable man could be entrusted with power over the Abbey, over its unique theological college and its three libraries. So not a muscle in his face betrayed the slightest emotion to the gendarme, who was still standing to attention.

"Father Andrei! Good Lord, how terrible! We were expecting him this morning – he was due back from Rome. How could such an accident have happened?"

"*Accident*? It's too early to use that word, Reverend Father. The few indications that we have suggest another line of inquiry. The passenger cars used on the Rome express are old models, but the doors are locked as soon as the train departs, for the entire journey. Your colleague can only have *fallen out of the window* in his compartment. When the ticket inspector did his last check before arrival in Paris, he saw that this compartment was empty: not only was Father Andrei no longer there – although his suitcase was where he'd left it – but the two other passengers had disappeared without leaving any luggage behind them. Three seats in the compartment had been reserved, but had remained unoccupied ever since Rome: so there was no witness. The inquiry is only just starting, but our initial hypothesis rules out any accident: it looks more like a crime. It seems possible that Father Andrei was pushed out of the window by one or both of the passengers as the train was moving. Do you mind coming with me for the identification?"

Father Nil had taken a discreet step backwards, but he had the impression that a flood of emotions was going to burst through the dam of his superior's face, however implacably it had been fashioned to stem the waves.

But the Father Abbot immediately mastered his feelings.

"Go with you? Now? That's not possible: this morning I am seeing the bishops from the Centre-Val-de-Loire Region, and my presence here is indispensable."

He turned round to Father Nil and said, with a heavy sigh, "Father Nil, could you go with this gentleman and carry out this painful formality?"

Nil bowed his head in sign of obedience: his study of the conspiracy around the death of Jesus would have to wait. It was Andrei who had just been crucified – and *this* death had taken place only the night before.

"Of course, Reverend Father: I'll go and get our coat, it's cold… It'll just take me a moment, Monsieur, if you don't mind waiting…"

Monastic poverty forbade a monk from proclaiming himself to be the owner of the least little object: *our* coat had for years been used solely by Father Nil – but it would have been inappropriate to say so. The Father Abbot asked the gendarme to step into the empty gatehouse and took him familiarly by the arm.

"I don't wish to prejudge the final result of your inquiry. But a *crime* – that's just not possible! Can you imagine what the press, the television, the journalists will make of it? The Catholic Church would come out of it badly, and the Republic would be gravely embarrassed. I'm certain it's a *suicide*. Poor Father Andrei... do you follow my meaning?"

The gendarme gently pulled his arm away: he followed all too well, but an inquiry is an inquiry, and it's no easy matter to climb through the open window of a speeding train while two innocent passengers watch. And he didn't like a civilian telling him what to do – not even one wearing a pectoral cross and a pastoral ring.

"Reverend Father, the inquiry will take its course. Father Andrei can't have fallen out of the window all by himself: it's up to Paris to decide what happened. Allow me to tell you that, right now, everything seems to indicate that this was a crime."

"No, I'm sure you mean a suicide..."

"A monk committing suicide? At his age? Highly unlikely."

He stroked his chin: all the same, the Father Abbot was right, this business was likely to cause quite a stir, and in high places too...

"Tell me, Reverend Father, did your Father Andrei suffer from... from psychological problems?"

The Father Abbot looked relieved: the gendarme seemed to understand.

"He did indeed! He was being treated for them. In fact, I can confirm that he was in a state of great mental fragility."

Andrei was known among his colleagues for being remarkably well balanced, physically and psychologically, and in forty

20

years of monastic life he had never once needed the infirmary. He was a studious man, surrounded by manuscripts; a scholar whose heart rate can never have risen above sixty beats per minute. The prelate smiled at the gendarme.

"A suicide is, of course, a horrible sin for a monk – but all sin deserves mercy. Whereas a crime…"

The wan light of morning enveloped the scene. The body had been moved away from the tracks so that the investigation would not get in the way of the trains, but the stiff corpse had not changed its posture: Father Andrei's left forearm was still pointing heavenwards, his fist clenched. On the ride over, Nil had had time to prepare himself for the shock. But he still found it difficult to approach, to kneel down, to draw back the cloth that had been placed over the head, twisted awry.

"Yes," he murmured with a sigh. "Yes, it's Father Andrei. My poor friend…"

There was a moment's silence, which the gendarme respected. Then he touched Father Nil on the shoulder.

"Stay with him: I'll draw up the statement of identification in the car, you'll just need to sign it and then I'll drive you back to the Abbey."

Nil wiped away a tear trickling down his cheek. Then he noticed the body's clenched fist that seemed, in a last gesture of despair, to be cursing the heavens. With difficulty he managed to prise open the dead man's chill fingers: in the hollow of the palm there was a crumpled little square of paper.

Nil glanced round: the gendarme was leaning over the dash-board of his car. He peeled the scrap of paper from his friend's hand, and his eyes fell on a few lines written in pencil.

Nobody was looking at him: he adroitly slipped the paper away into his coat pocket.

6

Gospels according to Matthew and John

A few days before the evening of the last supper, Peter had been waiting outside the walls. The Judaean came through the gate, greeted by the sentries who recognized him as the proprietor of one of the local villas. He took a few steps; the shape of the fisherman emerged from the shadows.

"*Shalom!*"

"*Ma shalom lek'ha.*"

He did not hold out his hand to the Galilean. For a week, apprehension had been gnawing away at him: whenever he met them, on the hillside outside the city where they spent each night in the friendly, secluded darkness of a vast olive grove, the Twelve spoke of nothing other than the imminent assault they were about to launch against the Temple. Never again would the circumstances be so favourable, they argued: thousands of pilgrims were encamped pretty much everywhere around the city. The crowd had been worked on by the Zealots, and were ready for anything. Jesus's popularity had to be exploited to set off the explosion, now.

They would fail – that much was obvious. And Jesus risked being killed for no reason at all, in a Jewish-style riot. The Master deserved better: he was worth infinitely more than all the rest of them, and he needed to be protected from his fanatical disciples. A plan had been hatching in the Judaean's head – now he just needed to convince Peter.

"The Master has asked if he can come to supper at your house," Peter said, "in the upper room. It's impossible for him to cele- brate Passover this year – we're being watched much too closely. Instead, a solemn meal, following the Essene rite – that's all."

"You're all completely mad! You want to come and do that *in my house*? Two hundred yards away from the High Priest's palace, in a part of town where your Galilean accent will get you arrested straight away?"

The fisherman from the Lake gave him a crafty smile.

"Exactly: your place is just where we'll be safest. The authorities will never think of coming to look for us in the protected district, especially not in the house of a friend of the High Priest!"

"Oh... 'friend' is going a bit far. We're neighbours. There's no way a former Essene like me and the highest dignitary in the clergy could be 'friends'. When do you plan on holding this supper?"

"Thursday evening, at nightfall."

It was a crazy but cunning idea. Hidden away inside his house, the Galileans would evade all notice.

"All right. Tell the Master that I'll be honoured to welcome him into my home, and everything will be ready for a solemn meal. One of my servants will help you slip past the patrols: you'll recognize him from the pitcher of water that he'll be carrying for the ritual ablutions of your meal. Meanwhile, come along with me, we need to talk."

Peter followed him. They climbed over a pile of bricks. There was a gleam of metal from under his cloak: the *sica*, the short sword the Zealots used to gut their victims. So he never went without it these days! Jesus's apostles were ready for anything...

In a few words, the Judaean told him of his plan. So the uprising was going to occur on the occasion of the feast, was it? An excellent idea: the crowd of pilgrims would be easy to manipulate. But given that Jesus preached only peace and pardon, how would he react, in the heat of the moment? And wasn't there the risk of his being wounded, or worse? If he were slain by a legionary's sword, their coup would fail…

Peter listened, his interest suddenly aroused.

"So are you saying we should ask him to go back to Galilee, where he doesn't run any risk? It's all going to happen so quickly, and we can't have him four days' journey away from here…"

"And who's asking you to send him away from Jerusalem? No, not at all: you need to bring him into the heart of the action, but in a place where a Roman arrow can't reach him. You want to have your meal in the part of town where Caiaphas's palace is, since you think it's where you'll be safest. A good idea. In the same way, what I'm telling you is this: just before the action, get Jesus into a really safe place, *right inside the palace*. Have him arrested and taken to Caiaphas on the eve of Passover. He'll be locked away in the cellars and, as you know, they're not allowed to hold trials during the feast. When it's over… power will have changed hands! You can go and fetch him in triumph, he'll appear on the balcony of the palace, the crowd will howl for joy at being finally delivered from the caste of priests…"

Peter interrupted him, after being completely stupefied.

"Have our Master arrested by our sworn enemies?"

"You need Jesus to be safe and sound. You're the ones who can take care of the violent stuff; then he can speak and take the people along with him – as only he knows how. Shelter him from the uproar of a violent insurrection, and then go and fetch him afterwards!…

And when you fail, the Judaean thought grimly – and you *will* fail, you're up against Roman troops – Jesus at least will still be alive. What happens then will be quite different from what you're dreaming of. Israel needs a prophet, not a gang leader.

They took a few steps in silence across the rocky crest that looked down over the Vale of Gehenna.

Suddenly Peter looked up.

"You're right: he'll be in the way if we start any violent action – he won't approve of it. But how can we ensure he gets arrested at just the right time? Things can change from one hour to the next!"

"I've thought of that. You know that Judas is completely devoted to him. You're a former Zealot like him, so you can explain things to Judas. He'll need to bring along the Temple guard at the precise time and place where they'll be sure to find him, separated from the crowd that's always protecting him. For example, just after the supper at my house, on Thursday night, in the Garden of Olives."

"Will Judas agree to that? And how will he make contact with the Jewish authorities? He's just an ordinary Galilean – how can he get into the High Priest's palace? How's he going to negotiate with the man he dreams of eliminating? Why on earth do you think he went over to the Zealots? I know those people: *this* is what *they* negotiate with!"

He slapped the *sica* rubbing against his left thigh.

"You can tell him it's for the good of the cause, to protect the Master. You'll find the right words: he'll listen to you. And I'll take him to Caiaphas. I'm allowed to enter and leave the palace at will: they'll let Judas in, if he's with me. Caiaphas will fall for it – the priests are so scared of Jesus!"

"Fine… So if you say you can bring him to Caiaphas, if you think he can pretend to betray Jesus while in fact protecting him… It's risky, but what isn't risky right now?"

As they passed back through the gate into the City, the Judaean gave a friendly wave to the guards. In a few days, many of these men would be dead or wounded, and the

Romans would easily suppress the revolt. As for the gang of Twelve, the Land of Israel would soon be rid of them once and for all.

And Jesus's mission, his real mission, could then begin.

7

Nil had spent the whole morning – from the time the gendarme had brought him back to the Abbey – slumped on his stool. He had not opened the notes and papers relating to his ongoing research into the circumstances of the death of Jesus. A monk's cell never contains a chair on which he might rest his back and daydream. And yet this is just what Nil was doing, mulling over his memories. The Abbey was silent, as if shrouded in cotton wool: all the classes in the theological college had been suspended until Father Andrei's funeral. There was still an hour to go before the conventual mass.

Andrei... the only one to whom he could ever talk about his research. The only one who seemed able to understand his conclusions, and sometimes even to reach them before he did himself.

"You should never fear the truth, Nil: it was to find the truth, to *know*, that you entered this abbey. But the truth will turn you into a solitary, and it might even destroy you: never forget that it was truth that led Jesus to his death, and others after him. I have come near the truth in the manuscripts I have been decrypting for forty years. Since few people can follow me in my speciality, and as I never talk about my conclusions, people trust me. And it was in the Gospels themselves that *you* discovered... certain things. Beware: if these things have long been kept hidden away in the oubliettes of the Church, it's because it's dangerous to talk about them openly…"

"St John's Gospel is on the syllabus in the theological college this year. I can't avoid the question: *who* was its author? What role did the mysterious *beloved disciple* play in the plot, and in that crucial period following the death of Jesus?"

Andrei, the son of Russian émigrés who had converted to Catholicism, had an amazing gift for languages, and this had led to his being put in charge of the three libraries of the Abbey, a sensitive position that only a trustworthy man could fill. Whenever he smiled, he looked like an old *starets*.

"Ah, my friend… Ever since the start, *this question has been evaded*. And you're starting to understand why, aren't you? So do the same as all those who came before you: don't say everything that you know. Your students in the theological college wouldn't be able to take it… and in that case, I'd fear for your safety!"

Andrei had been right. For the past thirty years, the Catholic Church had been undergoing an unprecedented crisis. Lay people were deserting it, joining sects or becoming Buddhists, and the Christian world was suffering from a profound malaise. You could no longer find any *reliable* teachers able to impart sound doctrine in the seminaries, which in any case were now emptying.

So Rome had decided to bring together the hard core of the remaining seminarists in a monastic school, a theological college of the kind found in the Middle Ages. There was a score of them, entrusted to the care of the Abbey and to the instruction of its scholars. Had the monks chosen to flee this corrupt world? Then they would provide the young men in the theological college with what they would most need for their survival: a breastplate of truth.

Father Nil was entrusted with the task of teaching exegesis – that is, explaining the Gospels. What did it matter if he wasn't really a specialist in ancient languages? He would work with Father Andrei, who could read Coptic, Syriac and many other dead languages fluently.

These two solitaries became collaborators and ended up as friends: what monastic life made difficult, the love of ancient texts enabled.

This only friend Nil had now lost in tragic circumstances. And this death filled him with anguish.

At the same moment, a hand was nervously dialling an international number beginning with 390, the main (and highly confidential) line of the Vatican State. It bore a ring adorned with a very simple opal: the Archbishop of Paris felt it was his duty to set an example of modesty.

"*Pronto?*"

In the shade of Michelangelo's dome, it was a hand with immaculately manicured fingernails that lifted the receiver. Its episcopal ring was topped by a curious green jasper: an asymmetric lozenge shape, in a chiselled silver mount on which it looked like a small lid. It was a jewel of great value.

"Hello, Monsignor, it's the Archbishop of Paris here... Ah, you were just about to phone me?... Yes, a most regrettable business, it really is – but... you've already heard?..."

(How can that be possible? The accident only happened last night...)

"Complete discretion? That will be difficult, the inquiry is in the hands of the Paris police – it seems it's a criminal affair... The Cardinal? Of course, I quite understand... Suicide, is that right? Yes... though it's painful for me to say so: suicide is a sin against which divine mercy has always been powerless. As you say… shall we let God decide?"

The Archbishop moved the receiver away from his ear just long enough to smile. In the Vatican, they rather enjoy telling God what to do.

"Hello? Yes, I can hear you… Now's the time to do a bit of networking? Of course, we're on excellent terms with the Ministry of the Interior. Fine… Well, I'll look after it. You can reassure the Cardinal: it will be reported as a suicide, and the file will be closed. *Arrivederci, Monsignore!*"

He always took care not to squander his credit with the Government. How could the death of a monk, an inoffensive scholar, justify a request for the inquiry to be taken no further? The Archbishop of Paris heaved a sigh. You couldn't quarrel with an order given by Mgr Calfo, especially when he was passing it onto you at the explicit request of the Cardinal Prefect.

He phoned the switchboard.

"Could you put me through to the Minister of the Interior? Thank you, I'll hold…"

8

Gospels according to Matthew and John

Thursday night was drawing to an end, and it was almost daybreak on Friday morning. The Judaean came over to the flames and held out his hands towards their welcoming warmth. Because of the cold, the guards had lit a fire in the courtyard of Caiaphas's palace, and they respectfully allowed him to come over to it: a wealthy local landowner, an acquaintance of the High Priest… He turned round: Peter was skulking in a corner, no doubt terrified to be there, at the very heart of a power that he was planning to overthrow in a few hours' time. If he behaved like a conspirator caught in the act, the Galilean would start to arouse suspicions.

He beckoned him over to the fire. The fisherman hesitated, then diffidently slipped into the circle of servants enjoying the warmth.

Everything had gone exceptionally well. Two days previously, he had dragged Judas along with him – Judas, who was completely amazed to find himself for the first time in the district where the Jewish dignitaries lived. The interview with Caiaphas had got off to a good start – the High Priest seemed delighted to be presented with an opportunity to hustle Jesus away into the shadows, without any bother, nice and quietly. Then Judas had stiffened: perhaps he suddenly understood whom exactly he was talking to, and realized he was actually going to hand his Master over to the Jewish authorities.

"And how am I to know that, once Jesus is in your hands, you won't put him to death?"

The High Priest solemnly raised his right hand.

"Galilean, I swear before the Eternal: Jesus the Nazorean will be judged fairly by our Law, which does not sentence a wandering preacher to death. His life will not be in any danger. To reassure you, I will give you a token of my promise: the Eternal is henceforth witness between you and me."

With a smile, he handed over to Judas thirty pieces of gold.

Without a word, Judas pocketed the gold. The High Priest had just made a solemn commitment: Jesus would be arrested, but there would be a trial. That would take time, and in three days Caiaphas would no longer be the most powerful leader in the country. He would no longer be anything at all.

* * *

But what on earth were they doing up there? Why wasn't Jesus already in the shadows of a dungeon in the cellars? In the shadows – safe and secure?

The Judaean had seen several members of the Sanhedrin grumbling as they climbed the steps up to the first storey of the palace, where Jesus had been taken on his arrival.

Since then, no further news had found its way down to the courtyard. He didn't like the way events were turning out: to hide his jumpiness, he headed out to the exit and walked a few steps down the street.

He bumped into a shadow flattened against the wall.

"Judas... what are you doing here?"

The man was trembling like the leaf of a fig tree in the wind of Galilee.

"I... I came to see. I'm really worried about the Master! Can anyone trust a promise made by a man like Caiaphas?"

"Look, just calm down: everything's going just as it should. Don't stay here, you risk getting arrested by the first patrol to come along. Go to my place; in my upper room you'll be safe."

He headed to the palace gate. Turning round, he saw Judas standing there motionless. He wasn't going to leave.

The cocks were starting to crow. Suddenly the door of the room opened and the light of the torches lit up the veranda. Caiaphas came out and glanced down into the courtyard: quickly, the Judaean moved away from the light of the fire – this was no time to be noticed. Later, when the uprising had failed, he would go to see the High Priest and demand that the Master be set free.

Then Jesus appeared, coming down the stairs. He was being held at the elbows by two guards, and his arms were tightly bound behind him.

Why? There was no need to tie him up just to take him down into the cellars!

The group passed on the other side of the fire, and he heard Caiaphas's shrill voice:

"Take him to Pilate, and don't hang about!"

An icy chill broke out on his forehead.

To Pilate! If he was being taken to the Roman procurator, there was only one single explanation: Caiaphas had broken his sworn promise.

Judas had not left his observation post. At first he just saw the light of a torch, dazzling him: he shrank back into a doorway and held his breath. A patrol?

It wasn't a patrol. In the midst of a group of Temple guards, he spotted a man who staggered as he walked, his arms shackled behind his back. The officer at the head of the group barked out an order as he strode past Judas, who was still hidden in the shadows.

"Get a move on! To Pilate's palace!"

With a sense of horror, Judas clearly made out the face of the man being roughly pushed along: it was Jesus.

The Master was very pale, and his features were drawn. He passed by the door without seeing anything – his gaze seemed focused within. Stricken with dismay, Judas stared at the Master's wrists: they were very tightly bound, there were bloodstains on the rope, and his twisted, knotted hands were completely blue.

This nightmare vision faded: the armed group had just turned right, heading for the Antonia fortress, where Pilate resided whenever he was in Jerusalem.

Every Jew knew the Law: in Israel, blasphemy brought a death sentence. You were immediately taken out and stoned to death. If they had not stoned Jesus in the courtyard, it must have been because he had refused to declare himself equal with God, which would have been the supreme blasphemy. So the leaders of the Jewish nation were seeking a sentence based on political grounds – and given that the Romans were jumpy throughout the feast of the Passover, they would no doubt get it.

Judas staggered out of the city. Jesus would not be given a proper trial, Caiaphas had broken his promise and decided on his death. And so that he would die – since they had not been able to convict him of blasphemy – he was being handed over to the Romans.

And the Romans were never short of crosses…

He arrived in front of the imposing mass of the Temple. In the depths of his pocket the thirty pieces of gold were still clinking – the derisory token of an agreement concluded between himself and the High Priest, an agreement that had just been broken, a promise that had been scorned. Caiaphas had duped him.

He would go and confront him inside the Temple, remind him of his promise. And if he persisted in his treachery, Judas would appeal to the Eternal, whom Caiaphas had called on as a witness.

"Priests of the Temple, the hour of God's judgement on you is at hand!"

9

Nil gave a start: the first bell for mass was ringing, he would soon need to go down into the sacristy to get ready. One last time, he reread the scrap of paper he had wrested a few hours earlier from the grip of Andrei's fingers stiffened in death:

Tell Nil: Coptic manuscript (Apoc.)
Apostle's letter
M M M.
Stone slab in G.
Find the link between them. Now.

Warding off any thought of his inquiry into the role played by Judas in the death of Jesus, he came down to earth with a bump. What did these words mean? They were a scribbled reminder, of course. Andrei wanted to tell him about a Coptic manuscript: the one from Rome, or another? Several hundred photocopies were filed away in the drawers of his office: which of them was it? He had written *Apoc.* in brackets: a Coptic manuscript about the apocalypse? This was not much to go on: there are dozens of apocalypses, Jewish as well as Christian. And though Nil was able to read Coptic, he felt unable to translate a difficult text correctly.

The second line awoke in him the memory of one of his conversations with the librarian. Was it the apostolic letter that Andrei had obliquely mentioned one day, dropping a fleeting hint, a mere conjecture, as he called it, a hypothesis for which he had no proof? He had refused to tell him any more about it.

What did the triple letter *M* underneath mean?

Only the last but one line was clear to Nil. Yes, he needed to go back and photograph the stone slab in Germigny again, as he had promised his friend he would just before he left.

As for the last line, *find the link between them*, this was something they had often discussed: for Andrei, it was the main part of his work as a historian. But why *now*, and why was this word underlined?

He tried to focus his thoughts. On the one hand there was

his research on the Gospels, which Andrei had often asked him about. Then the time the librarian had been called in for questioning in connection with the Coptic manuscript. And finally, the discovery at Germigny that had deeply disturbed him. All of this suddenly seemed to have assumed such significance for his friend that he urgently wanted to discuss it with Nil as soon as he returned.

Had Andrei discovered something in Rome? Something they might have referred to during their many private conversations? Or had he, in Rome, finally ended up talking about the things he should have kept secret?

The gendarme had used the word "crime". But what could have been the motive? Andrei had no possessions, and lived reclusively in his library, far from the gaze of all others. Of all others, that is, except the Vatican. And yet Nil could not accept the idea of a murder carried out at the behest of Rome. The last time the Pope had deliberately had his own priests assassinated was in Paraguay, in 1760. The political situation of the time had made that collective murder of innocent people expedient: things were different in those days. At the end of the twentieth century, the Pope would not get rid of an inoffensive scholar!

"Rome no longer sheds blood. The Vatican committing a crime? Impossible."

He remembered the frequent warnings uttered by his friend. The disquiet that had been dwelling in him for some time made his stomach tighten.

He glanced at his watch: four minutes to go before mass; if he didn't go down to the sacristy right now, he'd be late. He opened his desk drawer and pushed the note to the back, under a pile of letters. His fingers ran over the snapshot taken a month earlier in the church of Germigny. *Andrei's last wishes...*

He rose, and left his cell.

Before him stretched the dark, chill corridor of the second storey – the "corridor of the Reverend Fathers" – reminding him where he was: in the Abbey. And now he was alone. Never again would the librarian's conspiratorial smile lighten up this corridor.

10

"Take a seat, Monsignor."

Calfo repressed a grimace, and allowed his plump body to settle back into the soft curves of the armchair, opposite the imposing desk. He didn't like the way Emil Catzinger, the very powerful Cardinal Prefect of the Congregation for the Doctrine of the Faith, had summoned him to a formal meeting. As everybody knows, the serious business isn't done around a desk, but over a shared pizza, or going for a stroll after a *spaghettata* in a shady garden, with a fine cigar wedged between your index and middle fingers.

Alessandro Calfo had been born in the *quartiere spagnolo*, the working-class heart of Naples, from a lineage that had vegetated in the wretched promiscuity of a single-room flat overlooking the street. Immersed in a populace whose volcanic sensuality was nourished by a generous sun, he very soon perceived that he had an irrepressible need for pleasure. The flesh was there, soft, inviting, quivering, but inaccessible to a poor boy who learnt to dream of his desires and to desire his dreams.

Alessandro was cut out to be a real Neapolitan, obsessed by the cult of the god Eros – the only possible way of forgetting about the poverty of the *quartiere* into which he had been born. But in a patriarchal society, acting out your desires is even more of a tricky business than proving that the annual miracles promised by San Gennaro have been performed.

It was at this point that his father sent him to the unwelcoming North. There were too many children to feed in this one-room flat: this *figlio* would become a man of the Church, but not just anywhere. His father, a bashful admirer of Mussolini, had heard that *lassù* – up there – real patriots were rebuilding the seminaries in the spirit of Fascism. Since God was a good Italian, there was no question of going anywhere else to train for his service. At the age of ten, Alessandro, now ensconced in the plain of the Po, put on a cassock – he would wear it permanently from now.

But this cassock covered – without being able to contain them – the permanent frustrations of this son of Vesuvius, always on the verge of erupting.

In the seminary, he made his second discovery: comfort and affluence. Mysteriously, funds flowed here along the countless channels of the European extreme right. The poor boy from the *quartiere* learnt the importance of money – money which can do anything.

At seventeen he was sent to learn his faith in the shadow of the Vatican, and in the language of God: Latin. Here he made his third discovery: power. And he saw that wielding power can, more than any obsession with pleasure, fill a life and give it meaning. To be sure, the cult of Eros is one approach to the mysteries of God – but power turns the person who possesses it into the equal of God himself.

His natural inclination towards Fascism meant that, one day, he came across the Society of St Pius V. He realized that his three successive discoveries would find a table ready-laid for them. His appetite for power would grow and flourish in the ideological totalitarianism of the Society. His crimson-hemmed cassock would remind him of belated spiritual aspirations, while elegantly acting as a cover for the fulfilment of his carnal desires. And finally, money would come flowing into his hands, thanks to the hundreds of files the Society carefully kept up to date – files which spared no one.

Money, power and pleasure: Alessandro was ready. At the age of forty he was promoted to the title of *Monsignor*, and became the rector of the highly mysterious and highly influential Society, a prelature which answered directly to the Pope and was subject to his authority alone. Then the unexpected happened: he conceived a real passion for the mission with which he had been entrusted, and became the fanatical defender of the founding dogmas of a Church to which he owed everything.

He ceased to repress the itch of his senses. But in allowing it to find expression, he gave it a dimension compatible with his priestly office: now he saw it as the quickest way to reach mystical union, by means of carnal transfiguration.

Two people – and two alone – knew that the all-powerful Rector of the Society of St Pius V was this little man with his honeyed tones: the Pope and Cardinal Emil Catzinger. For everyone else, *urbi et orbi*, he was merely one of the humble *minutanti* of the Congregation.

In theory, at least.

"Take a seat. Two questions – one external and one internal."

This distinction is a habitual one in the inner circles of the Vatican: here "internal questions" are those that crop up in the Church – a friendly, normal, controllable world. And "external questions" refer to what happens on the rest of the planet – a hostile, abnormal world that needs to be controlled as much as possible.

"I've already spoken to you about this rather worrying problem – the French Benedictine Abbey…"

"Yes, you asked me to do the necessary. But we didn't need to take any action, as the unfortunate Father Andrei committed suicide, I think, and we can draw a line under it all."

His Eminence hated being interrupted: even if Calfo was trying to get him to forget the fact, *he* was in charge here. He would soon put him in his place.

Catzinger was an Austrian. He had been chosen by the Pope, who found that his reputation as an enlightened theologian would be useful. But he rapidly revealed himself to be a formidable conservative, and since this was also, deep down, to the taste of St Peter's new successor, the honeymoon between the two men turned into an enduring union.

"Suicide is an abominable sin – God have mercy on his soul! But it seems there's another black sheep in this monastery, where the flock of the faithful really needs to be above reproach. Look at this" – he passed a file over to Calfo – "a denunciation of this person from the Father Abbot. Perhaps it's of no importance: you be the judge, and we'll come back to it. There's no urgency, at least not yet."

The Cardinal's relation to his own past was fraught. His father had been an officer in the Austrian *Wehrmacht*, the *Anschluss* division. While he had distanced himself from Nazism to the utmost, he had preserved one of its instincts: his conviction of being the sole possessor of a truth that alone was capable of uniting the world, around a Catholic faith that was non-negotiable.

"The internal question concerns you directly, Monsignor…"

Calfo crossed his legs and waited to hear the rest.

"You know the Roman proverb: *una piccola avventura non fa male* – a little adventure does no harm… so long as the prelate remembers his position and is, above all, properly discreet. Well, I've learnt that a... common whore is threatening to sell her story to the paparazzi in the anti-clerical press, who are promising to pay her a fortune in exchange for her revelations concerning certain... how shall I put it?... certain private conversations you are alleged to have had with her."

"Spiritual conversations, Your Eminence: we are together making progress along the path of mystical experience."

"I'm sure you are. But anyway, the sums mentioned are considerable – what do you intend to do?"

"Silence is the first of Christian virtues: Our Lord himself refused to reply to the slanders of the High Priest Caiaphas. So silence has no price – I think that a few hundred dollars..."

"You must be joking! This time you need to add a zero. I'm inclined to help you out, but make this the last time: the Holy Father will not fail to see the paragraph published in *Il Paese*. This is a warning to us. It really is deplorable!"

Emil Catzinger slipped his hand into his crimson cassock and pulled out of the inside pocket a little silver-gilt key. He leant forwards, inserted the key into the bottom drawer of his desk and opened it.

The drawer contained a score of bulging envelopes. From even the smallest parish of the Catholic empire, a tax is gathered for the Apostolic seat. Catzinger directed one of the three congregations which ensured the collection of this manna, as regular and innocent as the fine drizzle of Brittany.

He delicately took hold of the first envelope, opened it and rapidly counted the notes with his fingertips. Then he proffered the envelope to Calfo, who half-opened it. He didn't need to stick his hand in to find out exactly how much it contained: a Neapolitan can count a bundle of banknotes with a glance.

"Your Eminence, I can't say how touched I am. You can rest assured of my gratitude and devotion!"

"I'm sure I can. The Pope and I appreciate your zeal for the most sacred cause there is – touching as it does the person of Our Lord Jesus Christ himself. *Va bene, Monsignore* – calm down this young woman's hankerings for publicity and, from now on, please lead her along the paths of spirituality in a... less demanding way."

A few hours later, Catzinger found himself in the office overlooking Bernini's colonnade, on the right-hand side, with its window directly onto St Peter's Square. Ever since his election, the Pope had chosen to travel extensively, leaving the management of everyday affairs to the men who live in the shadow of the Vatican. Nobody ever mentions them, but they steer St Peter's vessel in the right direction: that of the restoration of the old order.

His Eminence Emil Catzinger was the man who in secret ruled the Catholic Church – and he ruled it with a rod of iron.

A trembling hand held out to the Cardinal, who was standing respectfully in front of the old man's armchair, a copy of *Il Paese*. He found it difficult to enunciate his words.

"And this story in which the name Calfo appears... ah, er... is it *our* Monsignor Calfo?"

"Yes, Holy Father, it is. I saw him today: he'll do what is necessary to prevent these hateful slanders from spattering the Holy See with mud."

"And... how can we prevent?..."

"He'll take care of it in person. And you know that, thanks to our Vatican Bank, we control the press group on which *Il Paese* depends."

"No, I wasn't aware of that. All right, make sure that peace returns, *Eminenza*. Peace – that is what I yearn for, at every moment!"

The Cardinal bowed with a smile. He had learnt to love the old Pontiff, even though his past life meant that he felt different from him in every fibre of his being. Every day, he was moved by the older man's struggle against illness, his courage in suffering.

And he admired the strength of his faith.

11

The Father Abbot was the last to enter the huge refectory, where the monks were waiting respectfully in front of their stools, lined up in impeccable order. In his melodious voice, he began the ritual. After the chant *Edent pauperes*, forty hands laid hold of their stools and slipped them with an identical movement under their habits. Their hands lay folded on the edge of the tables of deal wood, and forty heads bowed to listen in silence to the beginning of the reading.

The midday meal had just begun.

Opposite the prelate, at the far end of the refectory, a whole table was filled by the students of the theological college. Impeccable clerical garb, a few cassocks designating the most traditionalist of them; tense faces with shadows under their eyes: the elite of the future French clergy making ready to pick up the metal soup tureens overflowing with the lettuce that had been picked that very morning by Brother Antoine. The academic year had begun, and would not end until June.

Father Nil liked the start of autumn, when the fruits of the orchard reminded him that he was living in the garden of

France. But for the past few days he had lost his appetite. His theology classes here were taking place in an atmosphere that left him feeling uneasy.

"So it is obvious that the Gospel according to St John is a composite work, and the final result of a long process of literary development. Who was its author? Or rather, who were its authors? The comparisons we have just drawn between different passages of this venerable text display a vocabulary and even a content that are extremely different. The same man cannot have written the vivid scenes, sketched from the life, that he obviously saw with his own eyes, *and* the long discourses in elegant Greek through which we can glimpse the ideology of the Gnostics, those philosophers of the Orient."

He had given his students permission to intervene during his lectures, so long as their questions were brief. But ever since he had come to the heart of the matter, he had been confronted by a score of frozen statues.

"I know we're straying away from the beaten track, that this isn't what they taught you in catechism classes. But the text gives us no choice… You're in for quite a few more surprises!" Such had been his line.

His classes were the result of years of solitary study and re-flection. Time and again he had sought in vain, in the library of the Abbey to which he had access, for certain books which, as he knew from a specialized review to which Father Andrei as librarian subscribed, had only just been published.

"Well, Father Nil, the fact is: they've finally brought to light a new batch of Dead Sea scrolls! I'd never have believed it… The jars were discovered fifty years ago in the caves at Qumran, and nothing's been published since Yigael Yadin died: more than half these texts are still unknown to the public. It's an incredible scandal!"

Nil smiled. In the intimacy of this office, he had discovered in Father Andrei a man of passion, who was aware of all the latest developments. He loved their long conversations behind closed doors. Andrei listened as he told him about his research, his head bent slightly forwards. Then with a word or two, or sometimes a silence, he would give his disciple his approval, or point him the way forward as he came out with his most daring hypotheses.

The man he could now see in front of him was so different from the starchy librarian, the strict guardian of the three keys, who had always been such a familiar figure in the Abbey on the river Loire!

The building had been rebuilt after the war, and the cloister had been left unfinished: it formed a U shape open to the plain. The libraries occupied the top storey of the three wings – central, north and south – just under the roofs.

Four years earlier, Father Andrei had seen considerable sums of money coming in, with instructions to purchase particular titles in the fields of dogma and history. He had been thrilled at this opportunity to place his knowledge at the service of these miraculous gifts of cash. The shelves filled up with rare books, editions that were difficult to find or out of print, in all languages both ancient and modern. The opening of the special theological school, closely followed by the Vatican, was obviously responsible for the creation of this marvellous research tool.

There was, however, an unusual restriction. Each of the eight teaching monks appointed to the theological college possessed just *one key*, the key corresponding to the subject he taught. Nil, who taught the New Testament, had been given the key to the central wing, over whose entrance was a wooden notice engraved with the words: *Biblical Studies*. The libraries of the northern wing (*Historical Studies*) and the southern wing (*Theological Studies*) remained obstinately closed to him.

Only Andrei and the Father Abbot possessed the keys to all three libraries, held together on a special keyring, which they never let out of their sight.

Right at the start of his research, Nil had asked his friend for permission to gain access to the historical library.

"There are certain books I really need and I can't find them in the central wing. You told me one day they'd been catalogued and placed in the north wing – why on earth can't I get in? It's ridiculous!"

For the first time, Nil saw his friend's face grow distant. Looking strained and edgy, Andrei eventually told him, with tears in his eyes:

"Father Nil... If I told you that, I was wrong to do so. Forget what I said. Please, *never* ask me for the key to one of the two libraries to which you no longer have access. You must understand, my friend, I can't do just what I want. Father Abbot's orders are strict, and they come... from a higher authority. Nobody can have access to all three wings of our library. It keeps me awake at night: it's not ridiculous, it's tragic. *I* have access to all three libraries, and I've often passed my time there ferreting around and reading. For the peace of your soul, in the name of our friendship, I beg you: just stick to what you find in the central wing."

Whereupon he had relapsed into a heavy silence, which was unusual when he found himself alone with Nil.

Feeling out of his depth, the teacher of exegesis had had to satisfy himself with the treasures that his one key opened up for him.

* * *

"His narrative shows that the principal author of the Gospel according to St John knows Jerusalem well, and has friends and acquaintances there: he's a wealthy, cultivated Judaean, whereas the Apostle John lives in Galilee, and is poor and illiterate… how could he be the author of the text that bears his name?"

As he spoke, the faces before him darkened into frowns. Some shook their heads disapprovingly – but nobody spoke up. This silence on the part of his audience disquieted Nil more than anything else. His pupils had come from the most traditionalist families in the country. They had been hand-picked to form the spearhead of tomorrow's Church. Why had he been appointed to this post? He was so happy when he could work in peace and quiet, all by himself!

Nil knew that he would not be able to present them with all his conclusions. He would never have dreamt that teaching exegesis would one day be a perilous acrobatic exercise. When he'd been a student in Rome, together with his friend, the warm and brotherly Rembert Leeland, it had all seemed so easy…

The first bell for mass started slowly to chime.

"Thank you. See you next week."

The students rose and started to tidy away their notes. At the back of the room, a seminarist in a cassock, his skull clean-shaven, lingered for a moment as he wrote a few lines on a small piece of paper – of the sort used by monks in order to communicate with one another without breaking the silence.

He folded the paper in two, pursing his lips. Nil absent-mindedly noted that his fingernails were bitten. Finally the student got up and walked past his teacher without even looking at him.

* * *

While Nil robed himself in his sacerdotal apparel in the sacristy that smelt pleasantly of fresh wax, a man in a cassock slipped into the common room and went over to the pigeonholes reserved for the reverend fathers. After he had glanced all round to ensure there was nobody else in the room, a hand with well-chewed fingernails slipped a piece of paper folded in two into the pigeonhole of the Reverend Father Abbot.

12

If it had not been for the Venetian bracket lamps that shed a warm, diffuse light, the room might have appeared sinister. It was long and narrow, without windows, and the only furniture in it was a table of waxed wood, behind which were aligned thirteen seats, backs to the wall. In the centre was a sort of throne in Neapolitan-Angevin style, covered in scarlet velvet. And, on either side, another six simple chairs, their arms ending in lions' heads.

The elegant panelling on the entrance door concealed a thick layer of reinforced sheeting.

The table was about five yards away from the wall, which was completely bare. Completely? No. There was a panel of dark wood set into the brickwork. Against the dark mahogany, the livid pallor of a bloody crucifix of Jansenist inspiration stood out, forming an almost obscene stain of colour under the combined glare of two spotlights hidden just above the central throne.

This throne had never been occupied, and it never would be: it reminded the members of the assembly that the presence of the Master of the Society of St Pius V was entirely spiritual, albeit eternal. For four centuries, Jesus Christ, the resurrected God, had sat here in spirit and in truth, flanked by twelve faithful apostles, six on his right hand and six on his left. Just as at the last supper he had shared with his disciples, two thousand years ago, in the upper room in the western part of Jerusalem.

Each of these twelve chairs was occupied by a man wearing a very loose-fitting alb, the cowl flung forward over the head. In front of each face, a simple piece of white linen was fastened by two buttons level with the cheekbones: the lower half of the face was masked, and only two eyes and a strip of forehead could be seen.

Lined up facing the wall as they were, they would all have needed to lean forwards and turn their heads forty-five degrees to see the silhouettes of their companions at table. Such contortions were obviously forbidden, just as it went without saying that they would show their hands as rarely as possible. Their arms were folded on the table, and the openings of their wide sleeves were designed to fit into one another easily, covering the wrists and hands of the participants.

Thus it was that, whenever they spoke, the members of this assembly did not address each other directly, but spoke to the bleeding image placed opposite them. If they could all hear – without turning their heads – what was said, it was because the Master, mute on his cross, gave his consent.

In this room whose very existence is unknown to the common run of mortals, the Society of St Pius V was holding its three thousand six hundred and third meeting since its foundation.

Set at the right of the empty throne, a single participant had placed, flat on the table – which was completely bare – his chubby hands: on his right-hand ring finger, a dark green

48

jasper glittered when he rose; he mechanically smoothed down his alb over his slightly protruding abdomen.

"My brothers, three exterior questions that we have already discussed in this very place need to occupy our minds today, and there is a fourth... one that is painful for all of us."

A complete silence greeted this declaration: everyone waited to hear what would come next.

"At the request of the Cardinal Prefect of the Congregation, you have been informed of a little problem that has arisen recently in France, in a Benedictine abbey that is under very strict surveillance. You gave me carte blanche to deal with it. Well, I have the pleasure of being able to tell you that the problem has been solved in a satisfactory manner: the monk whose recent remarks were giving us cause for alarm is no longer in any position to harm the Holy Catholic Church."

One of those present slightly raised his forearms, folded under his sleeves, to signify that he wished to speak.

"You mean that he has been... suppressed?"

"I would not use that term, *offensivum auribus nostris*. I have to inform you that he inopportunely fell from the Rome express that was taking him back to the Abbey, and that he died instantly. The French authorities have decided it was suicide. I thus commend him to your prayers: suicide, as you know, is a terrible crime against the creator of all life."

"But... Brother Rector, wasn't it dangerous to call on the services of a foreign agent to make this... suicide possible? Can we really be sure of his discretion?"

"I met the Palestinian while I was staying in Cairo, several years ago: ever since then, he has proved most reliable. His interests coincide with ours on this occasion, as he perfectly well understood. He obtained help from an old acquaintance of his, an Israeli agent: the men from Hamas and those from

Mossad are at each other's throats, but they know how to lend each other a hand when they have a common cause – and this is the case here, a fact which serves our own plans. Only the result matters: the means employed must be efficacious, rapid and definitive. And I can vouch for the absolute discretion of these two agents. They are being very well remunerated."

"Indeed: the thousands of dollars you have mentioned to us represent a considerable sum. Is this expense really justified?"

The Rector turned to his questioner, something he very rarely did.

"My brother, this investment is paltry in comparison with the profits that it can generate. These I estimate to be, not in the thousands, but in the millions of dollars. If we achieve our aims, we will at last have the wherewithal to accomplish our mission. Remember the sudden, vast wealth acquired by the Templars – well, we shall be drawing on the same sources as they did. But we will succeed where they failed."

"And the Germigny slab?"

"I was coming to that. The discovery of the slab would have passed unnoticed if Father Andrei had not been alerted to it because of the geographical proximity of his abbey. He had the unfortunate idea of going to visit the spot straight away, so he was the first to read the inscription. We knew of its existence thanks to the file on the Templars."

"You have already told us this."

"On his recent trip to Rome, he reluctantly passed some comments which seemed to prove that he was linking together all the information in his possession. This is extremely dangerous; we never know where it will all end, and our Society was founded by the sainted Pope Pius V to avoid" – and here he bowed, first to the empty throne on his left and then to the crucifix before him – "any sullying or tarnishing of the Master's memory and image. During the Church's long history, all those who have tried to do so have been eliminated. Often in time, but sometimes too late – and then there was the most dreadful turmoil, and it caused considerable suffering: think of Origen, Arius or even Nestorius, as well as many others... The team from the Rome express will do whatever is necessary, at my request: the Germigny slab will soon be safe from prying eyes, in this very place."

All present heaved a sigh of relief.

"But we now have another problem that has risen from the first," the Rector added.

Several heads automatically turned towards him.

"For some time, the late Father Andrei seems to have been arousing the curiosity of a kind of disciple: one of the monks, a professor in the special theology college of the abbey in question. Oh, it may be nothing more than a false alarm, triggered by a message that the Father Abbot has forwarded to us. A student attending the exegesis course of this professor – a certain Father Nil – has revealed that he had heard him putting forward positions that undermine sound teaching on the Gospel according to St John. Given the recent circumstances, the Father Abbot decided it was best to warn us straight away."

Several brothers looked up: the Gospel according to St John was at the very heart of their mission, and everything that might affect it needed to be closely analysed.

"Normally, the orthodoxy of a Catholic exegete concerns the Congregation, and this monk is not the first whom that body will have had to put in his place..."

There was the ghost of a smile under the veils covering the faces of some of those present.

"…but the circumstances here are rather special. The late lamented Father Andrei was a scholar of exceptional ability, and he had an acute and inventive intelligence. He is no longer capable of inflicting any harm, but what did he manage to suggest to his disciple Nil? As the Father Abbot has explained to us, a close friendship – always regrettable in an abbey – bound together these two intellectuals. In other words, might the poison that had seeped into Father Andrei's mind also have infected Father Nil? We have no means of knowing."

One of the brothers lifted his folded arms.

"Tell me, Brother Rector… This Father Nil… does he ever happen to take the Rome express too?"

"He might well do so. But a second suicide among the monks of the Abbey is something we can't envisage. Neither the French Government nor public opinion would be easy to convince, given the closeness of the events. As it happens it is a matter of some urgency, since this monk teaches on a regular basis and seems bent on bringing his students up to date with his… well, with some of the conclusions he has drawn from his research. What are they? We don't know, but we cannot run any risks: the Cardinal is placing a great deal of hope on the monastic theology college of St Martin, and he wants it to be absolutely beyond reproach."

"What do you suggest?"

The Rector sat down and withdrew his hands and his ring into the shelter of the sleeves of his alb.

"I do not know yet; it's all happened so recently. The first thing we need to do is find out what this monk knows, or – if he doesn't as yet know anything very serious – work out how far he might go. I'll let you know."

He paused, and stared intently at the crucifix, whose ivory was stained by a blood which seemed to have dried and clotted over the centuries. The next question was going to be more difficult: he couldn't beat around the bush. Every brother, after all, expected the Society to apply its statutes.

Even when these required the death of one of their number.

"Each of you knows nothing, or almost nothing, about the brother sitting next to him at this moment. So it falls to me to carry out the terrible task of protecting our Society, should the need arise."

The Rector of the Society of St Pius V was appointed for life. When he felt close to death, he designated from among the brothers the one who would succeed him – and who, in turn, would be the only one to know the identity of his eleven companions, and to be known by them. Most of the rectors, since 1570, had had the good taste to die before they became incapable. Sometimes, it had been necessary to give a helping hand to those who clung to life more than to their Master: the Eleven kept rigorous tabs on the capabilities of their leader. There was a protocol for such cases – and it was precisely this protocol that was about to be applied, but this time to a brother.

"One of us, I very much regret to say, has recently demonstrated his inability to respect our principal rule, that of complete and utter confidentiality. His venerable age, no doubt, has weakened his reflexes."

One of those present started to tremble, and the sleeves of his alb slipped down to reveal bony hands with prominent veins.

"Brother, please cover yourself!... Very well: you know the procedure applied to the guilty man. I am giving you due warning, so that this very evening you may begin the time of fasting, prayer and severe penitence that always accompanies the definitive end of a brother's mission. We must help him to make ready, and keep him company on the path that he is now to take. Total abstinence on the day before our next gathering, and discipline with the metal scourge morning and evening, every day, for as long as it takes to recite the *Miserere* – or longer if you wish. We will not stint our affection for the brother who has shared our responsibilities for so long, and from whom we will soon need to be parted."

Calfo did not like having to apply this protocol to one of the Twelve. He gazed intently at the crucifix: ever since he had presided over the gatherings of his Society, the Master had seen and heard many such cases.

"Thank you. We have until the next session to prove to our brother, in secret, the strength of the love we bear him."

The brothers rose and made their way towards the armour-plated door at the far end.

13

Gospels according to Matthew and John

As the sun rose on the Saturday of Passover, its gleam caught the tiles of the *impluvium*. Sitting on the rim of the basin in the centre, exhausted after two days that had witnessed the total destruction of so many hopes, the Judaean sighed: he would have to go up to the upper room where the Eleven had taken refuge in a panic-stricken flock. Jesus had been delivered to Pilate, crucified at noon the day before... It was a catastrophe beyond their worst imaginings.

He finally made up his mind to move and slowly climbed the steps leading to the first storey, where he pushed open the door through which he had watched Judas exit on Thursday evening. A single small light was burning in the huge room. He made out shadows sitting here and there on the floor. Nobody was speaking. These terrorized Galileans, forced into hiding – so this was all that remained of the Israel of the new age.

A shadow detached itself from the wall and came over to him.

"Well?"

Peter stared arrogantly at him.

"He will never accept that we've failed," he thought to himself. "He will never accept having to be in my debt by taking refuge at my home like this, just as he never accepted my privileged relationship with Jesus."

"Well, Pilate authorized Jesus's body to be taken down from the cross yesterday evening. As it was too late to give him the ritual treatment, he was placed provisionally in a nearby tomb, which happens to belong to Joseph of Arimathea, a sympathizer."

"Who transported the body?"

"Nicodemus carried the head and Joseph the feet. And some women, acting as mourners – the usual ones, we know them well: Mary of Magdala and her friends."

Peter bit his lower lip and punched the palm of his left hand.

"How shameful! What a… a humiliation! The final homage is always paid to a dead man by the members of his family! Neither Mary, nor his brother James were there… just sympathizers! The Master really died like a dog."

The Judaean gazed at him ironically.

"Is it the fault of Mary his mother, of James and his three other brothers, or his sisters, that the preparations for your insurrection were carried out in the greatest secrecy? Is it their fault that everything went wrong, in just a few hours, in such a tragic and unexpected way? Is it their fault that Caiaphas lied, that Jesus was taken before Pilate yesterday morning? That he was crucified without further ado, without any trial? Whose fault is it?"

Peter bowed his head. It was he who had teamed up with his old Zealot friends, it was he who had convinced Judas to do the dirty work, it was he who was ultimately responsible for everything. He knew as much, but he could not acknowledge it. Not in front of this man, this usurper, who continued his tirade.

"Where were *you* when they laid Jesus on the beam of wood, when they hammered the nails into his wrists? Yesterday at midday, I was there, hiding in the crowd. I heard the horrible noise of the hammer blows, I saw the blood and the water flowing from his side when the legionary finished him off with a thrust of his spear. I am the only one here who can testify that Jesus the Nazorean died like a man, without complaining, without uttering a word of reproach to us, even though we had allowed him to fall into this trap. Where were you all?"

Peter did not reply. The treachery of Caiaphas, Jesus delivered to the Romans, all these unexpected events had rendered their preparations for the insurrection futile. Like the others, at the very moment the Master was dying in agony, he had been hiding somewhere in the Lower City. As far away as possible from the Roman legionaries, as far away as possible from the western gate of Jerusalem and its crosses. Yes, this man alone had been present, he was the only one to have *seen*; he alone would now be able to testify to the death of Jesus, to his courage and his dignity. From now on he would be able to milk this fact for all it was worth, to strut and boast every hour of the day – the impostor!

He needed to seize back the initiative. *He* was the leader here. He drew the other man over to the window.

"Come. We need to talk."

Peter gazed out into the night for a few moments. Everything was dark in Jerusalem. He turned round and broke the heavy silence.

"Two urgent problems. First, Jesus's body: none of us can accept seeing it being thrown into a common grave, like all those condemned to death. It would be an insult to his memory."

The Judaean glanced at the indistinct shapes slumped along the walls of the upper room. Obviously, none of them would be able to offer the dead man a decent burial place. Joseph of Arimathea would not accept having Jesus in his family vault for ever. They needed to think of something else.

"There might be a way out... The Essenes always viewed Jesus as one of them – even if he never agreed to join their sect. For a long time I was part of their lay community: I know them well. They will certainly be prepared to place his body in one of their burial grounds in the desert.

"Can you get in touch with them? Right away?"

"Eliezer lives nearby, I'll take care of it all. And the second problem?"

Peter looked the other man straight in the eye – just then, the moon emerged from behind a cloud and heightened his rugged features. It was the former Zealot who replied, in harsh tones:

"The other problem is Judas. And I'll take care of *him*."

"Judas?"

"Did you know that this morning he went to the Temple to kick up a fuss? Did you know that he accused the High Priest of

57

felony, and that he called God to witness between Caiaphas and himself, in front of the crowd? According to Jewish superstition, one of the two must now die at God's hand. Caiaphas knows as much, and he'll have him arrested: then he'll talk. Both you and I will be unmasked. Me in particular. For the priests, it's of no importance. But think of the sympathizers: if they learn that it's because of us that Jesus was captured – even if we had no other intention than of ensuring his safety – then we have no future to speak of. Do you see what I'm saying?"

The Judaean stared in stupefaction at the Galilean. "What future?" he thought. "You've only just managed to save your wretched skin from a botched venture. What future do you have, other than going back to your fishing nets? You should never have left them in the first place!"

He said nothing. Peter bowed his head, and his face was again plunged into darkness.

"This man has lost his head, he's become really dangerous. We need to do something to eliminate that danger. Don't you worry about it, I'll look after Judas."

And his hand instinctively caressed his left thigh, where his *sica* rubbed against his flesh.

14

Acts of the Apostles

Leaving the Judaean standing there open-mouthed, Peter left the room, crossed the *impluvium* and slipped out of the house. The day was dawning tremulously on this Passover Saturday. The streets would be empty: he knew where he could find Judas.

He threaded his way through the labyrinth of ever narrower streets in the Lower City, where the cobblestones ran out and the sand crunched under his sandals.

He knocked at a door.

The anxious face of a veiled woman peered out.

"Peter! But... at this time of day?"

"It's not you I've come to see, woman. It's the Iscariot. Is he here?"

She still did not let him in, and lowered her voice.

"Yes, he arrived in the middle of the night. He was in a real panic. He really seemed out of his wits... He begged me to hide him until the end of the festival. He said that he had publicly accused the High Priest Caiaphas of treachery, and he called God to witness – now one of them must die."

"You don't believe all that, do you?"

"I am a disciple of Jesus, like you: he has delivered us from all those fables that keep the people in thrall."

Peter smiled at her.

"In that case," he said, "you have nothing to fear: I've come to reassure Judas. God is just, he knows that he has an upright heart. Judas was wrong to call him to witness between himself and the High Priest. Ask him to step outside, I want a word with him."

The woman hesitated, stared at Peter for a while and closed the door in his face.

The apostle wandered a little further on. There were three low-roofed houses at the dead end of the street; their outside shutters were drawn. Jerusalem was still asleep, after spending the night reciting the Passover Seder.

A noise made him start. He turned round. Judas was standing in front of him.

"Peter! *Shalom!*"

He was deadly pale. There were shadows under his eyes, and his hair was unkempt, giving him a haggard air. He stared at Peter in some disquiet. Peter did not return his greeting, but merely nodded. Judas took the initiative.

"If only you knew... We were betrayed, Peter, betrayed by the High Priest in person. He had sworn that Jesus's life would be safe. And yesterday at dawn, I saw the master being led before Pilate in chains. Then..."

"Then you lost your head!" Peter replied in cutting tones.

"Then I wanted to remind Caiaphas of our agreement. And I called God to witness between him and me."

"Do you know what that means, according to your absurd beliefs?"

Judas lowered his head and wrung his hands.

"Every oath that is sworn calls on the Everlasting. Caiaphas swore an oath to me, he gave me money as a token of his good faith, and yet Jesus died as a malefactor! Ah yes, only the Everlasting can be judge of such infamy."

"Didn't Jesus tell us again and again that we were not to swear by God's throne, since this was insulting to him?"

Judas shook his head.

"God judges, brother; God must judge the infamy of men..."

Peter thought: "This is what the priests have done to us – made us the slaves of absurd beliefs. This is what we need to free Israel from, first and foremost – and if this doesn't happen with Jesus, it will have to happen without him. But Judas is doomed. It's too late for him."

"Well, Judas?" he said.

"Well, it's all over. All we can do now is go back home to Galilee to expiate the Master's death for as long as we live. It's all over, Peter!"

The apostle took a step towards Judas, who stared at him mistrustfully. To reassure him, Peter smiled at him. "This man is a victim of Jewish power, let him die in peace!" Then he unsheathed his *sica,* and with a sudden thrust, as he had once learnt from the Zealots, he plunged it into Judas's belly. With a grimace of disgust, he jerked it upwards until he felt the sternum obstructing his weapon.

"God has judged, Judas," he whispered into his face. "God always judges: Caiaphas will continue to live – so much the worst for Israel."

With his eyes widening in horror, Judas, without a cry, toppled forwards, his belly slashed open and his entrails spilling out onto the sand.

Peter stepped back, slowly, and looked up and down the dead-end street: nothing had moved, there would be no witnesses. Slowly, he wiped his short sword on the inside of his tunic. Then he looked up. The cheerful Passover sun was shedding its light on the land of Israel, reminding him of their departure from slavery in the land of Egypt, and the miraculous parting of the waters of the Red Sea.

On that day, a people had been born: the People of God. Twelve tribes had then wandered through the desert before settling in Canaan: the old Israel, which was now on its last legs. A new Israel needed to come into being, and this time it would be led by twelve apostles. So there were only eleven of them left? God himself would appoint a replacement for Judas.

But never would the Judaean, the so-called beloved disciple, be one of the Twelve.

Never.

* * *

Peter stepped over Judas's body. When it was discovered, everyone would think it was a settling of accounts between Zealots: disembowelling their enemies was their calling card. He took a last glance at the body.

"From now on, I am the rock on which the Church will be built, and death will not prevail against us. It is not all over, Judas."

15

Two days had gone by since the death of Andrei. Nil gazed at his table strewn with papers, the result of years of research. He thought he had elucidated the circumstances of the death of Judas: the plot had been hatched during the final days preceding the crucifixion. Judas had been murdered; he had not hanged himself. The events that ensued could be understood only if the texts were scrutinized in detail, so that one could discover, behind what they openly said, what they merely hinted at. History is not an exact science: its truth comes from the juxtaposition of accumulated clues.

Now he needed to apply the same method to the mysterious note he had found in the hand of his dead friend. For this, he needed to gain access to the historical library. The new librarian would be appointed only after the funeral, which was to take place the following day.

He closed his eyes and allowed the memories to rise up within him.

"Father Nil, I have just learnt that, while working on the restorations at Germigny, the workers have unearthed an ancient inscription. I'd like to see it. Do you think you could come with me? I need to photograph some manuscripts in Orléans, and the road goes past Germigny-des-Prés…"

They parked on the square in the little village. Nil was pleased to see this church again. Charlemagne's architect had wanted to reproduce in miniature the cathedral of Aix-la-Chapelle, built in about 800. Its marvellous stained glass in alabaster created a powerful atmosphere inside, a sense of intimacy and meditation.

They made their way to the threshold of the sanctuary.

"See how it is still wrapped in mystery!"

Andrei's whispering was rendered barely audible by the noise of the hammers attacking the end wall: to remove the windows, the workers had been obliged to remove the coating surrounding them. In between two openings, just where the nave continued, one could make out in the gloom a gaping hole. Andrei went over to the men.

"Excuse me, gentlemen, I'd like to take a look at a slab that I gather you found while you were doing the restoration."

"Oh, the stone? Yes, we found it under a layer of coating. We pulled it down from the wall and placed it in the left transept."

"Can we examine it?"

"No problem: you're the first people to take an interest in it."

The two monks walked a little further on and noticed on the floor a square slab, the edges of which bore the traces of having been embedded. Andrei bent over, then went down on one knee.

"Ah… the embedding is clearly original. When it was *in situ*, this slab would have been directly in view of the faithful. So it assumed a particular importance… Then – look – it was covered with a coating that seems more recent."

Nil shared his companion's excitement. These men never

referred to history as a period that was over and done with: the past was their present. At this precise moment, they could hear a voice from across the centuries: the voice of the emperor who had ordered this slab to be engraved and wished it to be embedded in such a remarkable spot.

Andrei took out his handkerchief and delicately wiped the surface of the stone.

"The coating is of the same type as those in Romanesque churches. So this slab must have been covered with it two or three centuries after being set in place: one day, the need was felt to hide the inscription from the public. So in whose interest was it to hide it away?"

Characters were starting to appear under the coating as it crumbled into dust.

"Carolingian script. But... it's the text of the *Symbolon* of Nicaea!"

"The text of the Creed?"

"Indeed. I wonder why they wanted it to be so prominent, under full view of all, in this imperial church. In particular, I wonder..."

Andrei knelt looking at the inscription for a long while. Then he stood up, dusted himself down and placed his hand on Nil's shoulder.

"My friend, in this reproduction of the Nicene Creed, there's something I don't understand: I've never seen it before."

They quickly took a snapshot, and left just as the workers were downing tools for lunch.

Andrei remained silent until Orléans. As Nil was preparing the camera for their work session, he stopped him.

"No, not with that film, it's the one we used for the slab. Put it to one side, and use another film for these manuscripts, if you don't mind."

The journey home was glum. Before he got out of the car, Andrei turned to Nil. His face looked particularly grave.

"We'll develop the Germigny photo and make two copies. I'll take one and fax it straight away to an employee at the Vatican Library with whom I have been corresponding: I'd like to have his opinion; there are very few people capable of understanding the particularities of inscriptions from the High Middle Ages. The second copy... you can keep it and take good care of it in your cell. You never know."

A fortnight later, Andrei had phoned Nil in his office. He seemed worried.

"I've just received a letter from the Vatican: they've told me to go and explain the translation of the Coptic manuscript I told you about. Why do they want me to go there? With the letter there was a note from the employee in the Vatican telling me he'd received the photo of the Germigny slab. But he didn't add anything by way of comment."

Nil was just as surprised as his friend.

"When are you leaving?"

"Father Abbot came this morning to give me a ticket for the Rome express that leaves tomorrow. Father Nil... please, while I'm away, go back to Germigny. The snapshot that we took isn't clear: take another photo in a raking light."

"Father Andrei, can you tell me what you are thinking?"

"I can't tell you any more today. Find some excuse or another to leave the Abbey, and quickly go and take that photo. We'll examine it together as soon as I'm back."

Andrei had left for Rome the following day.

And he had never returned to the Abbey.

* * *

Nil opened his eyes. He would go as soon as he possibly could to carry out his friend's last wishes. But without him, what would be the use of a new snapshot of the inscription?

The tocsin started to chime lugubriously, announcing to the whole valley that, the next day, a monk was going to be solemnly borne to his last resting place. Nil half-opened the drawer in his table, and slipped his hand under the pile of letters.

His heart started to beat. He pulled the drawer open fully: *the photo taken at Germigny had disappeared, and so had Father Andrei's note.*

"Impossible! It's impossible!"

He had poured the contents of the drawer out onto the table: there was no denying it – the snapshot and the note were just not there.

Monks take a vow of poverty, so they possess absolutely nothing, cannot lock anything away, and not a single cell in the Abbey had a lock. Only the offices of the steward and that of the Father Abbot had locks – and the three libraries, the keys to which had been distributed parsimoniously, as already mentioned.

But a monk's cell is the inviolable domain of his solitude: nobody is ever allowed in when its occupant is not there, or without obtaining his formal permission. Except for the Father Abbot who, ever since his election, had made it a point of honour to respect this intangible rule, which underlines the choice made by his monks to live in a community, but alone in the face of God.

Not only had *someone* violated Father Nil's sanctuary, but *someone* had rummaged around and stolen what he found. He glanced at the folders scattered in disorder across the table. Yes, *someone* had not been content with ferreting around in the drawer: the most voluminous of his files, the one on the Gospel according to St John, was not in its usual place. It had been slightly moved, and opened. Nil, who had used it every day since his classes had started, immediately saw that some of his notes were not in their right order, the logic of which was known to him alone. He even thought that some pages had disappeared.

A rule of Benedictine life had just been violated – he had evident proof of the fact. And there must be an extremely serious reason for that. He had the vague sense that there must be a link between the unusual events of these last few days – but what?

He had become a monk against the wishes of his family, who were non-believers. He remembered himself as a young novice. *The truth...* he had pledged his whole life to seeking it out. Two men had understood this: Rembert Leeland, his co-disciple during the four years he had been a student in Rome, and Andrei. Leeland was now working somewhere in the Vatican, and Nil found himself alone, facing questions that he was unable to answer – and filled with a barely contained anguish that had not left him since the end of summer.

His hand smoothed down the thick file on St John's Gospel: it was all there. In fact, Andrei had not ceased to tell him as much, while refusing to give him any more information or to allow him into the library in the north wing. He could do no other: obedience was the rule. But Andrei was dead, perhaps because of that obedience. And his own cell had been searched, in violation of the immutable rules of the Abbey.

He had to do something.

There was an hour to go before vespers. He got up, went out into the corridor and made his way resolutely towards the stairs leading to the libraries.

* * *

Thanks to his good visual memory, he had recorded every little detail of Andrei's note in his mind. *Coptic manuscript (Apoc.)* – probably a Coptic apocalypse. *Apostle's letter*, then the three mysterious *M M M*, and the stone slab at Germigny. The thread linking all these mysterious elements must be lying unnoticed somewhere in the books of the library.

He came to Andrei's office, situated just next to the wing devoted to Biblical Studies. Ten yards further on was the corner of the north wing, and the entry to the library of Historical Studies.

The librarian's door had no more of a lock than any other cell in the monastery. He went in, switched the light on and sat heavily on the chair where, for so many happy hours, he had enjoyed conversations with his friend. Nothing had changed. Along the walls, the bookshelves with their piles of freshly labelled books: recent acquisitions, waiting to be definitively catalogued in one of the three wings. Underneath, the metal drawers in which Andrei filed the photocopies of the manuscripts on which he was working. The Coptic Apocalypse must be somewhere among them. Should he begin here?

Suddenly he gave a start. On a shelf, there were several rolls lying in disorder: the negatives of his manuscripts... Among them, in the first row, he immediately recognized the one he had used to photograph the Germigny slab. Andrei had left it there, without giving it another thought, before his departure for Rome.

Nil's photo had just been stolen, but they hadn't thought about the negative, or maybe they hadn't had time to inspect the librarian's office. Without hesitating, Nil got up, took the roll off the shelf and slipped it into his pocket. The last wishes of a dead man are sacred...

Just in front of him, hanging from the back of the chair, he recognized the jacket and trousers that Andrei had been wearing at the time he died. He would be buried the next day in his big monastic habit: nobody would ever wear this garment again, which was now of no further use to the inquiry. A mist of tears veiled Nil's eyes; then a crazy idea took hold of him. He seized the trousers and slipped his hand into the left pocket: his fingers tightened round a leather object. Quickly, he drew it out of the pocket: a bunch of keys! Without a moment's hesitation, he opened the clasp.

Three keys. The longest of them, exactly the same as his, was that to the central wing – the two others must be those of the north and south wings. *The special bunch of keys, the one which only the librarian and the Abbot possessed.* Perturbed by the dramatic events affecting his abbey, the Father Abbot had not yet thought of recovering these keys – which he would hand over to Andrei's successor when he had made up his mind about this delicate appointment.

Nil hesitated for a while. Then, in his mind's eye, he saw the face of his friend sitting opposite him on this chair. "The truth, Nil: it was to find the truth that you entered this Abbey!" He slipped the bunch of keys into his pocket and walked the few yards down the corridor to the north wing and the library in it.

Historical Studies: if he crossed this threshold, he would become a rebel.

He glanced behind him: the two corridors of the central wing and the north wing were empty.

Resolutely, he inserted one of the two little keys into the lock of the north wing: silently, the key turned.

* * *

Father Nil, the peaceable professor of exegesis, the observant monk who had never infringed the slightest rule of the Abbey, opened the door and stepped forward. By entering the north library, he was making himself a dissident.

16

Gospel according to Matthew

"What are they doing up there?"

They were sitting on one of the stone benches in the *impluvium*. The day was just dawning, the Sunday of Passover; the house was silent. Like his host, Peter was exhausted. "Two sleepless nights," he thought, "we haven't had a proper meal since Thursday evening, in the upper room with Jesus. Then, the arrest and death of the Master. And Judas eliminated."

His face was hollow, there were deep shadows under his eyes. He repeated his question.

"What are they doing up there?"

"You should know: didn't you spend all of yesterday locked away here, while I was busy negotiating with the Essenes?"

The Judaean did not mention the brief sortie that Peter had made the morning before. When he had seen him slipping out into the street, his hand flattened against his left thigh, he had understood. Later on that day, he had heard the rumours sweeping Jerusalem: the Galilean murdered by a Zealot was the man who had called God to witness between Caiaphas and himself the day before. His death was in the run of things: God had judged, and had chosen the Iscariot.

"I think..." Peter smiled bitterly, "that most of them are asleep right now. Tell me, are the Essenes inclined to help us?"

"Yes, I've had some good news. They consider that Jesus is one of the Just of Israel, and are ready to offer him a place of burial in one of their cemeteries. The transferral cannot take place until the sounding of the shofar to announce the end of Passover. You know that the Essenes are real sticklers when it comes to questions of ritual impurity; they'll never touch a body until the festival is officially over. In an hour's time."

Peter shot a sidelong glance at him.

"Where are they going to bury him? Qumran?"

The Judaean took his time answering. He looked Peter straight in the eye.

"I don't know, they haven't told me."

They will tell me – he thought – but you'll never know.

Not you. Never.

17

Nil gently closed the library door. Once he had been able to enter this place freely. But when the theology college had been set up, they had changed the locks: he hadn't set foot in this part of the north wing for four years.

He recognized the familiar smell, and at first glance he had the impression that nothing had changed. How many times had he come here to pick up a new book! And that meant making the acquaintance of a new friend, striking up a new dialogue. Books are companions you can rely on: they give themselves totally, without reserve, to anyone able to question them with tact but also with persistence. And Nil had been extraordinarily persistent.

From his earliest years he had been brought up in a completely materialist environment, where the only god venerated was social success. But one day he had glimpsed the light. How? His memory had lost all trace of how it had happened – but that day, he had *known* that reality is not limited to what we can perceive of it, to mere appearances. And the realization had dawned on him that finding out what lies *beyond appearances* constituted the most difficult of undertakings, the one that justified a man in mobilizing all the strength at his command.

This inner venture seemed to him, from this moment on, to be the only one capable of justifying the life of a free man. And the quest for what lay beyond appearances seemed the only quest not subject to any pressure from outside.

What he does not know, at the moment he enters the library in the north wing, is that he is wrong – wrong because it is against the rules that he is crossing this threshold, and because his only friend in the Abbey is dead – perhaps for crossing it too often.

In front of him, the world's historical knowledge was lined up within dozens of book stacks.

"Books don't give us knowledge," Andrei had told him. "They're a form of raw food. It's your task to digest it, in other words to deconstruct it as you read it, and then to reconstruct it within yourself. I have studied a lot, Nil, but I have learnt little. Do not forget what you are seeking: the very mystery of God, which lies beyond words. The words and ideas contained in books will lead you in very different directions, depending on the way you put them together. It's all there, present in these books – but most people simply see them as stones scattered in disorder on the bookshelves. It's up to you to build a coherent edifice out of them. But beware: not all architectural designs are acceptable, and not all are accepted. So long as you cling to what is ideologically correct, you won't have any problems. Repeat what people have said before you, rebuild the same edifice that has already been consecrated by the past, and you will be honoured. But if, with these same stones, you erect a new building, then beware..."

Nil recognized the nearest book stacks: twentieth century. The post-war librarian – he now rested in the cemetery – had not rigorously followed the Dewey Universal Classification, but one that was more convenient for the monks: a chronological one. The book stacks that interested Nil were thus at the very far end. He moved towards them.

And his eyes opened wide in amazement.

Four years previously, two book stacks had been enough to contain the first-century materials, catalogued by geographical origin: Palestine, the rest of the Middle East, the Latin West, the Greek West... But now he had half a dozen book stacks in front of him. He moved along to the ones devoted to Palestine: almost two entire book stacks! Texts that he had sought in vain in the only part of the library to which he had access, the Midrashim of the Pharisean epoch, the Psalms and wisdom texts that appear neither in the Old nor in the New Testament...

He moved along a little further, and came to a book stack on which the only label was: "Qumran". He started to leaf through the books, and then suddenly stopped. There, catalogued between the different editions of the Dead Sea Scrolls, his finger had just come to rest on a thick volume. There was no name of author or publisher on the spine, but simply three letters in Father Andrei's handwriting: *M M M*.

Nil, his heart beating fast, pulled the book out. *M M M*... the three letters Andrei had written just before he died!

In the faint gleam of the ceiling lights, he opened the work. It was not a book, but a bundle of photocopies: Nil immediately recognized the characteristic calligraphy of the Dead Sea Scrolls. So M M M simply meant *Manuscrits de la Mer Morte*, "Dead Sea Manuscripts"... Where did these texts come from?

At the foot of the first page, he spelt out a rubber-stamp mark in faded blue ink: "Huntington Library, San Marino, California".

The Americans' manuscripts!

One day, Andrei had told him the story – lowering his voice even though the door to his office was closed.

"The Dead Sea manuscripts were discovered just before the creation of the State of Israel, in 1947–48. In the turmoil of those chaotic days, there was a free-for-all in which everyone tried to buy – or steal – as many of those scrolls as possible, since it was suspected that they would revolutionize Christianity. The Americans got their hands on a significant number of them. Ever since then, the international team entrusted with publishing these texts has gone out of its way to delay their appearance. Seeing this, the Huntington Library decided to publish everything it possessed, in photocopies, and available only to a select few. I hope that one day" – and here he smiled maliciously – "we will be able to possess a copy here. These are in samizdat: just as in the worst Soviet period, we're obliged to circulate these texts surreptitiously!"

"Why, Father Andrei? *Who* is blocking publication of these manuscripts? And why are they frightened to reveal them?"

As sometimes happened in their conversations, Andrei had withdrawn into an awkward silence. And started to talk about something else.

Nil hesitated for a moment: in the normal run of things,

he was not allowed to borrow this work. Every time a monk takes a book from the bookshelves, he is supposed to leave in its place a "phantom", a slip bearing his signature together with the date of borrowing. This system means that books do not get lost, but it also means that the intellectual work being done by the monks can be kept under surveillance. Nil knew that for some time this surveillance had been strict.

His mind was soon made up. "Andrei's replacement has not yet been appointed. With any luck, nobody will notice that a book has disappeared for a single night without being replaced by a 'phantom'."

Like a thief, clutching his booty to his chest, he headed to the exit and slipped out of the library: the north-wing corridor was deserted.

He had one night: a long night of secret labour.

In the "Qumran" book stack of the history library, a big empty gap without its "phantom" signalled that a monk had today violated one of the strictest rules of St Martin's Abbey.

18

A few miles away, in the middle of the night, as Nil turned the pages of the *M M M* under the lampshade of his cell (he had blocked his window with a towel, the second dissident thing he had done that day), two men silently climbed out of a dust-covered car. The driver, blowing on fingers stiff with the November cold, gazed at the little church whose alabaster stained-glass windows glimmered in the night. Feeling a powerful wave of excitement surge up in him, he shivered, and his face suddenly became set.

The other passenger took a step forwards and inspected the environs: the village was asleep. Before them, the loose planks cordoning off the building site would be easy to shift, and it would be no trouble getting the stone slab out. Child's play!

He turned round.

"*Bismillah, yallah!*"

"*Ken, baruch atah Adonai!*"

A few minutes later they re-emerged, dragging along a heavy stone slab. As they wriggled their way between the planks of the fence, the driver tried to stifle the beating of his heart. "I must calm down…"

The village square was as silent and deserted as before. They hoisted the slab into the boot, then he took his place at the wheel and heaved a sigh: they faced a long journey to Rome… Before he pulled the door shut, the little roof light lit up his blond hair, and the scar that stretched from it down to his left ear.

The jasper on Mgr Calfo's finger, with its red highlights and silver frame, glinted briefly, while with his chubby hand he stroked the girl's lovely hair. He wished he could have mimicked, now, in the last years of the twentieth century, some of the refinements of Antiquity: the remains buried under Rome show that brothels and temples always formed a single organic unity. The same door led to the sources of one and the same ecstasy.

In the tranquillity of his apartment near Castel Sant'Angelo, from which if you leant forward you could see the majestic dome hanging over the tomb of Peter, he was happy on this particular evening to be wearing nothing other than his bishop's ring.

"The union of the divine and the carnal... If God became man in Jesus Christ, it was to make this union real. So, my beauty, make me rise up heavenwards!"

19

Gospels according to Mark and Luke

From the Temple, the guttural blast of the shofar greeted the sun, marking the end of Passover on this Sunday morning, 9th April. Four young men strode resolutely to the cemetery situated outside the west gate of Jerusalem. One of them was carrying a lever: a tombstone would need to be rolled away, and tombstones were always extremely heavy. But the young men were used to it.

On entering the tomb, they found the body of an executed man placed simply on a central slab, bearing the deep traces of flagellation and the marks of crucifixion. On one side, an open wound was still slightly bleeding. They uttered a groan.

"Eternal One! See what they do to your sons, the prophets of Israel! May the curse of this spilt blood fall on their heads! So much suffering for this just man!"

After reciting *Kaddish*, they slipped on their long white robes: transferring a corpse into pure earth represented a religious act for them, and it was obligatory to wear white. Furthermore, it would identify them to Jewish pilgrims – who were used to seeing Essenes transporting certain corpses for reburial in their own cemeteries.

Only two of them made ready to lift up the body. Everything had happened very fast on Friday evening, and the dead man's relatives would certainly be coming to finish preparing the body for burial. If they discovered an empty tomb, panic would ensue: they needed to be warned.

So the other two men, still wearing their white robes, settled down comfortably, one at the head and the other at the foot of the burial slab, while their companions took up the body and started out on the long journey towards one of the Essenian burial grounds in the desert.

The two who had stayed behind did not have long to wait: the sun was still low on the horizon when they heard furtive footsteps. Women from Jesus's entourage.

When they saw the heavy tombstone rolled to one side, the women gave a sudden start. One of them took a step forward and screamed in terror: two beings dressed in white were standing in the dark cave mouth of the tomb and seemed to be waiting for them. In her terror she stammered out a question to which they calmly replied. When the white apparitions started to come out, to explain further, the women turned on their heels and fled, screeching like a flock of birds.

The two Essenes shrugged. Why had Jesus's apostles sent women instead of coming themselves? Anyway, their own mission was over. They simply needed to tidy the place up before leaving.

They took off their white robes and tried to roll back the tombstone – in vain. There were now only two of them, and it was too heavy. So leaving the tomb open, they came out of the garden and sat in the sunshine. The Judaean who had organized it all would be coming to see them: they just needed to wait for him.

20

Calfo twirled the whip again and then lashed his shoulders with it. The metal discipline, which he prescribed to the Society only on rare occasions, is a skein of small cords with small aluminium balls threaded along them. Normally, drops of blood should start to appear at around verse 17 of the psalm *Miserere* – which thus acts as a kind of hourglass for this penance. At the twenty-first and final verse, it is seen as a good thing for a few red drops to spatter the wall behind the flagellant.

This mortification recalled the thirty-nine lashes received by Jesus before his crucifixion. When administered by a sturdy legionary, the Roman whip, with its balls of lead each as big as an olive, dug into the flesh and laid bare the bone: it was often enough to kill its victim.

Alessandro Calfo had not the slightest intention of succumbing to the flagellation he was inflicting upon himself: it was *another* who would soon be dying, and to whom this suffering offered a mystical witness of fraternal solidarity. He did not even have any intention of breaking the delicate skin on his chubby back: the girl would be returning on Saturday evening.

"Three days before the 'end of the mission' of our now senile brother."

When he had sent the girl to him, his Palestinian agent had informed him:

"Sonia is Romanian, Monsignor, she is a reliable girl. With her, you need have no fear of the problems caused by the previous one... Ah yes, *bismillah*, in the name of God!"

His years as Apostolic Nuncio in Egypt had taught him

how to carry out the necessary negotiations when faced with contradictory and urgent impulses. With a grimace, he prepared to give his shoulders another lashing: to negotiate does not mean to give in. Despite the weekend of pleasure that he could look forward to with Sonia, he would not suppress the exercise of the discipline, tangible proof of his solidarity towards one of the members of the Society. He would compromise between his fraternal love and that other imperative, the integrity of his velvety skin: the penance would last no longer than a *De profundis*.

This is a penitential psalm, like the *Miserere*, and it conferred a very satisfying value on the suffering that he was inflicting upon himself out of Christian virtue.

But there are only eight verses in the *De profundis*, which lasts merely a third of the time taken by the interminable *Miserere*.

21

Nil took off his glasses, rubbed his sore eyes and smoothed down his short-cropped grey hair. He had spent a whole night working his way through the photocopies of the *M M M*. He pushed back his stool, rose to his feet and went over to pull away the towel blocking his window. Lauds, the first office of the morning, was about to be rung: no one would be surprised to see light in his cell.

Through his window pane, he gazed for a moment at the black sky of the wintry Val-de-Loire. Everything was dark, both outside him and within.

He went back to his table and sat down wearily. His body was short and slender, and yet to himself he seemed massively heavy. In front of him rose several piles of handwritten notes that he had taken in the course of this long night, carefully classified into different heaps. He heaved a sigh.

His research into the Gospel according to St John had led him to the discovery of a hidden actor, a Judaean who kept appearing furtively in the text and who played an essential role in the last days of Jesus's life. Nothing was known of him, not even his name, but he called himself the "beloved disciple", and claimed to have been the very first to meet Jesus on the banks of the Jordan, before Peter. And he also said he had been among the guests at the Last Supper, in the upper room – a room that was certainly situated in his own house. He recounted that he had been lying next to the Master, in the place of honour. He described the crucifixion and the empty tomb in the style and in the truthful tone of voice of an eyewitness.

A man who was essential for learning about Jesus and the origins of Christianity, a friend whose testimony is of the highest importance. Curiously, the existence of this capital witness had been carefully eradicated from every text in the New Testament. Neither the other gospels, nor Paul in his letters, nor the Acts of the Apostles mentioned his existence.

Why had they been so bent on suppressing a witness of such importance? Only an extremely serious reason could have motivated his radical removal from the memory of Christianity. And why were the Essenes never mentioned in accounts of the early Church? There had to be some reason – Nil was convinced of the fact, and Andrei had encouraged him to follow the mysterious thread linking the different events that had for ever left their mark on the history of the West.

"The man you have discovered by studying the gospels is the same man I think I have encountered in my own field – manuscripts from the third to the seventh centuries."

Sitting opposite him in his office, Nil had started.

"Do you mean you have found traces of the 'beloved disciple' in texts postdating the gospels?"

Andrei's eyes had narrowed in his round face.

"Oh, clues that would never have attracted my attention if you yourself had not kept me up with your own discoveries! Almost imperceptible traces – until the Vatican sent me this Coptic manuscript discovered at Nag Hammadi" – and he pointed to his folder.

He gazed pensively at his companion.

"We each pursue our research by ourselves. Dozens of exegetes and historians do the same without being the least bit worried by the fact. On one condition: their work has to remain partitioned off; nobody must try to link together all this different information. Why do you think that access to our libraries is restricted? As long as everyone sticks to his own speciality, he risks neither censorship nor sanctions – and all churches can proudly assert that freedom of thought within them is total."

"All the churches?"

"As well as the Catholic Church, there is the vast constellation of Protestants – including the fundamentalists whose power is rising right now, especially in the United States. Then there are the Jews, and Islam…"

"The Jews, well, up to a point – though I don't see how the exegesis of a New Testament text could concern them, since they only recognize the Old Testament. But the Muslims?"

"Nil, Nil… You live in the first century, in Palestine, but my investigations stretch forward to the seventh century!

Muhammad put the final touches to the Koran in 632. You absolutely must study this text, without delay. And you'll discover that it is closely linked to the fortunes and destiny of the man you are seeking – if he indeed existed!"

There was a silence. Nil was working out how exactly to continue the conversation.

"*If he existed…* Do you doubt that this friend of Jesus's existed?"

"I would doubt it if I hadn't followed your own research step by step. Without realizing it, you led me to scrutinize certain passages in the literature of antiquity that had hitherto remained unnoticed. Without being aware of it, you enabled me to understand the meaning of an obscure Coptic manuscript on which I'm supposed to be presenting my report to Rome – I received a photocopy of it six months ago, and I still don't know how to spin my report, I'm in such an awkward position. Rome has rapped my knuckles once already, and I am frightened they'll call me in for questioning if I delay any further."

Andrei had indeed been called to Rome.

And he had never returned to this peaceful office.

The bell chimed in the November night: Nil went down and took his habitual place in the monastic choir. A few yards to his right, one of the choir stalls remained obstinately empty: Andrei… But his mind refused to focus on the slow melismata of Gregorian chant; he was still absorbed in the manuscripts which he had just spent all night deciphering. Over some time now, his lifelong faith had been torn to shreds, piece by piece.

And yet, at first sight, there was nothing sensational about the manuscripts of the *M M M*. Most of them came from the scattered library of the Essenes of Qumran: rabbinical-style commentaries on the Bible, fragmentary explanations on the struggle between good and evil, the sons of light and the sons of darkness, the central role played by a Master of Justice... it is now known that Jesus could not have been that Master of Justice. The general public, momentarily filled with excitement by the discoveries on the Dead Sea, had quickly been disappointed. Nothing spectacular... and the texts over which he had laboured all night long were no exception.

But for a mind as alert as his, what he had just read confirmed a whole set of details that he had carefully noted down over years of study. Notes which never left his cell, and of which nobody knew anything – except Andrei, from whom he kept nothing secret.

They completely threw into doubt everything that had been said hitherto about the origins of Christianity – in other words, about the culture and civilization of the entire West.

"From San Francisco to Vladivostok," Nil thought, "everything rests on a single postulate: Christ was the founder of a new religion. His divinity was revealed to the Apostles by the tongues of fire that settled upon them at Pentecost. There was a time *before* that day, the Old Testament, and a time *after* – the New Testament. But that is not the whole truth – in fact, it's false!"

Nil suddenly realized to his surprise that he was standing up in church, while all his fellow monks had just prostrated themselves to chant the *Gloria Patri*. Swiftly, he bent down like the others in his row of choir stalls – from the stalls opposite, the Father Abbot had looked up and was observing him.

He tried to follow the divine office more closely, but his mind was galloping along like a wild horse. "In the manuscripts of the Dead Sea I have discovered the basis of the notions by which Jesus was turned into a god. The apostles were not well educated, and could never have carried out such an operation: they drew on things that were being said around them, and we knew nothing about these – until the discoveries at Qumran."

This time, he found that he was the only one facing the opposite choir stalls, while the rest of the community had just turned as one towards the altar, to chant the *Our Father*.

The Father Abbot was not looking at the altar either: he had turned his head to the right and was gazing pensively at Nil.

As he left lauds he was grabbed by a student, who urgently needed some advice on his ongoing dissertation. When he had finally got rid of this unwanted interruption, he swept into his cell, picked up the *M M M* from his crowded table and slipped it without further ado under his scapular. Then, as naturally as possible, he headed to the library in the central wing.

The corridor was empty. With a beating heart, he stepped through the door of Biblical Studies, then into Andrei's office, and continued until he reached the corner where the two wings of the Abbey joined: the long north-wing corridor was equally deserted.

Nil went up to the door that he was not authorized to open – that of Historical Studies – took out of his pocket Father Andrei's bunch of keys and inserted one of the two small ones into the lock. A last glance down the corridor: still empty.

He went in.

Nobody would be in the library at such an early hour in the day. However, he did not want to take the risk of switching on the main lights, which would have indicated his presence. A few low lights remained permanently on and cast a wan, yellowish light. He headed to the far end of the library: he needed to get to the first-century book stacks, and put the *M M M* back in the place he had taken it from the evening before. Then disappear before anyone saw him.

* * *

Just as he was coming up to the third-century bookshelves, feeling his way along with his right hand, he heard the muffled noise of the door opening at the other end. Almost immediately, a glaring light flooded the whole library.

He found himself right in the middle of the central bay, his right arm stretched forwards, a forbidden book under his left arm, in a place he should never have entered, and to which he was not supposed to possess the key. It seemed to him as if the book stacks were moving away to either side of him so as to leave him even more alone and exposed to every gaze. Pitilessly, the spotlights shone out from the wall and berated him: "Father Nil, what are you doing here? How did you get hold of that key? What's that book? And why, yes, why did you borrow it yesterday evening? So what are you looking for, Father Nil? You did nothing else but sleep last night? Why were your wits so far away during this morning's office?"

He was about to be discovered, and he suddenly remembered Andrei's frequent warnings.

And he also remembered his friend's body rigid in death, lying by the tracks of the Rome express, his fist raised in anger against the sky.

As if he were accusing his assassin.

22

Gospel according to St John

Early on that Sunday morning, the women came back from the tomb, stupefied from finding it empty. They told the incredulous apostles a story about men in white so mysterious that they could only be angels. Peter told them to be silent. "Angels! Old wives' tales!" The Judaean signalled to him. They slipped out of the house.

They walked for a while in silence, and then started to run. Peter was soon outdistanced, and was out of breath by the time he reached the garden: the two Essenes had left without waiting for him, but the Judean, who had arrived first, told the apostle how he had been able to speak to the Essenes. Yet again he had the advantage, yet again he was the privileged witness.

Peter, furious, returned to the upper room alone: without a word of explanation, the Judaean had headed off in another direction and was making for a wealthy-looking house in the west district.

The sect of the Essenes had come into being two centuries previously. It comprised monastic communities living separate from the world, as in Qumran, and lay communities who led more normal lives within Jewish society. The Jerusalem community was the biggest, and had even given its name to the western district of the city. Eliezer Ben-Akkai was its leader.

He gave his visitor a warm greeting.

"You were one of us for a long time – if you had not become one of Jesus's disciples, you'd probably have been my successor. As you know, the temple Jews hate us and refuse to accept the fact that we bury our dead in burial grounds that are separate from theirs. Some of these are hidden in the middle of the desert. Impure hands must never profane our tombs."

"I know all that, Rabbi, and I share your desire to preserve the last dwelling place of the Just Men of Israel."

"Jesus the Nazorean was one of those Just Men. His final place of burial must remain secret."

"Eliezer… you are old now. You must not be the only person to know where Jesus's tomb lies."

"My two sons, Adon and Osias, are carrying his body at this very moment. They know the place, as do I, and they will transmit the secret of the tomb."

"What if something were to happen to them? You must entrust the secrets to me too."

Eliezer Ben-Akkai stroked his sparse beard for a long time. His visitor was right; peace with Rome was extremely fragile, and it could all explode at any moment. He placed his hands on his visitor's shoulders.

"Brother, you have always been worthy of our trust. But remember: if you were to deliver the remains of our dead into the hatred of our enemies, the Eternal One himself would be judge between us and you!"

He glanced into the room, where Essenes were coming and going. He moved away to the corner of a window and beckoned his companion to follow him.

He leant forwards, and murmured a few words into his ear.

When they separated in silence, the two men gazed at each other for a long time. Their faces were particularly grave.

As he went home, the Judaean smiled. Jesus's tomb would not be the object of any power struggle.

23

Still dazzled by the glaring light that had flooded the library, Nil glanced down the nearest row of books: it was empty in the middle, and as smooth as the palm of a hand. He stepped forwards: at the far end of the second-century book stack, two big boxes had been placed – books that needed to be catalogued. He quickly slipped behind them, hearing as he did so the characteristic rustle of an approaching robe. Was it a monk's habit, or the cassock of one of the traditionalist students? If they were coming to fetch a book from the second-century stacks, he was doomed. But perhaps the person approaching wasn't coming for a book? Perhaps he'd seen Nil enter, and was harbouring quite different intentions?

Nil crouched down.

The visitor passed the second-century stacks without stopping. Nil, hidden away in the shadows at the far end, behind the boxes, held his breath. He heard the man going into the first-century stacks from which he had taken away the *M M M* on the previous day, and he suddenly regretted that he had not thought to shift the neighbouring books on the bookshelf to disguise the big empty gap.

There was a moment of silence, then he made out the visitor's footsteps passing his stack, heading away towards the library entrance. He had not been spotted. Who was the intruder? A monk's footsteps can be recognized from those of a thousand others: he never attacks the ground with his heel, but slides his foot forwards and seems to be walking on a cushion of air.

It wasn't one of the students.

The main lights suddenly went out, and Nil heard the sound of the door closing, which automatically locked the door. His forehead was drenched with perspiration. He waited for a moment, then rose. Everything was dark and silent.

When he came out, having put the *M M M* back in its place, the north-wing corridor was empty: now he had to put the keys back where he had taken them from. The door to the librarian's office was still not locked. Nil went in and switched on the light: Andrei's clothes were still hanging over the back of his chair.

His heart was beating as he seized the trousers and thrust the bunch of keys into one of the pockets. He knew that he would never return to this office – never as he had done before. One last time he gazed round at the bookshelves in which Andrei stacked the books he had received before putting them in the library.

At the top of one pile, he noticed a book that did not have a label with its access number. His attention was drawn to the title:

LAST COPTIC APOCRYPHA FROM NAG HAMMADI
Critical Edition
by Fr Andrei Sokolwski, O.S.B.
Paris: Gabalda Editions

"The edition of the Apocrypha he had been working on for ten years – finally published!"

Nil opened the work: a remarkable piece of scholarship, published with the aid of the CNRS, the French research centre. On the left-hand page, the Coptic text patiently established by Andrei and, on the right, a translation. His friend's last work: a testament.

He had lingered in this office for too long, and he came to a sudden decision. *Someone* had stolen from his cell Andrei's last note, addressed to him alone like a message from beyond the grave. Well, this book that his friend had received just before leaving, into which he had poured all his knowledge and all his love – this book belonged to *him* – to Nil. It was not yet labelled, and so had not been entered into the catalogue of the Abbey: nobody in the world could possibly know that he was appropriating it today. He wanted this book for himself. From beyond death it was like a hand held out by a man who would never publish anything again – would never again sit down in this chair to listen to him, his head bent forwards, a mischievous gleam in the narrow slit of his eyes.

Resolutely, he slipped the edition of the Apocrypha of Nag Hammadi under his scapular, and went back out into the corridor.

As he headed for the stairs, his mind filled with the solitude in which he would henceforth dwell, he did not notice the shadowy figure flattened against the wall next to the high door of Biblical Studies. The shadow was that of a monk's habit.

On the smooth fabric a pectoral cross was dangling; the monk's right hand was caressing it nervously. On his ring finger, a very simple metal ring reflected no light.

Nil went back to his cell, closed the door behind him and stood stock still. When he had gone down for the office of lauds a while ago, he had left the labours of the night before meticulously arranged in small separate heaps. The pages were now scattered everywhere, as if by a gust of wind.

But it was November, and his window was closed. It had been closed since the day before.

Someone had again come into his cell. They had come in and searched it. They had searched it and perhaps taken away some of his notes.

24

Acts of the Apostles

"Peter, what has happened to Jesus's body?"

Peter looked all round. Three weeks had already gone by since Jesus's death, and all that time he had not left the upper room. Just a hundred or so sympathizers were there on this particular morning, and the same question was being urgently asked on every side.

At the far end of the room, their host was the only man standing, leaning against a wall. A score of men were sitting around him, turning their eyes alternately towards him and then to the window, at the foot of which the Eleven were all gathered together. Supporters, perhaps? "Now," thought Peter, "it's him or me."

The apostle looked at his ten companions. Andrew his brother, who was biting his lower lip; John and James, the sons of Zebedee; Matthew, the former customs officer... None of them possessed the stature of a leader.

Someone would have to stand up in the midst of this rudderless crowd. Stand up and speak out – for, just now, this was the only way to seize power.

Peter took a deep breath and stood up. The light from the window illumined him from behind, leaving his face in the shadow.

"Brothers..."

In spite of all his efforts, he had not managed to find out where the Essenes had buried Jesus's body after removing it from the tomb. "He is the only witness apart from me? Does *he* know? I must grab the attention of these people and assert my authority once and for all." He decided to ignore the questions of the throng, and measured them with his gaze. They were about to find out that it was he who had executed God's judgement. God had used his abilities, and God would use them again.

"Brothers, Judas had to endure his destiny. He was one of the Twelve, and he was a traitor: he fell on his face, his belly opened, and his entrails were shed on the sand."

A deathly silence fell on the room. Only the man who had murdered Judas could know these details. He had just publicly confessed that the hand which had held the dagger was not that of some Zealot, but his own.

He out-stared each of those who had noisily been demanding details of the fate of Jesus's body: under his gaze, one by one, they lowered their eyes.

The beloved disciple, at the far end of the room, was still saying nothing. Peter raised his hand.

"We must replace Judas; someone else needs to take over from him. Let him be chosen from among those who accompanied the Master, from the encounter on the banks of the Jordan up to the end."

A murmur of approval swept through the gathering, and all eyes turned towards the beloved disciple. He alone could complete the college of the twelve apostles: he had been the first to meet the Master by the Jordan, and he had been his close associate right up to the end. He was obviously the right man to replace Judas.

Peter perceived which way the crowd was inclining.

"We are not the ones who will choose! God must designate the twelfth apostle. We must draw lots. Matthew, take your calamus and write two names on these pieces of bark.

Before Matthew could obey, Peter leant towards him and murmured something in his ear. The former customs officer stared at him in surprise. Then he nodded, sat down and wrote quickly. The two pieces of bark were placed on a kerchief, of which Peter lifted the four corners.

"You there, come over here and draw one of these two names. And may God speak in our midst!"

A young boy rose to his feet, stretched out his hand, plunged it into the kerchief and took out one of the two pieces of bark.

Peter seized it and handed it to Matthew.

"I can't read: tell us what's written there."

Matthew cleared his voice, looked at the piece of bark and proclaimed:

"The name written here is Matthias!"

Protests erupted from the crowd.

"Brothers!" Peter had to shout to make himself heard. "God himself has just designated Matthias as the man to take Judas's place! There are twelve of us again, as at the last meal that Jesus ate before he died, in this very room!"

On every side men were rising to their feet while Peter drew Matthias to himself, embraced him and made him sit amid the Eleven. Then he stared at the beloved disciple, from whom he was separated by the throng of those sitting on the floor. A compact group of sympathizers was surrounding him now, standing erect, their faces sombre. Shouting above the tumult, Peter cried:

"Twelve tribes spoke for God: twelve apostles will speak for Jesus, in his place or in his name. Twelve, and not a single one more: *there will never be a thirteenth apostle!*"

The beloved disciple stared back at him for a long time without flinching, then leant over and murmured a few words in the ear of a curly-headed teenage boy. Suddenly feeling alarmed, Peter slipped his hand into the slit in his tunic and seized the handle of his *sica*. But his rival signed to those surrounding him, and silently made his way towards the door. Thirty or so men followed in his footsteps, their faces inexpressive.

* * *

As soon as he was out in the street, he turned round: the teenage boy had run up to his side, and held out to him the other piece of bark, the one that had slipped from the kerchief abandoned by Peter after the proclamation of God's choice. He asked the young boy:

"Yokhanan, are you sure nobody saw this piece of bark?"

"Nobody, *abbu*. Nobody other than Matthew who wrote the name, Peter who dictated it to him, and now you."

"Well then, my child, give it to me, and then forget all about it."

He glanced at the second voting slip that had been put forward in God's ballot, and smiled at Yokhanan: the name written on it was not his.

"So, Peter," he thought, "you have decided to keep me out of the New Israel for good! Now there is war between us: may it never crush this child, and those who will come after him."

25

Now that Father Nil had been brutally torn away from his studies and the patient reconstitution of the past, his stable, peaceful world collapsed: for the second time, his cell had been searched. And more papers had disappeared from his table.

The notes that had been taken on this particular morning contained details of his research into the beginnings of the Church. He had been aware that he was venturing down a path that had always been forbidden to Catholics. And now someone in the monastery knew what he was seeking, what he had already found. Someone who was spying on him, slipping into his cell when he was not there, and did not hesitate to steal. The impalpable danger he had sensed around him suddenly became more real – and he did not know from where it was coming, nor why.

Was it possible that studying might become dangerous?

His mind elsewhere, he mechanically turned the pages of his friend's last published work. At every moment he could tell how great was the void left by his death: nobody would be there to listen to him any more, to guide him... Feeling abandoned in the midst of the vast solitude of this monastery, a new feeling overwhelmed him: fear.

Andrei's last thoughts had been of him: he needed to overcome this fear and pursue his investigation using a mere brief note as a starting point. The first line mentioned the manuscript of a Coptic apocalypse: doubtless one of the many that his friend kept in the drawers of his office. But the mysterious visitor to the north library, who had almost caught him there that morning, had certainly spotted the big empty gap left on the bookshelf by the *M M M* he had borrowed. This book could have been taken only by a monk who did not have access to the library – without this, he would have left in its place a "phantom" with his signature, as was the rule.

They would soon discover the bunch of keys left in Andrei's trouser pocket, and they would put two and two together: the office would immediately be locked up, and Nil would lose any hope of getting back in there to find the mysterious manuscript.

Feeling quite crestfallen, he closed the book, mechanically slipping his index finger between the cover and the end paper. And jumped in surprise.

He had just felt a bump on the inside face of the cover.

A flaw in the book's manufacture?

He brought the book over to his lamp and opened it under the light: it was not a problem in the binding. The edge of the cover had been unglued and then glued back. Inside, one could make out the presence of a slender rectangular object.

With the greatest of care, he slit open the end paper that covered the board, pulled it away, and tipped the book so that the bright light could shine into it: there was a document folded into four on the inside.

Just before he left, Andrei had slipped into his final work a piece of paper that he had taken the greatest care to conceal.

Picking up a pair of tweezers, Nil cautiously started to extract the piece of paper from its place of concealment.

26

That evening, the Father Abbot, sitting at his office, was on the verge of feeling really rather cross.

He had been asked to be put through to Cardinal Catzinger in Rome, but his number seemed to be permanently engaged. Finally, the prelate's muffled voice came through.

"I hope I'm not phoning at an inconvenient time, Your Eminence... I need to ask for your advice, and perhaps your help, in the case of that monk we've already spoken about... Father Nil, the professor of exegesis in the theological college. You'll remember that I alerted you to... yes, that's right. I've recently noticed quite a big change in his patterns of behaviour. He's always been a very disciplined monk, attentive during the church services. Since poor Father Andrei died, he hasn't been the same. And something quite unprecedented has just happened: while the post of librarian remains unfilled, I've been checking the books borrowed from our library myself. Well, early this morning, I discovered that Father Nil had *stolen* a rather sensitive book from the north wing. Sorry? Well, it's, you know, the *M M M* of the Americans…"

He was obliged to hold the receiver away from his ear. The private line of the Vatican, used as it was to a higher degree of unctuousness, was now transmitting the Cardinal's wrath in high fidelity.

"I share your disquiet, Your Eminence: you'll be receiving without delay a small sample of the notes that Father Nil himself has been taking… Yes, I've been able to procure a few for myself. Then you'll be in a position to judge whether it would be appropriate to take measures, or whether we can leave dear Father Nil to pursue his scholarly studies in peace. You'll look after the matter personally? Thank you, Your Eminence… *Arrivederci*, Your Eminence."

Heaving a sigh of relief, the Father Abbot hung up. It was quite without enthusiasm that he had consented to the purchase of such dangerous works as the *M M M* – but how can one fight against the attacks of the enemy unless one knows which weapons he can deploy?

He knew that he was responsible before God for his monks, for their spiritual as well as their intellectual lives – and as for violating the sacred sanctuary of the cell of one of his sons, twice over… no, that was something he did not like having to do.

In his office at the Vatican, Emil Catzinger furiously pressed a button on his switchboard.

"Get me Mgr Calfo. Yes, straight away. I know perfectly well it's Saturday evening! He must be in his apartment in Castel Sant'Angelo – just get hold of him."

27

Father Nil's hand was trembling slightly. He had just carefully pulled out from the cover of Andrei's book a photocopy. He brought it nearer his lamp, and immediately recognized the elegant script of Old Coptic.

A Coptic manuscript.

The photo was perfectly legible, and showed a fragment of well-preserved parchment. Very often, Nil had examined the treasures that Andrei pulled out of his drawer so as to show them off. He had familiarized himself with the script used in the great manuscripts from Nag Hammadi, collated for the first time by the Egyptologist Jean Doresse after their discovery in 1945, on the left bank of the Middle Nile. As an expert in Hebrew and Greek manuscripts, he knew that calligraphy evolves over time, in a process tending towards greater simplification.

The script of this parchment was of the same kind as that of famous apocrypha such as the Gospel of Thomas from the end of the second century, which attracted worldwide attention. But this one was obviously later.

The fragment was really small, and must have been deemed obscure and of little interest to Doresse, who had let it go. And it had ended up in Rome, like so many others – to be, one fine day, exhumed by an employee in the Vatican Library, and sent to the Abbey. Andrei, as a recognized authority, often received documents of this kind to analyse.

Nil knew that the apocrypha of Nag Hammadi dated from the second and third centuries, and that from the fourth century onwards nothing else had been written in the Coptic village. So this late fragment dated from the end of the third century.

A third-century Coptic manuscript.

Was this the manuscript that had placed Andrei in such a difficult position that he dared not send his final report to Rome? But in that case, why had he taken such pains to conceal the photocopy, instead of filing it away with the others?

Andrei was no longer around to answer his questions. Nil buried his head in his hands and closed his eyes.

He seemed to be seeing the first line of the note discovered in his friend's hand: *Coptic manuscript (Apoc.)*. He had spontaneously translated *Apoc.* as "apocalypse" – the traditional abbreviation as used in editions of the Bible. Nil decided to check, and opened the very latest translation of the ecumenical Bible, the one Andrei used. In this recent version, now viewed as authoritative, the abbreviation for the Book of the Apocalypse was not *Apoc.*, but *Ap*.

Andrei was always au fait with the latest developments, and a meticulous scholar. If he had intended to allude to the Book of the Apocalypse, he would surely have written *Ap.*, and not *(Apoc.)*. So... what had he been thinking of?

And all of a sudden, Nil realized that *(Apoc.)* didn't mean "apocalypse", but "apocrypha"!

This is what Andrei had meant: "I need to talk to Nil about a Coptic manuscript that I hid away in my edition of the apocrypha, just before I left". The same edition that he had picked up in his office that morning, the one he was now holding. A manuscript the contents of which were of such great importance that he wanted to talk to him about them _now_, after his trip to the Vatican.

"It's the Coptic manuscript sent by Rome!"

Nil had in his hands the text that had led to the librarian of St Martin's Abbey being summoned to Rome.

He picked up the photocopy and examined it closely. The fragment was very small: Nil was no specialist in Old Coptic, but he could read it quite fluently, and the script was so clear that there would be no problem in deciphering it.

Could he translate it? Not an elegant translation, admittedly, but a transliteration, an approximate word-for-word version – that he could probably manage. Look up every word in a dictionary and assemble them all together: the meaning would start to emerge.

He rose to his feet. After a moment's hesitation, he placed the precious photocopy on the plank of wood that monks use as a wardrobe and went out into the corridor. Nobody would come into his cell during the few minutes he needed to be away.

He quickly headed to the only library to which he had access: Biblical Studies.

In the first stack, where reference works were kept, he found Cerny's Coptic-English etymological dictionary. He pulled it out, replaced it with a "phantom" with his name written on it and returned to his cell, his heart pounding. The precious piece of paper was where he had left it.

The first bell for vespers rang out: he laid the dictionary on his table, thrust the photocopy into the inside pocket of his habit and went down to the church.

Another sleepless night lay ahead of him.

28

Acts of the Apostles, Epistle to the Galatians, 48 AD

"*Abbu*, you can't let them get away with it!"

Eighteen years had elapsed since the death of Jesus. Standing at the side of the beloved disciple, Yokhanan was seething with impatience. The representatives of the "Christians" – as they had just started to be called – had now gathered together for the first time in Jerusalem, in order to lance a boil, namely the struggle between the "Jewish" believers, who refused to abandon the stipulations laid down by the Law – especially circumcision – and the "Greeks", who rejected that particular surgical intervention, but wanted a new god for a new religion. Jesus, rebaptized "Christ", would be this god: the idea was in the air, it was being whispered more and more insistently.

This ideological struggle concealed a fierce fight for predominance: the pious Jews associated with James, Jesus's younger brother and a rising star, versus the disciples of Peter – a majority, on whom the old leader kept an iron grip. And against all these the Greeks of Paul, a newcomer who dreamt of transforming the little house built by the apostles into an edifice of world stature. They had abused one another, hurled the most terrible insults at each other – *false brother, intruder, spy* – they had all but come to blows.

The Christian Church as it came into being was holding its first council in Jerusalem, the city that kills the prophets.

"Look at them, Yokhanan! They're fighting over a corpse, and all they can think of is tearing his memory to pieces!"

The young curly-headed man seized his arm.

"You were the first to meet Jesus, before any of the rest. You must say something, *abbu*!"

Heaving a sigh, he rose to his feet. Even though he had been sidelined by the Twelve, the prestige enjoyed by this man was still considerable: they all fell silent and turned towards him.

"I've been listening to you discussing it all ever since yesterday, and I have the impression you're talking about another Jesus than the one I knew. Everyone recreates him in his own way: some claim that he was simply a pious Jew, others would like to turn him into a god. I received him at my table, and there were thirteen of us around him that evening, in the upper room of my house. But the next day, I was the only one to hear the sound of the hammers, see the lance being thrust in, be present as he died – all the rest of you had taken to your heels. I bear witness that this man was not a god: God does not die, God does not suffer the agony he experienced under my very eyes. I was also the first to arrive at his tomb, the day it was found to be empty. And I know what happened to his tortured body, but I will say no more of that than the desert that now shelters him."

A simultaneous outburst of imprecations prevented him from carrying on. Some were still hesitant to admit to the divinity of Jesus, but they all agreed that he had indeed arisen from the dead. This idea of resurrection attracted the crowds, who found in it a means of putting up with a life that otherwise was devoid of hope. This man had few disciples – did he want to send thousands of converts home empty-handed?

Fists were being brandished in front of him.

"They want to use Jesus for their own ambitions? Let them do it without me." He left, leaning on Yokhanan's shoulder.

103

* * *

Yokhanan had still been a small child when the Roman legionaries crushed Sepphoris, the capital of Galilee. He had seen thousands of crosses erected in the streets, and the crucified dying a slow and agonizing death in the hot sun. One day they came for his father: horror-stricken, he saw him being whipped, then stretched out on the beam of wood. The hammer blows on the nails echoed in the very heart of him, he saw the blood spattering his wrists, heard the howl of pain. When they raised the cross against the sky of Galilee, he passed out. His mother wrapped him in a shawl and fled to the countryside, where they hid.

The child stopped speaking. But at night, in his restless sleep, he kept murmuring over and over: "*Abba!* Father!"

When he emerged from his torpor, they came and settled in Jerusalem. His mother dedicated him to God by making him take the vows of a Nazarite: he would no longer cut his hair. He was now a pious Jew – but he still would not speak.

Like everyone in the city, he learnt of the crucifixion of Jesus: the horror which torture and death on the cross inspired in the boy was so great that he drove this man out of his memory. A Messiah is awaited, he thought; he will come soon, and it can't be Jesus: the Messiah would never allow himself to be crucified. The Messiah will be strong, he will drive the Romans out and restore the Kingdom of David.

And then he had met this Judaean, reserved just as he was, a man who had looked on him with friendship, without taking umbrage at his silence. A man who spoke of Jesus as if he had lived very close to him and seemed to know him from within. When his mother died, this man, who loved the Master so dearly and called himself his beloved disciple, took him into his home. He became his *abbu*, the father of his soul.

One day, to show him that he had understood the new world revealed by Jesus, Yokhanan took a pair of scissors and cut the long locks of his hair short. Without taking his eyes off his *abbu*, since he was still not speaking, and expressed himself only in gesture.

Then the beloved disciple held out his thumb and traced on his forehead, his lips and his heart an immaterial cross. Here again, Yokhanan understood, and silently stuck out his tongue, which was also marked with the terrifying sign.

The following night, for the first time he slept without throwing off his blanket of pure wool. And the next day, his tongue spoke again, from the abundance of his heart healed by Jesus.

As he approached his house, the beloved disciple placed his hand on his shoulder.

"This evening, Yokhanan, you will go and see James, the brother of Jesus. Tell him I want to meet him. Ask him to come to my house."

The young man nodded and grasped his *abbu*'s hand in his own.

29

The night was far gone by the time Nil laid the dictionary down on his cluttered table. How far away he now seemed from the dramatic council in Jerusalem, whose swiftly changing events he had been examining just a few days earlier! And yet it was on that day, eighteen years after Jesus's death, that the beloved disciple had been definitively excluded from the nascent Church.

He had managed to translate the fragment of parchment, discovered in the book published by his friend. Two short and apparently unrelated sentences:

The rule of faith of the twelve apostles
Contains the seed of its destruction.

Let the epistle be everywhere destroyed
So that the place may remain in place.

Nil rubbed his brow: what on earth could it mean?

The "rule of faith of the twelve apostles": in antiquity, this was the name given to the *Symbolon* of Nicaea, the Creed of the Christian Churches. The one they had found engraved in Germigny, the one that had so intrigued Andrei. In what did this "seed of destruction" consist? It had no meaning.

"Let the epistle be everywhere destroyed": the Coptic word he had just translated by "epistle" was the very same one that designates the epistles of St Paul in the New Testament. Was it one of these epistles that was meant? The Church has never condemned any of Paul's epistles. Might the manuscript have been written by a group of dissident Christians?

The last line had posed another problem for Nil: "so that the place may remain in place". The dictionary gave several meanings: "dwelling place", or "house", or even "assembly". What was certain was that the same Coptic root was used twice in succession. So there was a deliberate play on words – but what was its significance?

He had just decrypted the meaning of the terms, but not that of the whole message. Had Andrei grasped this meaning? And what relation had he been able to establish between this message and the other clues on his posthumous note?

The librarian had died after being summoned to Rome to explain his translation. Did these four lines have anything to do with his brutal death?

Nil found himself facing a game of chess in which the pieces had all been scattered and lay in disorder. Andrei had patiently put them into place before him. And as he returned from Rome, in the train, he had written: _now_. So he had made, during his stay near the Apostle's tomb, a decisive discovery – but what was it?

For him, nothing would now ever be the same. Was his whole life in question? Can one still call oneself a Christian if one doubts the divinity of Jesus?

There were still a few hours of night-time left. Nil turned off the light and lay down in the dark.

"God – no man has seen God. And Jesus, even if he was not God, remains the most fascinating man I have ever encountered. No, I have not been wrong to dedicate my life to him."

A few minutes later, Father Nil, a Benedictine monk and the keeper of secrets too heavy for him, was sleeping peacefully.

30

"Take a seat, Monsignor."

The Cardinal's chubby face, crowned by a helm of white hair, looked anxious. He glanced at Calfo as he sat down with a sigh in the ample armchair.

Emil Catzinger had been born at the same time as Nazism. Like all the boys of his age, he had found himself enrolled, reluctantly, in the Hitler Youth. Then he had bravely distanced himself from the Führer, managing to evade the Gestapo purges. But he had remained deeply marked by the traumatic impact of these events on his childhood.

"I'm obliged to you for breaking off your activities on a Saturday evening."

The Rector, who had just abandoned the young Romanian woman in the middle of a particularly promising discourse, nodded gravely.

"When it's a question of serving the Church, Your Eminence, there's no such thing as a bad time or a delay!"

"Quite so. Well now… This afternoon I had a phone conversation with the Father Abbot of St Martin's Abbey."

"An excellent prelate, worthy in every respect of the trust you place in him."

"He informed me that the Father Nil of whom we have already spoken had *stolen* from a library – to which he does not have official access – a volume of the texts published by dissidents."

Calfo merely raised an eyebrow.

"And he has just faxed me a sample of his personal notes, which are giving me serious cause for concern. He might be able to approach the secret jealously guarded by our Holy Church, and by your Society of St Pius V."

"Do you think he has made much progress down this perilous path?"

"I don't as yet know. But he was very close to Andrei, who – as you know – had indeed gone far down that forbidden road. You know what is at stake here: the very existence of the Catholic Church. We need to find out how much Father Nil knows. What do you suggest?"

Calfo smiled in satisfaction, leant slightly backwards and took from his cassock an envelope, which he proffered to the Cardinal.

"If Your Eminence would be so good as to have a quick look at this... The minute you mentioned this Father Nil to me, I asked my brothers in the Society to carry out a twofold investigation. Here is the result and, perhaps, the reply to your question."

Catzinger pulled from the envelope two folders marked *confidenziale*.

"Take a look at the first of those folders... You'll see that Nil was a brilliant student at the Benedictine University in Rome. That he's a... how shall I put it?... an idealist – in other words, he is completely devoid of any personal ambition. An observant monk who derives joy from study and prayer."

Catzinger stared at him from above the rim of his glasses.

"My dear Calfo, you don't need me to tell you that the most dangerous of all are the idealists. Arius was an idealist, so were Savonarola and Luther... A good son of the Church believes in the dogmas and doesn't ask questions about them. Any other ideal may well turn out to be extremely harmful."

"*Certo, Eminenza*. During his studies in Rome, he became friends with an American Benedictine: Rembert Leeland."

"Well, well! *Our* Leeland? How very interesting!"

"Yes indeed: Mgr Leeland. I've picked up his dossier – it's in the second folder. He's a musician first and foremost, a monk in Kentucky, at St Mary's Abbey, where there's a musical academy. He was elected Abbot there. And then, following some rather controversial statements..."

"Yes, I know the story, I was already Prefect of the Congregation at the time. He was appointed bishop *in partibus* and sent to Rome, in accordance with the excellent principle *promoveatur ut amoveatur*. Oh, he wasn't really dangerous: a musician! But we had to nip in the bud the scandal caused by his public declarations on married priests. He's a *minutante* somewhere or other these days, I think?"

"At the Secretariat for Relations with the Jews: after Rome, he lived for two years in Israel, where he spent much more time studying music than Hebrew. Leeland is apparently an excellent pianist."

"And?…"

Calfo gazed pityingly at the Cardinal.

"But *Eminenza*, don't you get it?"

He suppressed his furious longing to light up the cigar making a bulge in his inner pocket. The Cardinal doesn't drink and doesn't smoke. But the Society of St Pius V held a certain dossier on his past, crammed to the brim with swastikas – so its Rector could feel quite safe.

"So long as Father Nil stays at St Martin's, we'll never know what's going through his mind. He needs to come here to Rome. However, he won't divulge his ideas in my office – nor in yours, Eminence. But just get him to meet up with his friend Leeland on some pretext or another, and give them time to open their hearts to one another. The artist and the mystic will soon be telling each other their secrets."

"What pretext could we invent?"

"Leeland is interested in ancient music, much more than he is in Jewish affairs. We will discover that he suddenly needs the help of a specialist in old texts."

"And you think he'll be… cooperative?"

"That's my business. You know we have him in our power: he'll collaborate.".

There was a silence. Catzinger was weighing up the pros and cons. "Calfo is a Neapolitan," he reflected. "He's used to tortuous manoeuvres. He's no fool."

"Monsignor," he said eventually, "I'm giving you carte

blanche. Take whatever steps you need to get that James Bond of exegesis here. And make sure he's feeling chatty."

As he left the Congregation, Calfo had a fleeting vision of a thick carpet of green banknotes leading to Castel Sant'Angelo. Catzinger thought he was informed about everything, but he did not know the most important things. He alone, Alessandro Calfo, just a poor boy from a poor family who was now the Rector of the Society of St Pius V – he alone had an overall view.

He alone would do the necessary. Even if it meant using the same means that had led to the Templars being burned alive in fourteenth-century Europe.

Without knowing it, perhaps, Philippe le Bel and Nogaret had saved the West. Now it was his task, and that of the Society of St Pius V, to fulfil this lofty and dangerous mission.

31

Jerusalem, 48 AD

"Thank you for coming, Iakov."

The beloved disciple called James by his familiar Hebrew name. The setting sun was illuminating the *impluvium* of his house with its red and gold light; they were alone. Jesus's brother had removed his phylacteries, but he was still wrapped in his prayer shawl. He looked scared.

"Yesterday, Paul returned to Antioch. The Church's first council almost ended badly. I had to impose a compromise, and Peter emerged greatly diminished. He hates you, the same way he hates me."

"Peter's not a bad man. Meeting Jesus made him face up to his destiny as a poor man, and it was quite a shock: he refuses to retreat, and loathes anyone who might take the first place away from him."

"I am Jesus's brother: if either of us has to withdraw, it's going to be him. He'll have to go and set up the seat of his dominion elsewhere!"

"He'll go, James, he'll go. When Paul has established the new religion he dreams about, the focus will shift from Jerusalem to Rome. The race for power has only just begun."

James lowered his head.

"Ever since he assassinated Ananias and Sapphira in public, Peter no longer bears weapons, but some of his faithful followers do. I heard them yesterday: they view you as a man from the past, someone opposed to those who are building the future. *There cannot be a thirteenth apostle*, as you know: your life is in danger. You can't remain in Jerusalem."

"The murder of Ananias and his wife happened a good while ago, and it was all a question of money. These days, money is flowing into Jerusalem from all the churches in Asia."

"It's not a question of money: you're casting doubt on everything they're working for. Together with Judas, you were the disciple my brother Jesus liked best. We know how Peter got rid of Judas, how he eliminates any obstacles on his path. If you disappear as the Iscariot did, a whole portion of memory will disappear too. You need to get away, quickly, and this may be the last time we'll see each other. So I beg you, tell me in which place the Essenes buried Jesus's body. Tell me where his tomb is!"

This man had neither Peter's ambition nor Paul's genius: he was just an ordinary Jewish man asking after his brother. He replied with some vehemence.

"I lived with Jesus for a much shorter time than you did, Iakov. But none of you can possibly understand what I understood about him. You, because you're viscerally attached to Judaism. Paul, because he's always been familiar with the pagan gods of the Empire, and dreams of replacing them with a new religion based on a Christ reconstructed in his own way. Jesus doesn't belong to anyone, my friend, neither to your followers nor to Paul's. He rests in the desert now. The desert alone can protect his body from the Jewish or Greek vultures of the new Church. He was the freest man I have ever met: he wanted to replace the Law of Moses by a new law written not on tablets, but in men's hearts. A law with no other dogma than love."

James's face darkened. Nobody can touch the Law of Moses: it is the very identity of Israel. He preferred to change the subject.

"You need to leave. And take my mother Mary far away from here: she seems so happy with you…"

"We have a great deal of affection for each other, and I venerate Jesus's mother: her presence at my side fills every minute with joy. You're right, I no longer have any place in Jerusalem or Antioch – I'm leaving. As soon as I know where I'm going to pitch my wanderer's tent, I'll ask Mary to come and join me. Meanwhile, Yokhanan can act as a go-between. For him, she's practically a second mother."

"Where do you think you'll go?"

The beloved disciple gazed around. The shadows were now lengthening in the *impluvium*, but the window in the upper room was still lit up by the light of the setting sun. It was the room of the last supper with Jesus, eighteen years ago. He needed to leave this place, which was now nothing but an illusion. And seek reality where Jesus himself had found it.

113

"I'll head east, into the desert: it was during his stay in the desert that Jesus accomplished his transformation, it was there that he realized what his mission would be. I often heard him say, with a smile, that he was surrounded by wild beasts there and that they had respected his solitude."

He looked Jesus's brother full in the face.

"The desert, James... Perhaps that is now the only land which the disciples of Jesus the Nazorean can call their own. The only place where they can feel at home."

32

As he took off his choir vestments after the office of lauds, the Father Abbot noticed how drawn and pale Nil's face appeared.

Just as he reached his office, the telephone rang.

Twenty minutes later, when he hung up, he was both perplexed and relieved. He had been surprised to hear Cardinal Catzinger in person informing him that a great honour was to be bestowed on his abbey: the skills of one of his monks were urgently required in the Vatican. An ancient music specialist who worked in the Curia needed help for his investigations into the origins of Gregorian chant. This was important research, which the Holy Father himself hoped would greatly improve relations between Judaism and Christianity. In short, Father Nil was expected forthwith in Rome, so as to put his expertise at the service of the Universal Church. He would be absent for only a few weeks, and he should take the first train: he would be staying at San Girolamo, the Benedictine abbey in Rome.

Just as the late lamented Father Andrei had done.

You don't quarrel with orders from Cardinal Catzinger, the Father Abbot reflected. And Father Nil's recent behaviour had been giving him cause for concern. It was better to shift problems as far away as possible.

Mgr Calfo had been obliged to interrupt his Sunday of pleasures for a moment and hurry over to his nearby office, but he had not managed to reach his Cairo counterpart. He strode briskly up the steps of his apartment block: what awaited him upstairs made him forget the drawbacks of his very Neapolitan paunch, and gave him wings.

My beloved, naked, knowing my desires,
Was wearing nothing but her clinking jewels.

Actually, the only jewels on the body of Sonia as she slept were the glints in her hair. Calfo gazed at them appreciatively. "Ah, Baudelaire, what a poet! But personally, I never give them jewels: just a money shot, as it were."

Mukhtar had been quite right: not only did Sonia turn out to be extremely talented in the erotic arts, but she was also perfectly discreet. Taking advantage of her slumber, he quickly picked up his telephone and dialled the Cairo number again.

"Mukhtar Al-Quraysh, please... I'll hang on, thanks."

This time they'd managed to get hold of him: he was just back from prayers at the Al-Azhar mosque.

"Mukhtar? *Salam aleikom.* Tell me, are your students leaving you any free time right now? That's great. Get a flight to Rome and we can meet up. It's about continuing the little mission I entrusted you with, for the good of the cause... Collaborating with your favourite enemy? No, it's too early for that, if necessary you can contact him in Jerusalem. Oh, a few weeks at most! That's right, at the Teatro di Marcello, as usual: *discrezione, mi raccomando!*"

He hung up, smiling. The man to whom he had just been speaking was occasionally invited to lecture at the celebrated Al-Azhar University: he was a fanatic, an ardent defender of Islamic dogma. Getting an Arab and a Jew to work together, two sleeping agents of the most formidable special services in the Middle East, so as to protect the most precious secret of the Catholic Church – all very ecumenical, of course.

It was during his time as Papal Nuncio in Cairo that he had first come across Mukhtar Al-Quraysh. The diplomat and the dogmatic theologian had each discovered that the other was burning with the same hidden inner fire, and this had created an unexpected bond between them. But the Palestinian was not seeking, as he was, to reach transcendence by means of erotic celebrations.

Sonia uttered a little moan and opened her eyes.

He laid the phone down on the bedroom floor, and leant over to her.

33

"Go back to Rome, Mukhtar. The Council of Muslim Brothers has managed to persuade Hamas of the importance of this mission. Their terrorist attacks would not be enough to protect Islam if the revealed nature of the Koran were to be undermined, or if the sacred person of the Prophet – blessed be his name – risked being sullied by the least little insinuation of doubt. But there is one thing…"

Mukhtar Al-Quraysh smiled; he had been expecting this. His dark skin, his muscular build and his shortness of stature brought out in contrast the tall silhouette of Mustapha Mashlur, venerated by all the students at the Al-Azhar University of Cairo.

"It's your relations with the Jewish guy. The fact you're friends with him…"

"He saved my life during the Six Days' War in '67. I was alone and unarmed in front of his tank in the desert, our army had been routed: he could have driven right over my body, it's what happens in war. He halted, gave me a drink and allowed me to live. He's not a Jew like the others."

"But he *is* a Jew! And not just any Jew, as you know full well."

They stopped in the shade of the Al-Ghari minaret. Even now, at the end of November, the old man's translucent skin felt vulnerable to the sting of the sun's rays.

"Do not forget the words of the Prophet: 'Be the enemies of the Jews and Christians, they are friends with each other! Anyone who takes them as friends is siding with them, and Allah does not lead a people who are in error'."

"You know the Holy Koran better than anyone, Murshid" – he called the man by his title of "Supreme Guide" to show his respect. "The Prophet in person did not hesitate to form an alliance with his enemies for a common cause, and his attitude is binding in law, even in the case of Jihad. It is not in the interests of either Jews or Arabs to see the age-old foundations of Christianity being shaken to the depths."

The Supreme Guide gazed at him with a smile.

"We reached that very conclusion a good while before you did, and that's why we'll let you get on with it. But never forget that you are a scion of the tribe that saw the birth of the Prophet – blessed be his name. So behave like a Quraysh, since you bear that glorious patronymic: your friendship for that Jew should never let you forget who he is, or who he is working for. Oil and vinegar may come temporarily into contact – but they will never mix."

"You can be reassured, Murshid, that the vinegar of a Jew will never bite into a Quraysh: I am thick-skinned. I know that man, and if all our enemies were like him, we might have peace in the Middle East."

"Peace… There will never be peace for a Muslim until the entire earth bows down five times a day before the kiblah indicating the direction of Mecca."

They left the protective shade of the minaret and walked in silence towards the entrance of the madrasa, whose dome sparkled in the sun. Before going in, the old man placed his hand on Mukhtar's arm.

"And the girl – you trust her?"

"She's better off in Rome than in the brothel in Saudi Arabia where I took her from! She's behaving herself for the moment. And she has no desire at all to be sent back to her family in Romania. This mission is simple, we're not using any sophisticated tricks: just the good old home-made methods."

"*Bismillah Al Rahim*. It'll soon be time for prayers, let me go and purify myself."

For the Supreme Guide of the Muslim Brothers, the successor of their founder Hassan al-Banna is, in the eyes of Allah, just one *Muslim* – one submissive human – among others.

Mukhtar leant against a pillar and closed his eyes. Was it the caress of the sun? He could see the scene in his mind's eye: the man had leapt down from his tank and walked towards him, his right hand raised so that his gunner wouldn't shoot. All around them, the Sinai desert was again swathed in its usual silence, the routed Egyptians were fleeing. Why was he still alive? And why was this Jew not going to kill him there and then?

The Israeli officer seemed to hesitate, the features of his face totally immobile. Suddenly he smiled, and held out a water gourd. As he drank, Mukhtar noted the scar across his forehead, where his hair was cut very short.

Years later, the Intifada exploded in Palestine. In a back alley in Gaza, Mukhtar was cleaning out a block of hovels that the Israelis, coming under pressure and being forced to retreat, had only just abandoned. He came into a yard gutted by grenades: a Jew lay slumped at the foot of a low wall and was groaning quietly as he clutched at his leg. He wasn't wearing the uniform of Tsahal – he was probably a Mossad agent. Mukhtar pointed his Kalashnikov at him and was about to open fire. But when the Jew saw the barrel of the weapon aimed at his chest, his face, crumpled in pain, grew more animated, and he sketched a smile. There was a scar extending from his ear to under his helmet.

The man from the desert! The Arab slowly stopped aiming his gun at the Jew, cleared his throat and spat. He slipped his left hand into his short pocket, and threw the man a small bundle of emergency bandages.

Then turned on his heel and barked out a brief order to his men: keep advancing, there's nothing and no one in this dive.

Mukhtar sighed: Rome is a beautiful city, plenty of girls to be found there. More than in the desert, that was certain.

He would indeed go back to Rome. With pleasure.

34

Three days later, Nil was trying to settle down on the uncomfortable seats of the Rome express.

He had been completely taken aback to learn he had been summoned to Rome, without any explanations being given. Ancient music manuscripts! The Father Abbot had handed him a train ticket for the following day – it would be impossible for him to go back to Germigny and take a second photo of the stone slab. As well as his files – for he mustn't leave anything compromising in his cell – he had slipped into his suitcase the negative he had stolen from Andrei's office. Would he be able to get anything out of it?

With surprise he noticed that his compartment was almost empty, and yet all the vacant seats were reserved. Just one passenger, a slender middle-aged man, seemed to be asleep, huddled in the corner by the corridor. Since they had left Paris, they had simply nodded to one another. His head was haloed by a mass of blond hair, with a long scar running through it.

Nil took off his clerical jacket and placed it – folded so that it would not get crumpled – on the seat to the right of him.

He closed his eyes.

The aim of monastic life is to track down the passions and eliminate them at their root. From the time he had entered the novitiate, Nil had been well schooled: St Martin's Abbey turned out to be an excellent establishment of self-renunciation. Since all his strength was bent on his search for truth, this caused him little pain. On the contrary, he was glad to be freed from those instincts that enslave humanity, for its greater woe. He could not remember getting angry – a degrading passion – for a long time now. So he hesitated to put a name to what he had been feeling for the past few days. The death of Andrei, the sloppy inquiry, the line hastily drawn under it all: verdict, suicide – a shameful end. In the monastery they were spying, searching rooms, stealing belongings. Now he was being packed off to Rome like a parcel.

Anger? At all events a mounting irritation, as irritating for him as the sudden epidemic of an illness that had long been kept at bay by regular vaccination.

He decided to postpone examining this pathological outbreak. "Wait till I get to Rome. The city has survived everything."

He had patiently reconstructed the events surrounding the death of Jesus, when the beloved disciple had been given a new lease of life. He had continued to exist after the Council of Jerusalem. The hypothesis of his flight to the desert seemed the most likely to Nil: it was there that Jesus himself had taken refuge, on several occasions. It was in the desert that the Essenes, and then the Zealots (at least until the Bar Kokhba revolt) had taken shelter.

The trace of his steps was lost in the desert sands. In order to pick it up, Nil needed to listen to a voice from beyond the grave, that of his dead friend.

Pursuing this research would serve to sublimate the anger he sensed mounting within him.

He tried to find a comfortable position and get a bit of sleep.

The gentle rattle of the train lulled him into a doze. The lights of Lamotte-Beuvron sped by.

Then it all happened extremely quickly. The man in the corner next to the corridor left his seat and came over, as if to take something from the luggage rack above him. Nil mechanically looked up: the luggage rack was empty.

He had no time to think: the blond head of hair was already leaning towards him, and he saw the man's hand reaching out towards his clerical jacket.

* * *

Nil was just about to protest at the cavalier manners of his travelling companion – "He's like a robot!" he thought.

But the door of the compartment clattered open.

The man quickly straightened; his hand fell to his side, his face grew more animated, and he smiled at Nil.

"'Scuse me for disturbing you, gentlemen." It was the ticket inspector. "The passengers who had reserved the empty seats in your compartment haven't turned up. I've got a couple of nuns with me who couldn't find seats next to each other in the train. Here you go, Sisters, sit where you like, plenty of room in the compartment. Enjoy your journey!"

While the nuns came in and greeted Father Nil ceremoniously, the other passenger went back to his seat without a word. A moment later his eyes were closed and he was nodding off.

"Funny chap! What came over him?"

But getting the new arrivals settled occupied his full attention. A suitcase had to be hoisted onto the luggage rack, and bulky cardboard boxes pushed under the seats – and then he had to put up with their interminable chattering.

Night had fallen. As he sought sleep, Nil noted that the mysterious fellow opposite him had not moved an inch, huddled in his corner.

Awoken by daybreak, when he opened his eyes the seat next to the corridor was empty. To get to the restaurant car for breakfast, he had to walk the full length of the train – no sign of the man.

He returned to his compartment, where one of the nuns obliged him to have a sip of disgusting coffee from her Thermos. He was forced to bow to the evidence: the enigmatic traveller had disappeared.

Part Two

35

Pella (Jordan), 58 AD

"How are your legs, *abbu*?"

The beloved disciple heaved a sigh. His hair had turned white, and his features were hollowed. He looked at the man in the prime of his life standing next to him.

"It's been twenty-eight years since Jesus died, and ten years since I left Jerusalem. My legs have carried me here, Yokhanan, and they may need to carry me elsewhere, if what you tell me is true…"

They were taking advantage of the shade of the peristyle, the floor of which was covered by a magnificent mosaic depicting Dionysus. From here, the dunes of the nearby desert could be seen.

Pella, founded by veterans of Alexander the Great on the eastern bank of the Jordan, had been almost entirely destroyed by an earthquake. It seemed to him, when he was forced to flee from Jerusalem to escape the threats of Peter's followers, that this city situated outside Palestine would be safe enough for him. He settled here with Jesus's mother, and they were soon joined by a core of his disciples. Yokhanan came and went between Pella and neighbouring Palestine, or even Syria;

Paul had established his headquarters in Antioch, one of the capitals of Asia Minor.

"What about Mary?"

Yokhanan's affection for Jesus's mother was touching. "That child has adopted the mother of a crucified man, and has adopted me to replace his own crucified father," thought the beloved disciple.

"You'll be seeing her later on. Tell me more about what's going on: I'm so out of it here..."

"My news is several weeks old. James, the brother of Jesus, finally won. He's now the head of the Jerusalem community."

"James! But... what about Peter?"

"Peter resisted for as long as he could. He even went to try and dethrone Paul in his own lair in Antioch – but he got sent away with a flea in his ear! Anyway, he's just taken ship to Rome."

The two men laughed. Seen from here, on the edge of the desert and its vast emptiness, struggles for power in the name of Jesus seemed derisory.

"Rome... I knew it! If Peter is no longer number one in Jerusalem, Rome is the only place big enough for his ambitions. It's in Rome, Yokhanan, at the heart of the Empire, that the Church of which he dreams will grown and become mighty."

"There's something else: your disciples left in Judaea are more and more marginalized, and sometimes hassled. They're asking if they ought to get away as you have, and come and join you here."

The old man closed his eyes. This too was something he had been expecting. The Nazoreans were neither Judaizers like James, nor prepared to deify Jesus like Paul: caught between the two tendencies that were violently opposed in the young Church and refusing to be assimilated to either of them, they risked being crushed.

124

"Those who can't put up with the pressure can come and join us in Pella. We're safe here – for the time being."

Yokhanan made himself comfortable sitting beside him, and pointed to the bundle of sheets of parchment scattered across the table.

"Have you been reading, *abbu*?"

"All night long. Especially this collection, which you tell me is circulating in Asia."

He showed the thirty or so sheets, bound by a woollen cord, that he was holding.

"For all these years," said Yokhanan, "the apostles have been transmitting Jesus's words orally. So that the memory of them won't be lost when they die, they have set them down here, in no particular order."

"Yes, it is his teaching, just as I heard it. But the apostles are cunning. They don't put words into Jesus's mouth that he never said: they merely change one word here, add a nuance there. They invent commentaries, or attribute to themselves things they never really said. For example, I've read that, one day, Peter fell to his knees before Jesus and proclaimed: 'Truly, you are the Messiah, the Son of God!'"

He threw the book down on the table.

"Imagine Peter saying something like that! Jesus would never have accepted such a claim, neither from Peter nor from anyone else. Listen, Yokhanan: in exiling me, the apostles managed to gain exclusive control of the testimony. In their hands the Gospel has become a tool of power. The transformation of Jesus will continue apace, that much is obvious. How far will they go?"

Yokhanan kneeled at his feet, and placed his hands on his knees in a familiar gesture.

"You can't let that happen. They are writing down their memories – you should write yours. You ought to record in writing the things you teach your disciples here – and circulate the text the way they are circulating theirs. Tell the whole story, *abbu*: talk about the first encounter on the banks of the Jordan, the healing of the lame man by the pool of Bethesda, Jesus's last days... tell the story of Jesus the same way you told it to me, so that he doesn't die a second time!"

He kept his eyes fixed on the face of his adoptive father, who picked another bundle of parchment off the table.

"As for Paul, he knows what he's doing. He knows that people can only put up with their wretched lives thanks to their faith in the resurrection. He says to them: you will rise from the dead, *because* Jesus rose from the dead first. And if he rose from the dead, it means he's God – only a god can raise himself from the dead."

His face clouded over, and Yokhanan took his hands in his own.

"I didn't want to tell you: Eliezer Ben-Akkai, the leader of the Essenes in Jerusalem, is dead. Is he going to take the secret of Jesus's tomb with him?"

The old man's eyes filled with tears. The death of the Essene meant his whole youth had been wiped away.

"It was Eliezer's own sons, Adon and Osias, who carried the body. They know – that makes three of us, and that's quite enough. You have learnt from me how to encounter Jesus from beyond his death. What would you gain from knowing where his final grave lies? His tomb is respected by the desert – it would not be respected by men."

Yokhanan quickly rose to his feet and went off for a few minutes. When he came back, he was holding a bundle of virgin parchment in one hand, and in the other pen of buffalo horn and an earthen inkwell. He set them down on the table.

"So, write, *abbu*. Write, so that Jesus may remain alive."

126

36

"I now declare this solemn session open."

The Rector of the Society of St Pius V noted with satisfaction that some of his brothers were not leaning against the backs of their chairs: those were the ones who had made good use of the psalm *Miserere* to measure out their application of the metal discipline.

The room was still just as empty, with two exceptions: opposite him, at the foot of the bloody crucifix, an ordinary chair had been placed. And, on the bare table, a liqueur glass contained a colourless liquid, which gave off a faint odour of bitter almonds.

"My brother, please take your place for the proceedings."

One of the participants rose, walked round the table and sat on the chair. The veil masking his face was trembling, as if it were an effort for him to breathe.

"For many long years, your service in our Society has been beyond reproach. But recently you have committed a grave error: you have given away confidential information concerning the current business, one which is of capital importance for our mission."

The man raised supplicant hands to those present.

"The flesh is weak, my brothers, I beg you to forgive me!"

"That is not the question!" the Rector replied in trenchant tones. "The sin of the flesh is remitted by the sacrament of penance, just as Our Lord remitted the sins of the woman caught in adultery. But by speaking to that girl about our recent anxieties…"

"She's no longer in any position to cause us problems!"

"Indeed. We had to make sure that she would *never again* be able to cause problems, which is always regrettable and ought to remain the exception."

"So… since you have been so kind as to resolve this problem…"

"You do not understand, my brother."

He turned to address the assembly.

"There is a great deal at stake in this mission. Until the middle of the twentieth century, the Church kept control over the interpretation of the Scriptures. Ever since Pope Paul VI of unhappy memory suppressed the Congregation for the Index in 1967, we no longer control anything. Absolutely anybody can publish absolutely anything, and the Index, which relegated pernicious ideas to the forbidden sections of libraries, has fallen away like a finger attacked by the leprosy of modernism. These days, an ordinary monk, far away in his abbey, can become a grave menace to the church by providing the proof that Christ was just an ordinary man.

A shudder ran through the assembly.

"Ever since our Society was created by the sainted Pope Pius V, we have struggled to preserve the public image of Our Saviour and God made man. And we have always succeeded."

The brothers all nodded.

"Times are changing, and they demand extraordinary measures. We need money to isolate the problem, set up *sound* seminaries, control the media throughout the planet and block certain publications. A lot of money to influence governments when it comes to cultural politics and education, so that the Christian West is not invaded by Islam or by sects. Faith can move mountains, but the lever it uses is money. Money can do everything: when used by pure hands it can save the Church, which is today threatened in its most precious belonging – the dogma of the Incarnation and that of the Trinity."

A murmur of approval could be heard running through the room. The Rector gazed intently at the crucifix, under which the accused sat trembling.

"Well, we get nothing more than a trickle of funds. You will remember the sudden vast fortune of the Templars? Nobody has ever known where it came from. And now the inexhaustible source of that fortune may perhaps be within our reach. If we possessed it, we would have unlimited means to carry out our mission. On one condition…"

He lowered his gaze to the wretched brother who seemed to melt away on his chair under the violent glare of the two spotlights illuminating the crucifix.

"That condition is that no indiscretion should compromise our activities. And you have committed that indiscretion, my brother. We have managed to draw out the thorn you thrust into the flesh of Our Lord, but it was a near-run thing. We no longer have any confidence in you, and so your mission is today at an end. I ask the ten apostles present to confirm, by their vote, my sovereign decision."

All at the same time, ten hands stretched out towards the crucifix.

"My brother, our affection goes with you. You know the procedure."

The condemned man undid his veil. The Rector had often met him face to face, but the others had never seen anything but his two hands.

The veil fell to reveal the features of an elderly man. There were dark rings under his eyes, but his gaze was no longer imploring: this last act was part of the mission he had accepted when he became a member of the Society. His devotion towards Christ as God was total and it would not flinch today.

* * *

The Rector rose, followed by the ten apostles. They slowly held out their arms until their fingers were touching.

Facing the bloodstained crucifix, the ten men, their arms held out as if on a cross, gazed at their brother who rose to his feet. He was no longer trembling: when Jesus had stretched out on the wood, he had not trembled.

The Rector raised his voice and said, in neutral tones:

"My brother, the three Persons of the Trinity know with what dedication you have served the cause of one of them. They welcome you to their company, in that divine light that you have not ceased to search for throughout your life."

Slowly, he picked up the liqueur glass from the table, raised it for a moment like a chalice, and then presented it to the old man.

With a smile, he took a step forwards, and held out his bony hand to the glass.

37

"Welcome to San Girolamo! I am Father John, the hosteller."

On emerging from the Rome express, Nil rediscovered his bearings from his days as a student, and unhesitatingly set off for the bus stop where he could catch a bus to the Catacombs of Priscilla. He was so happy to be seeing the city again that he forgot the odd events that had taken place on his journey.

He got off just before the terminus, at the stop of the sloping Via Salaria. The San Girolamo Abbey, situated in a still green and leafy spot, is an artificial creation of Pope Pius XI, who wanted to bring together Benedictines from all over the world to establish a revised version of the Bible – but in Latin. The

Society of St Pius V kept a close eye on each of these monks, until they were obliged to admit that Latin was now spoken only in the Vatican: the modern world condemned their labour. Ever since then, San Girolamo had been living on its memories.

Nil set down his suitcase at the entry to the dingy yellow cloister, adorned in the middle by a basin over which hung a melancholy clump of bamboos. A faint whiff of pasta and oleander were the only signs that the visitor was in Rome.

"The Congregation told me yesterday that you would be arriving. At the beginning of the month, we received the same request for your Father Andrei, who stayed here for several days…"

Father John was as voluble as a Roman from Trastevere. He guided the new arrival to the staircase that led to the upper floors.

"Give me your case… Phew! It's heavy! Poor Father Andrei, nobody knows what came over him, but he left one morning without telling anyone. And he packed his bags in a hurry, since he left several of his things in his room. I left them there – it's the room you'll be occupying. Nobody's set foot in there since the sudden departure of your unfortunate colleague. So, you're here to work on Gregorian manuscripts?"

Nil had stopped listening to this torrent of words. He would be staying in Father Andrei's room!

As soon as Father John had finally left him to himself, he surveyed the room. Unlike the cells in his abbey, it was filled with several articles of furniture. A big wardrobe, two sets of bookshelves, a mattress-and-frame bed, a huge table with a chair, an armchair… The indefinable smell of monasteries hung in the air, an odour of dry dust and wax polish.

The objects left by Father Andrei had been placed on one of the bookshelves. Shaving equipment, handkerchiefs, a plan of Rome, an appointments diary… Nil smiled at the latter: a monk didn't have many appointments to note!

He heaved his suitcase up onto the table. It was almost entirely filled with his precious notes. He was about to arrange them on the bookshelf, but then thought better of it: there was a key in the wardrobe. He placed the papers in there, pushing the negative from Germigny right to the back. Then turned the key in the lock and pocketed it, without conviction.

Then he stopped: on the table, there was an envelope. Addressed to him.

Dear Nil,

You have come to help me with my research. Bienvenue à Rome! *To be frank, I don't really understand why: I never asked them to request that you come! Anyway, I'm delighted to see you. Call round to my office as soon as you can: Secretariat for Relations with the Jews, in the Congregation building.* À bientôt!

Your old friend, Rembert Leeland

A broad smile lit up his face. *Remby*! So he was the man he was here to help! He might have guessed as much, but he hadn't seen his friend from their student days in Rome for over ten years, and the idea that he might be summoned to Rome by him had never so much as crossed his mind. *Remby, what a pleasure!* This trip would at least allow them to catch up with each other.

Then he reread the letter: Leeland seemed every bit as surprised as he was himself. *I never asked them…* It wasn't Leeland who had asked him to come.

So who was it?

38

The old man in the white alb took the glass proffered to him by the Rector, raised it to his lips and swallowed the colourless liquid in one draught. He grimaced and sat down on his chair.

It was very quick. In front of the eleven apostles, their arms still extended as on a cross, the man hiccuped, then bent double with a groan. His face turned purple, contracted into a horrible rictus, and he collapsed on the ground. The spasms lasted for about a minute, and then he stiffened for the last time. From his mouth, opened as if to gulp the air, a thick trail of slime trickled down his chin. His wide-open eyes stared at the crucifix above him.

Slowly, the apostles lowered their arms and sat down. In front of them, on the ground, the white shape was motionless.

The brother who was furthest from the Rector on his right stood up, a cloth in his hand.

"Not yet! Our brother must hand on the torch to the man who is to succeed him. Be so kind as to open the door, please."

In the half-light, a white shape was standing there, apparently waiting.

"Come forwards, my brother!"

The new arrival was dressed in the same alb as those already present, his cowl pulled over his head and the white veil fastened to either side of his face. He took three steps forwards and then stopped, seized by horror.

"Antonio," the Rector reflected, "such a charming young man! I feel sorry for him. But he must take up the torch, it's the rule of apostolic succession."

Faced with the spectacle of the old man whose brutal death had convulsed his body, the new brother's eyes remained wide open and staring. They were curious eyes: the iris was almost perfectly black, and his pupils, dilated by his sense of revulsion, gave him an odd appearance, which was made even odder by a pale matt brow.

The Rector beckoned him across.

"My brother, it is you yourself who must cover this apostle's face, as you are today to succeed him. Look closely at his features: they are those of a man totally dedicated to his mission. When he ceased to be capable of fulfilling that mission, he willingly brought it to an end. Receive his torch from him, so that you may serve as he served, and die as he died, in the joy of his Master."

The new arrival turned towards the man who had opened the door to him and was now handing him the cloth. He seized it and kneeled next to the dead man, whose purple face he contemplated for a long time. Then he wiped away the foam that stained his mouth and chin and, lying prostrate, gave to the lips that had turned blue in death a lingering kiss.

Then he straightened up, spread the cloth on the face that was now slowly swelling, and finally turned to the motionless brothers.

"Good," said the Rector warmly. "You have just undergone the final trial, and it has made you the twelfth of the apostles who sat at either side of Our Lord in the upper chamber in Jerusalem."

Antonio had been forced to flee his native Andalusia: Opus Dei is very reluctant to allow its members to leave it, and a certain distance seemed wise. In Vienna, the collaborators of Cardinal Catzinger had spotted this taciturn young man with his dark eyes. After several years of observation, his file was sent to the Prefect of the Congregation, who placed it, without further comment, on Calfo's desk.

It required another two years of close investigations led by the Society of St Pius V. Two years of tailing him, tapping his phone conversations, keeping his family and friends back in Andalusia under surveillance... When Calfo asked him to come to his apartment in Castel Sant'Angelo for a series of interviews, he definitely knew Antonio better than the Andalusian knew himself. In Vienna, a city of pleasures, they had tempted him in every way: he had resisted. Pleasure and money were of no interest to him – just power and the defence of the Catholic Church.

The Rector motioned to him. "Andalusian, Moorish blood," he reflected. "Criticized the methods of Opus Dei. Arabic melancholy, Viennese nihilism, the disenchantment of a southerner: an excellent recruit!"

He told him: "Take your place among the Twelve, my brother."

Facing the bare wall on which the only decoration was the bleeding image of the crucified, the Twelve were once more gathered around their Master in their full complement.

"You know our mission. You will start contributing to it straight away; you are to keep under close surveillance a monk who has arrived today in San Girolamo. I have just learnt that an outside agent almost interrupted a capital process concerning this monk, in the Rome express. This was a regrettable incident – he had received no orders to this end, and I do not control him directly."

The Rector sighed. He had never met this man, but he had a full dossier on him. He remembered its contents.

"Unpredictable. A compulsive need to act out his ideas. When it's not a musical challenge, it's the excitement of danger. Mossad has withdrawn his licence to kill."

"Here are your first instructions," he said, holding an envelope out to the new brother. "The next ones will reach you when the time is ripe. And remember whom you are serving!"

He pointed with his right hand to the cross, the image on which stood out against its mahogany panel. The green jasper of his ring glinted.

"Lord! Never perhaps since the Templars have you been in such danger. But once your Twelve possess the same weapon as they did, they will use it to protect You!"

39

Cardinal Emil Catzinger motioned to his guest to sit down – a tall, slim man with a broad forehead over a pair of rectangular glasses.

"Please, Monsignor…"

Behind his glasses, Rembert Leeland's eyes were sparkling. He had the long face of an Anglo-Saxon, but the fleshy lips of an artist. He gazed interrogatively at His Eminence.

"You must be wondering why I have asked you here… First tell me this: do relations with our Jewish brothers occupy your whole time?"

Leeland smiled, which gave his face the expression of a mischievous student.

"Not really, Your Eminence. Luckily I also have my musicological studies!"

"*Precisamente*. That brings me to my point. The Holy

Father himself is extremely interested in your research. If you can demonstrate that the origins of Gregorian chant lie in the psalmody of the synagogues of the High Middle Ages, it will be an important element in our rapprochement with Judaism. So we've brought in a specialist to help you decipher the ancient texts you are studying... A French monk, an excellent exegete... Father Nil, from St Martin's Abbey."

"I heard as much yesterday. We were students together."

The Cardinal smiled.

"So you know each other then? It will be pleasant to mix business with pleasure – I'm always glad when friends get an opportunity to meet like this. He's just arrived – see him as often as you like. And listen to him: Father Nil is a fund of knowledge, he has a great deal to say, and you will learn a lot from him. Let him talk about his interests. And then... from time to time, just drop me a report on the tenor of your conversations. In writing – I'll be the one and only addressee. All right?"

Leeland opened his eyes in the greatest surprise. "What does that mean?" he thought. "He's asking me to get Nil to talk, and then to make a report on him? Who does he take me for?"

The Cardinal was observing the American's expressive features. He could read him like a book. He added with an avuncular smile:

"Don't be afraid, Monsignor, I'm not asking you to act as an informer. Merely to keep me abreast of the research your friend is doing, the things he is writing. I'm extremely busy, and I won't have time to invite him in. But I too am very curious to keep up with the most recent advances in exegesis… You'll be doing me a favour if you can flesh out what I already know."

When he saw that he had not convinced Leeland, his tone became sharper.

"I would also like to remind you of your position. We were obliged to bring you over from the United States to your appointment here, with the rank of a bishop, to draw a line under the scandalous polemic that you had provoked over there. The Holy Father will not tolerate anyone questioning his refusal – an absolute and justified refusal – to ordain married men as priests. And then it would be the turn of women – why not? He will tolerate even less a Benedictine Abbot, at the head of the prestigious St Mary's Abbey, publicly giving him advice on this subject. You now have, Monsignor, an opportunity to redeem yourself in the Pope's eyes. So I am counting on your discreet, efficient and total collaboration. Do you understand?"

His head lowered, Leeland did not reply. Then the Cardinal put on the tone of voice his father had used, in bygone days, when he returned from the Eastern Front.

"I have the painful duty to remind you, Monsignor, that it is also for *another reason* that we were obliged to make you leave your country as a matter of urgency and bestow on you the episcopal dignity that protects you at the same time as it honours you. Now do I make myself clear?"

This time, Leeland lifted to the Cardinal the eyes of a sad child, and nodded. God forgives all sins, but the Church makes its members expiate them.

At great length.

40

Pella, end of 66 AD

"Father, I thought I'd never make it here!"

The two men embraced effusively. Yokhanan's drawn features showed how exhausted he was.

"The Roman XII Legion has put the coastal region to the fire and the sword. It's just retreated in front of Jerusalem, with considerable losses. They're saying that Emperor Nero is going to bring General Vespasian in from Syria, to reinforce the position with the V and X Legion – the formidable Fretensis. Thousands of seasoned soldiers are converging on Palestine – it's the beginning of the end!"

"And Jerusalem?"

"Safe, at least for the time being. James fought for as long as he could against the deification of his brother, then he finally accepted it in public: for the Jewish authorities this was blasphemy, and the Sanhedrin had him stoned. The Christians are anxious."

"James! With him, the last check on the Churches' ambitions has gone."

"Any news of Peter?"

"Still in Rome. There are rumours of persecutions there. Nero views Christians and Jews with an indiscriminate hatred. Peter's Church itself is under threat. Perhaps it's the end there too."

He showed his satchel, containing a few parchments.

"James, Peter... They belong to the past, *abbu*. Now there are several Gospels in circulation, as well as other of Paul's epistles..."

"I've received all of them, thanks to our refugees." He stretched his hand out towards the table in the peristyle, laden with documents. "Matthew has rewritten his text. I saw he was drawing inspiration from Mark, the first to compose a sort of history of Jesus, from the encounter by the Jordan to the empty tomb. In fact, Matthew himself didn't write it, since, you see, it's in Greek. He must have written it in Aramaic and had it translated."

"Exactly. There's a third Gospel in circulation, also in Greek. The copies come from Antioch, where I managed to meet the author, Luke, a friend of Paul."

"I've read those three Gospels. They're increasingly putting into Jesus's mouth words he never said: they make him say he was the Messiah, or even God. It was inevitable, Yokhanan. And... what about my narrative?"

He had finally agreed to write it, not a Gospel constructed like those of Mark and the others, but a narrative – which Yokhanan had copied and put into circulation. He started by relating his own memories: the encounter by the Jordan, the overwhelming experience of those first days. But he had not left Judaea, whereas Jesus had returned to live and teach further north, in Galilee. On what had happened there, he had almost nothing to say. His narrative resumed from the time when the Twelve and their Master had returned to Jerusalem, a few weeks before the crucifixion. Until the finding of the empty tomb.

Obviously, no reference was made to what had followed, the removal of the body by Adon and Osias, the two sons of Eliezer Ben-Akkai. The role played by the Essenes in the disappearance of the body of the condemned man needed to remain an absolute secret.

As did the location of Jesus's tomb.

Between these two periods, the beginning and the end, he had added the memories of his Jerusalem friends: Nicodemus, Lazarus, Joseph of Arimathea. A narrative composed directly in Greek, describing the Jesus he had known: a Jew first and foremost, but filled with a dazzling light whenever he revealed how his Father dwelt in him, that God whom he called *abba*. Never before had a Jew dared to use that familiar term to designate the God of Moses. He repeated:

"And what about my narrative, Yokhanan?"

The young man's face darkened.

"It's in circulation. Among your disciples, who know it off by heart, but also in the Churches of Paul, as far as Bithynia, apparently."

"And it doesn't get the same reception there, does it?"

"No. In Judaea, the Jews criticize you for describing Jesus as a prophet superior to Moses. And among the Greeks, they find your Jesus too human. Nobody dares to destroy the testimony of the *beloved disciple* but, before reading it out in public, they correct it, they 'fill it out', as they say – to an increasing extent."

"They can't rip my guts out like they did to Judas, so they're eliminating me by the pen. My narrative will turn into a fourth Gospel, one that fits in with their ambitions."

As in bygone days, Yokhanan kneeled before his *abbu*, and took his hands in his own.

"So then, father, write an epistle for us, your disciples. I'll put it in a safe place, while there's still time: the fanatical Jews of Jerusalem won't hold out for long. Write the truth about Jesus and, so that nobody can travesty it, say what you know about his tomb. Not the one in Jerusalem, the one that's empty: the real one, the one in the desert, the one in which his remains lie."

The refugees were now flooding into Pella from all sides. Sitting on the edge of the peristyle, the old man gazed out at the valley. Already, from the other side of the Jordan, plumes of smoke could be seen rising from the burning farms.

Pillagers, of the kind that always accompany invading armies. It was the end. He must transmit it to future generations.

Filled with resolve, he sat at his table, picked up a sheet of parchment and started to write: "*I, the beloved disciple of Jesus, the thirteenth apostle, to all the Churches...*"

The next day, he came up to Yokhanan, who was saddling a mule.

"If you make it through, try to hand over this epistle to the Nazoreans in Jerusalem and Syria."

"What about you?"

"I'll stay in Pella until the last moment. When the Romans approach, I'll take our Nazoreans south. As soon as you get back, go directly to Qumran: they'll tell you where to find me. Look after yourself, my son."

With a lump in his throat, he silently handed over to Yokhanan a hollow reed, which the young man slipped under his belt. Inside it was a simple scroll of parchment, rolled up, bound by a linen cord.

The letter of the thirteenth apostle to posterity.

41

Nil first walked along the Villa Doria Pamphili and then took the Via Salaria Antica that was hemmed in between its walls. He loved to tread the uneven surface of the ancient imperial roads, on which the Roman paving is still evident. During his student years, he had passionately explored this city – the *Mater Praecipua* – the mother of all the peoples. He joined the Via Aurelia, which leads out onto the Vatican City from behind, and unhesitatingly headed towards the building in which the Congregation for the Doctrine of the Faith was housed.

The Secretariat for Relations with the Jews is located in an annex of the building, on the side of St Peter's Basilica. He had to climb up three flights of stairs before coming to a corridor of small bays directly under the eaves: the offices of the *minutanti*.

Mons. Rembert Leeland, O.S.B. He knocked discreetly.

"Nil! *Bonjour, mon ami!* It's so good to see you!"

His friend's office was tiny, separated from its neighbours by a mere partition. He just had space enough to slide onto the single chair facing the strangely bare table. Noticing his astonishment, Leeland gave him an embarrassed smile.

"I'm only a minor *minutante* in an unimportant secretariat… Actually, I tend to work mainly at home; here I'm so hemmed in I can hardly breathe."

"It must be quite a change from the plains of Kentucky!"

The American's face darkened.

"I'm in exile, Nil, for having said aloud what a lot of people think…"

Nil looked at him affectionately.

"You haven't changed, Remby."

They had both been students in the period just after the Second Vatican Council and had shared the hopes of a whole younger generation which believed in the renewal of the Church and of society: their illusions, gone with the wind, had left traces within them.

"Don't delude yourself, Nil, I've changed a great deal, more than I can say: I'm no longer the same guy. But what about you? Last month we learnt about the brutal death of one of your monks, in the Rome express. I heard talk of suicide, and now I see you turning up here without my even asking. What's happening, *mon ami*?"

"I knew Andrei well: he wasn't the type of man to commit suicide, quite the opposite – he was passionate about the research we'd been involved in for years, not working together but in parallel. He'd discovered things that he wouldn't – or couldn't – tell me clearly, but I have the impression that he was urging me on to discover by myself. I was the one who went to identify the body officially: in his hand I discovered a note written just before his death. Andrei had jotted down four points he wanted to talk to me about as soon as he got back: it wasn't the letter of someone who's planning to commit suicide, but rather the proof he had plans for the future, and wanted me to be associated with them. I didn't show this note to anyone, but it was stolen from my cell, and I don't know who by."

"*Stolen?*"

"Yes, and that's not all: some of my notes were taken too."

"And what about the inquiry into Father Andrei's death?"

"In the local paper there was a brief article that called it an accidental death, and in *La Croix* a simple notice of death. We don't read any other paper, we don't listen to the radio or the television; monks only know what the Father Abbot wishes to tell them in the chapter meetings. The gendarme who discovered the body said it was a murder, but he was taken off the inquiry."

"A murder!"

"Yes, Remby. I can't believe it either. I want to know what happened, why my friend died. His last thoughts were of me, and I have the sense that something has been entrusted to me, that I need in turn to transmit. The last words of a dead man are sacred, especially when it's a man of the scale of Father Andrei."

* * *

Hesitantly at first, Nil told him of his research on St John's Gospel, his discovery of the beloved disciple. Then he described his frequent conversations with Andrei, the unease the latter had felt at Germigny, and the fragment of the Coptic manuscript concealed in the binding of his last book.

Leeland listened without interrupting him.

"Nil, I've never been any good at anything except music. And computers, for processing the manuscripts I study. But I don't understand how a labour of erudition can lead to such dramatic events and cause you such anguish."

He prudently omitted any mention of the Cardinal Prefect's request.

"Andrei was forever telling me in veiled terms that our research touched on something much more important, which I can't discover. It's as if I had all the threads of a tapestry in front of me and no idea of the design they're supposed to form. But now, Rembert, I've decided to go all the way: I want to know why Andrei died, I want to know what is hidden behind this mystery. I've been going round and round in circles trying to solve it for years."

Leeland looked at him, surprised by the grim determination he could read on a face that in his experience had always looked so placid and tranquil. He rose, walked past the chair and opened the door.

"I'll leave you with all the time you need to carry on with your research here. But right now, we need to go to the Vatican library stacks. I have to show you the building site on which I'm labouring, and you need to show your face there: don't forget that the reason you're in Rome is my manuscripts of Gregorian chant."

Leeland recalled his summons to Catzinger's office: perhaps there was *another* reason, too? In silence, they made their way along the labyrinth of corridors and staircases that led to the exit on St Peter's Square.

In the office next to Leeland's, a man pulled off two earphones linked to a box fixed by a suction pad to the wooden wall. He was dressed elegantly in clerical garb, and let the earphones dangle round his neck while he rapidly sorted sheets of paper covered in tiny shorthand. His unusually black eyes shone with satisfaction: the sound had been of excellent quality, the partition was not very thick. Not a single word of the conversation between the American *monsignore* and the French monk had been lost. It would be quite enough just to leave the two of them together, they'd never stop talking.

The Rector of the Society of St Pius V would be happy: the mission was off to a good start.

42

"The book stacks are located in the Vatican basement. I had to get accreditation for you, since access to this part of the building is strictly controlled – you'll understand why when you get there."

They walked along the high wall of the Vatican City and went in through the entry on the Via di Porta Angelica, where the main guard post is situated. The two Swiss guards in traditional uniforms let them in without stopping them, and they crossed a series of inner courtyards, until they reached the Belvedere Court. Surrounded by high walls, it protects the Lapidary Gallery of the museums and the Vatican Library. Despite the fact it was still early, figures could be seen walking along behind the glass panes.

Leeland motioned Nil to follow him and headed towards the opposite corner. At the foot of the imposing wall, there was a little metal door with a small keypad. The American typed in a code and waited.

"A few hand-picked people have permanent accreditation, like me. But you're going to have to prove you're a bona fide visitor."

A papal policeman in civilian clothes opened the door and scrutinized the two visitors suspiciously. When he recognized Leeland, he gave him a brief smile.

"*Buongiorno, Monsignore.* Is this monk with you? May I see his papers and accreditation?"

Nil had dressed in his monastic habit – it makes things easier here, Leeland had explained to him. They went into a sort of airlock, and Nil handed over a piece of paper with the coat of arms of the Vatican. The policeman took it without a word and went off.

"The controls are strict," the American whispered. "The Vatican Library is open to the public, but its stacks contains ancient manuscripts that only a few scholars are allowed to see. You'll meet Father Breczinsky, the guardian of the place. Given the priceless value of the treasures stored here, the Pope appointed a Pole to this post, a timid and self-effacing man, but one who's totally dedicated to the Holy Father.

The policeman returned and handed Nil's accreditation back to him with a nod.

"You'll need to show that paper every time you come here. You're not allowed in by yourself, but need to be accompanied by Mgr Leeland, who has a permanent pass. Follow me."

A long corridor, sloping gently downwards, bent off under the building and led to a reinforced door. Nil had the impression he was entering a citadel that was prepared for a siege.

"This spot is buried under the thousands of tons of St Peter's Basilica. The tomb of the Apostle isn't far." The policeman inserted a magnetic card and typed in a code: the door opened with a swish.

"You know your way around, Monsignor. Father Breczinsky is waiting for you."

The man standing at the entry to a second reinforced door had a face whose pallor was set off by his severe black cassock. Round glasses on his short-sighted eyes.

"Good morning, Monsignor – and this is the French visitor for whom I have received accreditation from the Congregation?"

"The very man, my dear Father. He'll be helping me with my work: Father Nil is a monk at St Martin's Abbey."

Breczinsky started.

"Are you by any chance a colleague of Father Andrei?"

"We were colleagues for thirty years."

Breczinsky opened his mouth as if he were about to ask Nil a question, but then thought better of it and concealed his unspoken curiosity behind a quick nod. He turned to Leeland.

"Monsignor, the room is ready – if you will follow me…"

In silence he led them down a series of vaulted rooms, each communicating with the next by a broad arched opening. The walls were covered with glass-fronted shelves, the lighting was uniform, and a low hum indicated the hygrometer necessary for the safe conservation of ancient manuscripts. Nil's gaze darted along the shelves as they passed them: Antiquity, Middle Ages, Renaissance, *Risorgimento*… From the labels, he surmised that these were the most precious witnesses of Western history, and had the impression he could survey it all within a few dozen yards.

148

Amused by his astonishment, Leeland whispered:

"In the music section, the only one I can use, I'll show you autograph scores by Vivaldi, pages from Handel's *Messiah*, and the first eight bars of Mozart's *Lacrimosa* – the last notes he ever wrote as he was dying. They're all here…"

The music section was in the last room. In the centre, under the adjustable lighting, a bare table covered with a sheet of glass on which you would have sought in vain for a single grain of dust.

"You know your way around, Monsignor, I'll leave you to it. Er…" He seemed to be in a state of some mental turmoil. "Father Nil, could you come into my office? I need to find you a pair of gloves that will fit, you need them to handle the manuscripts."

Leeland looked surprised, but allowed Nil to follow the librarian to an office that opened directly onto their room. Breczinsky carefully closed the door behind them, took a box off a shelf and then turned to Nil with an embarrassed look.

"Father… may I ask you exactly what was the nature of your relations with Father Andrei?"

"We were very close. Why?"

"Well, I… he and I wrote to one another – he sometimes asked for my advice on the medieval inscriptions he studied.

"So… *it's you?*"

Nil thought to himself, "I sent the photo of the stone slab of Germigny to a Vatican employee. He wrote back to say that he had received it, but made no comment."

"Andrei had told me about his correspondent in the Vatican Library – I didn't know it was you and didn't think I'd get to meet you!"

With downcast eyes, Breczinsky was mechanically fingering the gloves in the box.

"He would ask me for technical details, the same way other scholars do: we had established a relation of trust, albeit at a distance. Then one day I found, as I was sorting out the Coptic holdings, a tiny fragment of a manuscript that seemed to come from Nag Hammadi and had never been translated. I sent it to him: he seemed most disturbed by this piece, which he sent me back without his translation. I wrote to him about this, and he then faxed me the photo of a Carolingian inscription found in Germigny, asking me what I thought of it."

"I know, we took the photo together. Andrei kept me up to date with his work. Almost all of it."

"Almost?"

"Yes, he didn't tell me everything, and made no bones about it – something that always surprised me."

"Yes, he came here: it was the first time we'd ever met, a very... intense meeting. Then he vanished, I never saw him again. And I learnt of his death in *La Croix* – an accident, or suicide..."

Breczinsky seemed to be very ill at ease, and his eyes evaded those of Nil. Finally he handed him a pair of gloves.

"You can't stay with me too long, you need to get back into the room. I... we will talk again, Father Nil. Later on – I'll find some means. Beware of everyone here, even Mgr Leeland."

Nil's eyes opened wide in amazement.

"What do you mean? I'll probably not be seeing anyone apart from him here in Rome, and I trust him completely: we were students together, I've known him for ages."

"But he's been living in the Vatican for a while. This place transforms all those who come near it, and they're never the same afterwards... Anyway, forget what I've just told you, but look after yourself!"

On the table, Leeland had already spread out a manuscript.

"Say, he sure took his time finding you some gloves! There's a drawer full of them in the room next door, every size…"

Nil did not reply to his friend's anxious glance, and went over to the big rectangular magnifying glass placed over the manuscript. He glanced at it.

"No illumination, probably before the tenth century – to work, Remby!"

At noon they ate sandwiches brought to them by Breczinsky. Suddenly all smiles, the Pole asked Nil to explain what his work would be consisting in.

"First deciphering the Latin text of these manuscripts of Gregorian chant. Then translating the Hebrew text of the ancient Jewish chants which have similar melodies and comparing them… I'm only looking at the words, of course. Mgr Leeland is doing the rest."

"Ancient Hebrew is all Greek to me, like medieval scripts!" explained the American with a laugh.

When they came out, the sun was low on the horizon.

"I'll head straight back to San Girolamo," said Nil apologetically, "this air-conditioned atmosphere has given me a headache."

Leeland stopped him: they were in the middle of St Peter's Square.

"Seems to me you've made a big impression on Breczinsky: usually he doesn't say more than a few sentences. So, *mon ami*, I have to warn you: beware of him."

"Oh Lord!" reflected Nil. "What kind of place have I come to?"

Leeland insisted, a serious expression on his face.

"Make sure you don't make any faux pas. If he talks to you, he's trying to worm things out of you – here, nobody's

151

innocent. You don't know what a dangerous place the Vatican is – you have to mistrust each and every one here."

43

A whirlwind of thoughts was still swirling around in Nil's head when he entered his room in San Girolamo. He first assured himself that nothing had disappeared from the wardrobe – which was still locked – and then went over to the window: the sirocco, that terrible south wind that covers the city in a fine film of sand from the Sahara, had just started to blow. Rome, usually so luminous, was immersed in a yellowish, watery haze.

He closed the window to keep out the sand. This would not stop him suffering from the brutal drop in atmospheric pressure that always comes with the sirocco and causes the population migraines that Roman justice considers to be an attenuating circumstance in cases of crimes committed under the influence of the baleful wind.

He went over to the shelves to take an aspirin to keep headaches at bay, and halted at the sight of the objects left by Andrei. Nil had been rejected by his family when he had entered the monastery, and wounded by the death of his friend; he was easily swayed by emotion, and his eyes misted over with tears. He gathered together what were now precious souvenirs for him, and slipped then into his suitcase: they would find a place in his cell at St Martin's.

He mechanically opened the diary and leafed through it. A monk's calendar is as uneventful as his life: the pages were empty up until the start of November. Here, Andrei had jotted down the date and time of his departure for Rome, then his appointments at the Congregation. Nil turned the page: a few lines had been hastily scribbled down.

His heart thumping, he sat down sideways on the chair and lit the lamp on the desk.

At the top of the left-hand page, Andrei had written, in capitals: LETTER OF THE APOSTLE. There followed, a little lower, two names: Origen, Eusebius of Caesarea – the latter followed by three letters and six figures.

Two Fathers of the Greek Church.

On the opposite page, he had scrawled: "SCV Templars". And, opposite, another three letters, followed by just four figures.

What were the Templars doing in the company of the Fathers of the Church?

Was it an effect of the sirocco? He was starting to feel a little light-headed.

Letter of the Apostle. In their conversations, Andrei had, rather vaguely, mentioned something of this kind. And it was one of the four leads on the note he had written on the Rome express.

Nil had often wondered what to make of this mysterious allusion. And here was his friend again talking to him about this letter, as if he were still at his side. Andrei seemed to be telling him that he would learn something about it from the writings of two Fathers of the Church, from whom he had here noted down something that looked like a scholarly reference.

He needed to track down these two texts. But where?

Nil went over to the washbasin for a glass of water and dropped his aspirin in it. As he watched the cloudy column of bubbles swirl up, he started to think hard. Three letters followed by figures: these were the classification marks from the Dewey system, telling you where to find a book in a library. But which library? The advantage of the Dewey system is that it is infinitely extendible: librarians can adapt it to their needs without having to stray outside it. With a good deal of luck, the two last figures could enable you to find one library among hundreds.

If you asked every librarian. Throughout the entire world.

Nil swallowed his aspirin.

Finding a book just from its Dewey classification mark was like looking for a particular car in a car park with four thousand spaces without knowing either where it was parked nor what make it was. Nor the name of the attendant at the entry. Nor even what car park it is…

He rubbed his temples: the pain was coming on more quickly than the aspirin.

The three letters after Origen and Eusebius were followed by six figures: so this was a complete classification mark, giving the precise position of a book on a particular shelf. But the three letters accompanying "SCV Templars" were followed by only four figures: they indicated a book stack, or perhaps a zone in a given library, without giving the exact position.

Was SCV the abbreviation of the name of a library? In what part of the world?

Now Nil's head was grasped in a painful vice that prevented him from thinking. For years, Father Andrei had been in communication with librarians from all across Europe, often by means of the Internet. If one of these classification marks were that of a library in Vienna, he could hardly see himself asking the Reverend Father Abbot to book him a return ticket for Austria.

He took a second aspirin and went up to the terrace that looked out over the local district. In the distance, you could make out the lofty dome of St Peter's Basilica. The Apostle's tomb had been dug into the *tufo* of the Vatican Hill that was in those days outside Rome; here Nero had built an imperial residence and a circus. It was here that thousands of Christians and Jews, pursued by the same indiscriminate hatred, were crucified in 67 AD.

His research had revealed an unexpected face of Peter, a man filled with murderous impulses. The Acts of the Apostles attest that two Christians from Jerusalem had perished by his hand, Ananias and Sapphira. The killing of Judas was only a hypothesis, but one that was supported by some highly persuasive evidence. And yet his death in Rome had been that of a martyr. "I believe" – says Pascal – "those who die for their faith." Peter had been born ambitious, violent, calculating – perhaps, in the last moments of his life, he had finally become a true disciple of Jesus? History is no longer in a position to decide, but he had to be given the benefit of the doubt.

"Peter must have been like all of us: a two-sided man, capable of the best after doing the worst…"

Nil had just been warned to mistrust everything and everybody. This idea was intolerable to him; if he dwelt on it for too long, he'd jump into the first train, just like Father Andrei.

So as not to lose his equilibrium, he needed to concentrate on his research. He should live in Rome as if it were the monastery, and in the same solitude.

"I will seek. And I will find."

44

Vatican Hill, 67 AD

"Peter... If you won't eat anything, you can at least drink!"

The old man pushed away the pitcher proffered to him by his companion, who was wearing the short tunic of slaves. He leant over, picked up a straw and slipped it between his back and the bricks of the *opus reticulatum*. He shuddered: in a few hours he would be crucified, and his body coated in pitch. At nightfall, the executioners would set fire to these living torches, which would provide light for the show the Emperor was putting on for the people of Rome.

Those who had been condemned to death had been penned up in these long vaulted tunnels that came out directly onto the arena of the circus. Through the entrance grille you could see the two stone markers – the *metas* – set at either end of the race track. It was here, around the great central obelisk of the circus, that every evening "Jewish" men, women and children were indiscriminately crucified, being allegedly responsible for the huge fire that had destroyed the city a few years earlier.

"What's the point of eating or drinking, Linus? You know it's going to be this evening: they always start with the eldest. You'll live a few more days, and Anacletus will see you leaving; he'll be among the last to join us."

He stroked the head of a child sitting at his sides on the straw. The child gazed at him with veneration, his big eyes underscored by dark shadows.

As soon as he had arrived in Rome, Peter had taken the Christian community in hand. Most of the converts were slaves, like Linus and the boy Anacletus. They had all passed through the mystery religions from the East, which exercised an irresistible spell on the people. They offered them the prospect of a better life in the beyond and spectacular, bloody cults. The austere and unadorned religion of the Jews who had converted to Christ – who was both God and man – experienced a meteoric success.

Peter had finally admitted that Jesus's absolute divinity was indispensable for the spread of the new religion. He forgot the scruples that had held him back right at the start, when he had still been living among the Jerusalem converts. "Jesus is dead," he had thought. "The Christ-God is alive. Only someone alive can bring these throngs of people to the new life."

The Galilean became the uncontested head of the community in Rome. No more was heard about the thirteenth apostle.

He closed his eyes. On his arrival here, he had told the prisoners how soldiers had captured him on the Via Appia as he fled with those trying to escape Nero's persecution. Revolted by what they considered to be an act of cowardice, many of the Christians arrested for their courage gave him the cold shoulder in this prison.

His life was abandoning him – would he hold out until evening? He must. He wanted to suffer this hideous death, rejected by his own, to redeem himself and become worthy of God's forgiveness.

He motioned to Linus, who sat beside Anacletus, on the mildewed paving. After midday, the roars of the wild animals had fallen silent: they had all been massacred by the gladiators during a huge fight that morning. The odour of a menagerie mingled with the nauseating stench of blood and excrement. He had to force himself to speak.

"You may live, you and this boy. Three years ago, after the fire, the youngest prisoners were released, when the crowd grew weary of so many horrors displayed on the sand of the circus. You will live, Linus, you have to."

The slave gazed at him intently, tears in his eyes.

"But if you're not here any more, Peter, who will lead our community? Who will teach us?"

"You will. I knew you when you'd just been sold at the market near the Forum, just as I watched this child grow. You and he will live. You are the future of the Church. I'm no more than an old tree now, already dead inside…"

"How can you say that? You knew Our Lord, you followed him and you served him without fail!"

Peter bowed his head. The betrayal of Jesus, the successive murders, the vicious struggle against his enemies in Jerusalem, so many sufferings of which he had been the cause…

"Listen to me carefully, Linus: the sun is already setting, there isn't much time left. You have to know: I've failed. Not only by accident, as happens to each of us, but over a long period, and repeatedly. Tell it to the Church, when it's all over. But tell them too that I die at peace – because I have acknowledged my faults, my countless faults. Because I have asked forgiveness from Jesus himself, and from his God. And because a Christian should never – *never* doubt God's forgiveness. That's the very heart of Jesus's teaching."

Linus placed his hands on Peter's: they were frozen. Was it his life withdrawing from him? Several had died in this tunnel, even before being led out to execution.

The old man looked up.

"Remember, Linus – and you, child, listen – on the evening of the last supper we took with the Master, just before his capture, there were twelve of us with him. *There were only twelve apostles with Jesus.* I was there, I call God to witness before I die. Perhaps you will one day hear of a thirteenth apostle; neither you, nor Anacletus, nor those who will come after you must tolerate so much as the mere mention of any apostle other than the Twelve – not so much as an allusion to one. It's a matter of the Church's life and death. Will you swear solemnly to obey, before me and before God?"

The young man and the child nodded gravely.

"If he ever emerged from the shadows, that thirteenth apostle could completely destroy everything we believe in. Everything that will enable those men, those women" – and he motioned to the indistinct shadowy figures lying prostrate on the ground – "to die in peace this evening, perhaps even with a smile. Now leave me. I have a lot to say to my Lord."

Peter was crucified at sunset, between the two *metas* of the Vatican circus. When they set fire to his body, it lit up, for an instant, the obelisk, which was just a few yards away from the cross.

Two days later, Nero proclaimed the end of the games: all those who had been sentenced to death were freed, after being subjected to the thirty-nine lashes of the whip.

Linus succeeded the Apostle, whose body he buried at the summit of the Vatican Hill, some distance from the entrance to the circus.

Anacletus succeeded Linus, the third on the list of popes proclaimed at every Catholic mass throughout the whole world. It was he who built the first chapel on Peter's tomb. This was later replaced by a basilica erected by the Emperor Constantine, who already wanted the building to be one of great majesty.

The solemn oath sworn by the two popes who succeeded Peter was transmitted from century to century.

* * *

And the obelisk in front of which Father Nil paused for a moment, that morning – the sirocco had dropped, and Rome was sparkling in all its glory – was the very same one at the foot of which, nineteen centuries earlier, one of Jesus's disciples, reconciled with his God by penitence and pardon, had willingly faced up to a terrible execution.

For Peter had hidden the truth from the Christians: he alone knew that he did not deserve their veneration, and wished to die a shameful death, scorned by all. But he had not fled the persecution. Quite the opposite: he had gone to hand himself over to Nero's police to expiate his faults. And to be able to get Linus to swear that he would transmit the secret.

Ever since, that secret had gone no further than the Vatican Hill.

The thirteenth apostle had not spoken.

45

Nil loved to stroll and daydream in St Peter's Square early in the morning, before the tourists got there. He moved out of the shadow of the obelisk to enjoy the already warm sunshine. "They say that it's the obelisk that stood in the centre of Nero's circus. In Rome, time doesn't exist."

His left hand kept a tight hold on his bag, in which he had placed, on leaving San Girolamo, the most precious of his notes, extracted from the papers he had placed on the bookshelves. His room could be searched here just as easily as in the Abbey, and he knew that now he had to mistrust everyone. "But not Remby – never!" As he left, he slipped into his bag the roll with the negative of the snapshot he had taken in Germigny. One of the four leads that Andrei had left behind, though he still didn't know what to make of it.

When Leeland reached his office, while Nil was still day-dreaming at the foot of the obelisk and musing on the empires that are consolidated by time, he found a note summoning him immediately to see a *minutante* of the Congregation. A certain Mgr Calfo, whose path he had sometimes crossed in a corridor, without altogether knowing what place he occupied in the organization chart of the Vatican.

Two storeys and a labyrinth of corridors further down, he was surprised to see the prelate installed in an almost luxurious office, whose single window looked out directly over St Peter's Square. The man was short, podgy, and looked both self-confident and smooth-tongued. "An inhabitant of the Vatican galaxy," reflected the American.

Calfo did not ask him to sit down.

"Monsignor, the Cardinal has requested me to keep him informed of your conversations with Father Nil, who has come to give you a hand. His Eminence – and it would be surprising if this were not the case – takes a close interest in the studies of our specialists."

On his desk, in full view, lay the note handed over by Leeland to Catzinger the day before: in it, he summarized his first conversation with Nil, but said nothing whatever about his friend's confidential remarks on his research into St John's Gospel.

"His Eminence has passed your first report on to me: it shows that there is a friendly, trusting relation between yourself and the Frenchman. But that's inadequate, Monsignor, quite inadequate! I can't believe that he told you nothing about the nature of the talented work he has been doing, and for so long!"

"I didn't think that the details of a general conversation could interest the Cardinal to such an extent."

"All the details, Monsignor. You need to be more precise, and less reserved, in your reports. They will save a lot of the Cardinal's valuable time, since he wants to follow every new scientific advance – it's his duty as Prefect of the Congregation for the Doctrine of the Faith. We expect you to collaborate, Monsignor, and you know why – don't you?"

A feeling that Leeland could not suppress, an upsurge of muted anger, overcame him. He pursed his lips and said nothing.

"Do you see this episcopal ring?" Calfo stretched out his hand. "It's an admirable masterpiece, fashioned at a period when people still understood the language of precious stones. Amethyst, which most Catholic prelates choose, is a mirror of humility and reminds us of the ingenuousness of St Matthew. But this is a jasper, which is the reflection of faith, associated with St Peter. At every instant it forces me to face anew the thing for which my life is one long struggle: the Catholic faith. It is that faith, Monsignor, which is concerned at the work being done by Father Nil. You must hold back nothing of what he tells you – as you have done."

Calfo dismissed him in silence, then sat at his desk. He opened the drawer and drew from it a bundle of pages torn from a notepad: the shorthand account of the previous day's conversation. "I'm still the only person who knows that Leeland isn't playing the game. Antonio has worked well."

As he made his way back along the corridors to his office, Leeland tried to stifle his anger. That *minutante* knew that he had concealed a whole swathe of his conversation with Nil. How did he know?

"Someone's been overhearing us! I'm being bugged, here in the Vatican!"

Once again the hatred welled up in him. They had made him suffer too much, they had destroyed his life.

As he came into Leeland's tiny office, Nil apologized for being late.

"Sorry, I was having a stroll out on the Square…"

He sat down, propped his bag against one of the chair legs, and smiled.

"I've put all my most precious notes together in there. I need to show you my conclusions – they're provisional, but you'll start to understand…"

Leeland interrupted him with a wave of his hand, and scribbled a few words on a piece of paper, which he held out to Nil, placing his forefinger on his lips. In surprise, the Frenchman took the paper and glanced at it. "They're listening in on us. Don't say anything, I'll explain. Not here."

He raised his eyes to Leeland in astonishment. In a tone of volubility, the latter carried on:

"So, settled into San Girolamo okay? Yesterday there was quite a sirocco – hope it wasn't too uncomfortable for you?"

"Er… oh, yes, actually, I had a headache all evening. What…"

"There's no point in us going back to the Vatican book stacks today: I'd like to show you what I've got on my computer, you'll see what I've already done. It's all over at my place. Would you like to come with me? Now? It's ten minutes' walk, Via Aurelia."

He nodded imperiously at the flabbergasted Nil and rose to his feet without waiting for him to answer.

Just as they were leaving the corridor for the stairwell,

163

Leeland let Nil go on ahead of him and turned round. From the office next to his own he saw a *minutante* emerge, someone he didn't know. The man quietly locked the door and started to come towards them. He was wearing elegant clerical costume, and in the darkness of the corridor Leeland could make out only his dark gaze, both melancholy and disquieting.

He quickly caught up with Nil, who was waiting for him on the first steps of the stairwell, looking just as bewildered.

"Let's go down. Quick."

46

They crossed Bernini's colonnade. Leeland looked all round and took Nil's arm in a familiar gesture.

"My friend, this morning I obtained the proof that our conversation yesterday was overheard."

"Like in an embassy in Soviet times!"

"The Soviet Empire no longer exists, but here you're at the nerve centre of another empire. I'm dead certain about what I'm saying, don't ask me any more. *Mon pauvre ami*, what hornet's nest have you got yourself embroiled in?"

They walked in silence. The traffic was extremely heavy on the Via Aurelia, and made any conversation impossible. Leeland stopped outside a modern apartment block at the corner of the next street.

"Here we are, I've got a studio on the third floor. The Vatican pays the rent, my salary as a *minutante* wouldn't be enough."

As they crossed the threshold of Leeland's studio, Nil whistled in quiet admiration.

"Monsignor, what a wonderful place!"

164

A spacious living room was divided into two. The first part contained a baby grand piano, around which a whole battery of electro-acoustic equipment was scattered. An openwork bookshelf filled with books separated off the second part: two computers linked to the most sophisticated peripherals – printers, a scanner and keypads that Nil was unable to identify. Leeland invited him to make himself comfortable and uttered an embarrassed little laugh.

"It's my American abbey that gave me all this stuff. It's worth a fortune! They were furious at the way I was dismissed from my post as abbot – which I'd been elected to in the proper way – for reasons of church politics. The Vatican requires me to sign in at my office mornings and evenings. Then I go off to work in the book stacks or come back here. Breczinsky has authorized me to photograph certain manuscripts, which I've scanned into the computer."

"Why did you tell me not to trust him?"

Leeland seemed to hesitate before replying.

"During the years when we were students in Rome, you could see the Vatican from the Aventine Hill, a mile or so away: it was a long way, Nil, a really long way. You were fascinated by the prelates dancing their ballet round the Pope, you enjoyed it as a spectator, proud to belong to a machine that possesses such a prestigious bodywork. Now you're not a spectator any longer: you're an insect, pinned to the canvas, caught in the spider's web, stuck there like a defenceless fly."

Nil listened to him in silence. Ever since Andrei's death, he had sensed that his life had been turned upside down, that he had entered a new world of which he knew nothing. Leeland continued:

"Josef Breczinsky is a Pole, one of those they call 'the Pope's men'. Totally dedicated to the person of the Holy Father, and thus torn between the different tendencies in the Vatican, all the more violent because they bubble away underground. For years I've been working ten yards away from his office, and I still know nothing about him – except that he bears the weight of an infinite suffering – you can read it in his face. He seems to have taken a liking to you: take great care about what you tell him."

Nil restrained his desire to seize Leeland by the arm.

"And what about you, Remby? Are you also an… an insect stuck in the spider's web?"

The American's eyes misted over with tears.

"Me?… My life's over, Nil. They destroyed me, because I believed in love. The same way they can destroy you, because you believe in truth."

Nil realized he should not persist. "Not today," he thought. "Such distress in his eyes!"

The American got a grip on himself.

"I'm completely unable to collaborate with you on your scholarly work, but I'll do my very best to help you: Catholics have always tried to ignore the fact that Jesus was Jewish! Make the best use of your stay in Rome, the Gregorian manuscripts can wait if necessary."

"We'll work in the book stacks every day, so as not to arouse suspicions. But I'm resolved to pursue Andrei's research. His note mentioned four leads that can be followed. One of them concerns a recently discovered stone slab in the Germigny church, with an inscription dating back to the period of Charlemagne. We took a quick snapshot opposite it, the inscription had greatly surprised Andrei. I have the negative here – do you think that with your computer equipment you can maybe develop it?"

Leeland seemed relieved: talking technology enabled him to escape the ghosts he had just referred to.

"You've no idea what a computer can do! If they're the characters of a language that it possesses in its memory, it can reconstitute letters or words from a text that has been eroded by time. Show me your negative."

Nil picked up his bag and held the roll over to his friend. They moved to the other part of the room, and Leeland switched on the boxes that started to blink. He opened one of them.

"Laser scanner, latest generation."

Fifteen seconds later, the slab appeared on the screen. Leeland manipulated the mouse, tapped away at the keyboard, and the surface of the image started to be swept, very smoothly, by a sheaf of light.

"It'll take twenty minutes. While it's getting on with it, come over to the piano, I'll play you *Children's Corner*."

While Leeland, eyes closed, brought Debussy's delicate melodic lines to life under his fingers, the sheaf of light from the computer passed untiringly over the reproduction of a mysterious Carolingian inscription.

Photographed, in the twilight of the twentieth century, by a monk led to his death by this snapshot.

At the same moment, Mgr Calfo was picking up his mobile phone.

"So they've left the office of the Congregation and headed straight off to the *Americano*'s apartment? Okay, stay in the neighbourhood, keep a discreet eye on their movements, and this evening you can write your report for me."

He mechanically stroked the elongated lozenge shape of his green jasper.

47

On the computer screen, the inscription on the Germigny slab now showed up more clearly.

"Look, Nil: it's perfectly legible. They're Latin letters, the computer has restored them. And then look, at the beginning and end of the text there are two Greek letters – alpha and omega- which it had identified beyond any possibility of error."

"Can you do a copy for me?"

Nil was contemplating the inscription on the printout. Leeland waited for him to speak.

"Yes, it's the text of the *Symbolon* of Nicaea, the Creed. But it's set out in a completely incomprehensible way…"

They brought their chairs closer to each other. "It's like before," thought Nil, "when I went to his room to study with him, side by side under the same lamp."

"Why has the letter alpha been added before the first word in the text," he continued, "and the letter omega after the last one? Why are those two letters, the first and the last in the Greek alphabet, artificially put down on a text written in Latin and considered to be unalterable? Why have the words been chopped up like that, without their meaning being taken into account? I can see only one possible explanation: we mustn't bother about the meaning, since there isn't one, but about the way the text has been set out. Andrei told me he had never seen this; he certainly suspected that this way of cutting up the text had a particular meaning, and he had to come to Rome before realizing that the Creed, modified in this way, had something to do with the three other clues jotted down in his note. Right now, I've only deciphered one, the Coptic manuscript."

"You haven't told me about that…"

"That's because I've discovered the meaning of the words, but not the sense of the whole message. And the sense may lie in the incomprehensible way this text was inscribed in the eighth century."

Nil reflected, then continued:

"As you know, for the Greeks alpha and omega signified the beginning and end of time…"

"As in the Apocalypse of St John?"

"Exactly. When the author of the Apocalypse writes, 'I saw a new heaven and a new earth', he has Christ in glory say:

'I am Alpha and Omega,
the first and the last,
the beginning and the end.

"The letter alpha means that a new world is beginning, and the letter omega indicates that that world will last for eternity. Framed between those two letters, the odd way the text has been cut up seems to allude to a new world order, one which cannot ever be modified: 'a new heaven and a new earth', something that must last until the end of time."

"Are alpha and omega frequently used as symbols in the Bible?"

"Not at all. They are found only in the Apocalypse, traditionally ascribed to John. So the conclusion seems to be that if this text is 'set' between the alpha and the omega in this way, the arrangement must have something to do with St John's Gospel."

Nil got up and stood right in front of the closed window.

"The text is arranged independently of the meaning of the words, and has some link to St John's Gospel. That's all I can say, until I can sit down at my desk and look at this inscription every which way, as Andrei must have done. In any case, everything gravitates around the Fourth Gospel, and that's why my research was of such interest to my old friend."

Nil motioned Leeland to join him at the window.

"You won't see me tomorrow: I'll be locked away in my room in San Girolamo, and I'm only coming out when I've found the meaning of this inscription. Let's meet up the day after tomorrow; I hope I'll have a better idea by then. Then you'll have to let me use the Internet, I need to do research in all the great libraries of the world."

He jutted his chin towards the cupola of St Peter's dome, emerging from above the rooftops.

"Perhaps Andrei died because he'd come across something that threatened all *that*..."

If, instead of gazing at the Vatican dome, they had glanced down into the street, they would have spotted a young man having a quiet smoke, sheltering from the December chill in a carriage entrance. Like any casual passer-by, he was wearing light-coloured trousers and a thick jacket.

His dark eyes never left the third floor of the apartment block on the Via Aurelia.

48

Late that evening, Catzinger's office was the only one with its lights on in the Congregation building. He told Calfo to come in, and addressed him in tones of command:

"Monsignor" – the Cardinal was holding a simple sheet of paper – "late this afternoon I received Leeland's second report. He's kidding around with us. According to him, the only thing they discussed today was Gregorian chant. But you tell me they stayed locked up together in the apartment on the Via Aurelia all morning long?"

"Until 2 p.m., Your Eminence, when the Frenchman left and went back to San Girolamo, where he closeted himself away in his room. My information is completely reliable."

"I don't want to know who your source is. Sort out a way of finding out what they're saying to each other in Leeland's apartment: we *must* discover what that Frenchman's up to. Understood?"

Early next morning, a tourist seemed to be taking a close interest in the sculpted capitals of the Teatro di Marcello, which marks the site of the cattle market in ancient Rome, the Foro Boario. Not far away rise the rigid columns of the Temple of Virile Fortune, topped by a Corinthian acorn; they remind the informed visitor who the Temple was dedicated to. Just next to them, a small round temple is dedicated to the Vestal Virgins, who offered their perpetual chastity to the divinities of the city and maintained the sacred fire. As he walked past these two contiguous buildings, the tourist smiled with pleasure, reflecting: "Virile fortune, and perpetual chastity. A deified Eros next door to divine purity: the Romans had already understood. Our mystics merely developed their insights."

His elegant trousers did not quite conceal an eloquent posterior, and the reason he kept his right hand thrust into the pocket of his suede jacket was that he wanted to hide the very fine jasper adorning his ring finger – never, in any circumstances, did he take off that precious jewel.

He was joined by a man who was ostentatiously holding a thick tourist guide to Rome.

"*Salam aleikom*, Monsignor!"

"*We aleikom salam*, Mukhtar. These were the arrangements for transporting the Germigny slab. Nice work."

From his pocket there emerged an envelope that changed hands. Mukhtar Al-Quraysh quickly fingered the envelope without opening it, and offered his colleague a smile in exchange.

"I went over to inspect the apartment block on the Via Aurelia: there's no flat to let. But there's a studio for sale on the second floor, just beneath the *Americano*'s."

"How much?"

When he heard the figure, Calfo pulled a face: but, before long, perhaps the Society of St Pius V would no longer need to count its pennies. He opened his jacket and took out of his inner pocket another envelope, bigger and thicker than the first one.

"Go and have a look at it straight away, settle the purchase immediately and get hold of the key. Leeland will be kept busy at the Congregation this afternoon, you'll have three hours to do whatever's necessary."

"Monsignor! In just one hour, the microphones will be installed."

"Has your favourite enemy gone back to Israel?"

"Straight after our little trip. He's preparing for an international tour starting with a series of concerts here in Rome, for Christmas."

"Perfect, a wonderful cover – you may yet need to call on his services."

Mukhtar looked at him with a ribald glint in his eye.

"And Sonia – happy with her?"

Calfo suppressed his irritation. He replied drily:

"I'm very satisfied, thank you. Let's not waste any time, *mah salam*."

The two men nodded to each other and left. Mukhtar crossed the Tiber via the Isola Tiberina bridges, while Calfo took a short cut across the Piazza Navona.

"Christianity couldn't have come into being anywhere but Rome," he thought as he gazed in passing at the sculptures of Bernini and Brunelleschi, set opposing each other in a dramatic stand-off. "The desert leads to the inexpressible – but in order to express himself in incarnate form, God needs the quiverings of the flesh."

49

Qumran, 68 AD

Dark clouds were piling up over the Dead Sea. In this natural basin, clouds never bring rain: they announce a catastrophe.

Yokhanan motioned his companion to keep going. In silence they approached the enclosure wall. A guttural voice rooted them to the spot:

"Who goes there!"

"*Bene Israel!* Jews."

The man who had stopped them stared at them suspiciously.

"How did you get this far?"

"Over the mountain – then we slipped through the Ein Feshka plantations. It's the only way to get here: the legionaries are encircling Qumran."

The man spat on the ground.

"Sons of darkness! And what are you here for? Seeking your deaths?"

"I've come from Jerusalem, we have to see Shimon Ben-Yair. He knows me – take us to him."

They climbed over the enclosure wall and halted in amazement. What had once been a peaceful place of prayer and study was now nothing much than a huge caravanserai. Men were polishing derisory weapons, children were hurtling around yelling, and the wounded were lying on the ground. Yokhanan had already been here, some time ago, accompanying his adoptive father, who liked to meet up with his old Essene friends. In the gathering gloom, he stopped, unsure what to do, in front of a group of aged men sitting against the scriptorium wall where he had so often spent hour after hour watching the scribes tracing Hebrew characters on their parchments.

The lookout came over and whispered a few words into the ears of one of the old men.

"Yokhanan! Don't you recognize me? True enough: I've aged a century in the last month. Who's that with you? My eyes are infected, I'm half-blind."

"Of course I recognize you, Shimon! It's Adon, the son of Eliezer Ben-Akkai."

"Adon! Give me a hug!… But where's Osias?"

Yokhanan's companion lowered his head.

"My brother died in the plain of Ashkelon, killed by a Roman arrow. It was a miracle that I managed to get away from the V Legion: its legionaries are invincible."

"They will be conquered, Adon; they are the sons of darkness. But we will die before they do – Qumran is ripe for plucking. Vespasian has taken over the X Fretensis Legion that's got us encircled, he wants to attack Jerusalem from the south. All day long we've been able to observe their preparations. We have no archers, and they can manoeuvre right in front of our eyes. It's going to happen tonight."

174

Yokhanan gazed in silence at the poignant spectacle of these men, in the grip of a History from which they could not escape. Then he continued:

"Shimon, have you seen my *abbu*? I've spent over three months crossing the country. No news of him, nor of his disciples: I found Pella completely abandoned."

Through his purulent eyes, Shimon contemplated the sky: the setting sun was lighting up the clouds from below. "The most beautiful sight in the world, just as on the morning of creation! But this evening our world is going to end."

"His flight brought him this way. With him there were at least five hundred Nazoreans – men, women and children. He wanted to send them into Arabia, to the shore of the Inner Sea. He was right: if they escape from the Romans, they'll be persecuted by the Christians, who hate them. Our men have accompanied them as far as the edge of the desert of Edom."

"Did my father go with them?"

"No, he left them at Beersheba and let them carry on towards the south. We have a small community of Essenes in the desert of Idumaea: that's where he's waiting for you. But will you be able to get there? You've just got tangled in a net whose mesh is closing in on the sons of light. Will you live the Day with us, and enter its brightness – this very night?"

Yokhanan stepped to one side and exchanged a few words with Adon:

"Shimon, I have to join my father: we're going to try and get out. But before that, I've got something I need to put somewhere safe. Please help me."

He went over to the old man and murmured a few words in his ear. Shimon listened attentively, and then nodded.

"All of our sacred scrolls have been placed in caves that are inaccessible to anyone who doesn't know the mountain. One of our men will take you there, but he won't be able to go up with you – listen…"

From the Roman camp the blare of trumpets could be heard. "They're sounding the attack!"

Shimon gave a brief order to the sentinel. Without a word, the man motioned Yokhanan and Adon to follow him, as a first shower of arrows came plummeting down on the Essenes, to shrieks of terror from the women and children. They made their way against the stream of haggard men rushing to the eastern wall, and went through the gate facing the mountain.

It was the beginning of the end of Qumran.

Mechanically, Yokhanan slipped his hand under his belt: the hollow bamboo, the one his father had given him in Pella, was still there.

Khirbet Qumran is built into the slopes of a high cliff, and the buildings were constructed on a plateau overlooking the Dead Sea. A complicated system of small canals open to the sky brought water to the central pool, where the Essenes practised their baptismal rites.

Yokhanan and Adon, preceded by their guide, initially followed the line of the channels. Bent double, they ran from tree to tree, in short, swift spurts. The tumult of a fierce battle reached them from not very far behind.

Yokhanan, panting, motioned to them that he needed a rest. He was no longer young… He looked up. In front of them, the cliff seemed at first to be nothing but a bare wall, plunging down in a fearful precipice. But when he looked more closely, he saw that it was comprised of huge rocky concretions that formed a complicated interweaving pattern of footpaths and ravines hanging over the void.

Here and there you could make out black patches: the caves, to which the Essenes had moved their entire library. How had they managed it? It seemed completely inaccessible!

On the summit of the cliff he could make out the mobile arms of the Roman catapults that were starting to toss their murderous freight towards the camp. A line of archers, spread out along a hundred yards or so, were unleashing their arrows at a terrifying rate. He felt a pang in his heart, and didn't look back.

Their guide showed them the path they could take to get to one of the caves.

"Our main scrolls are there. I myself put our community's *Manual of Discipline* there. Along the left wall, third jar from the entrance. It's a big one: you can slip your parchment in with it. May God preserve you! My place is down there. Shalom!"

Still bent double, he set off running in the opposite direction. He wanted to live the Day with his brothers.

They resumed their ascent. For another eight hundred yards or so, they were in the open: continuing along the line of trees that bordered the canals, they darted from one to the other. Their travelling bags, slung down their haunches, hampered their movements.

Suddenly a hail of arrows fell all around them.

"Adon, up there, they've seen us. Let's run to the foot of the cliff!"

But these two shadows, unarmed and heading away from the battle, soon ceased to interest the Roman archers. Out of breath, they finally managed to reach the relative safety of the precipice. Now they needed to climb.

Between the rocky outcrops they managed to find goats' trails. When they reached the cave, night was falling.

"Quick, Adon – we've only got a few minutes' light left!"

The cave entrance was so narrow that they were obliged to wriggle into it feet first. Curiously, the interior seemed brighter than outside. Without a word, the two men felt their way along the ground on the left: several conical shapes emerged from the sand. Terracotta jars, half-buried, sealed by a kind of bowl-shaped lid.

With the help of Adon, Yokhanan carefully opened the third jar from the cave mouth. Inside, a scroll surrounded by scraps of cloth soaked in tar filled half the space. With great respect, he opened the hollow reed that he had pulled from his belt, and drew from it a simple sheet of parchment, bound by a linen cord. He slipped it into the jar so that it would not get stuck to the tar on the scroll. Then he put the lid back on, and piled the sand up to the jar's neck.

"There. *Abbu*, we can die: your epistle is safe here, safer than it would be anywhere else. If the Christians manage to destroy all the copies I've had made of it, the original is here."

From the mouth of the cave they could see Qumran, where the blazing buildings hinted at scenes of horror. The square formations of the legionaries were advancing methodically towards the enclosure wall, climbing over it and combing the whole space inside – leaving nothing behind them but the bodies of slaughtered men, women and children. The Essenes were no longer defending themselves. Around the central pool, they could make out an indistinct mass of people on their knees. In the middle, a man in a white robe was raising his arms to the sky. "It's Shimon! He's asking the Eternal to welcome the sons of light, this very moment!"

He turned to Adon.

"Your brother and you carried Jesus's body to the place where it rests. Osias is dead: now you are the only one to know

178

where the tomb is, you and my *abbu*. His epistle is safe here: if God requires our lives, we've done what we had to do."

Darkness was filling the basin of the Dead Sea. The whole area around Qumran was guarded. The only possible way out was the oasis right next to Ein Feshka, the same way they had come. As they approached it, they spotted a group armed with torches coming towards them. Someone shouted to them, in bad Hebrew:

"Halt! Who are you?"

They started to run, and a hail of arrows came flying after them. Seeking the cover of the first olive trees, Yokhanan sprinted along as fast as his legs would carry him, his travel bag bumping against his hip, when he heard a muffled cry just behind him.

"Adon! Are you wounded?"

He ran back, and leant over his companion: a Roman arrow was fixed in his back between his shoulder blades. He just had enough strength to murmur:

"Leave now, brother! Leave, and may Jesus be with you!"

Hunkered down in a grove of olive trees, Yokhanan saw from afar the legionaries drawing their swords to finish off the second son of Eliezer Ben-Akkai.

Now only one man knew the location of Jesus's tomb.

50

Nil walked with a spring in his step; radiant sunlight was shining through the high walls on either side of the Via Salaria. He had spent all of the previous day shut away in his room, and shared the monks' meals without attending their infrequent services. He had been obliged to suffer the never-ending chatter of Father Jean only when they took coffee, sitting in the cloister.

"All of us here lived through the golden age of San Girolamo, when it was hoped we could offer the world a new version of the Bible in Latin. Since modernity has condemned us, we're working in a vacuum, and the library has been abandoned."

"It's not just modernity that's condemning you," thought Nil as he swallowed a liquid that was an insult to Rome, the city where you can enjoy the best coffee in the world. "Perhaps the truth condemns you too."

But this morning he felt as light as air, and could almost forget the oppressive ambience in which he had been forced to live since his arrival – the way everybody mistrusted everybody else, and Leeland's private remark: "My life's over, they've destroyed my life". What had become of that tall student, both serious and childish, who rested his unchanging gaze on every thing and every person, filled with an optimism as indestructible as his faith in America?

He'd struggled with the inscription on the slab, looking at it from every possible angle. Just when he was about to give up, he had had the idea of comparing the mysterious text with the Coptic manuscript: that had been a real inspiration. One of the two phrases had enabled him, as night fell, to reach his goal.

Andrei had seen the problem clearly: you had to *put everything in perspective*. Bring together the scattered elements, each of them written at a different period – first century for the Gospel, third century for the manuscript, eighth century for Germigny. He was starting to see a thread that linked them all.

And he mustn't lose this thread. "The truth, Nil: it was to find the truth that you entered the monastery." The truth would avenge Andrei.

* * *

When he came into the studio on the Via Aurelia, Leeland had switched all his lights on and was playing a Chopin étude; he greeted him with a smile. Nil suddenly wondered whether the same man had, only two days previously, given him a glimpse into an abyss of despair.

"During the years I was in Jerusalem, I spent a lot of time with Arthur Rubinstein, who had gone there to live out his last days. There were a dozen of us students, Israelis and foreigners, who used to meet at his place. I had the privilege of seeing him playing this étude over and over. Anyway, have you managed to understand the rebus?"

Nil motioned Leeland to come and sit next to him.

"Everything became clear when I had the idea of numbering the lines of the inscription one by one. This is the result:

1   αcredo in deum patrem om
2   nipotentem creatorem cel
3   i et terrae et in iesum c
4   ristum filium ejus unicu
5   m dominum nostrum qui co
6   nceptus est de spiritu s
7   ancto natus ex maria vir
8   gine passus sub pontio p
9   ilato crucifixus mortuus
10 et sepultus descendit a
11 d inferos tertio die res
12 urrexit a mortuis ascend
13 it in coelos sedet ad dex
14 teram dei patris omnipot
15 entis inde venturus est
16 iudicare vivos et mortuo

17   s credo in spiritum sanc
18   tum sanctam ecclesiam ca
19   tholicam sanctorum commu
20   nionem remissionem pecca
21   torum carnis resurrectio
22   nem vitam eternam amen.ω

"Twenty-two lines," murmured Leeland.

"Exactly twenty-two. So I asked myself the first question I'd already raised: why were an alpha and an omega added to the beginning and end of the text?"

"You've already told me: to engrave into the marble a new world order, one that would be immutable, for all eternity."

"Yes, but I've managed to take it much further than that. Each individual line is devoid of meaning, but when I counted the number of characters – in other words, letters and spaces – I realized that each of them is of the same length, exactly twenty-four characters. So my first conclusion was: this is a *numerical code*, one based on the symbolism of numbers – a very widespread hobby horse in Antiquity and at the start of the Middle Ages."

"A numerical code? What's that?"

"You know that twelve plus twelve is twenty-four?"

Leeland gave a low whistle.

"I bow before your genius: you spent a whole day to end up with that result!"

"No jokes. Just listen. The numerical basis of this code is the figure 12, which in the Bible symbolizes the perfection of the chosen people: twelve sons of Abraham, twelve tribes of Israel, twelve apostles. If twelve represents perfection, two times twelve means that perfection raised to the absolute. For instance, in the Apocalypse, God in majesty appears surrounded by four-and-twenty elders, two times twelve. Each line of the inscription contains two times twelve characters: so each line is absolutely perfect. But two letters are missing for regular lines of twenty-four letters to be obtained: so as to obtain this result, they added a letter alpha at the beginning and a letter omega at the end. This way, they killed two birds with one stone, since they also introduced a transparent allusion to the Apocalypse of St John: 'I am alpha and omega, the beginning and the end'. By its code, the text establishes a new, immutable world. Do you follow me?"

"So far, so good."

"Now if two times twelve represents absolute perfection, the square of this perfection, i.e. twenty-four times twenty-four, is eternal perfection: in the Apocalypse, the ramparts of the Heavenly Jerusalem – the eternal city – measure one hundred and forty-four cubits, which is twelve squared. So that it can represent eternal perfection in accordance with this particular code, the Creed would need to be set out in twenty-four lines, each of then consisting of twenty-four characters: a perfect square. Okay?"

"But there are only twenty-two lines!"

"Exactly: there are two lines missing to form a perfect square. Now, it so happens that the text adopted at the Council of Nicaea contains twelve professions of faith. A very ancient legend relates that on the evening of the last supper in the upper room, each of the twelve disciples wrote down one of these professions of faith. This was a naive way of guaranteeing the apostolic origin of the Creed. Twelve apostles, twelve professions of faith, in twelve phrases each of them spread over two lines of twenty-four characters: in the rigorous language of a numerical code, that should have produced a perfect square, twenty-four lines of twenty-four characters. And as you see, there are only twenty-two lines: the square isn't perfect – there is an apostle missing!"

"What are you driving at?"

"When they arrived in the upper room, on the evening of the last supper, there were twelve of them with Jesus – *plus* the prestigious host, the beloved disciple: thirteen men to bear witness. Halfway through supper, Judas left to go and make preparations for his Master's arrest: twelve men remained. But one of the twelve was the one who would subsequently be fiercely eliminated from all the texts, and from men's memories. This one could not be counted as one of the apostles, of those who wished to found the Church on their testimony. He had to be got rid of at any price, so that he could never be considered one of the Twelve. Dividing the text into twenty-four lines would have meant admitting that this person too had, that evening, written one of the twelve professions of faith in the Creed. So it would have meant authenticating his testimony, on a level with that of the other apostles. The missing double line, Rembert, is the *incised* place of the man who lay next to his Master on the evening of Thursday 6th April 30 AD, but who was rejected from the group of the Twelve when the Church was founded. It is the tacit admission that there was indeed, at Jesus's sides, a thirteenth apostle!"

Nil opened his folder and drew out the photocopy of the Coptic manuscript, which he handed to Leeland.

"Here is my translation of the first phrase: *The rule of faith of the twelve apostles contains the seed of its destruction.* In other words, if the beloved disciple had added his testimony to that of the eleven apostles – if there had been twenty-four lines instead of twenty-two – the Creed would have been destroyed, and the Church founded on it annihilated. This inscription engraved into marble, in the eighth century, the elimination of a man: the thirteenth apostle. Many others apart from him, throughout the centuries, have opposed the deification of Jesus, but none of them have been pursued by such enduring hatred. So there was something particularly dangerous about him, and I wonder whether Andrei didn't die because he had discovered what this was."

Leeland rose to his feet and played a few chords on the piano.

"Do you think that the text of the Creed was coded right from the start?"

"Evidently not. The Council of Nicaea was held in 325, under the control of Emperor Constantine, who demanded that the divinity of Jesus be definitively imposed on the whole Church. Arianism needed to be vanquished – it refused to accept this deification and endangered the unity of the Empire. We have several accounts of the discussions: nothing indicates that the elaboration of the *Symbolon*, which in any case is closely based on an older text, obeyed any but political considerations. No, it was much later, at the start of the Middle Ages – an era besotted with esoteric knowledge – that the need was felt to code this text and engrave it on a slab placed in a prominent spot in an imperial church. This was because they wanted to reaffirm – a long time later, but insistently – the elimination of a testimony that was deemed extremely dangerous."

"And do you really think that the unlettered peasants of the Val-de-Loire could understand the meaning of the inscription that they found in front of their eyes when they came into the church at Germigny?"

"Certainly not, numerical codes are always very complicated and can be understood only by a very few initiates – who in any case already know what the code contains. They aren't

185

made, as the capitals of our Romanesque churches are, to instruct the ordinary people, but for a minority who enjoy the knowledge available only to initiates. No, the slab was engraved by imperial power to remind the elite who shared a part of that power – especially the bishops – of its mission: to maintain for all eternity, *alpha and omega*, the belief in the divinity of Jesus affirmed by the Creed, the belief that lies at the foundation of the Church – which itself was the main bulwark of imperial authority."

"Incredible!"

"The really incredible thing is that from the end of the first century a kind of conspiracy seems to have been set up in order to conceal a secret linked to the thirteenth apostle. It appears periodically. There's evidence of it from the third century in the Coptic manuscript, and more evidence in the eighth century in the Germigny inscription – maybe other clues here and there: I haven't finished looking yet. A secret maintained by the ruling religious classes, one that runs through the history of the West... and, in Andrei's footsteps, I'm about to put my finger on it. There's just one thing I know: this secret could imperil the basis of the faith defended by the hierarchy of the Church."

Leeland was silent, like an animal darting back into its lair. It was his life that this hierarchy had imperilled. He rose to his feet and slipped on his coat.

"Let's get over to the Vatican, we're running late... What do you think you'll do?"

"Tomorrow I'm going to sit down in front of your computer and start surfing the Web. I'm after two works by Church Fathers, identified only by their Dewey classification – they're in a library, somewhere in the world."

* * *

On the second storey, Mukhtar had listened in to the whole conversation. The "For Sale" sign had been taken down from the studio door and, the day before, he'd had time to move in. On a whitewood table, some electronic equipment had been set up, with a tangle of wires draped over it. One of these wires ran across the ceiling and led to the exact place on which one of the feet of the baby grand piano rested. A microphone, no bigger than a small lens, was concealed under its hinge. You would need to have completely dismantled the piano to see it.

The spools on the tape recorders linked up to this wire had been turning from the moment Nil arrived on the storey above.

Earphones in place, he hadn't missed a single word of the conversation, but he hadn't understood much. Nothing, at all events, affecting his real mission. He took the tape off the second recorder: this would be going to the Vatican, and he'd get Calfo to pay for it. The first tape was for the Al-Azhar University in Cairo.

51

"My brothers…"

This was the first meeting of the Society of St Pius V since the admission of the new brother. Modestly, Antonio was sitting in the place of the twelfth apostle at the far end of the table.

"My brothers, I am in a position to reveal to you one of the proofs of the secret which it is our mission to protect: it has recently been brought to light, and has been in our possession for just a short while. I am referring to the inscription placed by Emperor Charlemagne in the church at Germigny – its hidden meaning could be grasped by only a few scholars. It is with great joy that I now present it for you to pay it your devotions. Second and third apostles, if you please…"

Two brothers rose and stood before the crucifix, to the left and right of the Rector. The latter seized the nail piercing the Master's feet. His two acolytes did likewise to the nail fixed into his right hand and his left. He nodded, and each of them twisted his nail in accordance with a numerical code.

There was a click: the mahogany panel slid away.

It revealed behind it a recess, in which there were three shelves. The one at the bottom, level with the floor, contained a stone slab erected on its base.

"My brothers, you may approach to venerate the slab."

The apostles rose, and each in turn went over to kneel before the slab. The coating on it had been completely cleaned away: the Latin text of the Nicene Creed was perfectly readable, divided into twenty-two lines of equal length and framed by two Greek letters. Each brother bowed deeply, lifted his veil and placed his lips on the alpha and the omega. Then he straightened up and kissed the episcopal ring which the Rector held out to him, as he stood erect under the crucifix.

Antonio was deeply moved when his turn came. This was the first time that he had seen the recess opened: inside, there were two material proofs of the secret whose preservation in itself justified the existence of the Society of the Twelve. Above the slab, on the middle shelf, there was a casket of precious wood, gleaming faintly. *The treasure of the Templars!* It would soon be offered to the brothers for them to venerate, on the next Friday, the 13th.

The upper shelf was empty.

As he straightened up, he too placed his lips on the Rector's ring. Dark red highlights glinted here and there in the dark green jasper, cut in the shape of an oblong lozenge and set in a chiselled silver mount that gave it the shape of a miniature coffin. *The ring of Pope Ghislieri!* His heart pounded as he went back to his seat at the twelfth place, while the Rector pushed back the mahogany panel, which slid automatically shut with a click.

"My brothers, the upper shelf of this recess was meant one day to harbour the most precious of all treasures, that of which the treasures we possess here are merely the shadow or the reflection. We suspect that this treasure does indeed exist, but we still do not know where it is to be found: our current mission will perhaps enable us to find it and place it in our guard, safe at last. Then we really will have the means to accomplish that for which we have devoted our lives to the Lord: we will be able to protect the identity of the risen Christ."

"Amen!"

The eyes of the Eleven were lit up with joy, as their Rector went back to his place to the right of the central throne with its red-velvet cover.

"I have relieved the twelfth apostle of the task of listening in on the conversations of the two monks: such surveillance would have required his presence for long periods, and this would have kept him immobilized to no purpose. My Palestinian agent will take over, and I will soon be in a position to bring you up to date on the contents of the first tapes – which I am analysing right now. The twelfth apostle will keep the Vatican book stacks under discreet surveillance. Father Breczinsky has not met him yet, and this will make things easier. For the time being I will keep track of all the information received by the

189

Cardinal. As for the Holy Father, we will continue to keep him completely in the dark – such anxieties would only weigh him down."

The Eleven nodded their approval. This mission had to be carried out with great precision – the Rector had shown how efficient he could be.

52

Desert of Idumaea, 70 AD

"Did you get any sleep, *abbu*?"

"Ever since I came into the desert, I have been waiting for you and keeping close watch over the tremulous life still within me. Now that I've seen you again, I can depart into a different kind of sleep... What about you?"

Yokhanan's left arm dangled inertly at his side, and deep wounds scarred his naked torso. He stared anxiously at the old man, whose face bore the lines and wrinkles of illness. He did not answer, but sat down with an effort, next to him.

"Once the legionaries had finished off Adon, they caught up with me at the Ein Feshka oasis and left me for dead there. Some Essene fugitives, who had managed to escape from the capture of Qumran and the ensuing massacre, slung me over their shoulders: I'd lost consciousness, but was still alive. For several months they looked after me in the community in the desert of Judaea where they had taken refuge. As soon as I could walk again, I begged them to come with me, to find you here – you can't imagine my wanderings across this desert."

The thirteenth apostle was lying on a simple mat in front of the cave mouth. He stared at the deep defile that opened up before them, hollowed out by erosion in the red ochre rocks. In the far distance rose the mountain chain leading to Horeb, where God had, long ago, given his Law to Moses.

"The Essenes… If it hadn't been for them, Jesus would never have lived in the desert for forty days, in that solitude that transformed him. If it hadn't been for them, I wouldn't have met him when he came to John the Baptist, and he would never have met Nicodemus, Lazarus and my friends from Jerusalem. It was in one of the jars of the Essene caves that you placed my epistle, at Qumran… We owe so much to them!"

"More than you think. In the desert of Judaea they are continuing to copy every kind of manuscript. Before I left them, they gave me this…" He placed a bundle of parchments on the edge of his mat. "It's your Gospel, Father, as it is now circulating throughout the Roman Empire. I've brought it for you to read."

The old man raised his hand: he seemed to be keeping every movement to a minimum.

"Reading exhausts me these days. You read it to me!"

"Their text is much longer than your original narrative. They've stopped just correcting: they're inventing new things. The way you described him to me, Jesus used to express himself as a Jew talking to Jews…"

A faint flush of colour returned to the cheeks of the thirteenth apostle. He closed his eyes, as if he were reliving scenes that were deeply etched into his memory.

"Listening to Jesus was like hearing the wind blowing across the hills of Galilee, like seeing the ears of corn bending down, ripe for harvest, and the clouds floating across the sky above our land of Israel… When Jesus spoke, Yokhanan, he was the flute player in the market square, the tenant farmer hiring his labourers, the guests going in to the wedding feast, the

191

bridegroom arrayed for her bride… It was the whole of Israel, in its living flesh, its joys and pains, the sweet golden haze of evenings on the lakeside. He was a piece of music emerging from our native clay, raising us to his God and our God. Listening to Jesus meant that you received, like pure water, the tenderness of the prophets enveloped in the mysterious song of the Psalms. Ah, yes! He was indeed a Jew talking to Jews."

"This Jesus you knew – they're now putting long speeches in his mouth, making him sound like the Gnostic philosophers. And they are turning him into the Logos, the eternal Word. They say: 'All things were made by him; and without him was not any thing made that was made.'"

"Stop!"

From his closed eyes two tears trickled solely down his hollow cheeks, with their straggling beard.

"The Logos! The anonymous divine principle of hand-me-down philosophers who pretend they've read Plato and harangue the crowds until they've got those idlers in their pockets – not to mention a few silver pieces too! Already the Greeks had transformed the blacksmith Vulcan into a god, and that whore Venus into a goddess, and a jealous husband into a god, and a boatman into a god too. Oh, how easy it is, a god with a human face – and how the public just love it! By deifying Jesus they are thrusting us back into the darkness of paganism from which Moses had rescued us."

He was weeping now, weeping gently to himself. After a moment's silence, Yokhanan continued:

"Some of your disciples have joined the new Church, but others have remained faithful to Jesus the Nazorean. They are driven from the Christians' gatherings and persecuted, and some of them have even been killed."

"Jesus had warned us: *You will be driven out of the assemblies, you will be handed over to torture and you will be killed*… Do you have any news of the Nazoreans that I had to abandon in order to take refuge here?"

"I've had some information from nomads. After leaving Pella with you, they continued their exodus as far as an oasis on the Arab peninsula, I think it's called Bakka – a stage on the commercial route to Yemen. The Bedouin who live there worship some sacred stones, but they call themselves sons of Abraham like us. Now a seed of the Nazorean faith has been planted in Arabia!"

"That's good, they'll be safe there. What about Jerusalem?"

"It's under siege by Titus, the son of Emperor Vespasian. The city is still holding out, but who knows for how long…"

"Your place is there, my son: this is my journey's end. Go back to Jerusalem, defend our house in the western district. You have a copy of my epistle, keep it in circulation. Perhaps they will listen to you. In any case, they won't be able to transform that the way they have done to my Gospel."

The old man died two days later. One last time he awaited the dawn. When the flames of the sun enveloped him, he uttered the name of Jesus and stopped breathing.

In the depths of a valley in the desert of Idumaea, a sarcophagus of dry stones arranged in a simple pattern now indicated the tomb of the man who had called himself the beloved disciple of Jesus the Nazorean, the thirteenth apostle who had been his close friend and his best witness. And with him, there vanished for ever the memory of a similar tomb situated somewhere in this desert. One which, even today, contains the remains of a Just Man, unjustly crucified by the ambition of men.

Yokhanan spend the whole night sitting at the entrance to the valley. When, in the clear bright sky, he could see only the star of the watcher still shining, he rose and headed for the North, accompanied by two Essenes.

53

"It's the first time I've managed to identify so clearly the direct influence of a rabbinical melody on a medieval chant!"

They had spent several hours leaning over the glass table of the book stacks, comparing, word for word, a manuscript of Gregorian chant and a manuscript of music from the synagogues, both of them dating to before the eleventh century and composed on the same Biblical text. Leeland turned to Nil.

"Could the synagogue chant really be at the origin of the chant sung in church? I'll just go and fetch the next text in the Jewish Manuscripts room. Take a break while I'm gone."

Breczinsky had greeted them this morning with his habitual discretion. But he had taken advantage of a moment when Leeland wasn't there to say to Nil, in a hurried undertone:

"If you can... I'd like to have a word with you today."

His door was a few yards away. Nil, alone at the table, hesitated for a moment. Then he took off his gloves and went over to the office of the Polish librarian.

"Please, take a seat."

The room was in the image of its occupant, austere and dingy. There were shelves with lines of folders and, on the desk, a computer screen.

"Each of our precious manuscripts appears in a catalogue which is used by scholars from all over the world. I'm right now setting up a video service which will enable them to be consulted via the Internet – as you'll have noticed, not many people come here these days. Having to travel places to study a text will become more and more of a waste of time."

"And you will be more and more alone," thought Nil. A silence fell between them, and Breczinsky seemed unable to break it. Finally, he spoke, in a hesitant tone:

"Can I ask what your relations with Father Andrei were?"

"I've already told you, we were colleagues for a very long time."

"Yes, but… did you know about his latest research?"

"Only partly. And yet we were very close, much more than is usually the case with members of a religious community."

"Ah, so you were… close to him?"

Nil didn't understand what he was driving at.

"Andrei was a very dear friend to me, we weren't just brothers in religion but on intimate terms. I've never shared so much with anyone else in my life."

"Yes," murmured Breczinsky, "that's what I thought. And to think that when I saw you arriving, I thought you were… one of the collaborators of Cardinal Catzinger! That changes everything."

"*What does it change*, Father?"

The Pole closed his eyes, as if he were seeking for some inner strength buried deep within himself.

"When Father Andrei came to Rome, he wanted to meet me: we had been corresponding for a long time, but had never met. When he heard my accent, he switched to Polish, which he could speak fluently."

"Andrei was a Slav, and could speak a dozen or so languages."

"I was amazed to discover that his Russian family came from Brest-Litovsk, in the Polish province annexed in 1920 by the USSR, on the frontier of the territories placed under German administration in 1939. This unhappy plot of territory, which had always been Polish, never ceased to be coveted by the Russians and the Germans. When my parents got married, it was still under the heel of the Soviets, who populated it with Russian colonists forced to go and live there against their will."

"Where were you born?"

"In a little village near Brest-Litovsk. The native Polish populace were treated very harshly by the Soviet administration, who despised us as a subject people – and then, to crown it all, we were Catholics. Then came the Nazis, after the invasion of the Soviet Union by Hitler. Father Andrei's family lived next door to mine, and there was just a hedge between their house and ours. They protected my unfortunate parents from the terror that was raging in this border district before the war. Eventually, under the Nazis, they fed us first and then hid us. Without them, without their daily generosity and their courageous aid, my folks would never have survived and I would never have been born. Before she died, my mother made me swear never to forget them, or their descendants and relatives. So you were Andrei's close friend, his brother? Well, his brothers are my brothers, my blood belongs to them. What can I do for you?"

Nil was completely taken aback. He realized that the Polish librarian had divulged as many personal details as he was going to today. In this basement under the city of Rome, the great winds of history and war were suddenly catching up with them.

196

"Before he died, Father Andrei wrote a short note, various things he wanted to tell me when he came back. I'm striving to understand his message, and I'm continuing along a path that he had ventured along before me. I find it difficult to believe that his death wasn't accidental. I'll never know if he was really killed, but I have the feeling that from beyond his death he has bequeathed his research to me, rather like a posthumous command, a mission. Can you understand that?"

"Yes, especially since he confided various things to me that maybe he said to no one else, not even to you. We'd just discovered we had a common past, a closeness born of particularly painful circumstances. In this office, the ghosts of deeply loved men and women arose, covered in blood and mire. It came as a shock, for him as for me. This is what led me, two days later, to do for Father Andrei something which… which I should never have done. Never."

"Nil, my boy," thought Nil to himself. "Take it easy with him, don't rush. Drive those ghosts away."

"To begin with, I have one problem I need to sort out: I have to find two references that Andrei left behind – Dewey classifications, more or less complete, for works by Church Fathers. If I don't manage to track them down on the Internet, I'll ask you to help me. Up until now I haven't dared ask anyone: the further I go, the more the things that I'm discovering strike me as dangerous."

"More dangerous than you think." Breczinsky stood up to indicate the conversation was over. "Let me tell you again: a close friend, a brother of Father Andrei is my brother too. But you need to be extremely careful: what's said between these four walls must remain strictly between us."

Nil nodded and went back into the room. Leeland had returned to the table, and was starting to arrange a manuscript under the lamp. He glanced up at his companion, then lowered his head without a word and continued to adjust the light. His face was sombre.

54

Jerusalem, 10th September 70 AD

Yokhanan came through the south gate that was still intact and stopped, gasping in dismay: Jerusalem was no more than a field strewn with ruins.

Titus's troops had entered it at the beginning of August, and for a month a fierce battle raged relentlessly, street by street, house by house. The men of the X Fretensis legion, driven to fury by the resistance, systematically destroyed each stretch of wall still standing. The city is to be razed – these had been Titus's orders – but its Temple spared. He wanted to find out what the effigy of a God capable of inspiring such fanatical behaviour and of leading a whole people to sacrificial death could look like.

On 28th August, he finally managed to enter the parvis leading to the Holy of Holies. It was here, so they said, that the presence of Yahweh, the God of the Jews, resided. His presence, and thus his statue, or something equivalent.

He drew his sword and slashed through the veil of the sanctuary. Took a few steps forwards and halted, unable to believe his eyes.

Nothing.

Or rather, set on a table of pure gold, two winged creatures, *cherubim* of the kind he had seen so often in Mesopotamia. But, between their extended wings, nothing. A void.

So the God of Moses, the God of all these maniacs, did not exist – since, in the Temple, there was no effigy that made his presence manifest. Titus burst out laughing, and emerged from the Temple filled with merriment. "It's the greatest scam ever! There's no god in Israel! All that blood shed for nothing." Seeing his general guffawing, a legionary hurled a flaming torch into the Holy of Holies.

Two days later, the Temple of Jerusalem had almost finished slowly burning. Of the splendid monument barely finished by Herod, nothing remained.

On 8th September 70, Titus left the ruins of Jerusalem and marched to Caesarea.

Yokhanan waited until the last legionary had left the city before he ventured in: the western district no longer existed. Making his way with difficulty through the rubble, he recognized, from its enclosure wall, Caiaphas's luxurious villa. The house of the beloved disciple, the house of his happy childhood, was two hundred yards away. He found his bearings and walked on.

You could not even make out the basin of the *impluvium*. Everything had burned down and the roof had collapsed. It was here, under this pile of charred tiles, that the remains of the upper room lay. The room in which Jesus had taken his last meal forty years earlier, surrounded at first by thirteen, and then by twelve men.

For a long while he stood there, gazing at the ruins. One of the two Essenes accompanying him finally touched him on the arm.

"Let us leave this place, Yokhanan. There is no memory in these stones. Memory resides in you. Where do we go now?"

"The memory of Jesus the Nazorean," thought Yokhanan. "That fragile inheritance, coveted by everyone."

He replied: "You're right. Let's head north, to Galilee: Jesus's words still echo there among its hills. I have an inheritance with me that I need to hand on."

He took a sheet of parchment out of his pocket and brought it up to his lips. "The copy of the epistle written by my *abbu*, the thirteenth apostle."

Three centuries later, a well-to-do Iberian woman, Etheria by name, who had treated herself to the very first organized tour that enabled one to participate in the Holy Week celebrations in Jerusalem, saw as she passed along the Jordan an engraved stele, tilting rather forlornly to one side. Filled with curiosity, she stopped her litter: was this another souvenir of the time of Christ?

The inscription was legible. It stated that at the time of the destruction of the Temple of Jerusalem, a Nazorean, Yokhanan by name, had been massacred at this very spot while fleeing from the ruins of Jerusalem. Titus's legionaries must have caught up with him, Etheria reflected; they had slaughtered him and thrown his body in the nearby river. She exclaimed:

"A Nazorean! It's been ages since any of them were around. This poor man must have been the last of them, and that's probably why they erected this stele on the site where he was killed."

What the pious Christian lady did not know was that Yokhanan was not the last of the Nazoreans.

Ever since that day, only two copies of the epistle written by Jesus's thirteenth apostle had been in existence. One was hidden away at the bottom of a jar, inaccessible in its cave perched in the middle of a cliff overlooking the ruins of Qumran on the Dead Sea.

And the other was in the hands of the Nazoreans who had escaped from Pella. And taken refuge in an oasis in the Arabian desert named Bakka.

55

Mgr Calfo slipped on his purple-hemmed cassock. To receive Antonio, he needed to be dressed in the attributes of his episcopal dignity. Young recruits should never forget who they are dealing with. Once the preliminary interviews had been conducted, he rarely invited the members of the Society in to see him. They all knew his address, but the demands of confidentiality are better respected in one of the discreet trattorie of Rome. And sometimes, Sonia's fragrance would float in his studio long after she had left.

It was with pleasure that he opened his door to the twelfth apostle.

"Your mission will now consist in keeping an eye on Father Breczinsky. He's a *pauvre type*, a loser. But that type of man is always unpredictable. He might react impulsively."

"What do I need to get out of him?"

"First, he needs to keep you informed about what the two monks might be telling each other during their sessions in the book stacks of the Vatican. Then remind him where he comes from, who he is and who the Cardinal is. That simple reminder should keep him faithful to his mission. You are now one of the very few men to know of the extremely confidential documents he has in his guard. Don't forget that he has a terrible wound lodged in his memory: we just need to prod that, and we'll get what we want from him. You need have no scruples: the only thing that counts is the current mission."

Once Antonio had been given his instructions, he left the building and ostentatiously took a right turn, towards the Tiber, as if he were heading back into town. Without looking up, he could sense the eyes of the Rector staring down at the back of his neck from the window of his apartment. But once he reached the corner of Castel Sant'Angelo, he took another right turn, and after another sudden swerve he started to walk away from town, towards St Peter's Square.

Rome's ochre-coloured walls still gleamed in the wan December sunlight. For centuries she had watched the incessant ballet of the intrigues and plots of her Catholic prelates. Eyes half-closed, she lay in a maternal doze, enjoying the long winter of her splendour; she no longer attached any importance to the games of power and glory unfolding around the tomb of the Apostle.

"Come in, my friend," exclaimed Catzinger with a smile. "I was expecting you."

The young man bent forwards to kiss the Cardinal's ring. "He escaped two successive purges," he reflected, "that of the Gestapo first, then that of the Liberation. Honour and respect to those fighting for the West."

He sat down opposite the desk and fixed his strange black eyes on His Eminence.

56

Nil had asked Leeland to go to the Vatican book stacks without him.

"I want to work on a phrase I discovered in the diary left by Andrei at San Girolamo. I need to use the Internet – it'll take me maybe a couple of hours. If Father Breczinsky asks you any questions, invent some excuse for my absence."

Now that he was alone at the computer, he was starting to feel discouraged, lost in the midst of a tangle of paths leading in every direction. The texts photocopied by the Huntington Library merely confirmed what he had been sensing would be the case since he had been studying the manuscripts of the Dead Sea. The Coptic manuscript? Its first phrase had enabled him to understand the code introduced into the *Symbolon* of Nicaea. That left the second phrase, and the mysterious apostle's letter. He had decided to follow up this last clue, a trace of which he had found in Andrei's diary. All these leads must come together somewhere or other. This had been his friend's last message: *link things together*.

Rembert Leeland... What had become of the friendly, confident student of bygone days, the laughing young man who played his life the same way he played his music, with brio and optimism? Why had he succumbed to that brief attack of despair? Nil had perceived within him a wound that went too deep for him to tell an old friend about it.

As for Breczinsky, he seemed completely isolated in the glacial and deserted basement of the Vatican Library. Why had he made those private remarks to him? What had passed between himself and Andrei?

He decided to concentrate on the apostle's letter. He needed to find a book, somewhere in the wide world, just from its Dewey classification. He connected to the Internet, called up Google, and typed *university libraries*.

A page with eleven sites came up. At the foot of the page, Google indicated that twelve similar pages had been selected for him. About a hundred and thirty sites altogether.

With a sigh, he clicked on the first site.

* * *

When he came back shortly after noon, Leeland was irritated to find that there was just a brief note propped up in front of the computer: Nil had returned to San Girolamo as a matter of urgency. He would be returning to Via Aurelia in the course of the evening.

Had he found anything? The American had never been much of a Biblical scholar. But Nil's work was starting to interest him to the highest point. As he sought to discover what had led to Andrei's death, his friend was filled with the desire to avenge his memory – as for himself, it was his own ruined life that he now dreamt of avenging. For he sensed that those who had destroyed his existence were also those who had caused the fatal accident that had befallen the librarian of St Martin's Abbey.

The setting sun gave a dark red tinge to the cloud of pollution hanging over Rome. Leeland had headed back to the Vatican. In the apartment underneath, the Palestinian suddenly heard someone come in, then sit down at the computer: it must be Nil. The tape recorder was merely recording the clatter of the keyboard.

Suddenly the aural landscape came to life: Leeland had just arrived in his turn. They were going to talk.

57

Egypt, second to seventh centuries

Forced by the war to leave Pella, the Nazoreans were welcomed by the Arabs in the Bakka oasis, where they settled. But the second generation found the austerity of the desert of Arabia difficult to live in: some of them decided to carry on to Egypt. They moved to a place north of Luxor, a village in the jebel El-Tarif called Nag Hammadi. Here they formed a community kept together by the memory of the thirteenth apostle and his teaching. And by his epistle, of which every family possessed a copy.

They soon came into conflict with Christian missionaries from Alexandria, whose Church was undergoing rapid expansion. Christianity was indeed spreading across the Empire with all the impetuosity of a forest fire: the Nazoreans, who refused to accept the divinity of Jesus, were forced to submit – or disappear.

Transform Jesus into the Christ-God? Be unfaithful to the epistle? Never – they were persecuted by the Christians. From Alexandria came orders written in Coptic: this epistle must be destroyed, in Egypt and everywhere else in the Empire. Each time a Nazorean family was driven out into the desert, where death awaited them, their house was searched and the letter of the thirteenth apostle destroyed. It spoke of a tomb containing the bones of Jesus, somewhere in the desert of Idumaea – but Jesus's tomb needs to remain empty, so that the Christ may live.

However, one single copy did escape the persecutors and reached the Library at Alexandria, where it was buried away among the five hundred thousand volumes of that eighth wonder of the world.

Shortly after the year 200, a young Alexandrinian by the name of Origen started to frequent the Library with great assiduity. He was a tireless researcher, and he was fascinated by the person of Christ. He had a prodigious memory.

* * *

When he became a teacher, Origen was persecuted by his bishop, Demetrius. This was due to jealousy: Origen's charisma was luring the elite of Alexandria to hear him. But it was also due to mistrust, since Origen did not hesitate to use in his teaching texts that were forbidden by the Church. Finally, Demetrius drove him from Egypt and Origen took refuge in Caesarea, Palestine – but he took his prodigious memory with him. As for the letter of the thirteenth apostle, it remained buried in the huge library, known to nobody: there are few scholars that have the genius of an Origen.

When, in 641, Alexandria fell into the hands of the Muslims, General Amr ibn al-As ordered all the books to be burned, one by one. "If they are in agreement with the Koran," he proclaimed, "they are superfluous. If they are not in agreement, they are dangerous." For six months, the memory of antiquity heated the boilers in the public baths.

By burning the Library of Alexandria, the Muslims had achieved what the Christians had never succeeded in doing: now there was not a single copy of the epistle anywhere to be found.

Except for the original, still buried in a jar protected by the sand, on the left as you go into one of the caves looking out over the ruins of Qumran.

58

"So, have you found anything?"

Leeland, his face looking tense, had just arrived in the studio. Next to the computer, several sheets of paper were lying scattered. Nil seemed tired; without replying, he went over to the window and glanced out. Then he came back to his seat, resolved to ignore the warnings of Breczinsky and to tell his friend everything.

"After you'd left, I started to look in the biggest libraries in the world. Around midday, I came across the librarian from Heidelberg, who has lived in Rome. We started to chat online, and he told me that the Dewey classification probably came from – guess where?"

"From the Library of San Girolamo, and that's why you rushed back there!"

"I should have thought – it was the last library that Andrei used before his death: he came across a book and jotted down the details on what he had at hand, his diary – probably intending to consult the work a second time. And then he hastily left Rome, leaving the now superfluous diary behind him."

Leeland sat next to Nil. His eyes were shining.

"And you've found the book?"

"The San Girolamo Library was built up out of odds and ends, following the whims of the successive librarians who followed each other in quick succession. You can find something of everything there. But the books are more or less all catalogued, and I did indeed discover the one that had attracted Andrei's attention, a catena by Eusebius of Caesarea – a rare edition from the seventeenth century, I'd never heard of it."

Leeland asked, in some embarrassment:

"Excuse me, Nil, I've forgotten pretty much everything except my music. What's a catena?"

"In the third century there was a fierce struggle over Jesus's divinity, which the Church was seeking to impose. They were destroying all the texts they could find that didn't conform to the new dogma. After condemning Origen, the Church methodically burnt all of his writings. Eusebius of Caesarea greatly admired the Alexandrine, who died in his city. He wanted to save what he could of his work, but – so as to avoid being condemned in his turn – he chose excerpts from it and had them circulated. He arranged them one after the other like the links of a chain: a *catena*. Later on they picked up on his idea, and many ancient works are now accessible to us only through these excerpts. Andrei guessed that this unfamiliar catena might contain passages from Origen that were barely known. He sought, and he found."

"Found what?"

"A phrase in Eusebius that had hitherto passed unnoticed. In one of his now lost works, Origen said that he had seen, in the Library of Alexandria, a mysterious *epistola abscondita apostoli tredicesimi*: the secret – or hidden – epistle of a thirteenth apostle, which would provide *proof* that Jesus was not divine in nature. Andrei must have suspected the existence of this epistle – he had vaguely alluded to it in my presence. I can see he was looking for it, since he took care to note that unexpected and welcome reference."

"What credit can we give an isolated phrase in a minor text that has been forgotten?"

Nil rubbed his chin.

"You're right," he said, "this mere link in a chain is of no use by itself. But remember: in his posthumous note, Andrei suggested bringing together the four leads he had found. I've been mulling over the second sentence in the Coptic manuscript I found in the Abbey for weeks and weeks – the sentence that reads: '*Let the epistle be everywhere destroyed, so that the place may remain in place*'. Thanks to Origen, I think I've finally got it."

"A new code?"

"Not at all. At the beginning of the third century, the Church was putting the final touches to the dogma of the Incarnation that would be proclaimed at the Council of Nicaea, and it was seeking to eliminate everything that might oppose it. This fragment of a Coptic manuscript – which had alerted Andrei – is probably what's left of a directive from Alexandria, ordering this epistle to be destroyed wherever it was found. Finally, there is a play on words on a Coptic term which I have translated, *faute de mieux*, by 'place', but which may also mean 'assembly'. In Greek, the official language of Alexandria, 'assembly' is *ekklesia* – the Church. The meaning of the sentence then becomes clear: this epistle must be everywhere destroyed, *so that the Church may remain* – so that the Church itself may not be annihilated! Only one of the two could survive: the letter of the thirteenth apostle or the Church."

Leeland gave a low whistle.

"I see…"

"Then the leads start to come together: the Germigny inscription confirms that in the eighth century, a thirteenth apostle was deemed to be so dangerous that he had to be got rid of for ever – *alpha and omega* – and we know that he is none other than the beloved disciple of the Fourth Gospel. Origen tells us that, in Alexandria, he saw an epistle written by that man, and the Coptic manuscript confirms that there were one or more copies at Nag Hammadi, since it orders them to be destroyed."

"But how did this epistle reach Nag Hammadi?"

"We know that the Nazoreans took refuge in Pella, in present-day Jordan, perhaps with the thirteenth apostle. After that, the trail goes cold. But Andrei had asked me to read the Koran – which he knew well – attentively. So I did, comparing several scientific translations that I had in the Abbey. I was surprised to find frequent mention of the *nasara* – the Arabic word for 'Nazorean' – who are the text's main source of information on Jesus. After Pella, the disciples of the thirteenth apostle must have taken refuge in Arabia, where Muhammad would have known them. Why might they not have continued as far as Egypt? To Nag Hammadi, taking the copies of the epistle with them?"

"The Koran... Do you really believe that the Nazorean fugitives had any influence on its author?"

"Obviously: the text bears several traces of it. I'd rather not tell you any more just now: I still have one lead to follow, a work, or series of works, concerning the Templars, with an incomplete classification. We'll talk about the Koran some other time, it's late and I need to get back to San Girolamo."

Nil stood up, and again looked down into the street filled with shadows. As if talking to himself, he added:

"So the thirteenth apostle wrote an apostolic epistle, *to be everywhere destroyed*, pursued by the Church's hatred. What could there be in that letter that was so dangerous?"

On the floor below, Mukhtar had been listening closely. When Nil mentioned the Koran, Muhammad and the Nazoreans, he swore.

"Son of a dog!"

59

Desert of Arabia, September 622

The man galloped on through the dark night. It was towards Medina that he was fleeing, as fast as his camel, foaming at the mouth, could carry him. This night would come to be known as the Hegira, marking the beginning of time for Muslims.

He was fleeing from the oasis of Bakka, where he had been born into the prestigious clan of the Quraysh. He was fleeing because the Quraysh called themselves sons of Abraham, but in fact worshipped sacred stones.

In this caravan halt in the middle of the desert, a community from the Jewish diaspora had been vegetating ever since the dim and distant past. At his head, an erudite and fiery rabbi dreamt of bringing the whole of Arabia round to Judaism by means of his rabbinical tradition. The young Arab had allowed himself to be convinced by this hot-headed visionary: he became his disciple, and quietly converted.

But his rabbi asked more of him. The haughty Quraysh rejected the preaching of a Jew – perhaps they would listen to him, an Arab from the same clan as they were? Had he not become a Jew at heart? He wanted his disciple to proclaim what he taught him every day out in the open, in the oasis. "Tell them…" he kept saying. So that he would not forget anything of what he had heard, Muhammad took notes, which grew into quite a pile. They were in Arabic, since the rabbi had realized that one needed to speak to these men in their own language, and not in Hebrew.

For the Quraysh, it was all to much: one of their own, Muhammad, was also seeking to destroy the cult of the sacred stones that lay at the source of their wealth! They might, at a push, have tolerated his becoming a Nazorean: these dissidents of Christianity had arrived several centuries ago, and their prophet Jesus wasn't dangerous. The young Arab willingly listened to their teaching as well as that of his rabbi: seduced by Jesus, Muhammad would like to have grown closer to them. But the Quraysh did not give him time to do so, and drove him away.

Now he was fleeing towards Medina: his only baggage was his precious notes. Written day by day, from what he heard his rabbi say: *tell them…*

In Medina, he transformed himself into a warrior whose dazzling successes followed after one another, like flashes of lightning. He extended his power across a whole region and became a respected political leader. Laws were needed to organize those who joined him: he issued those laws, then wrote them down, and these pages joined the notes he had taken previously, building up day by day. Then he also started included anecdotes, accounts of his battles. His notes became a voluminous travel journal.

When he wanted to enrol the Jews under his banner, they refused point-blank. He was furious, and drove them out of the city, turning instead to the Christians in the north. Yes, these would be glad to help him in his conquests, but on one condition: he should convert to Christianity and recognize the divinity of Jesus. Muhammad cursed them, and included them in the fierce hatred he felt for the Jews.

Only the Nazoreans found grace in his eyes. And he filled his notebook with words of praise for them and their prophet Jesus.

When he returned victorious to Bakka, Muhammad drew his sabre and swept away all the sacred stones of the idolaters. But he came to a halt before the icon of Jesus and his mother, whom the Nazoreans had always venerated. He thrust his sabre back into its sheath, and bowed deeply.

Subsequently, the name "Bakka" underwent a slight transformation, as sometimes happens, and the oasis became generally known as "Mekka".

In other words, Mecca.

Two generations later, the Caliph Uthman edited, in his own way, Muhammad's travel journal, which he called the "Koran", deeming it to have been written by Muhammad under the direct dictation of God. Ever since, nobody who wished to stay alive could question the divine nature of the Koran.

Islam had never had its thirteenth apostle.

60

St Peter's Square was filled with people and all the hustle and bustle of grand occasions. An immense portrait of the newly beatified man had been hung on the façade of the basilica. The cold was less intense and the weather was sunny, which made it possible for this beatification to be performed in the open air, with the two arms of Bernini's colonnade embracing a motley, colourful crowd, delighted at the chance to see the Holy Father and to take part in one of Christianity's great festivals.

As Prefect of the Congregation, Cardinal Catzinger was officiating at the right hand of the Pope. He had been the driving force behind this beatification: next up was the founder of Opus Dei. The list of his supernatural virtues had been drawn up without any problem, but it was proving difficult to find the three miracles necessary for a canonization in accordance with the rules. Catzinger mechanically lifted one edge of the pontifical chasuble, which was slipping down as a result of the trembling which afflicted the aged pontiff. As the Pope pronounced the sacred words, the Cardinal smiled. "Miracles will be found. The first miracle of all is the permanence, across the centuries, of the Roman Catholic and Apostolic Church."

Catzinger had been privileged to know the saint-in-waiting personally. Before founding Opus Dei, Escrivá de Balaguer had been an active militant in the Spanish Civil War, on Franco's side; then he had been friends with a young officer in the Chilean Army, a certain Augusto Pinochet. His father would have subscribed to this canonization: he too had chosen the right side when he went to fight the Communists on the Eastern Front. To raise Escrivá de Balaguer to sainthood would be an act of justice towards his father, who had died for the West.

Lost amid the mass of prelates lined up on their benches in front of the papal platform, in the humble place his rank as *minutante* gave him, Mgr Calfo enjoyed the caress of the sun and the beauty of the spectacle. "Only the Catholic Church is capable of orchestrating the encounter between the divine and the human in the midst of so much beauty, and for such huge crowds." At the end of the ceremony, while the procession of dignitaries lined up behind the Pope, his eyes met those of the Cardinal, who nodded at him imperiously.

An hour later, the two men were sitting face to face in Catzinger's office. The latter's face wore the expression it habitually did on bad days.

"So then, Monsignor, where have we got to?"

Unlike his Prefect, Calfo seemed very relaxed. Sonia had played her part in this: he found her to be a priestess expert in the cult of Eros, but also a person who was prepared to listen to him.

"Your Eminence, we are making rapid progress. Father Nil is turning out to be gifted, very gifted, when it comes to research."

The Cardinal's brow furrowed. Leeland's reports were not only insipid, they were becoming more and more infrequent, and it was still too early to put pressure on Father Breczinsky: his grip on the Polish librarian was based on the obscure twists and turns of the human heart, and this was a lever he could use only once. And he needed to do it properly. But for now, Mgr Calfo held all the aces.

"What do you mean?"

"Well…" Calfo pursed his fleshy lips. "He has found the trace of a lost apostolic writing, which would confirm his analyses of St John's Gospel."

The Cardinal rose, motioned Calfo to follow him to the window and showed him St Peter's Square. The papal platform was still in place, and thousands of pilgrims seemed to be turning round and round this nerve centre like the water in a funnel around the whirlpool drawing it in. The crowd seemed happy: one big family discovering the links that unite it and how vast it actually is.

"Look at them, Monsignor. You and I are responsible for millions of believers like these, all of whom live in the hope of a resurrection made possible for them by the sacrifice of God incarnate. Is a single man going to undermine all that? We've never allowed it. Do you remember Giordano Bruno, a monk who was also very gifted when it came to research: he was burned half a mile away from here, on the Campo de' Fiori, in spite of his Europe-wide fame. What is at stake is the very order of the world: yet again, a monk seems capable of overthrowing it. It isn't possible for us – as it was in the past – to cure the body of the Church by cauterizing it with fire. But we need to bring Father Nil's research to a quick end."

Calfo did not reply straight away. The Eleven at their meeting had approved his line of conduct: he was to say just enough to the Cardinal to make him afraid, but reveal nothing of the Society's ultimate aims.

"Your Eminence, I don't think that's necessary. He's just an intellectual unaware of what he's doing. In my view, we should let him carry on; we have the situation entirely in hand."

"But if he goes back to his monastery, who's going to stop him divulging his conclusions?"

"*Pazienza*, Your Eminence. There are other ways, less spectacular than a train accident, of silencing those who stray from the Church's teaching."

The day before, he had been obliged to calm Mukhtar, who was furious to hear Nil questioning the revealed nature of the Koran and the person of the founder of Islam: the Palestinian wanted to take action immediately.

In just a few days, Nil had girded himself with a belt of explosives. Calfo didn't intend him to blow himself up before he had made himself *really* useful to the Catholic Church. With a mechanical gesture, he twisted his Episcopal ring on his finger and concluded with a reassuring smile:

"Father Nil is behaving in Rome as if he had never left his cloister: he leaves San Girolamo only to go to the Vatican stacks, communicates with nobody apart from his friend Leeland, has no contact with the press or dissident circles, and in fact seems to know nothing about them."

Calfo jutted his chin towards St Peter's Square.

"He doesn't represent any danger for those crowds, who will never hear of him and whom he has deliberately chosen to ignore by shutting himself away in a monastery. Let's allow him to carry on peacefully with his research. I have every confidence in the training he was given from his time as a novice at St Martin's onwards: that's a mould which shapes men for life. He'll fall into step; if he ever took it into his head to follow his own bent again, then we'd intervene. But that almost certainly won't be necessary."

216

As they separated, the two prelates felt equally satisfied: the first because he thought he had given His Eminence enough to worry about while preserving room for manoeuvre; and the second because he was meeting Antonio that very same evening, and would soon know nearly as much as the Rector of the Society of St Pius V.

61

"This morning, there's a ceremony of beatification: we won't be able to get across St Peter's Square. Let's take a detour."

Each of the two men was absorbed in his own thoughts as they turned into the Borgo Santo Spirito and headed back to the Vatican City via Castel Sant'Angelo, which had originally been the mausoleum of the Emperor Hadrian before becoming a fortress and a papal prison. Nil found it difficult to accept those heavy silences that had been so common between them ever since his arrival in Rome.

Finally, Leeland started to speak.

"I don't understand you: you haven't left your monastery for years, and yet here you live like a recluse. You loved Rome so much when we were students – you ought to make the most of it. Go and visit a few museums, meet up with the folks you used to know… You're behaving as if you'd transplanted your cloister into the heart of the city!"

Nil looked up at his companion.

"When I entered the monastery, I chose solitude in the midst of a universal community, the Catholic Church. Look at this crowd, they seem so happy at a new canonization! For a long time I thought they were my family, replacing the one that had rejected me. Now I know that my research into Jesus's identity excludes me from my adoptive family. You don't question the foundations of a religion with impunity – not when a whole civilization is based on that religion! I imagine that the thirteenth apostle must have experienced a similar solitude when he opposed the Twelve. I have only one friend left: the Jesus whose mystery I am seeking to penetrate."

He added, in a murmur:

"And you, of course."

By now they were walking along the high walls of the Vatican City. The American plunged his hand into one of his pockets, and took out two little cardboard boxes.

"I've got a surprise for you. I've been given two invitations to a concert by Lev Barjona at the Academy of Santa Cecilia – just before Christmas. I'm not giving you any choice in the matter: you're coming with me!"

"Who's this Lev Barjona?"

"A famous Israeli pianist. I got to know him back there when he was a pupil of Arthur Rubinstein. We became friends at the feet of the maestro. An amazing man, who's had a very unusual life. He's very kindly added a few personal words to his invitation, specifying that the second ticket is for you. He's playing Rachmaninov's Third Concerto – he's the best current interpreter of the piece."

They were now entering Vatican City.

"I'd be delighted," said Nil. "I like Rachmaninov and I haven't been to a concert for a very long time. It'll be a real change for me."

Suddenly he stopped dead and frowned.

"But... how come your friend sent a second ticket *especially for me?*"

Leeland seemed surprised at this remark, and was just about to reply when they had to separate: a luxurious official

218

limousine was just passing in front of them. Inside, they spotted the scarlet robes of a cardinal. The car slowed down to pass through the gate of the Belvedere, and Nil suddenly seized the American by the arm.

"Rembert, look at that car's number plate!"

"What about it? SCV, *Sacra Civitas Vaticani*, it's a Vatican number plate. We see them going by every day in these parts, you know."

Nil stood rooted to the spot in the middle of the Belvedere courtyard.

"SCV! But those are the three letters that Andrei noted in his diary, just before the word 'Templars'! I was racking my brains for days trying to work out what they meant: since they were followed by an incomplete Dewey classification, I was convinced that they must designate a library somewhere in the world. Rembert, I think I've got it! SCV followed by four digits is the place where you can find a series of books in one of the libraries of the Sacra Civitas Vaticani, the Vatican. I should have realized: Andrei was always sticking his nose into odd corners. In the San Girolamo Library he found a rare text by Origen, but it's right here that the second work he mentioned in his notebook is to be found."

Nil looked up at the imposing edifice.

"Right in there, hidden away somewhere, there's a book that will perhaps enable me to find out a little more about the letter of the thirteenth apostle. But there's one thing I don't understand, Rembert: what have the Templars got to do with all this?"

Leeland was no longer listening. Why indeed had Lev Barjona sent him *two* complimentary tickets?

Mechanically, he typed in the code at the entrance to the Vatican stacks.

* * *

Just as the bell rang, Breczinsky nervously seized the elbow of the man he was talking to.

"It must be them, I'm not expecting anyone else this morning. If you go out the front way, they are bound to see you. The stacks have stairs that lead directly to the Vatican Library: I'll take you there. Quick, they'll be here any minute!"

Dressed in an impeccable cassock, Antonio glanced at the Polish librarian, whose face betrayed complete consternation. It had all been easy: after a few moments' conversation in his office, Breczinsky had practically melted away before his eyes. The Cardinal knew the human heart intimately: you merely had to know where its hidden wound lay, and then prod it.

62

Sonia pulled her hair down over her breasts and gazed at the little man as he got dressed. He wasn't a bad chap after all. Just a bit off, with his mania for talking all the time while she did to him what he expected from her. When she had come to Saudi Arabia, drawn by the alluring offer of a job, she had found herself locked away in the harem of a dignitary of the regime. The Arab didn't utter a single word while making love, which he did with quick efficiency. But Calfo never stopped muttering incomprehensibly, and it was always something about religion.

Sonia was an Orthodox Christian, and shared the respect that all Romanians felt for religious dignitaries. But this one must be a bit cracked: he always made her move slowly, and sometimes he scared her with his eyes that stared intently at her. His unctuous voice intimated things to her that filled her with deep revulsion, coming from a bishop.

She couldn't mention this to Mukhtar, who had brought her to Rome. "You'll see," he had told her, "he's a client who pays well". This was true, the bishop was generous. But Sonia was now finding that the money was hardly worth it.

As he buttoned up the collar of his cassock, Calfo turned to her.

"You should go, I have a meeting tomorrow evening. An important meeting. Okay?"

She nodded. The bishop had explained to her that, in order to climb up the rungs of the *Ladder of Divine Ascent*, a dialectical tension had to be maintained between its two uprights, the carnal and the spiritual. She hadn't understood the least thing in this farrago of nonsense, but knew that she should not return for two days.

It was like this whenever there was an "important meeting". And tomorrow was a Friday 13th.

The twelve apostles were particularly solemn. Dressed in his white alb, Antonio slipped silently behind the long table and took his seat. His strange dark gaze, visible only behind the veil masking his face, was innocent and peaceful.

"As on every Friday 13th, my brothers, our meeting is a statutory obligation. But before we venerate the precious relic in our possession, I need to update you on the latest developments in the current mission."

For a moment, the Rector gazed at the crucifix opposite him, then continued, amid a total silence:

"Thanks to my Palestinian agent, we now have recordings of everything that gets said in the studio on the Via Aurelia. The Frenchman is showing himself to be a worthy imitator of Father Andrei. He has managed to break the code of the Germigny inscription, and to understand its meaning thanks to the first sentence in the Coptic manuscript. He has found the Origen quotation, and thanks to the second sentence in the manuscript he is on the trail of the letter of the thirteenth apostle – whose existence Andrei had merely suspected before coming here to Rome."

A frisson ran through the gathering, and one of the apostles raised his forearms.

"Brother Rector, aren't we playing with fire? Nobody, ever since the Templars, has come so close to the secret that it is our mission to protect."

"This gathering has already weighed up the pros and cons and come to a decision. Letting Father Nil carry on with his research is a risk – but a calculated risk. In spite of the efforts of our predecessors, not every trace of the epistle has completely disappeared. We know that its contents are of a nature to destroy the Catholic Church, and with it the civilization of which she is the soul and inspiration. And yet there may still be one copy that has escaped our vigilance. Let us not make the same mistake we did with Father Andrei: we've unleashed the ferret, this time let's not stop it running after its prey. If he manages to locate it, we'll act – and quickly. Father Nil is working for us…"

He was interrupted by an apostle whose white alb barely disguised his obesity.

"They are spending the majority of their time in the stacks of the Vatican: what means of surveillance do we have over what gets said in that strategic place?"

The Rector was the only person to know that this apostle was a highly placed member of the Congregation for the Propagation of the Faith, one of the most efficient secret services in the world. He answered with a nuance of respect: this man was au fait with all the information collected across the five continents, reaching down to the smallest country parish.

"One of us paid a visit to Father Breczinsky yesterday, and reminded him of a few things. He seems to have understood. I think that we will soon be in a position to know whether Father Nil is going to find the epistle. Now let's move on to the statutory meeting."

Helped by two apostles, he slid away the wooden panel and respectfully took hold of the casket on the middle shelf. In front of the eleven immobile men, he placed it on the table and bowed deeply.

"On Friday 13th October 1307, the Chancellor Guillaume de Nogaret arrested the Grand Master of the Temple, Jacques de Molay, and a hundred and thirty-eight of his brothers in the Templars' house in Paris. They were thrown into dungeons and relentlessly interrogated under torture. Throughout France, on that same day, almost all members of the Order were seized and rendered harmless. Christianity was saved. It is that Friday 13th, a date that has become unlucky throughout the world, which we are today commemorating as laid down by our statutes."

Then he bent forwards and opened the casket. Nil had found almost all the traces left in history by the letter of the thirteenth apostle: but this was one he had missed. The Rector took a step backwards.

"My brothers, please, it is time for veneration."

The apostles rose, and each of them drew near to kiss first the Rector's ring, then the contents of the casket.

When his turn came, Antonio paused for a moment over the table: placed there simply on a small cushion of red velvet, a gold nugget was gleaming. It was very smooth and shaped like a tear.

"*All that rests of the treasure of the Templars!*"

He bent down, his face dipping into the casket, and placed his lips on the golden tear. It struck him that it was still burning, and at that point a dreadful scene appeared behind his closed eyes.

63

Father Breczinsky had greeted them with a wan smile, and led them without a word to their work table. After a nod, he went into his office, leaving the door ajar.

Nil, still absorbed in his recent discovery, had not noticed the librarian's reserve. "SCV, a classification number in the Vatican library. It's one of the biggest libraries in the world! Finding a book there is going to be mission impossible."

He worked mechanically for a while, then heaved a deep sigh and turned to Leeland.

"Rembert, can you manage without me, just for a few minutes? Breczinsky is the only person who can help me find what the SCV classification corresponds to, the one Andrei left in his diary. I'm going to ask him."

A shadow passed across the face of the American, who whispered:

"Please, do remember what I told you: here you should trust nobody."

Nil did not reply. "I know things that you don't." And he took off his gloves and knocked on the library door.

Breczinsky was sitting at the screen of his computer. It was switched off, and his hands were lying flat on his desk.

"Father, you told me the other day that you were ready to help me. Can I call on your aid now?"

The Pole was staring at him in silence, his face haggard. Then he lowered his eyes to his hands and spoke in a low voice, as if talking to himself, as if Nil were not there.

"My father was killed at the end of 1940 – I never knew him. My mother told me how it happened: one morning, a senior Wehrmacht officer came to round up all the men in the village, ostensibly to do some work in the forest. My father never returned, and my mother died when I was six. A cousin from Cracow took me into his home, I was a war orphan and I had stopped being able to speak. The young priest from the parish next to ours took pity on that mute boy: he took care of me and made me feel life was worth living again. Then, one day, he made the sign of the cross on my forehead, my lips and my heart. The next day, for the first time in years, I talked. Then he made it possible for me to enter the diocesan seminary of Cracow, where he had become the bishop. I owe him everything; he's the very father of my soul."

"What was his name?"

"Karol Wojtyla. The present Pope. The Pope whom I serve with all my strength."

He finally lifted his eyes and fixed them on those of Nil.

"You are a true monk, Father Nil, just as Andrei was: you live in another world. In the Vatican, a web is woven around the Pope by men in whose interest it is that he should not know all that they do in his name. Never did Karol Wojtyla experience anything of the kind: in Poland, the clergy showed total solidarity, united against the common Soviet enemy. Everyone trusted everyone else blindly, and the Polish Church would never have survived any internal manoeuvrings. It was in this spirit that the Pope delegated his responsibilities onto men like Cardinal Catzinger. And here am I – the silent witness of many things."

He rose with an effort.

"I will help you, just as I helped Father Andrei. But I'm taking a considerable risk: swear that you're not trying to harm the Pope."

Nil replied gently:

"I am merely a monk, Father, nothing interests me other than the face and the identity of Jesus. The politics and the whole way of life of the Vatican are foreign to me, and I have nothing to do with Cardinal Catzinger, who knows nothing of my research. Like Andrei, I am a man of truth."

"I trust you – the Pope is also a man of truth. What can I do for you?"

Nil handed Andrei's diary to him.

"When he was in Rome, Father Andrei consulted a book. He noted its classification number here. Does it mean anything to you?"

Breczinsky examined the diary page attentively, then looked up.

"Of course. It's a classification from these stacks. It indicates all the shelves on which are stored the minutes of the Inquisition's trial of the Templars. When he came by, Father Andrei asked if he could consult them, even though he had no authorization to do so. Follow me."

In silence they walked past the table where Leeland, bent over a manuscript, did not look up. When they reached the third room, Breczinsky suddenly turned left and led Nil to a book stack in a recess.

"Here" – he showed him the shelves lining the wall – "you have records of the Inquisition's investigation into the affair of the Templars – the original records. I can tell you that Father Andrei spent most time looking at the minutes of the interrogation of the Templar Esquieu de Floyran by Guillaume de Nogaret, and the correspondence of Philippe le Bel. I put them back in their place after he had left. I hope you can work as quickly as he did: I'll give you two hours. And remember: you have *never* been in this part of the stacks."

He slipped away like a shadow. In this deserted nook, the only sound was the low hum of the air conditioning. A dozen or so cardboard boxes were lined up and numbered. In one of them, on a page written by the notary of the Inquisition in the presence of the prisoner exhausted by torture, could perhaps be found a trace of the thirteenth apostle that Andrei had discovered.

He resolutely pulled the first box towards him: *The Confessions of the Templar Brothers, Recorded in the Presence of Monseigneur Guillaume de Nogaret by Me, Guillaume de Paris, Representative of King Philippe le Bel and Grand Inquisitor of France.*

64

Shores of the Dead Sea, March 1149

"Keep going, Pierre, they're hot on our heels."

Esquieu de Floyran flung his arms round his companion. They were at the foot of an abrupt cliff, a pile of rocky concretions through which goat tracks meandered. Black holes could be seen here and there: the entrances to natural caves looking out onto emptiness.

Ever since they had met in Vézelay three years earlier, the two men had never left each other's sides. Fired with zeal by St Bernard's preaching, they had donned the white tunic with the red cross and joined the Second Crusade in Palestine.

Here, in Gaza, the Templars had fallen into a trap laid by the Seljuk Turks. Esquieu wanted to clear the fortress: at the head of some fifteen or so knights, he made a sort of diversion in broad daylight – which did indeed lure some of the besiegers after them. As they fled eastwards, his companions had fallen one after another. Now only the faithful Pierre de Montbrison was left at his side.

When they reached the Dead Sea, their mounts collapsed under them. The two Templars leapt over a crumbling wall, and came into a ruined enclosure that bore the traces of a terrible fire. They ran on past a vast reservoir dug into the rock, then followed the line of irrigation canals heading towards the cliff. Here they would be safe.

Just as they were emerging from the cover of the trees, Pierre uttered a cry and fell. When his companion bent over him, he saw that an arrow had pierced his abdomen, near his loin.

"Leave me, Esquieu, I'm wounded!"

"Leave you in their hands? Never! We'll take refuge in this cliff, and escape under cover of night. There's an oasis nearby, Ein Feshka: it's the road westwards, the road to safety. Lean on me, it's not the first arrow that's got you: we'll pull it out once we're up there. You'll see France again and your commandery."

The incandescent words of St Bernard still resounded in his ears: "The knight of Christ can deal out death in all security. If he dies, it is for his own good; if he kills, it is for Christ". But right now the important thing was to escape a gang of enraged Turks.

Allahu Akbar! Their cries were now very close. "Pierre can't manage. Lord, help us!"

Helping each other along, they started to climb the steep wall of the cliff.

228

They stopped at one of the cave mouths, and Esquieu glanced downwards: their pursuers seemed to have lost sight of them, and were discussing what to do. From their perch up here, he could see not only the charred ruins they had just come across, but also the cove of the Dead Sea glinting in the morning sun.

To his right, Pierre was leaning against the rock wall, deathly pale.

"You need to lie down, and I'll get this arrow out. Come on, let's wriggle into this hole, we can wait for nightfall."

The opening was so narrow that they had to enter feet first. Esquieu helped his groaning, bloodstained companion. Curiously, the interior of the cave was quite bright. He made the wounded man lie down on the left of the entrance, his head against a kind of terracotta bowl emerging from the sand. Then, with a swift tug, he pulled out the arrow: Pierre screamed, and lost consciousness.

"The arrow has pierced him right through the stomach, the blood is streaming out: he's not going to make it."

He poured the last drops of water from his gourd between the dying man's lips. Then he peered down into the valley below: the Turks were still there; he needed to wait until they had gone. But Pierre would be dead by then.

Esquieu was a man of letters, a scholar; he had allowed a priory of white-robed monks of the new order created by St Bernard to settle on his lands. He spent his free time reading the manuscripts they had gathered in their scriptorium, and studied the medicine of Galen in the original Greek: Pierre's lifeblood was draining away, forming a dark puddle under his body. He had maybe an hour to live, perhaps less.

At a loss, he glanced round the floor of the cave. All along the left-hand wall there were terracotta bowls sticking out of the sand. Choosing at random, he lifted the third one from the cave mouth: it was an earthenware jar, perfectly well preserved. Inside, he saw a thick scroll surrounded by rags, all of them soaked in oil. Against the wall there was a smaller scroll, kept well away from the other one. He took it out, without any difficulty. It was a good-quality parchment, tied by a simple linen cord that he easily untied.

He glanced across at Pierre: he was immobile, hardly breathing, and his face already had the ashen hue of corpses. "My poor friend... dying on foreign soil!"

He unwound the scroll. It was in Greek, perfectly legible. Elegant handwriting, and words that he recognized without difficulty: the vocabulary of the apostles.

He went over to the cave mouth and started to read. His eyes widened, and his hands started to tremble slightly.

"I, the beloved disciple of Jesus, the thirteenth apostle, to all the Churches..." The author related how, on the evening of the last supper in the Upper Room, there had not been twelve, but thirteen apostles, and he had been the thirteenth. He protested in solemn terms against the deification of the Nazorean. And stated that Jesus had not risen from the dead, but had been transferred after his death to a tomb, which was located...

"Pierre, look! An apostolic letter from Jesus's day, the letter of one of his apostles... *Pierre!*"

His friend's head had rolled gently to the side of the earthenware bowl sealing the first jar in the grotto. He was dead.

An hour later, Esquieu had taken his decision: Pierre's body would here await the final resurrection. But this letter by one of Jesus's apostles of whom he had never heard was something he *must* reveal to the Christian world. Taking the parchment with him would be too risky: made brittle by time, it would

230

quickly crumble away into pieces. And would he himself escape from the Muslims that night? Would he reach Gaza safe and sound? The original would remain in this cave, but he would make a copy. Immediately.

With great respect, he turned over his friend's body, opened his tunic and tore a long strip off his shirt. Then he whittled down a piece of wood to a fine point, and placed the cloth on a flat stone. Dipped his improvised pen into the pool of blood gleaming red on the ground. And started to copy the apostolic letter, as he had so often seen monks do in the scriptorium of their priory.

The sun was setting behind the cliffs of Qumran. Esquieu got up: the text of the thirteenth apostle was now inscribed in letters of blood on Pierre's shirt. He rolled up the parchment, tied the linen cord around it and gently placed it back in the third jar – taking great care not to touch the greasy scroll. He replaced the lid, carefully folded up the copy he had just made, and slipped it into his belt.

From the cave mouth, he glanced down: there were already only half as many Turks. Now that he was alone he would be able to evade them. He needed to wait for night, and pass across the plantation of Ein Feshka. He would succeed.

Two months later, a vessel whose sail was blazoned with the red cross cleared the narrows of Saint-Jean-d'Acre, and headed west. From its prow, a Knight of the Templar in a great white robe took one last glance at the land of Christ.

Behind him, he was abandoning the body of his best friend. It lay in one of the caves overlooking Qumran, a cave containing dozens of jars filled with strange scrolls. As soon as possible, he would have to go there. Collect the parchment from the third jar on the left from the cave mouth and take it back to France, with all the precautions that such a venerable document deserved.

Pierre's death would not have been in vain: he would hand his copy of an apostle's letter that nobody had ever heard of to the Grand Master of the Temple, Robert de Craon. Its contents would change the face of the world. And would prove to everyone that the Templars had been right to reject Christ and instead love Jesus passionately.

On his arrival in Paris, Esquieu de Floyran asked to see Robert de Craon alone. Once he was admitted to his presence, he brought out from his belt a roll of fabric covered with dark brown characters, and held it out to the Grand Master of the Temple, the second to hold that title.

Without a word, the Grand Master unrolled the strip of fabric. Still in silence, he read the text. It was perfectly legible. He sternly imposed absolute secrecy on Esquieu, on the blood of his friend and brother, and dismissed him with a mere nod.

Robert de Craon spent the whole evening and the whole night alone, at the table on which the scrap of cloth lay extended, covered with the blood of one of his brothers. On it could be read the most incredible, the most overwhelming lines that he had ever read.

The next day, grave-faced, he sent out across the whole of Europe an extraordinary summons to a general chapter of the Order of Templars. Not one of the capitulary brothers, seneschals or priors, titulars of illustrious fortresses as much as the smallest commandery, should be absent from this chapter meeting.

Not one.

65

When Nil joined his friend, still bent over the table in the stacks, his face was impassive. Leeland looked up from his manuscript.

"Well?"

"Not here. Let's go back to the Via Aurelia."

Rome was preparing to celebrate Christmas. Following a tradition peculiar to the Eternal City, every church, throughout this period, makes it a point of honour to display a *presepio*, a crib adorned with all the attributes of the baroque imagination. Romans spent their December afternoons strolling from one church to another, comparing the shows that each one had put on and appraising them with eloquent hands.

"It's impossible," thought Nil as he saw entire families crowding in through the church porches, "impossible to tell them that it's all based on an age-old lie. They need a god in their image, a child god. The Church can only protect its secret – Nogaret was right."

The two men walked on in silence. When they reached the studio, they sat next to the piano, and Leeland brought out a bottle of bourbon. He poured a slug out for Nil, who raised his hand to stop him.

"Come on, Nil, our national drink bears the name of the kings of France. A few sips will help you tell me what you were doing, alone all morning, in a part of the Vatican stacks to which in principle you have no access…"

Nil did not pick up on the allusion: for the first time he was going to hide something from his friend. The confidential remarks of Breczinsky, his terror-stricken face, had nothing to do with his research: he felt that he was the possessor of a secret that he wasn't going to share with anyone. He took a big sip of bourbon, pulled a face and coughed.

"I don't know where to start: you're not a historian, you haven't studied the minutes of the Inquisition's interrogations that I've just seen. I found the texts consulted by Andrei when he went into the stacks, and they immediately spoke to me: they said something both clear and obscure."

"Did you find anything relating to the thirteenth apostle?"

"The words 'thirteenth apostle' or 'apostolic epistle' don't appear in any interrogation. But now I know what we are looking for, there are two details that have drawn my attention, and I can't understand them. Philippe le Bel himself drew up the accusation of the Templars in a letter addressed to the royal commissioners on 14th September 1307, one month before the big round-up of all the members of the Order. It's kept in the stacks, I copied it out this morning."

He bent down and picked a sheet of paper out of his bag.

"I'll read you his first accusation: 'Here is a bitter thing, a deplorable thing, most assuredly horrible, a detestable crime…' What was it? 'That the Templars, when they enter their order, deny Christ three times and spit on his face as many times.'"

"Oho!"

"Then, from Friday 13th October 1307, until the final interrogation of Jacques de Molay on the stake on 19th March 1314, one question is asked again and again: 'Is it true that you deny Christ?' All the Templars, however great the severity of the tortures inflicted on them, acknowledge that, yes, they reject Christ. But that no, they do not reject Jesus, and that it is in the name of Jesus that they joined the militia."

"So?"

"So that's exactly what the Nazoreans said – the same ones whose texts Origen was able to consult in Alexandria. We know that this was the teaching of their master, the thirteenth apostle: if his epistle is capable, all by itself, of destroying the Church, if it must be *everywhere destroyed* as the Coptic manuscript demands, it is not only because it denies the divinity of Jesus – many others did the same after it – but because, according to Origen, it contains *proof* that he was not God.

"Might the Templars have been aware of the vanished letter of the thirteenth apostle?"

"I don't know, but I will say that in the fourteenth century Templars get themselves tortured and killed because they proclaim the same doctrine as the Nazoreans, and they confirm this choice by a ritual gesture – spitting at Christ. There is perhaps a second hypothesis" – Nil rubbed his forehead. "These men were for a long time in close contact with Muslims. The rejection of any god other than Allah recurs again and again in the Koran, and don't forget that Muhammad himself knew the Nazoreans and quotes them on several occasions…"

"What does that mean? You're mixing everything up!"

"No, I'm linking disparate elements together. It has often been said that the Templars had been influenced by Islam: perhaps, but their rejection of Jesus's divinity does not originate from the Koran. It's more serious than that: if you look through the accounts of the interrogations, some of them admit that the authority of Peter and the twelve apostles has, in their view, been transferred to the person of the Grand Master of the Temple."

"The Grand Master? So is he a sort of successor of the thirteenth apostle?"

"They don't say it in so many words, but state that their rejection of Christ is based on the person of their Grand Master, whom they consider to be an authority superior to the Twelve and the Church. It's just as if a hidden apostolic succession had been transmitted down the centuries, parallel with that of Peter. It originated with the thirteenth apostle and was then based on his Nazoreans, and then, after their extinction, on this mysterious epistle."

Nil took another swig of bourbon.

"Philippe le Bel levelled a second serious accusation against the Templars: 'When they enter their order, they kiss the man who receives them – the Grand Master – at first at the bottom of his back, then on his belly.'"

Leeland burst out laughing.

"Gosh! Queer Templars!"

"No, the Templars were not homosexuals, they took a vow of chastity and everything indicates that they respected it. This was a ritual gesture that took place in the course of a religious ceremony, a solemn and public affair. This gesture allowed Philippe le Bel to accuse them of sodomy, since he didn't understand it – while it certainly had a highly symbolic meaning."

"Kissing the backside of the Grand Master and then going round and kissing his belly – a symbolic ritual, in a church?"

"A solemn rite to which they attached great importance. So what meaning did this gesture have for them? At first I thought they were venerating the chakras of the Grand Master, those crossroads of spiritual energy that the Hindus locate in the belly and… the backside, as you put it. But the Templars did not know about Hindu philosophy. So I have no explanation, except this one: a gesture of veneration towards the person of the Grand Master, the apostle whose authority in their eyes supplanted that of Peter and his successors. Thus they seem to have attached themselves to another tradition, that of the thirteenth apostle. But why a kiss on that precise spot? I don't know."

* * *

That evening, Father Nil could not go to sleep. Questions spun round and round in his head. What did that sacrilegious gesture, which had sullied the memory of the Knights Templar for ever, actually mean? And above all, what relation was there with the letter of the thirteenth apostle?

Again, he turned over in his bed, and the springs of the mattress creaked. The next day he would be going to a concert. A welcome change.

66

Paris, 18th March 1314

"One last time, we adjure you to confess: have you rejected the divinity of Christ? Will you tell us the meaning of the impious ritual of admission into your Order?"

At the tip of the Île de la Cité, the Grand Master of the Temple, Jacques de Molay, had been hoisted onto a heap of faggots. His hands were bound under his white mantle bearing the red cross. Opposite him was Guillaume de Nogaret, the Chancellor and partner in crime of King Philippe le Bel. The people of Paris had amassed on both banks of the Seine: was the Grand Master about to recant at the last minute, thereby depriving the curious of a choice spectacle? The executioner, legs apart, was holding a flaming torch in his right hand, and had only one small move still to make.

Jacques de Molay closed his eyes and recalled the whole memory of his Order. It had begun almost two centuries earlier, in 1149. Not far from this stake where he was about to die.

* * *

The day following the trip to Paris of the knight Esquieu de Floyran, Grand Master Robert de Craon had urgently summoned an extraordinary chapter of the Order of the Temple.

In front of the assembled brothers, he had read aloud the letter of the thirteenth apostle, in the copy that had just miraculously reached him. It contained the undeniable proof that Jesus was not God. His body had never risen, but had been buried by the Essenes, somewhere on the edge of the desert of Idumaea. The author of this letter said that he rejected the testimony of the Twelve and the authority of Peter, whom he accused of having accepted that Jesus be deified in order to seize power.

The Templars were transfixed, and listened to him in a deathly silence. One of them stood up and said in a hoarse voice:

"Brothers, all of here have lived for several years in contact with our Muslim enemies. Everyone knows that their Koran rejects the divinity of Jesus, in terms exactly similar to this apostolic letter, and that this is the main reason for their fierce hostility to Christians. We need to bring this letter to the knowledge of Christendom, so that Jesus's true identity can finally be revealed: this will for ever put an end to the pitiless war that sets Muhammad's successors against Peter's successor. Only then will the two groups be able to live peacefully together, proclaiming as one that Jesus, the son of Joseph, was not a god but an exceptional man and an inspired guide!

Robert de Craon weighed the terms of his reply with care: never, he told the assembled brothers, never would the Church renounce its founding dogma, the source of its universal power. He had another plan; it was adopted after lengthy deliberation.

* * *

In the following decades, the wealth of the Templars grew amazingly. It was enough for the Grand Master to meet a prince or a bishop, and donations in land and precious metal would immediately come flowing in. This was because the successors of Robert de Craon had an unassailable argument at their disposal.

"Give us the means to fulfil our mission," they said, "or we will publish an apostolic document in our possession that will destroy you by totally undermining the Christianity from which you derive your power and all your wealth."

The kings and even the popes themselves paid up, and opulent Templar commanderies sprung up everywhere. A century later, the Templars were acting as bankers for the whole of Europe: the letter of the thirteenth apostle had become the sluice gate of a river of gold, flowing into the coffers of the Knights.

But the source of such wealth, the object of every covetous desire, was at the mercy of a theft: that fragile piece of fabric needed to be put somewhere safe. The physical person of the Grand Master, the continuer of the thirteenth apostle, one who like him held his ground against the Christianity founded by Peter, had become untouchable. One of them remembered the way prisoners from the East concealed their money by placing it in a metal tube that they slipped into their entrails and thus kept on their bodies, safe from every theft. He had a golden case made, placed in it the copy of the epistle, carefully rolled up, inserted it in himself, and from then on carried it around within his very body, that was now doubly sacred.

So that nobody would suspect the secret attached to the epistle, all trace of it, even the smallest, had to be effaced. The seneschal of the commandery of Patay heard of an inscription that had been carved in the church of Germigny, which was at that time on land belonging to him. A scholarly monk claimed that this inscription contained a hidden meaning that lurked in the remarkable way the text of the *Symbolon* of Nicaea had been transcribed. He said he was capable of deciphering this code.

The seneschal summoned the monk and shut himself away with him in the church of Germigny. When he came out, his face was grave, and he immediately had the monk taken under escort to his commandery at Patay.

The scholarly monk died there the next day. The slab was immediately covered with a layer of coating, and its mysterious inscription vanished from people's eyes as well as from their memory.

The ritual of admission to the Order of the Templars now included a curious gesture, which novices accomplished religiously: during the mass and before receiving their great white mantle, each of them had to kneel before the Grand Master and kiss first the bottom of his back, and then his belly.

Without knowing it, the new brother was in this way venerating the letter of the thirteenth apostle, that was pursued by the hatred of the Church whose existence it imperilled. Now it was contained in the entrails of the Grand Master, who would extract it from its precious case only to obtain, by threat, even more land and even more gold.

The treasure of the Templars lay in the cellars of several commanderies. But the source of this treasure, its inexhaustible source, was transmitted by each Grand Master to his successor, who protected it with the rampart of his own body.

* * *

On the stake, Jacques de Molay lifted his head. They had inflicted the torture of water and fire on him, and had put him on the rack, but they had not searched his entrails. With a mere contraction he could feel in the most intimate part of himself the presence of the gold case: the epistle would disappear with him, the sole weapon of the Templars against the kings and prelates of a Church that had become unworthy of Jesus. In an astonishingly strong voice, he replied to Guillaume de Nogaret:

"It was under torture that some of our brothers confessed to the horror of which you accuse me. In the face of heaven and earth I now swear that everything you have just said about the crimes and the impiety of the Templars is pure slander. And we deserve death for not having managed to resist the suffering inflicted by the Inquisitors."

With a smile of triumph, Nogaret turned to the King. Standing in his royal loggia that looked out over the Seine, Philippe raised his hand: at that very moment the executioner lowered his arm, plunging the lighted torch into the faggots of the stake.

The sparks flew into the air, right up to the towers of Notre-Dame. Jacques de Molay still had the strength to cry:

"Pope Clement, King Philippe! Before one year is up, I summons you to appear before the tribunal of God to receive your just punishment! Be accursed, you and those who will come after you!"

The stake collapsed in on itself, in an explosion of sparks. The heat was so great that it reached the banks of the Seine.

At the end of the day, the priest from Notre-Dame came to pray on the smoking remnants of the pyre. The archers had deserted the spot; he was alone and he kneeled down. Then he jumped in amazement: in front of him, amidst the hot ashes, an object was gleaming in the light from the setting sun. With the help of a branch, he pulled it towards him: it was a nugget of gold, gold melted by the heat of the brazier, gleaming and tear-shaped.

It was all that remained of the case that had contained the letter of the thirteenth apostle; all that remained of the last Grand Master of the Temple; all that remained of the real treasure of the Templars.

Like many other people, the priest knew that the Templars were innocent, that their terrible death was in fact a martyrdom: devoutly, he pressed his lips to the golden teardrop, which seemed to him to be still burning even though it was only tepid. It was the relic of a saint, the equal of all those who have given their lives for Jesus's memory. He entrusted it to the envoy of Pope Clement, who died within the year.

After many perilous adventures, the teardrop later fell into the hands of a Rector of the Society of St Pius V – who managed to discover its meaning, since not all the Templars had perished at the start of the fourteenth century. Nothing is more difficult to suppress than memory.

He kept this indirect testimony to the rebellion of the thirteenth apostle against the dominant Church as a precious addition to the Society's treasures.

67

The entrance hall was in fact the living room of a vast patrician residence. Just a skip and a jump from the buzz of the city centre, the Via Giulia offered to Rome the charm of its arcades covered with wisteria, and several old palaces transformed into hotels that were at once familiar, luxurious and convivial.

"Could you please tell Signor Barjona that I would like to see him?"

The receptionist, dressed with distinction in black, gazed at this early visitor. A middle-aged man, greying hair, nondescript clothes – an admirer, a foreign journalist? He pursed his lips.

"The *maestro* came back very late last night, we never disturb him before…"

As naturally as possible, the visitor pulled from his pocket a twenty-dollar bill and handed it to the receptionist.

"He'll be delighted to see me, and if that were not the case I would make it up to you by the same amount again. Tell him that his old friend from the club is waiting for him: he'll understand."

"What the hell's the idea, Ari, dragging me out of bed at this time, on the day before a concert? And to begin with, what are you doing in Rome? You ought to be enjoying your retirement in Jaffa in peace and quiet and leave me alone. I'm not under your command any more!"

"True, but nobody ever leaves Mossad, Lev, and you *are* under their command, still. Come on, relax! I was just passing through Europe, and I'm taking advantage of the opportunity to see you, that's all. How's your Roman tour going?"

"It's going well. But this evening I'm starting with Rachmaninov's Third – it's a terrifying monument, and I need to concentrate. So do you still have relatives in Europe?"

"A Jew always has relatives somewhere. *Your* family, well, they're really the service I trained you up in when you were still a teenager. And they're worried about you in Jerusalem. Whatever led you to follow that French monk onto the Rome

243

express after reserving his entire compartment? Who'd given you orders to do so? Did you want to do the previous operation all over again, but alone this time? Did I ever tell you to go solo in an operation?"

Lev pulled a face and lowered his eyes.

"I didn't have time to warn Jerusalem, it all went so quickly…"

Ari clenched his fists and interrupted him.

"Don't lie, not to me. You know perfectly well that, ever since your accident, you haven't been the same. You've been flirting with death for years now. There are times when you allow yourself to get overwhelmed by a hankering for danger – it has a perfume that arouses you like a drug. Then you don't think any more – just imagine what would have happened if Father Nil in turn had had an accident?"

"It would have been a real headache for the people in the Vatican. I hate them with all my soul, Ari: they were the ones who allowed the Nazis who had exterminated my family to escape to Argentina."

Ari looked at him with tenderness.

"It's no longer the time for hatred, but for justice. And it's inconceivable, unacceptable, that you should take political decisions at such a level without getting permission. You've shown you're no longer able to control yourself: we need to protect you against yourself. From now on, you are absolutely forbidden to carry out any operations in the field. The little Lev who used to play with his life as if it were a musical score has grown up. You're a celebrity now: carry on with the mission we've entrusted you with, keep tabs on Mukhtar Al-Quraysh, and concentrate on the French monk. No more direct action as far as you're concerned."

68

Nil was filled with excitement as he went into the Academy of Santa Cecilia. The last time he'd been to a concert was in Paris, just before he entered the monastery. That had been quite a while ago.

The auditorium is small and almost intimate in size. It was now humming with gossip and, in the middle of the gala costumes, the scarlet cassocks of several cardinals could be seen. Leeland held the two invitation cards to the usher, who led them to the twentieth row, slightly to the left.

"From here your view won't be interrupted by the lid of the piano, Monsignor; you'll be able to watch the soloist."

They sat in silence. Ever since his arrival in Rome, Nil had sensed that something had snapped between himself and Leeland: the complete and absolute trust that had enabled them to remain so close to one another in spite of their physical distance and the years of separation had broken down. It seemed to him that he had lost his last and only friend.

The orchestra was already in its place. Suddenly the lights in the hall dimmed, and the conductor made his entrance, followed by the pianist. Thunderous applause broke out, and the American leant towards Nil.

"Lev Barjona has already given several recitals here, the audience know and admire him."

The conductor bowed, but Lev Barjona went straight over to the piano and sat down, without looking at the audience. From his seat, Nil could see only the right side of his profile, crowned by a mane of blond hair. When the conductor climbed onto the podium, the pianist raised his eyes and smiled at him. Then he nodded, and the vibrant hum of the violins was heard, the steady beat of a deep pulse announcing the entry of the piano. As soon as this repetitive, obsessive cadence reached him, the pianist's face became set like that of a robot.

Nil suddenly had a flashback: he had already seen that expression somewhere. But Lev's hands were now on the piano, and the first-movement theme rose up like the nostalgic reminder of a lost world, that of the happiness that had been lost since the October Revolution. Nil closed his eyes. Rachmaninov's music swept him away in a sled, across frozen wastes of snow, then along the road to exile, to the gates of death and abandonment.

By the end of the second movement, the audience was enraptured. Leeland again leant across to Nil.

"The third movement is one of the most difficult pieces in the whole repertoire."

Lev Barjona was dazzling, but hardly acknowledged the audience, which had risen to its feet as one, before walking off into the wings. Flushed with pleasure, Leeland was clapping like mad. Then, suddenly, he stopped.

"I know Lev, he won't return to the stage, he never gives an encore. Come on, let's see if we can say hello to him."

They pushed their way through the crowd that was stamping with enthusiasm and crying, "Bravo! Bravo! Encore!"

In the box reserved for the Vatican, Cardinal Catzinger was applauding with detachment. He had received a note labelled *molto confidenziale* from the Secretary of State, warning him about the Israeli pianist. "He may be a dodgy character, perhaps, but what a virtuoso!"

Suddenly he froze: he had just spotted, down among the audience, Leeland's elegant silhouette, followed by the grey head of Nil. They were heading towards the left of the stage, making for the wings – the artists' dressing rooms.

* * *

"Rembert! *Shalom*, what a pleasure to see you!"

Surrounded by pretty women, Lev Barjona embraced Leeland and then turned to Nil.

"And this must be your friend... Pleased to meet you. Do you like Rachmaninov?"

Nil, transfixed, did not return his greeting. The Israeli was now standing in the full light, and for the first time he could see his face clearly: there was a scar running from his left ear right into his mane of hair.

The man from the train!

Lev was completely at ease and pretended that he had not noticed his stupefaction. He leant towards Leeland and whispered, with a smile: "You've come at just the right time, I was trying to get away from this bevy of female admirers. After each concert, I need a few hours to come back down to earth, a little oasis of calm and silence."

He turned to Nil.

"It would be a great pleasure for me if you would have dinner with me. We could go to a discreet trattoria – and with two monks, silence is absolutely guaranteed: you'll be the ideal dinner companions to help me emerge from the world of Rachmaninov. Wait for me at the artists' exit, I'll get away from these bothersome women, get changed and meet you there."

Lev Barjona's smile and charm were irresistible, and he obviously knew it: he didn't wait for a reply, and headed off into the wings, leaving Nil rooted to the spot in amazement.

The man from the train! What had he been doing alone with Nil in a crowded Rome express, and what had he been about to do when the ticket collector had suddenly come into their compartment?

He was going to have dinner with him, face to face...

247

Part Three

69

Late that evening, the phone rang in the apartment at Castel Sant'Angelo: Alessandro Calfo jumped. He had just convinced Sonia (she was starting to put up with his demands less and less readily), and was putting the final touch to a complicated scenario which needed to run flawlessly.

At a time like this, it could only be the Cardinal.

It was indeed. He had only just got back to the Vatican – the Academy of Santa Cecilia is very near. From the tone of his voice, Calfo immediately realized that something was wrong.

"Monsignor, did you know about this?"

"About what, Your Eminence?"

"I've just this minute got back from a concert by the Israeli, Lev Barjona. A few days ago, our services alerted me about this man, and to my amazement I learnt that the Society of St Pius V had... how shall I put it... used his hidden talents. Who has authorized you to bring in foreign agents to act in the name of the Vatican?"

"Your Eminence, Lev Barjona has never been a Vatican agent! First and foremost, he's an eminent pianist, and the reason I accepted his collaboration was that he's a son of Abraham like us, and he understands a great many things. But I've never actually set eyes on him."

"Well *I* have, just now, at Santa Cecilia. And guess who there was in the audience?"

Calfo sighed.

"Your two monks," continued Catzinger, "the American and the Frenchman."

"Your Eminence… what harm is there in going to listen to some nice music?"

"For one thing, a monk has no place going to a theatre. And above all, I spotted them heading for the wings at the end of the concert. They will doubtless have met Lev Barjona."

"I very much hope," thought Calfo, "that they have indeed met him."

"Your Eminence," he said aloud, "a long time ago in Jerusalem, Leeland made the acquaintance of Barjona, who was a pupil of Arthur Rubinstein. He shares a passion for music with him. It does not seem at all odd that…"

Catzinger interrupted him.

"May I remind you that Leeland works at the Vatican, and that it was *me* who authorized you to use him as a bait for Father Nil? It is highly dangerous to let them meet such a diabolical person as that Lev Barjona. You know just as well as I do that he's not just a talented musician. My patience is exhausted: during the week leading up to Christmas I have to celebrate mass every morning in my *titulum* of Santa Maria in Cosmedin, starting from tomorrow. Make sure Leeland is available to meet me tomorrow, in the early afternoon. I'll see him in my office and remind him of his responsibilities. As for you, don't forget that you are in the service of the Church, which rules out your taking certain… initiatives."

As he hung up, Calfo smiled. He would not like to be in the American's shoes: the bait was about to be swallowed by His Eminence. This was of no importance: he had played his role perfectly, first getting Nil to talk and then taking him to meet the Israeli. The bait was for the Cardinal. *He* was seeking to skitter the fish.

He returned to his bedroom and suppressed a gesture of exasperation: Sonia had removed her accoutrements and was sitting naked on the edge of the bed. Her face was stubborn, and tears were trickling down her cheeks.

"Come on, my pretty, it's not so terrible!"

He made her stand up and obliged her to put on a wimple, which masked her lovely hair, and to slip over it a starched cornet, the points of which fell onto her round shoulders. Thus attired as a nun from the olden days – "just her upper body, the rest is for me" – he made her kneel on a prie-dieu in red velvet, in front of a Byzantine icon. Always attentive, he had thought that an icon would allow the Romanian woman better to play the role he wanted her to play.

He took a step backwards: the tableau was perfect. Sonia was stripped bare, but her oval visage was nicely set off by the cornet, and her eyes were raised to the icon as she joined her delicate hands and seemed to be praying. "A virginal attitude in front of the Virgin's image. Very suggestive."

Rome was plunged into the silence of night. Mgr Calfo, kneeling behind Sonia and pushing against the curve of her back, started to celebrate the divine service. His shins rested on the prie-dieu, and he was thankful for its velvety surface. His hands took a firm grip of the young woman's breasts. For a moment he was uncomfortably aware of the gaze of the Byzantine virgin staring at him in what looked like mute reproach. He closed his eyes: in his quest for mystical union, nothing within him would come between the human and the divine, the carnal and the spiritual.

As he started to murmur words that made no sense to her,

Sonia, her eyes fixed on the icon, uncrossed her hands and wiped the tears that were clouding her eyes.

70

At the very same moment, Lev was raising his glass before the eyes of his companions.

"A toast! Good to meet up!"

He'd taken the two monks to a trattoria in Trastevere, one of Rome's more populous districts. The clientele was entirely composed of Italians swallowing gigantic portions of pasta.

"I recommend the *penne all'arrabbiata* here. It's home cooking, I always come here after a concert: they close very late, and we'll have plenty of time to talk."

Since their arrival in the restaurant, Nil had remained silent: it was impossible that the Israeli did not recognize him. But Lev, jovial and relaxed, seemed not to notice the silence of the man sitting opposite him. He exchanged with Leeland memories of the good old days, their meeting in Israel, their musical discoveries.

"At that time, in Jerusalem, we could at last start to live again after the Six Days' War. Commander Ygael Yadin would very much have liked me to stay with him in Tsahal…"

For the first time, Nil intervened in the conversation.

"The famous archaeologist? You knew him?"

Lev waited until three plates of steaming pasta had been set before them, then turned towards Nil. He pulled a face and smiled.

"I not only knew him, something really rather extraordinary happened to me thanks to him. You're a specialist in ancient texts, a scholar, it should interest you…"

Nil had the unpleasant sensation of falling into a trap. "How does he know that I'm a specialist and a scholar? Why has he brought us here?" Unable to reply, he decided to let Lev show his hand, and silently acquiesced.

"In 1947, I was eight years old and we were living in Jerusalem. My father was friends with a young archaeologist at the Hebrew University, Ygael Yadin: I grew up alongside him. He was twenty, and like all the Jews living in Palestine he led a double life: he was a student, but above all he was a fighter in the Hagana, and rapidly rose to become its commander-in-chief. I knew this and was full of admiration for him. I had only one dream: I too wanted to fight for my country."

"At the age of eight?"

"Rembert, the formidable fighters of Palmakh and Hagana were teenagers. They were intoxicated by the allure of danger. They didn't hesitate to call on children to transit their messages; we had no other means of communication. On the morning of November 30th, the United Nations accepted the creation of a Jewish State. We knew that war would break out: Jerusalem was covered all over with barbed-wire fences, and only a child could get about without a pass."

"And you did so?"

"Of course: Yadin started to make use of me daily. I listened to everything that was being said around me. One evening, he mentioned a strange discovery: a Bedouin had been chasing after a goat among the cliffs overlooking the Dead Sea, and had come across a cave. Inside, he had found jars containing gluey parcels that he sold for five pounds to a Christian cobbler in Bethlehem. Who eventually handed them over to the Metropolitan Samuel, the superior of St Mark's Monastery, in the part of Jerusalem that had just turned Arab."

253

Nil pricked up his ears: he had heard of the fantastic odyssey of the Dead Sea Scrolls. His mistrust suddenly evaporated: he was face to face with a direct witness. This was an opportunity he had never dreamt of.

As he tucked into his *penne*, Lev kept glancing over at Nil, whose sudden interest seemed to amuse him. He carried on:

"The Metropolitan Samuel asked Yadin to identify those manuscripts. It was necessary to cross the city to St Mark's. Every street was an ambush. Yadin gave me a schoolboy's apron and satchel and showed me which direction the monastery lay in. I slipped between the British barricades, the Arab tanks, the Hagana platoons. They all stopped shooting for a while to let this kid get to school! In my satchel I brought two scrolls back from the monastery and Yadin immediately realized what they were: the oldest manuscripts ever discovered in the land of Israel, a treasure that belonged by right to the new Jewish State."

"What did he do with them?"

"He couldn't keep them, it would have been theft. He returned them to the Metropolitan and told him he was prepared to buy all the manuscripts the Bedouins might find in the caves of Qumran. In spite of the war, the news got out: Americans from the American Oriental School and French Dominicans from the École Biblique de Jérusalem pushed up the bidding. One minute Yadin was commanding military operations, the next he was locked in secret negotiations with antiques sellers in Bethlehem and Jerusalem. The Americans were making off with everything…"

"I know," Nil interrupted. "I've seen the photocopies from the Huntington Library, in my monastery."

"Ah, you've managed to get hold of a copy? Very few people have been so lucky. I hope they'll get published one day. Well,

I then became an unwitting actor in an incident that ought to interest you…"

He pushed his plate away and poured himself a glass of wine. Nil noted how his face suddenly became set – just as in the train, or when he was playing Rachmaninov!

After a silence, Lev pulled himself together and continued his story.

"One day, the Metropolitan Samuel told Yadin that he had come into possession of two exceptionally well-preserved documents. The Bedouin man had found them on his second visit to the cave, in the third jar on the left going in, next to the skeleton of what must have been a Templar, since he was still wrapped in the white tunic with the red cross. I once more made my way across the city, and brought the contents of the jar to Yadin: a big scroll wrapped in oil-soaked cloth and a little parchment – a single sheet, tied up with just a single linen cord. In the room that he used as headquarters, when the bombs were falling, Yadin opened the scroll that was covered by Hebrew characters: it was the *Manual of Discipline* of the Essenes. Then he unrolled the sheet: it was written in Greek, and he translated the first line aloud to me. I was a child, but I still remember: 'I, the beloved disciple, the thirteenth apostle, to all the Churches…'"

Nil turned pale and gripped his knife and fork tightly, trying to master his emotion.

"You're sure? *That's* what you heard? 'The beloved disciple, the thirteenth apostle'?"

"Absolutely. Yadin looked really downcast. He told me that he was only interested in Hebrew manuscripts, since these were the patrimony of Israel: this letter, written in the same Greek as that of the Gospels, concerned the Christians, and needed to be given back to the Metropolitan. He kept the *Manual of Discipline*, slipped a bundle of dollars into my satchel in exchange and added the little Greek parchment. Then he sent me off through the bombs to St Mark's."

Nil was transfixed. "This man," he thought, "has held in his own hands the letter of the thirteenth apostle, the only copy to have escaped the Church – perhaps even the original!"

Lev, his features still impassive, continued:

"I'd got to within about a hundred yards of the monastery when a shell fell in the street: I was flung into the air, and I lost consciousness. When I opened my eyes, a monk was leaning over me. I was inside the monastery, the skin on my skull was split from top to bottom" – grimacing, he touched his scar – "and my schoolboy's satchel had vanished."

"Vanished?"

"Yes. I'd been in a coma for twenty-four hours, between life and death. When the Metropolitan came to see me the next day, he told me that one of his monks had picked me up in the street and handed the satchel over to him. When he opened it, he realized the situation: Yadin was paying him in cash for the Qumran manuscript, but he wasn't interested in the Greek letter. He'd just sold the letter to a Dominican, with an assortment of odds and ends of Hebrew manuscripts that the Bedouins had brought him. He even added, with a laugh, that he'd bundled everything together, letter and manuscripts, in an empty crate of Napoleon brandy, which he was very partial to. And he told me the Dominican seemed completely unaware of the value of what he'd just acquired."

Questions were jostling to be answered in Nil's head.

"Do you think the Metropolitan read the letter before he sold it on to that Dominican?"

"I haven't the foggiest. But I'd be surprised. Metropolitan

Samuel was anything but a scholar. Don't forget we were at war: he needed money to feed his monks and look after the wounded who were being brought into the monastery in their dozens. It was no time to start analysing texts! He certainly didn't look closely at the letter."

"And what about the Dominican?"

Lev turned to him: he knew that his story would be of the greatest interest to the little French monk. "Well," he thought, "why do you think that I've invited you here to dinner this evening, Father? Just to enjoy the *penne all'arrabbiata*?"

"I told you," he said aloud, "these recollections had remained engraved in my memory. Much later, before he died, Yadin mentioned the letter again, and asked me to try and track it down. I carried out a small-scale inquiry thanks to Mossad – I'd become, let's say, one of their occasional agents. The best secret service in the world, apparently, after that of the Vatican!"

Lev was now sparkling, and his playful expression had returned: all tension had vanished from his face.

"The Dominican was in fact a lay brother, a good chap but a bit obtuse. Just after Israel's declaration of independence, the situation had become so tense in Jerusalem that many monks and priests were repatriated to Europe. Apparently the Dominican stuffed the crate of Napoleon brandy into his luggage, quite unaware of its value, and lugged it with him all the way to Rome, where he ended his days at the General Curia of the Dominicans, on the Aventine. We learnt that the crate was no longer there – when he died, all they found in his cell was an olive-wood rosary."

"And... where might it be?"

"A General Curia is an administrative body that doesn't allow itself to get snowed under with documents of no use.

It will have handed on the assorted material from Jerusalem to the Vatican, where it doubtless joined all the old stuff that nobody knows what to do with – or that nobody wishes to make use of. It must be gathering dust somewhere, in a corner of one of the libraries or some cubbyhole in the Holy City – if it had been opened, news would have got out sooner or later."

"Why's that, Lev?"

The Israeli's relaxed tone was contagious, and Nil had called him by his first name. Lev noticed, and poured him another glass of wine.

"Because Ygael Yadin *had* read the letter before he gave it back to the Metropolitan. And what he told me on his deathbed suggested to me that it contained a terrifying secret, the kind of secret that no Church, no State – even one as impenetrable and monarchical as the Vatican – can stop leaking out sooner or later. If anyone has seen that letter, Father Nil, either he's dead by now, or the Vatican and the Catholic Church would have imploded – and that would make more noise than the Arab-Israeli war of 1947, more than the Crusades, more noise than any other event in the history of the West."

Nil nervously rubbed his face.

Either he's dead by now…

Andrei!

71

The light Castelli wine was rather making Nil's head turn. He noticed with some surprise that the waiter was placing a cup of coffee in front of him: he had been so captivated by Lev's story that he had swallowed down, without noticing it, the *penne all'arrabbiata* and the *cotoletta alla milanese* that

258

had followed. Looking preoccupied, Leeland was stirring the coffee in his cup. He decided to ask Lev the question that Nil had confronted him with in the Belvedere courtyard.

"Tell me, Lev... Why did you send me two invitations to your concert, specifying in your note that it might be of interest for my friend? How did you know he was in Rome and, well, quite simply, how did you even know of his existence?"

Lev raised his eyebrows, looking surprised.

"But... you told me so yourself! The day after I arrived, I received a letter in my hotel on the Via Giulia. It had the Vatican coat of arms on it. Inside there were a few lines of typescript – if I remember rightly, something like 'Monsignor Leeland and his friend Father Nil would be happy to attend...' and so on. I thought you'd asked your secretary to tell me, and I simply thought it was maybe a bit hasty – but that's probably how things work in the Vatican, and I imagined the style had rubbed off on you."

Leeland replied gently:

"I don't have a secretary, Lev, and I never sent you a letter. I didn't even know what hotel you were staying at for your concert series in Rome. Tell me... did the letter have my signature?"

Lev swept his hand through his thick locks of blond hair.

"Gosh, I can't remember! No, it wasn't your signature, there was just an initial at the bottom. A capital C, I think, with a full stop. Anyway, Rembert, I was fully intending to see you while I was passing through, and I would inevitably have got to know Father Nil."

Leeland's face had suddenly darkened: Catzinger or Calfo? Anger again started to rise within him.

Nil, lost in his own thoughts, had been only half-following this conversation. He was assailed by many other questions, and suddenly remarked:

"Only the result matters, since thanks to this letter I've been able to hear a fabulous performance of the Rachmaninov concerto. But Lev... why are you telling us all this? You can guess what it would mean for Rembert and myself if a new apostle's letter had been discovered, miraculously dragged out of oblivion at the end of the twentieth century, and putting a question mark over our faith. Why have you told us all this?"

Lev replied with his most charming smile. He could not possibly tell Nil the truth – "because these are my instructions from Mossad".

"And who could be more interested in it all than you?"

He seemed to attach no importance to Nil's question, and gazed at him with a friendly expression.

"Father Nil... would a mere ancient document contesting the divinity of Jesus change anything for you?"

The last customers had just left the trattoria, and they were now alone in the dining room, where the manager was idly starting to tidy up. Nil thought for a long time before replying, as if he had forgotten whom he was addressing.

"You have told me this evening that an apostolic letter was discovered at Qumran at the same time as the Dead Sea Scrolls: I have been accumulating proof of its existence for several weeks now. In the third century in a Coptic manuscript, at the turn of the fourth century in a text by Origen. In the seventh century in allusions in the Koran, in the eighth century in a code introduced into the *Symbolon* of Nicaea at Germigny, and finally in the fourteenth century in the account of the trial of the Templars. All this after spending years decrypting the text from the end of the first century that started it all off: St John's Gospel. I've been able to follow the traces of the letter of the thirteenth apostle thanks to the shadow it has left on the history of the West."

He looked Lev right in the eyes.

"Now you have just told me that you transported it in your schoolboy satchel, as you attempted, while the bombs were falling, to carry out a mission for the head of Hagana. Then you tell me that it must be somewhere in the Vatican, hidden away or simply not known about. You heard Ygael Yadin tell you that it contained a terrifying secret. Even if I were to know of its contents – which must indeed be terrible to have given rise to so many expulsions, murders and plots – it would change nothing in my relationship with Jesus. I have met him personally, Lev, can you understand that? His person does not belong to any Church, and he does not need them in order to exist."

Lev seemed impressed. He gently placed his hand on Nil's forearm.

"I've never really practised my religion much, Father Nil, but any Jew will understand what you've just told me, since every Jew is descended from the lineage of the prophets, whether he wants to be or not. Let me tell you I've taken a real liking to you, and though I've told a lot of lies in my life, I'm being totally sincere when I tell you that."

He got up, as the manager was starting to hover round their table.

"With all my soul, I hope you succeed with your research. Don't think it concerns nobody except yourself, and I won't say any more about it. Beware: the prophets and those like them all met with a violent death. This too is something a Jew knows by instinct, and he accepts it, just as Jesus accepted it, long ago. It's 2 a.m. now: let me order a taxi for you to get back to San Girolamo."

261

* * *

Huddled in the back seat, Nil watched as the dome of the Vatican, gleaming softly in the cold December night, went by. Suddenly his eyes misted over with tears. Up until now this letter had merely been a hypothesis, with only a virtual reality. Now he had just shaken a hand that had actually touched it, his eyes had looked into the eyes which had seen that document.

All at once, the hypothesis had become a reality. The letter of the thirteenth apostle was probably somewhere behind the high walls of the Vatican.

He would keep going right on to the end. He too would see that letter with his own eyes.

And he would try to survive, unlike all those who had preceded him.

72

Leeland was playing a Bach prelude when Nil arrived at the studio in the Via Aurelia. Until dawn he had mulled over the revelations of Lev Barjona. His eyes, ringed with dark circles, betrayed the depths of his anxiety.

"I didn't sleep a wink all night: too many new things all at once! Never mind – let's go to the stacks, and I'll get down to your manuscripts of Gregorian chant, it will help perk me up. Just think, Rembert: the letter of the thirteenth apostle is probably in the Vatican!"

"We'll only be able to spend the morning there. I've just received a call from Mgr Calfo: the Cardinal's asked me to see him today at 2 p.m. in his office."

"Whatever for?"

"Oh..." Leeland closed the lid of the piano, looking embarrassed. "I think I know why, but I'd rather not tell you right now. If the mysterious epistle you've been chasing all these years really is in the Vatican, how are you going to get your hands on it?"

Now it was Nil's turn to look embarrassed.

"I'm sorry, Remby, but I prefer not to tell you straight away. You can see what the Vatican has turned us into: brothers who are no longer completely brothers, since they no longer tell each other everything..."

On the floor below, Mukhtar switched off his tape machines and uttered a low whistle. Nil had just said something that was worth a great number of dollars: *the letter of the thirteenth apostle was probably in the Vatican!* He had been right to listen to the orders from Cairo and not yet take action against the little Frenchman. Hamas knew almost as much as did Calfo about that letter and its vital importance for Christianity: the net was tightening around Nil, but they needed to let him get to the bottom of things.

Calfo protected Christianity, but he, Mukhtar, protected Islam, its Koran and its Prophet – blessed be his name.

As he walked down the long corridor leading to the office of the Prefect of the Congregation, Leeland felt his stomach tightening. Thick carpets, wall lights in Venetian glass, panelling in precious wood: this luxury suddenly struck him as intolerable. It was the ostentatious sign of the power of an organization that didn't hesitate to crush its own members to preserve the existence of a vast empire based on a succession of lies. Ever since Nil had arrived, he had started to realize that his friend had fallen victim to this power just as he had – but for quite another reason. Leeland had never really asked himself any questions about

263

his faith: Nil's discoveries had shattered him, and provided his inner rebellion with a new ambition. He knocked discreetly on the high door decorated with thin gold lines.

"Come in, Monsignor, I was expecting you."

Leeland had thought he would find Calfo sitting with him, but Catzinger was alone. On his empty desk lay nothing but a folder with a red stripe along it. The Cardinal's face, usually round and pink, was hard as stone.

"Monsignor, I won't beat about the bush. For three weeks you have been meeting Father Nil daily. Now you go dragging him off to a concert and let him meet a rather shady character, a man we have heard bad things about."

"Your Eminence, Rome is not a monastery…"

"*Sufficit!* We had made an agreement: you were to keep me informed of your conversations with Father Nil and how his personal research was progressing. No research can be *personal* in the Catholic Church: any thinking, any discovery must be useful to it. I've stopped getting any reports from you, and those you have sent me are, to put it mildly, far from informative. We know that Father Nil is heading in a dangerous direction, and we know that he is keeping you up to date with his work. Why, Monsignor, are you choosing the path of adventure rather than that of the Church, to whom you belong and who is a mother to you?"

Leeland lowered his head. What could he say in reply to the man in front of him?

"Your Eminence, I don't understand much about the scholarly work of Father Nil…"

Catzinger interrupted him sharply.

"I'm not asking you to understand, but to report on what you hear. It's painful for me to have to remind you, but you're in no position to choose."

He leant across the table, opened the folder and slid it over to Leeland.

"Do you recognize these photos? Here you're in the company of one of your monks at St Mary's at the time you were the Father Abbot. Here" – he waved a black-and-white photo in front of Leeland's nose – "you are face to face in the Abbey garden, and the look you are exchanging with him is pretty eloquent. And here" – this time the photo was in colour – "you're at his side, seen from behind, and your hand is placed on his shoulder. Between two monks, such postures are indecent."

Leeland had turned pale, and his heart thumped in his chest. *Anselm!* The purity, the beauty, the nobility of Brother Anselm! Never would this Cardinal understand anything of the feelings that had brought them together. But never would he allow himself to be sullied by that pop-eyed stare, or those words emerging from a mouth of rigid, icy marble.

"Your Eminence, I have proved – as you know full well – that nothing happened between myself and Brother Anselm that affected our vow of chastity. Never an act, or even the hint of an act, contrary to Christian ethics!"

"Monsignor, Christian chastity is not violated by acts alone; it has its seat in the mastery of one's mind, heart and soul. You failed in your vow by evil thoughts, as your correspondence with Brother Anselm" – he showed Leeland a dozen letters that had been carefully sorted under the photos – "abundantly proves. By abusing the authority that you had over him, you led this unfortunate brother towards a dangerous inclination, one that bubbles away inside you – even mentioning it fills me, as a priest, with horror."

Leeland blushed to the roots of his hair and stiffened. "How did they get hold of those letters?" he thought. "Anselm, my poor friend, what did they do to you?"

"Your Eminence, those letters contain nothing other than the evidence of the affection between a monk and his superior – an affection that was intense, admittedly, but chaste."

"You're joking! These photos, plus these letters, and finally your public stance on married priests, all come together to show that you have fallen into such a state of moral depravity that we have been obliged to shelter you behind the rank of a bishop so as to avoid a dreadful scandal in the United States. The Catholic Church in America is going through a terrible period right now, repeated cases of paedophilia have seriously undermined its credit among the faithful. Imagine what the press would do to us with that information! They'd be baying for blood. 'St Mary's Abbey, an outpost of Sodom and Gomorrah!' I've buried you away in the protective shadow of the Vatican and persuaded the journalists not to harass you personally – and it cost us a lot of money. This file, Monsignor…"

He carefully placed the photos on the pile of letters, and closed the folder with a peremptory gesture.

"…this file, well, I won't be able to keep it secret for much longer if you don't fulfil our contract in such a way as to keep me satisfied. From now on, you'll keep me informed directly of any progress in the work of your French colleague. In addition, by seeing that he meets nobody else in Rome other than yourself, you'll be ensuring your own safety as much as his. *Capito?*"

When Leeland found himself in the long empty corridor, he had to lean for a moment against the wall. He was panting: the effort he had just made to master his feelings had left him exhausted, and his T-shirt was sticking to his chest. Gradually he got a grip on himself, walked down the grand marble staircase and emerged from the Congregation building. Like an automaton, he turned right, following the first of the three steps that go round Bernini's colonnade. Then right again, and he headed towards the Via Aurelia. His head was empty, and he walked without looking to either side.

He had the impression he had been physically crushed by the Cardinal. Anselm! Could they know, could they even understand what love is? For these men of the Church, love seemed to be nothing more than a word, a category as devoid of content as a political programme. How can anyone love the invisible God when you have never loved a creature of flesh and blood? How could you be a "universal brother" if you are not your brother's brother?

Not quite knowing how he had got there, he found himself in front of the door to his apartment block, and walked up the three flights of stairs. To his great surprise, he found Nil sitting on a step, his bag between his legs.

"I couldn't stay in San Girolamo without doing anything – that monastery is a gloomy place. I needed to talk to someone, so I came to wait..."

Without a word, he ushered him into the living room. He too needed to talk – but would he be able to force off the iron hoop crushing his chest?

He sat down and poured himself a glass of bourbon: his face was still very pale. Nil gazed at him, his head leaning to one side.

"Remby, my friend... what's happening? You look distraught."

Leeland nursed his glass between the palms of his hands, and for a moment closed his eyes. "Am I going to be able to tell him?" he thought. Then he took another sip and addressed a shy smile to Nil. "He's my only friend now." He could no longer stand the duplicity to which he had been constrained ever since his arrival in Rome. With an effort, he began to speak:

"You know I was very young when I entered St Mary's conservatory, and that I went straight from the schoolroom to the novitiate. I had experienced nothing of life, Nil, and chastity was no burden since I didn't know what passion was. The year I took my vows, a young man entered the novitiate; like me he came from the conservatory and like me he was as innocent as a newborn child. I'm a pianist, he was a violinist. Music brought us together to begin with, then something of which I knew nothing, something against which I had no defences, something they never talk about in the monastery: love. I needed years to identify this feeling that was so new to me, to understand that the happiness I felt in his presence was love. For the first time in my life, I was in love! And I was loved, as I found out on the day when Anselm and I opened our hearts to each other. I loved a younger monk, Nil, someone like a clear spring flowing from a pure source... and I was loved by him!"

Nil stirred, but restrained from interrupting him.

"When I became the Abbot of the monastery, our relationship deepened. My election as Abbot meant that he had become my son in the sight of God; my love for him was tinged by a boundless tenderness..."

Two tears trickled down his cheeks – he wouldn't be able to go on. Nil took the glass out of his hands and placed it on the piano. He hesitated for a moment.

"That mutual love, that love of which you were both aware – did you express it in the form of any physical contact?"

Leeland looked up at him, his eyes swimming in tears.

"Never! Never, you hear me – if it's anything vulgar you're alluding to. I breathed in his presence, I perceived every vibration of his being, but our bodies never indulged in any coarse contact. I never stopped being a monk, and he never stopped being as pure as crystal. We loved each other, Nil, and knowing this was enough for us to be happy. From that day on, I understood the love of God better, and grew closer to it. Perhaps the beloved disciple and Jesus experienced something similar, all that time ago?"

Nil pulled a face. One shouldn't mix everything together, but stick to the facts.

"If *nothing happened* between you, if there was never any act and thus no matter for sin – I'm sorry, but that's the way the theologians argue – what is Catzinger concerned about? You've just come from his office, haven't you?"

"I once wrote some letters in which this love is evident – I don't know what pressures the Vatican exerted to get their hands on them – with two innocent photos in which Anselm and I are side by side. You know the Church's obsession with everything to do with sex: this was enough to feed their sick imagination, to accuse me of moral depravity, to sully a feeling that they can't understand and cover it with mud, make it stink. Are those prelates still human beings, Nil? I doubt it, they've never experienced the wound of love that brings a man to life, makes him really human."

"So," persisted Nil, "it's you Catzinger is pressurizing now. But do you know why? What has he told you, why are you so upset?"

Leeland lowered his head and replied in a murmur:

"On the day you arrived in Rome, he told me to go and see him. And he ordered me to report all our conversations to him, or else he'd throw me to the wolves in the press. I'll survive, perhaps, but Anselm is without defence, he doesn't have the strength to stand up to the mob, I know it will destroy him.

Just because I have experienced love, because I have dared to love, they asked me to spy on you, Nil!"

Once the first moment of surprise had passed, Nil stood up and poured himself a glass of bourbon. Now he could understand his friend's ambiguous attitude, his sudden silences. It all started to become clear: the documents stolen from his cell on the banks of the Loire must have landed on a desk in the Congregation very soon after. His summons to Rome on an artificial pretext, his meeting up with Leeland, it had all been planned out and arranged in advance. Had he been spied on? Yes, in the Abbey, immediately following the death of Father Andrei. Once he had come to Rome, poor Rembert had merely been a pawn on a chessboard in which he was the central piece.

He was deep in thought, but he soon came to a decision.

"Rembert, my research and Andrei's seem to be upsetting rather a lot of people. Ever since I discovered the presence of a thirteenth apostle in the upper room, next to Jesus, and the way he was relentlessly excluded by a deliberate and tenacious effort of will, things have been happening that I would have thought were no longer possible in the twentieth century. As far as the Church is concerned, I have become a black sheep because I have finally accepted what cannot be admitted, however convincing the proof: Jesus's transformation into Christ-God was an imposture. And also because I have discovered a hidden face to the personality of the first pope, and the manoeuvring for power at the origins of the Church. They won't let me carry on down this path: I'm now convinced that it was because he started down it that Andrei fell from the Rome express. I want to avenge his death, and only the truth will avenge it. Are you ready to come with me, all the way?"

Without hesitating, Leeland replied, in a hoarse voice:

"You want to avenge your dead friend, and I want to avenge my living friend, who is now reduced to shame and silence in my own abbey: he hasn't written to me for months. I want to avenge the way we have been spattered in mud, and the way something much too innocent to be understood by the men in the Vatican has been annihilated. Yes, I'm with you, Nil – at last we're back together again!"

Nil leant back in his chair and emptied his glass with a grimace. "I'm starting to drink like a cowboy!" he thought. Suddenly, he relaxed: once again he could share everything with his friend. Only action would allow them to escape being caught.

"I want to find that epistle. But I have a few questions about Lev Barjona: our meeting wasn't a matter of chance, it was deliberately arranged. Who fixed it, and why?"

"Lev is a friend, I trust him."

"But he's a Jew, and he's been a member of Mossad. As he told us, the Israelis know the letter exists, and perhaps they even know what it contains, since Ygael Yadin read it and spoke of it before he died. Who else is in the know? It seems that the Vatican doesn't know that the epistle is somewhere within its walls. Why did Lev drop that item of information? A man like him never does anything lightly."

"I have no idea. But how are you going to find a mere sheet of parchment, maybe jealously protected, or maybe simply gathering dust in some nook? The Vatican is huge, with all the different museums, the libraries, their annexes, the eaves and the basements containing an incredible jumble – from abandoned manuscripts in a cupboard to the copy of the Sputnik that Nikita Khrushchev gave John XXIII. Millions of barely catalogued objects. And this time you have nothing to guide you, not even a classification number."

271

Nil got up and stretched.

"Lev Barjona, perhaps unwittingly, gave us a valuable clue. In order to make use of it, I have just one trump card to play: Breczinsky. That man is a human fortress, barricaded on every side: I have to find some means of breaking through, he's the only one who can help me. Tomorrow we'll go and work in the stacks as usual, and you will let me take the necessary steps."

Nil was leaving the studio: Mukhtar took off his headphones and rewound the tapes. One was for Calfo. He slipped the other into an envelope that he would take to the Egyptian embassy. Thanks to the diplomatic bag, it would be in the hands of the Supreme Guide at the Al-Azhar University the following morning.

His lips pursed in disgust. Not only was the American in cahoots with Nil, but he was a queer. Neither of them deserved to live.

73

That same evening, Calfo called an extraordinary meeting of the Society of St Pius V. It would be brief, but events required that the Twelve demonstrate their total solidarity around their crucified Master.

The Rector glanced over at the twelfth apostle: his eyes modestly lowered under his cowl, Antonio was waiting for the session to begin. Calfo had given him the task of putting pressure on Breczinsky, and had pointed out the Pole's weak point: why hadn't the Spaniard come to report to him, as had been arranged? Might his trust in one of the twelve apostles be misplaced? This would be the first time that had ever happened.

He brushed away this disagreeable thought. Ever since his celebration, the night before, kneeling before Sonia transformed into a living icon, he had been afloat on a tide of euphoria. The Romanian girl had finally accepted all of his demands, keeping her nun's cornet on her delicate little head right until the end.

Emboldened by this success, he had, on sending her away, informed her that next time he would be organizing an even more suggestive act of worship, that would unite them on a very intimate level with the sacrifice of the Lord. When he explained to her the ritual that he wanted her to join him in, Sonia had turned pale, and then fled.

He wasn't worried: she'd be back, she had never refused him anything. This evening he needed to get through this meeting pretty quickly, so that he could return home where long and meticulous preparations needed to be done. He rose to his feet and cleared his throat.

"My brothers, the current mission is taking an unexpected and very satisfying turn. I've managed to get Lev Barjona, who is at present giving a series of concerts at the Academy of Santa Cecilia, to meet Father Nil. Actually, my intervention was superfluous: the Israeli intended to meet our monk in any event, which shows the extent to which Mossad too is interested in his research. In short, they've met, and in his conversations with the inoffensive intellectual, Lev casually dropped the information we had so long been looking for: the letter of the thirteenth apostle has not disappeared. There is indeed a copy in existence, and it is very probably in the Vatican."

A quiver ran through the gathering, expressive of its stupefaction as well as its excitement. One of the Twelve raised his crossed forearms.

"How can that be possible? We suspected that a copy of that epistle had escaped our vigilance, but... in the Vatican!"

"We are here at the centre of Christendom, an immense web whose strands cover the whole planet. Everything ends up in the Vatican one day or another, including ancient manuscripts or texts discovered here or there: this is what must have happened in this case. Lev Barjona didn't give away this information for free: he must be hoping that it will arouse Father Nil's curiosity and lead him to this document, which the Jews covet as much as we do."

"Brother Rector, is it necessary for us to run the risk of exhuming this letter? Oblivion has, as you know, always been the Church's most powerful weapon against the thirteenth apostle, oblivion alone has ensured that his pernicious testimony remained harmless. Isn't it better to prolong this salutary amnesia?"

The Rector seized this opportunity to remind the Eleven of the grandeur of their task. He solemnly extended his right hand, showing off the jasper of his ring.

"After the Council of Trent, St Pius V – the Dominican Antonio Ghislieri – was dismayed by the weakening of the Catholic Church, and did all in his power to save it from the shipwreck he sensed it was heading for. The most serious threat did not come from Luther's recent rebellion, but from an old rumour that even the Inquisition had not managed to stifle: the tomb containing Christ's bones existed and could be found somewhere in the deserts of the Near East. A lost epistle by a privileged witness of the Lord's last moments claimed that not only had Jesus not risen from the dead, but that his body had in fact been buried by the Essenes in that region. You know all this, don't you?"

The Eleven nodded.

"Before becoming Pope, Ghislieri had been Grand Inquisitor: he had learnt of the interrogations of the dissidents burnt alive for heresy, he had consulted certain minutes of the Templars' trial, all documents that have now disappeared. He became convinced of the existence of Jesus's tomb, and realized that its discovery would mean the definitive end of the Church. It was then, in 1570, that he created our Society, to preserve the secret of the tomb."

They knew this too. Sensing their impatience, the Rector lifted his ring, which shed a brief gleam in the light of the wall lamps.

"Ghislieri ordered this episcopal ring in the shape of a coffin to be cut from a very pure jasper. Since that time, its shape has reminded every rector – when he removes it from the finger of his dead predecessor – of the nature of our mission: to ensure that *no coffin* containing the bones of the Crucified of Jerusalem can ever be discovered."

"But," one of the brothers asked, "if the echo of the thirteenth apostle's letter has come down through the centuries, nothing proves that it indicates the exact location of the tomb. The desert is vast, and the sands have covered everything for ages!"

"Indeed, there was no risk of Jesus's tomb being discovered so long as the desert was crossed by nothing more than camels. But the conquest of space has placed at our disposal extraordinarily sophisticated means of research. If they've been able to detect traces of water on a distant planet like Mars, they can also these days pick out all the bones in the deserts of the Negev and Idumaea, even those covered by sand. This is something that Pope Ghislieri could not have imagined. If the existence of the tomb becomes public knowledge, hundreds of radar planes or space probes will start to comb the desert from Jerusalem to the Dead Sea. The sudden emergence of space technology creates a new risk, one that we cannot afford to run. We need to get our hands on that abominable document, and quickly, since the Israelis are on the same track as we are."

He devoutly raised the jasper coffin to his lips, before hiding his hands under the sleeves of his alb.

"This explosive document must be placed in the shelter of the casket opposite us. We need to find it, not only to place it out of reach of our enemies, but also to obtain, thanks to its presence here, financial resources that will enable us to fulfil our ambition: to stem the drift of the West. You know how the Templars managed to acquire their immense fortune; the relic that we venerate every Friday 13th reminds us of it. This fortune can become ours, and we shall use it to preserve the divine identity of Our Lord."

"What do you have in mind, Brother Rector?"

"Father Nil has picked up the scent of what might be the right trail: let's leave him to follow it. I've reinforced the surveillance around him: if he succeeds, we'll be the first to know. And then…"

The Rector knew that he did not need to finish his sentence. "And then" had already happened thousands of times, in the cellars of the palaces of the Inquisition whose walls were drenched with pain, or on the stakes erected to light up Christendom all throughout its history. In the present case, only the practical details of this "and then" would change. Nil would not be burned in public – Andrei had not been.

74

The sun was caressing the flagstones on the courtyard of the Belvedere when Nil and Leeland entered it. Relieved that he had told Nil those things about his private life, the American had slipped back into his usual playful demeanour, and throughout their walk he had talked of nothing but their youthful student days in Rome. It was ten o'clock when they presented themselves at the door of the stacks.

One hour earlier, a priest in a cassock had preceded them. Seeing his accreditation signed by Cardinal Catzinger in person, the policeman had bowed and deferentially accompanied him to the reinforced door, where Breczinsky, looking anxious, was waiting for him. This second interview had been brief, like the first one. As he left, the priest had fastened his black eyes on the Pole, whose lower lip was trembling.

Nil no longer paid much attention to his very pale, almost transparent face: on arrival he did not notice that the librarian looked distressed, and merely set the equipment out on the table while Leeland went off to fetch the manuscripts they would need to examine.

After an hour's work, he took off his gloves and whispered:

"Carry on without me, I'm going to try my luck with Breczinsky."

Leeland nodded in silence, and Nil went to knock on the librarian's door.

"Come in, Father, take a seat."

Breczinsky seemed happy to see him.

"You didn't tell me anything about your research in the Templars' book stack the other day – did you discover anything useful?"

"Better than that, Father: I found the text examined by Andrei, the one he'd noted the details of in his diary."

He took a deep breath and launched out:

"Thanks to my deceased brother, I'm on the trail of a document of capital importance that might put a question mark over the foundations of our Catholic faith. Forgive me if I don't tell you any more: ever since I arrived in Rome, Mgr Leeland has been subjected to considerable pressures because of me, and if I keep quiet, it's because I'm trying to ensure you don't get bothered in any way."

Breczinsky gazed at him in silence, then asked, timidly:

"But… who can exert such pressures on a bishop working in the Vatican?"

Nil decided to gamble everything. He remembered a remark the Pole had made at their first meeting: "To think that I imagined you were one of Catzinger's men!"

"From the Congregation for the Doctrine of the Faith, and more precisely from the Cardinal Prefect himself."

"*Catzinger!*"

The Pole mopped his brow; his hands were trembling slightly.

"You don't know anything about that man's past, or about what he lived through!"

Nil concealed his surprise.

"Yes, I don't know anything about him, except that he's the third principle person in the Church, after the Secretary of State and the Pope."

Breczinsky looked at him with his hangdog eyes.

"Father Nil, you've gone too far, now you need to know. What I'm about to tell you is something I've only ever told Father Andrei, since he was the only person who could understand. His family had been linked with the sufferings of mine. I didn't need to explain things to him; he understood straight away."

Nil held his breath.

"When the Germans broke the German-Soviet Pact, the Wehrmacht swept across what had been Poland. For some months the *Anschluss* division protected the rear of the invading army around Brest-Litovsk and, in April 1940, one of its superior officers, an *Oberstleutnant*, came to round up all the men in my village. My father was taken away with them into the forest, and we never saw him again."

"Yes, you told me."

"Then the *Anschluss* division joined the Eastern Front, and my mother tried to survive in the village with me, helped by Father Andrei's family. Two years later, we saw the last remnants of the German Army fleeing in the other direction as the Russians advanced. It was no longer the glorious Wehrmacht, but a gang of pillagers raping all the women and burning everything in their path. I was five; one day, my mother took me by the hand, she was terror-stricken: 'Hide in the cellar, it's the officer who took your father away, he's back!' Through the gap in the door, I saw a German officer come in. Without a word he unbuckled his belt, flung himself on my mother, and raped her right in front of my eyes."

Nil was horrified.

"Did you ever find out the officer's name?"

"As you can imagine, I was never able to forget it and never abandoned my quest to trace him: he died shortly afterwards, killed by Polish resistants. It was *Oberstleutnant* Herbert von Catzinger, the father of the current Cardinal Prefect of the Congregation for the Doctrine of the Faith."

Nil opened his mouth, but was incapable of uttering a word. Opposite him, Breczinsky seemed distraught. With an effort, he continued:

"After the war, Catzinger became Cardinal of Vienna. He asked a Spaniard from Opus Dei to carry out research in the Austrian and Polish archives, and he discovered that his father, for whom he had a boundless admiration, had been killed by Polish partisans. Ever since then, he has hated me, just as he hates all Poles."

"But... the Pope is Polish!"

"You can't understand: all those forced to experience Nazism, even unwillingly, were deeply marked by it. The old member of the Hitler Youth, the son of a Wehrmacht soldier killed by the Polish resistance, has rejected his past but he has not forgotten it: *nobody emerged from that hell intact.* As for the Polish Pope whose right-hand man he now is, I'm certain he has overcome his visceral aversion and has a sincere veneration for him. But he knows that I come from a village in which the *Anschluss* division was stationed, and he knows about my father's death."

"And… about your mother?"

Breczinsky wiped his eyes with the back of his hand.

"No, he can't know about that – I was the only witness, and his father's memory is intact. But *I know*. I can't… I just can't forgive, Father Nil!"

Nil's heart was filled with an immense sense of pity.

"You cannot forgive the father… or the son?"

Breczinsky replied in a whisper:

"Neither of them. For years, the Holy Father's illness has enabled the Cardinal to do – or allow to be done – things that go right against the spirit of the Gospels. He wants to restore the Church of bygone centuries, he is obsessed by what he calls 'the world order'. Under an appearance of modernity, it's a return to the iron age. I have seen theologians, priests and monks reduced to nothing, crushed by the Vatican with the same absence of pity which his father once showed towards the peoples enslaved by the Reich. You tell me he's been putting pressure on Mgr Leeland? It's not as if your friend were the only one, alas… I'm just an insignificant little pebble, but like the others I must be crushed so that the pedestal which supports the Doctrine and the Faith does not become cracked."

"Why you? Buried away in the silence of your stacks you don't bother anyone, you're not a threat to any of the powers that be!"

"But I'm one of the Pope's men, and the post I fill here is a more sensitive one than you can imagine. I... I can't tell you any more."

His shoulders were trembling slightly. He got a grip on himself and continued:

"I have never recovered from what I suffered as a result of the actions of Herbert von Catzinger, the wound has never closed – and the Cardinal knows this. Every night I wake in a cold sweat, haunted by the image of my father being led off into the forest at sub-machine-gun point, and those boots that forced my mother's body against our kitchen table. You can chain a man by threat, but you can also enslave him by keeping his sufferings fresh: you just have to revive his pain, make the wound bleed. Only someone who has known those men of bronze can understand, and this was Andrei's case. Ever since I entered the Pope's service here, I have been trampled under at every moment by two shiny boots, and Catzinger in his scarlet robes stands over me – just as his father, strapped into his uniform, once swaggered over my mother and his Polish slaves."

Nil was starting to understand. Breczinsky had never managed to escape from the cellar of his childhood, huddled down against the door behind which his mother was being raped. Never had he emerged from a certain forest path down which he advanced in a dream, behind his father who was about to die, cut down by a burst of sub-machine-gun fire. Night and day he was haunted by two waxed boots against a table, and deafened by the echo within him of the guttural order given by Herbert von Catzinger: "*Feuer!*"

His father had been cut down by German bullets in that forest, but Breczinsky himself never ceased to fall, to fall forever down into a dark, bottomless well. This man was one of the living dead. Nil hesitated:

"Does… the Cardinal come here, in person, to torment you by reminding you of your past? I can't believe that."

"Oh no, he doesn't act directly. He sends the Spaniard here, the one who carried out research for him in the Vienna archives. Right now, the man in question is in Rome, he's come to see me twice recently, he… he tortures me. He dresses as a priest – but if he really is a priest of Jesus Christ, then, Father Nil, it can only mean that the Church is finished. He has no soul, no human feelings."

There was a long silence, and Nil let Breczinsky continue.

"You can see why I helped Father Andrei, and why I'm helping you. Like you, he told me he was looking for an important document: he wanted at all costs to keep it out of Catzinger's hands, and give it to the Pope in person."

Nil thought quickly: not for an instant had he reflected on what he would do if he found the letter of the thirteenth apostle. Indeed, it was for the Pope to judge whether the future of the Church was compromised by its contents, and to do with it what he thought best.

"Andrei was right. I still don't know why, but it's clear that what I have discovered is an object that many people covet. If I manage to find this document lost for centuries, I do intend to alert the Pope and inform him of its whereabouts. Only the head of the Church can be the keeper of this secret, as he has been of the secrets of Fatima. I've just learnt that it could be buried away somewhere in the Vatican: think about it!"

"The Vatican is huge: don't you have any clues?"

"Just one, and it's a slender lead. If it has indeed come to Rome, as I believe, it must be somewhere among the Dead Sea manuscripts it was found with. The Vatican will have received it after the Israeli War of Independence, around 1948. Do you have any idea of the place where Essenian manuscripts from Qumran might be kept, the ones that have not yet been examined?"

Breczinsky rose to his feet. He looked worn out.

"I can't say right away, I need to think. Come and see me here in my office tomorrow afternoon: there won't be anyone apart from you and Mgr Leeland. But I beg you not to tell him about our conversation, I shouldn't have told you all this."

Nil reassured him: he could trust him, just as he had trusted Father Andrei. Their objective was the same: to inform the Pope.

75

"I raise my glass to the day the last Jewish settler leaves Palestine!"

"And I raise mine to the definitive establishment of the Greater Israel!"

The two men smiled before draining their glasses. Lev Barjona suddenly turned scarlet and choked.

"By my tefillin, Mukhtar Al-Quraysh, what the hell is it? Arab petrol?"

"*Centerbe*. A liqueur from the Abruzzi. Seventy degrees – a kind of drink that sorts out the men from the boys."

Ever since they had spared one another's lives on the battlefield, a strange complicity had grown between the Palestinian and the Israeli – of the sort that once existed between the officers of regular enemy armies, and as sometimes exists between adverse politicians or executives of big rival groups. Fighting in the shadows, they feel at ease only with their peers, who are engaged in the same conflicts as they are. They despise the society of ordinary civilians, their dull, flat lives.

More often than not they are locked in fierce confrontation with each other – but when they are not fighting, they won't refuse to share a glass, a girl or two, or a common operation, if the opportunity of some neutral terrain arises.

The present opportunity was provided by Mgr Calfo. He had proposed that they carry out one of those operations that the Church does not like to perform or even officially to admit – the sort where you get your hands dirty. *Ecclesia sanguinem abhorret* – the Church hates blood. Unable to get its dirty work done for it by a secular arm that tended to ignore it, the Church was now constrained to call in independent agents. These were usually men of the European extreme right. But they could not refuse the lure of media exposure, and always asked for their services to be rewarded with tiresome political manoeuvrings. Calfo appreciated the fact that Mukhtar had only asked for dollars, and that the two men had left no trace behind them. They had been as discreet as a breath of wind.

"Mukhtar, why did you ask me to meet you here? You know that if we were seen together it would be considered by our respective bosses as an extremely grave professional failing."

"Come on, Lev, Mossad has countless agents, they're all over the place. But not here: this restaurant only serves pork, and I know the manager – if he knew you were Jewish, you wouldn't be able to stay under his roof for a minute longer. We haven't met since the Germigny slab was brought to Rome, but you've just met our two scholar monks, and I listen in on them regularly. We need to talk."

"I'm all ears…"

Mukhtar signalled to the manager to leave the flagon of *centerbe* on the table.

"Let's not beat around the bush, Lev. We're playing the same game here. But I don't know everything, and it bugs me: the

Frenchman is starting to poke his nose into the Koran – there are things that Muslims won't tolerate, you know. Let me make this clear: I'm not just on this mission for Mgr Calfo, Hamas is concerned too. But what's less clear to me is the reason why you've got personal about it, meeting up with Nil and casually letting him in on information that's worth its weight in gold."

"Are you asking me why we're interested in that lost epistle?"

"Exactly: how does this story about the thirteenth apostle concern the Jews?"

Lev drummed his fingers nervously on the marble table: the *pizze al maiale* were a long time in coming.

"The fundamentalists in Likud keep a close eye on everything that's said in the Catholic Church about the Bible. For them, it's essential that Christians are never able to cast doubt on the divinity of Jesus Christ. We have intercepted information that Father Andrei was allowing to leak out to people in Rome and to his European colleagues. This was in fact the reason why I was authorized to join you in the Rome express operation. It was high time – that scholar had discovered certain things that worry the folks in Meah Shearim."

"But *why*, in the name of the jinn? What difference does it make to you whether the Christians suddenly realize that they've fabricated a false God, or rather a second God, for themselves? The Koran has been condemning them for that over the last thirteen centuries. On the contrary, you ought to be satisfied that they're finally admitting that Jesus was nothing other than a Jewish prophet, just as Muhammad says."

"You know full well, Mukhtar, that we're fighting for our Jewish identity on every level, not just that of territory. If the

Catholic Church were to question his divinity and recognized that Jesus never ceased to be anything other than a very great prophet, what would distinguish us from the Church? If Christianity turned back into something Jewish, went back to its historical origins – it would swallow up Judaism. Christians venerating the Jewish Jesus instead of worshipping their Christ-God would be a peril for the Jewish people, a risk that we can't allow ourselves to run. Especially since they'll immediately claim that Jesus is greater than Moses, that with him the Torah loses all its value – even though he taught quite the opposite: that he had come, not to abolish the Law, but to fulfil it. A Jewish prophet proposing a law more perfect than that of Moses: you know what Christians are like, the temptation would be too strong. They weren't able to get rid of us with their pogroms, but assimilation would wipe us out. The fire of the crematoria has purified us: if Jesus is no longer God, if he becomes Jewish again, Judaism will soon be nothing more than an annex of Christianity, chewed up, swallowed and soon digested in the Church's hungry belly. That's why research like Father Nil's worries us."

Two huge pizzas smelling appetizingly of fried bacon had just been set before them. Mukhtar tucked into his hungrily.

"Just try a mouthful of that and tell me what you think. And at least we'll know why we're going to end up in hell. Mmm... The big problem with you Jews is your paranoia. You go looking for things to worry about everywhere – going too far for us! But I know what you're like, and from your point of view you're right. Above all, no cosying up to the Christians, or you'll be diluted like a drop of water in the sea. Let the Pope shed tears at the Wailing Wall, but then everyone goes back to his own home. Agreed. Anyway, what are you going to do if little Nil persists in rummaging around?"

"I got rapped on the knuckles when I tried... well, let's just say I tried to put a stop to his work somewhat prematurely. Instructions are to let him carry on, and see what comes out of it. This is Calfo's policy too. By meeting the little French monk and talking to him, I've given him a nudge in the right direction – and perhaps, that way, he'll find what we're all looking for. What's more, Nil likes Rachmaninov, which proves he's a man of taste."

"You seem to like him?"

Lev swallowed a big mouthful of *pizza al maiale* and licked his lips: these goyim really knew how to cook pork.

"I think he's really nice, and even rather touching. This is something you Arabs can't understand, since Muhammad never understood a thing about the prophets of Judaism. Nil is like Leeland, they're both idealists, spirituals sons of Elijah – the hero and model for all Jews."

"I don't know if Muhammad understood anything about your prophets, but I've certainly understood Muhammad: the infidels must not live."

Lev pushed away his empty plate.

"You're a Quraysh and I'm a Barjona – a descendent of the Zealots who once upon a time terrorized the Romans. Like you, I'm defending our values and our tradition, unhesitatingly: the Zealots were also called *sicarii* because of their virtuosity at handling the dagger and their technique of disembowelling their enemies. But while I like Nil, Leeland has been my friend for twenty years. Don't do anything to them without warning me first."

"Your Leeland has been walking hand in hand with the Frenchman, he knows nearly as much as him. And then, he's a queer – our religion condemns men like him! As for the other guy, if he so much as touches the Koran and its Prophet, nothing will stop God's justice."

"Rembert, a queer? You're kidding! These men are pure, Mukhtar, I am certain of my friend's integrity. What goes on inside his head is something else, but the Koran only condemns acts; it doesn't go rummaging round in the brain. This mission concerns the integrity of the three monotheisms: don't touch a hair on their heads without warning me. In any case, if you want to apply Koranic law to them, you're not going to manage without me: it was child's play in the Rome express, but in the middle of this city it's going to be more difficult. Mossad leaves fewer traces behind it than Hamas does, as you know perfectly well... Here your methods are out of place."

When they went their separate ways, the flagon of *centerbe* was empty. But the two men walked down the deserted street as steadily as if they'd been drinking nothing but spring water.

76

Since daybreak, Sonia had been walking straight ahead, mechanically. She was mulling over what Calfo had asked her to do for him the next week: she wouldn't be able to go through with it. "I'm nothing more than a prostitute now, but that's just too much." She needed to talk to someone, she needed to share her distress. Mukhtar? He'd send her back to Saudi Arabia. He'd confiscated her passport and shown her photos of her family, photos taken recently in Romania. Her sisters and her parents would be threatened, they would pay dearly on her behalf if she didn't behave. She wiped her eyes and blew her nose.

She had been walking up the left bank of the Tiber, and realized that she had just passed a crossroads: it was busy at this time of the morning. At the end of a broad, clear street that turned off towards the Capitoline, two ancient temples and the pediment of the Teatro di Marcello were visible. She didn't want to go in that direction. There would be tourists, and she needed to be alone. She crossed the road: opposite her, the gate of Santa Maria in Cosmedin was open. She went through it and passed the Bocca della Verità without a glance; then she went into the church.

She had never been here before, and was struck by the beauty of the mosaics. There was no iconostasis, but the church very much resembled those she had frequented in her youth. There was a peaceful and mysterious atmosphere in here, the Christ in glory was the same as that of the Orthodox, and so was the fragrance of incense hanging in the air. Mass had just been celebrated at the main altar, and a choirboy was extinguishing the candles one by one. She went up and kneeled in the front row of the pews, on the left.

"A priest – I'd like to talk to a priest. Catholics respect the secrets of confession too, just as our priests at home."

At that very minute a priest was emerging through the door on the left – the sacristy, no doubt. He was wearing a broad surplice in white lace, without any particular distinguishing signs. His round, smooth face was that of a baby, but his white hair showed him to be a man of experience. She raised to him eyes made red by a night spent weeping, and was struck by the gentleness of his gaze. In an unthinking outburst, she straightened up as he walked by.

"Father…"

He looked her up and down.

"Father, I'm Orthodox… can I still make my confession to you?"

He smiled kindly at her: he very much liked the rare occasions when he could exercise his ministry of mercy in anonymity.

The light reflected from the golden mosaics conferred on Sonia's face, haggard with stress, the beauty of the Sienese Primitives.

"I won't be able to give you sacramental absolution, my child, but God himself will comfort you... Come this way."

She was surprised to find herself on her knees in front of him, without any grille or obstacle, in the Roman way. Her face was a few inches away from his...

"Well now, what do you have to tell me..."

As she started to speak, she had the impression that a weight was being lifted from her chest. She told him of the woman who had recruited her in Romania, then the Palestinian who had sent her to the harem of the Saudi dignitary. Finally Rome and the chubby little man, a Catholic prelate who had to be satisfied at all costs.

The priest's face suddenly moved away from hers, and his eyes narrowed.

"This Catholic prelate – do you know his name?"

"No, Father, but he must be a bishop: he wears a curious ring, of a kind I've never seen before. It looks a bit like a coffin – a jewel in the shape of a coffin."

The priest quickly slipped the gemstone of the episcopal ring he wore on his finger round so that it was hidden in his palm, and hid his right hand in the folds of his surplice. Sonia, absorbed in her confession, had not noticed this furtive gesture.

"A bishop... how dreadful! And you say that he makes you do..."

With some difficulty, Sonia told him of the scene in front of the Byzantine icon, the nun's cornet tightly fitted to her head, her naked body offered to the man kneeling behind her on the prie-dieu, murmuring incomprehensible words about union with the Unspeakable.

The priest brought his face closer to hers.

"And you tell me that, next time you go to see him, he wants…"

She related what the bishop had explained to her when he sent her away, causing her to flee in horror from his apartment. The priest's face was now almost touching hers, and had become as hard as the marble on the Cosmatesque flagstones on which she was kneeling. He spoke slowly, separating out each word:

"My child, God forgives you, as you have been abused by one of his representatives on earth and you had no choice. In His name, I today give you His peace. But you must not – you hear me: *you must not* – agree to go to the next meeting with this prelate: what he is making you do is an abominable blasphemy against Our Saviour Jesus Christ crucified."

Sonia lifted her distraught face towards him.

"That's impossible! What will happen to me if I don't obey? I can't leave Rome, my passport…"

"Nothing will happen to you. First because God is protecting you, your confession has shown him that your soul is pure. I'm bound by the secret of the confessional, as you know. But I know a few people in Rome, and without betraying this secret I can make sure nothing happens to you. You have, alas, fallen into the hands of a perverse bishop, who has made himself unworthy of the ring he wears. The coffin adorning his criminal hand symbolizes the spiritual death which has already befallen him. But you are also in God's hands – trust in him. Don't go and see that bishop on the day you mentioned."

* * *

The unexpected encounter with the priest was for Sonia like God's answer to her prayer. For the first time since she had rushed down the stairs of Calfo's apartment, she could breathe freely. This unknown priest had listened to her kindly, he had assured her of God's forgiveness! Delivered of the burden that had been crushing her, she seized his hand and kissed it as the Orthodox do. She did not notice that it was his left hand – his right hand was still obstinately thrust into his surplice.

As she headed towards the exit, the priest rose and went back into the sacristy. First he put his episcopal ring, bearing the arms of St Peter, back in its place. Then he took off his surplice to show his broad scarlet belt. With a precise gesture, he smoothed down his white hair and placed on the crown of his head a skullcap of the same colour, the Cardinal's scarlet.

Up until now, Catzinger had been dealt a less good hand of cards than the Neapolitan. Without knowing it, Sonia had just slipped in a crucial card. He would use this card: it would be Antonio who would play it, Antonio, that most faithful of servants who had managed to evade the vigilance of the Society of St Pius V – the Andalusian who had never compromised nor deviated from his path, who was as supple as a Toledo blade, bending only in order to spring back into place.

77

Sitting in front of the reinforced door, the papal police officer had let them pass without checking Nil's accreditation: they were well-known faces… Breczinsky took them to their table, where the manuscripts from the previous day were waiting for them.

Nil had told Leeland that they wouldn't be going to the Vatican until just after lunch: he needed to think things over. The trust the Pole had shown him had at first amazed and then scared him. "Has he talked because he's desperately lonely, or because he's manipulating me?" Never before had the quiet teacher from the Loire had to confront such a situation. He had set out to follow the trace of the thirteenth apostle: like him, he now found himself embroiled in conflicts that were too big for him to handle.

Breczinsky had said that he wanted to help him, but what could he do? The Vatican was a huge place; its different museums and libraries must each possess one or several annexes in which thousands of valuable objects lay gathering dust. Somewhere among them, there was perhaps a crate of Napoleon brandy containing an odd assortment of Essene manuscripts – and one sheet, one tiny little sheet of parchment bound by a twirl of linen. The description given by Lev Barjona had remained graven into Nil's memory, but what if the crate had been emptied and its contents dispersed at random by an over-hasty employee?

Around the middle of the afternoon, he took off his gloves.

"Don't ask me any questions: I need to see Breczinsky again."

Leeland acquiesced in silence, and smiled encouragingly at Nil before leaning back over the medieval manuscript that they were examining.

His heart thudding, the Frenchman knocked on the librarian's door.

Breczinsky's face was feverish, and behind his round glasses there were dark shadows under his eyes. He motioned to Nil to take a seat.

"Father, I prayed all night for God to enlighten me, and I have made my decision. What I did for Andrei I will also do for you – but I just have to tell you that I am again infringing the most sacrosanct instructions that were handed on to me when I took on this job. I've decided to go ahead because you've assured me that you're not working against the Pope, and indeed that you intend to communicate all your discoveries to him. Will you swear to do so, before God?"

"I'm only a monk, Father Breczinsky, but I have always sought to be a monk to the last fibre of my being. If what I discover represents a danger for the Church, the Pope will be the only person to know."

"Good… I believe you, just as I believed Andrei. Managing the treasures contained here is just one of my tasks, the only visible one and the least important of them. In the extension to the stacks, there is a room that you won't see on any plan of this set of buildings, and which you won't find mentioned anywhere, since it doesn't officially exist. It was ordered by St Pius V in 1570, just as they were putting the finishing touches to St Peter's Basilica."

"The secret archives of the Vatican?"

Breczinsky smiled.

"The secret archives are perfectly official, they are two floors above us, and their contents are made available to researchers in accordance with public rules. No, this particular room is known to very few people, and since it doesn't exist, it doesn't have a name. If you like, it's the secret collection of the Vatican, and most states across the planet have something similar. It doesn't have an officially appointed librarian – since, as I've already said, it doesn't exist – and its contents are neither classified nor catalogued. It's rather like what French librarians call an *enfer*, a hell – a private collection where sensitive documents are thrust into oblivion, so that they will never come to the attention of historians or journalists. I'm the only person in charge of them, and I answer to the Holy Father. Through the centuries, a great variety of disparate things have accumulated there, on the initiative of a pope or of a cardinal prefect of a dicastery. When anyone decides to send a document to the secret collection, it never emerges again, not even after the death of the person who sent it there. It will never be archived or exhumed."

"Father Breczinsky... why are you revealing the existence of this secret collection to me?"

"Because it's one of the two places in the Vatican where what you are seeking may be found. The other is the secret archives which are made public year by year, fifty years after the facts they concern. Unless a decision is made to the contrary – though this is generally given some official explanation. You have told me that a crate containing manuscripts from the Dead Sea came to the Vatican in 1948 at the time of the first Israeli-Arab war: if it had been classified in the secret archives, it would already have emerged. And if any item in that batch had been deemed too sensitive to be placed in the public domain, I would inevitably have known about it: that sometimes happens, and I then receive a file or a parcel that needs to be placed far from prying eyes in the secret collection. I alone am authorized to do so – and for five years I haven't received anything new, either from the secret archives or anywhere else."

"But... do you ever have a closer look at what you are supposed to classify away, definitively, in this secret collection? Have you ever been curious enough to glance at what your predecessors have been storing away there ever since the end of the sixteenth century?"

Breczinsky replied almost joyfully.

"Pope Wojtyla made me swear an oath never to seek to discover the contents of what was handed to me, or of what is already in that room. In fifteen years, I've only had to go in there three times, to place a new item there. I have been faithful to my oath, but I couldn't help noticing a series of shelves labelled *Dead Sea Manuscripts*. I don't know what's contained in that section of the room. When I talked to Father Andrei about it, after sharing all these same secrets with him, he begged me to let him have a look. Who could I ask for permission to do so? Nobody but the Pope – and it's the Pope whom Andrei and I wished to protect, though he didn't know this. I agreed, and let him look round the room for an hour."

Nil murmured:

"And it was the next day, I imagine, that he left Rome in such a hurry?"

"Yes. He took the Rome express the next day, without telling me a thing. Had he discovered something? Had he spoken to anyone? I don't know."

"But he fell from the Rome express during the night, and it wasn't an accident."

Breczinsky wiped his face with his two hands.

"It wasn't an accident. What I can tell you is that, by carrying on your colleague's work, you have placed yourself in the same perilous position. Your research has led you, as it led him, to the threshold of that non-existent room. I am prepared to let you too enter it, I trust you as I trusted him. Catzinger, and many others too, I fear, are on the same track: if you get to the goal before them, you will be in the same danger as Andrei. There is still time for you to drop it all, Father Nil, to go back to the room next door and carry on examining your harmless medieval manuscript. What is your decision?"

* * *

Nil closed his eyes. He imagined he could see the thirteenth apostle, placed at the right hand of Jesus in the upper room, listening to him with veneration. Then, having become the keeper of a weighty secret, struggling alone against the hatred of Peter and the Twelve, who wanted to remain twelve and to be solely in possession of the monopoly of the information to be transmitted. They condemned him to exile and silence, so that the Church that they were going to erect on top of the falsified memory of Jesus would endure for ever, *alpha and omega*.

The secret had lasted down the centuries before reaching him. Reclining at the table of the last supper, propped on his elbow, the beloved disciple of Jesus was at this minute asking him to take up the torch.

Nil rose.

"Take me there, Father."

They came out of the office. Leeland, bent over the table, didn't even look up when he heard them pass behind him. They walked through the successive rooms of the stacks. Breczinsky opened a little door, and motioned Nil to follow him.

A corridor sloped gently down in front of them. Nil tried to get his bearings. As if he had guessed what he was thinking, Breczinsky whispered:

"Here, we are under the right transept of St Peter's Basilica. The room was dug into the foundations, about forty yards away from the tomb of the Apostle discovered during the excavations ordered by Pius XII under the main altar."

There was a band in the corridor, which then came to a reinforced door. The Polish librarian unbuttoned his Roman collar and took out a little key that he carried on a chain dangling round his neck. Just before opening the door, he looked at his watch.

"It's 5 p.m., the stacks close at six: you have an hour. All our doors can be opened from the inside without a key: the same is true of this one. You just need to push it as you come out, and it will close automatically. Switch off the light before you leave, and come and join me in my office."

The armoured door opened without a sound, Breczinsky slipped his hand in against the inner wall and turned on a switch.

"Make sure you don't damage anything. Good luck!"

Nil went in: the door swung shut behind him with a muffled click.

78

He was standing at the beginning of a long vaulted tunnel, brightly lit. The right-hand wall was bare, in fashioned stone. Nil moved his hand over its surface, and immediately recognized the cutting technique. It was not the chisels of medieval masons, or the saw marks of recent times. The regular traces of the chisel marks and the way they were spaced out were the signature of Renaissance stonecutters.

Along the left-hand wall there were rows of shelves extending right back. Some were sculpted with art and refinement – the oldest ones. Others were simply in undressed wood, and must have been added over the centuries as new items were classified and stored.

Classified... At his first glance, Nil realized that no rational classification system had been adopted. Crates, boxes, containers, piles of folders were all stacked up on the shelves.

"Why should any order be introduced into a library hell? Nothing's ever going to get out of here."

He took a step forward to peer down to the end of the tunnel: about fifty yards. Dozens of stacks, thousands of documents: he had an hour to find a needle in this haystack. It wouldn't be possible. And yet Andrei had found something here, Nil was convinced of the fact: this alone could explain his flight and his death. He advanced down the rows, examining the stacks on his left.

There was no classification, but signs had been nailed onto the edges of the shelves, in a mixture of elegant old-fashioned calligraphy and more modern handwriting. He felt as if time had been abolished.

Cathars... Trial of the Templars... a whole stack. *Savonarola, John Huss, The Galileo Affair, Giordano Bruno, Sacerdoti rinnegati francesi* – the list of the priests who had sworn to support the revolutionary French republic, and were condemned by Rome as apostates in 1792. *Corrispondenza della S.S. con Garibaldi...* All the secret history of the Church in conflict with its enemies. Suddenly, Nil halted: a stack filled with cardboard boxes that looked recent bore a single label – *Operation Ratlines.*

Forgetting why he was there, Nil turned into the bay and opened one of the boxes at random: it was the correspondence between Pius XII and Draganovič, the former priest who had become head of the Ustaše, the Croatian Nazis who had committed atrocities during the war. He opened other boxes: the identity papers of notorious Nazi criminals, dockets of Vatican passports drawn up in their names, receipts for considerable sums of money. Operation Ratlines was the code name for the network that had enabled Nazi criminals, just after the war, to escape with impunity, aided by the Holy See.

Nil wiped his face. He wasn't learning anything new here. The Church's compromises, its crimes indeed, were the logical consequences of what the thirteenth apostle must have suffered in the middle of the first century. He came out of the bay, and his eyes were drawn to a dossier that was just lying there on a shelf: *Auschwitz, rapporti segreti 1942*. He repressed his desire to open it. "So the Holy See knew what was going on in Auschwitz as early as 1942..."

He looked at his watch: more than half an hour. He moved on.

Suddenly he halted: he had just spotted a label in recent writing:

Manoscritti del Mar Morto, Spuria.

A dozen dusty boxes were piled up there. He took the one on top and opened it: inside were several fragments of scrolls, half worn away by time. He regretted that he hadn't brought his gloves, and picked up one of the scrolls: bits of parchment came away and fell to the bottom of the box, which was strewn with them. "The Hebrew writing from Qumran!" They were indeed the manuscripts from the Dead Sea, but why had they been relegated to this library hell, doomed to fall to pieces when scholars from all over the world were looking for them? *Spuria* – "scraps and leftovers": had the worldwide community been deprived of these scraps because they were valueless... or because they represented the leftovers of history and needed to be concealed for ever, because that history had taken another direction?

He put the box back in its place. The one underneath it was made of deal, and bore on its side a printed inscription: *Cognac Napoléon, cuvée de l'Empereur*.

The crate of Metropolitan Samuel, the crate that had been given to the Dominican lay brother in Jerusalem!

His heart pounding, Nil pulled it from the pile. On the lid, three letters had been written: *M M M*. He recognized Father Andrei's bold handwriting.

His head started to turn. So when, in the train, Andrei had written *M M M* on his note, he had not simply been alluding to the batch of photocopies from the Huntington Library that were preserved in the library of St Martin's Abbey. He had been designating this box – the very same one that Nil had just discovered. Andrei himself had written these three letters on its lid so that it could be more easily identified one day: *this* was the one he had meant to tell him about. Its discovery, made possible by the encounter with Breczinsky, had been the end and goal of their research, and he had been intending to tell Nil everything.

That was why he had been killed.

Nil opened the box: the same heap of fragmentary scrolls. And, to one side, a single sheet of rolled parchment. Nil's hands were trembling as he undid the twist of linen tied around the manuscript. He unrolled it carefully: it was in Greek, an elegant hand, perfectly legible. The handwriting of the thirteenth apostle! He started to read:

"*I, the beloved disciple of Jesus, the thirteenth apostle, to all the Churches…*"

When he had finished reading, Nil was pale with emotion. The beginning of the letter had not told him anything he did not already know: Jesus was not God, the Twelve – driven on by their political ambitions – had deified him. But the thirteenth apostle knew that this would not be enough to preserve his Master's true face: he testified, in an irrefutable fashion, that on 9th April 30 AD he had met men in white, Essenes, in front of the tomb from which they had just taken

301

Jesus's body, and that they were about to carry this body to one of their desert burial grounds, to give it a proper funeral.

As for this tomb, he did not indicate its exact location. In a laconic phrase, he stated that only the desert sand would protect Jesus's tomb from the covetousness of men. Like all the prophets, the Nazorean was alive for all eternity, and the veneration of his bones might distract humanity from the only real way in which it could encounter him: prayer.

During all these months of research, Nil had believed that the mystery facing him was that of the thirteenth apostle, the role he had played in Jerusalem and what he had bequeathed to posterity. The man who had written these lines in his own hand knew that he was already eliminated from the Church, written out of its future. And he sensed that this future would have nothing to do with the life and teaching of his Master. He had entrusted to this parchment the secret that, perhaps one day, would enable the world to rediscover Jesus's true face. He had done this without any illusions: what did a slender sheet of paper represent when opposed by the consuming ambition of men who were ready to do anything to achieve their ends, by manipulating the memory of the man he had loved more than any other?

The thirteenth apostle had just brought him to the true secret: the real, physical existence of a tomb containing Jesus's bones.

Nil glanced at his watch: ten past six. "I hope Breczinsky's waiting for me!" He put the miraculously rediscovered letter back in its box, and the box back in its place. He would keep his word: the Pope would be alerted, via the Polish librarian, to the existence of this apostolic letter that neither the centuries nor the men of the Church had managed to destroy. Thanks to the inscription *M M M* it would be easy for Breczinsky to find it again and hand it over to him.

What happened after that no longer concerned a little monk like him. It concerned nobody but the Pope.

Nil came quickly out of the room, taking care to switch off the light: behind him, the door closed automatically. When he reached the room where Leeland and he had been working every day, it was empty and the ceiling lights had been switched off. He went over and knocked at the office door: no reply, Breczinsky had not waited for him.

Nil wondered, rather anxiously, whether all the doors leading to the Belvedere courtyard did indeed open from the inside: he was extremely reluctant to spend the night in the cramped, musty stacks. But Breczinsky had not lied to him: he got through the two armoured doors without any difficulty. The entrance airlock was empty, but the door leading outside was ajar. Without thinking, Nil walked out into the courtyard and took in a great gulp of fresh air. He needed to walk, to get his head round all that had happened.

He was in so much of a hurry to leave that he paid no attention to the tinted window behind which the papal policeman was smoking a cigarette. As soon as he saw him go out, the man picked up the internal Vatican City phone and pressed a button.

"Your Eminence, he's just left... Yes, he was alone: the other one left before him. *Di niente, Eminenza.*"

In his office, Cardinal Catzinger hung up with a sigh. It would be time for Antonio to act, very soon now.

79

Nil crossed St Peter's Square, and mechanically looked up: the Pope's window was lit up. Tomorrow he would speak to Breczinsky, tell him where to find the crate of brandy marked *M M M*, and entrust him with the task of giving the old Pontiff a message by word of mouth. He turned into the Via Aurelia.

When he reached the third-floor landing, he halted: through the door he could hear Leeland playing Erik Satie's second *Gymnopédie*. The melody, floating in air, expressed a sense of infinite melancholy, a feeling of despair tinged with a touch of humour and derision. "Rembert..." he thought. "Will your sense of humour enable you to overcome your own despair?" He knocked discreetly at the door.

"Come in! I couldn't wait for you to get here!"

Nil sat near the piano.

"Remby, why did you leave the stacks before I came back?"

"Breczinsky came to tell me when it was six o'clock: he had to lock up, he said. He seemed worried. But never mind that: tell me, did you discover anything?"

Nil did not share Leeland's carefree attitude: the absence of Breczinsky disquieted him. "Why wasn't he there as we'd agreed when I came back?" he wondered to himself, before pushing the question to the back of his mind.

"Yes, I found what Andrei and I had been seeking for such a long time: an intact copy of the letter of the thirteenth apostle – the original, in fact."

"Tremendous! But... is this letter really so terrible?"

"It's short, and I know it off by heart. Origen was right – it provides irrefutable proof that Jesus did not rise from the dead as the Church teaches. So he isn't God: the empty tomb in Jerusalem, on which the Church of the Holy Sepulchre is built, is a decoy. The real tomb, the one containing Jesus's remains, is somewhere out in the desert."

Leeland was stupefied.

"In the desert! And where, exactly?"

"The thirteenth apostle refuses to indicate the place with any precision, so as to preserve Jesus's body from human covetousness: he simply mentions the desert of Idumaea, a vast zone to the south of Israel whose limits have varied through the ages. But archaeology has made considerable progress: if you use the right tools, you'll find what you're looking for. A skeleton placed in an abandoned Essene burial ground located in that zone and bearing traces of crucifixion, carbon-14-dated to the middle of the 1st century, would have a shattering impact on the West."

"Are you going to publish the results of your research, make this epistle known to the public, and join the archaeological digs? Nil, do you really want this tomb to be found?"

Nil was silent for a while. Satie's melody was trotting round and round in his head.

"I will follow the thirteenth apostle right to the end. If his testimony had been preserved by the history, there would never have been any Catholic Church. It was because they knew this that the Twelve refused to accept him as one of them. Remember the Germigny inscription: there must only be twelve witnesses to Jesus, for all eternity, *alpha and omega*. Are we to question, twenty centuries later on, the edifice they have built over an empty tomb? The burial place of the apostle Peter today marks the centre of Christianity. An empty tomb has been replaced by a full tomb, that of the first among the Twelve. Then the Church created the sacraments, so that everyone on the planet might be able to enter into physical contact with God. If we take this away from believers, what will they be left with? Jesus asks us to imitate him day by day, and the only method he proposes for that is prayer. But the multitudes, and an entire civilization, can only be swayed by concrete and tangible evidence. The author of the epistle was right: placing Jesus's bones in the Holy Sepulchre would mean transforming that tomb into a unique object of adoration for the credulous masses. It would mean forever turning away the humble and the lowly from access to the invisible God via the means that they have always been given: the sacraments."

"So what will you do?"

"Inform the Holy Father of the existence of the epistle, and tell him where it is. He will be the keeper of yet one more secret, that's all. Once I'm back in my monastery, I will bury away the results of my research in the silence of the cloister. Except for one, which I want to publish without delay: the role played by the Nazoreans in the birth of the Koran."

On the floor below, Mukhtar had been scrupulously recording the two *Gymnopédies* of Satie, then, after Nil's arrival, the start of the conversation. At this particular moment he quickly put on his headphones.

"Has the letter of the thirteenth apostle taught you anything new about the Koran?"

"He addressed his letter to the Churches, but in fact it was meant for his disciples, the Nazoreans. At the end, he adjures them to remain faithful to his testimony and his teachings about Jesus, wherever their exile may lead them. He thus confirms something I already suspected: after taking refuge for a while at Pella, they must have hit the roads again, probably fleeing from the Romans in 70 AD. Nobody knows what happened to them, but nobody seems to have noticed that, in the Koran, Muhammad often mentions *nasara*, a term which has always been translated as 'Christians'! In fact, *nasara* is the Arabic translation of 'Nazoreans'!"

"What do you conclude?"

"Muhammad must have known the Nazoreans at Mecca, where they had escaped to after Pella. Attracted to their teaching, he almost became one of them. Then he fled to Medina, where he became a warlord: politics and violence took the upper hand, but he remained forever marked by the Jesus of the Nazoreans, the Jesus of the thirteenth apostle. If Muhammad had not been devoured by his desire for conquest, Islam would never have been born, and Muslims would be the last of the Nazoreans – the cross of the prophet Jesus would be floating on the flag of Islam!"

Leeland seemed to share his friend's enthusiasm.

"I can guarantee that in the United States, at all events, academics are going to be really excited about your research! I'll help to spread the word back there."

"Just imagine, Remby! Muslims might finally accept the fact that their sacred text bears the mark of someone close to Jesus, someone who was himself excluded from the Church for denying Jesus's divinity – just as they do! It would be a new basis for a potential rapprochement between Muslims, Christians and Jews. And probably the end of the Jihad against the West!"

Mukhtar's face had suddenly darkened. Overwhelmed by hatred, he was now only half-listening: Nil was now asking Leeland what his plans were, and what he would do to conceal all this from Catzinger. Would he be able to resist the pressure and give nothing away? What would happen if the Cardinal enforced his threats and made his close relationship with Anselm public?

307

They were babbling away like women: the Palestinian had lost interest, and took off his headphones. The two men had just crossed the forbidden limit: *nobody touches the Koran*. Christian scholars could dig out secrets buried away in their Gospels if they wanted to – that was their problem. Never would the Koran be subjected to the methods of their impious exegesis; the Al-Azhar University drew its strength from rejecting them. Nobody dissects the words of Allah as transmitted by his Prophet, blessed be his name.

Muhammad – a secret disciple of a Jew, Jesus! The Frenchman would apply his infidel methods to the sacred text, and he would publish the results with the help of the American. In the hands of America, Israel's lackey, his work would become a terrible weapon against Islam.

Frowning, he rewound the tapes and remembered a sentence he often quoted to his students:

"The infidels, seize them, kill them wherever you find them!"

Mukhtar felt relieved: the Prophet, blessed be his name, had made his decision.

80

All day long it had been raining. Swathes of mist were slowly rising up the slope of the Abruzzi on our side, then seemed to hesitate for a moment before crossing the crest and disappearing in the direction of the Adriatic. The flight of the birds of prey seemed as if drawn towards the horizon.

Father Nil had given me shelter in his hermitage cut into the rock. A straw mattress thrown down onto a bed of dried ferns and a small table in front of the tiny window. A rudimentary fireplace, a Bible on a shelf, some bundles of wood. Less than the essential – for here, the essential lay elsewhere.

He told me that we were coming to the end of his story. It was only after it had all happened, in the silence of these mountains, that he had understood all of its twists and turns. He betrayed emotion only once, and I perceived this from the trembling in his voice: when he told me about Rembert Leeland, about the inner torment that he had endured and that had led to such a tragic end within just a few hours.

As soon as he had laid hands on the lost manuscript, events had started to happen very fast. By exhuming this text from a bygone age and bringing it out of oblivion, he had opened the sluice gates. Behind them, men unknown to him were waiting grimly, each of them defending his own cause with a relentlessness whose violence still remained incomprehensible to him, even today.

81

That same evening, Mukhtar had telephoned Lev Barjona, arranging to meet up with him, in a bar this time. They ordered drinks and remained standing at the counter, talking in low voices in spite of the hubbub of conversation around them.

"Listen, Lev, it's serious. I've just handed over to Calfo the recording of a conversation between Nil and Leeland. The Frenchman has found the epistle – it was indeed in the crate of brandy that the Metropolitan Samuel had told you about. He has read it and left it in its place, in the Vatican."

"Good, very good! Now we just need to go about things nice and slowly."

"We need to act now, and act quickly. That dog claims that the letter contains the proof… or rather, confirms his deeply rooted conviction that the Koran was not revealed to Muhammad by God. He thinks the Prophet was close to the Nazoreans, before relapsing into violence when he went to Medina. He thinks Muhammad was blinded by ambition… You know what that means: you've known us since forever. He has crossed the line beyond which any Muslim will immediately react: he needs to be eliminated. Quickly, and his accomplice too."

"Calm down, Mukhtar – have you received any instructions from Cairo telling you to do as much? What about Calfo?"

"I don't need any instructions from Cairo, in this situation the Koran dictates how believers should act. As for Calfo, I don't give a damn. He's a depraved old fool, and the stories Christians concoct leave me indifferent. Let them sort out their own problems and get involved in whatever dirty little tricks they fancy: *I* have to protect the purity of the message transmitted by God to Muhammad. Every Muslim is ready to shed blood for this cause; God will not tolerate his name being sullied. I will defend God's honour."

Lev signalled to the barman.

"What do you intend to do?"

"I know all about their movements, the routes they take. In the evening, Nil returns to San Girolamo on foot, it takes him an hour – he goes down the Via Salaria Antica, which is always deserted at dusk. The American goes part of the way with him, but then retraces his steps and goes for a walk round Castel Sant'Angelo, where he dreams in the moonlight – there's never anyone there. Will you join me? Tomorrow evening."

Lev sighed. A slapdash operation, carried out under the impulse of anger, with no lucidity. When Mukhtar's fanaticism

310

went to his head, he lost all sense of proportion. The Bedouin hopped onto his camel and galloped off to wash away the insult with blood. Waiting was a sign of weakness, something that went against the law of the desert. The Arabs' pride, their inability to control themselves when honour was at stake, had always allowed Mossad to win out over them. And he remembered the instructions from Jerusalem, firmly transmitted by Ari: "No more action for you".

"Tomorrow evening I've got a rehearsal with the orchestra for my last concert. They know I'm in Rome: nobody would understand it if I didn't turn up. I have to keep my cover, Mukhtar. Sorry."

"So I'll act without you: first the one and then the other. Father Nil is as fragile as china, he'll break at the least little shove. As for the American, I'll just have to frighten him, he'll die of fear without me even having to touch him. I won't need to dirty my hands on someone like *him*."

When they went their separate ways, Lev headed towards the gardens of the Pincio. He needed to think.

As night fell, the Rector called an urgent meeting of the Twelve. When they were seated behind the long table, he rose.

"My brothers, once again we are here with the Master, just as the Twelve were in the upper room. This time it is not to accompany him to Gethsemane, but to offer him a second triumphal entry into Jerusalem. Father Nil has found the last and only remaining copy of the letter of the impostor, the so-called thirteenth apostle. It was simply in the secret collection of the Vatican, among the manuscripts from the Dead Sea that were stored away there permanently in 1948."

A murmur of intense satisfaction ran through the gathering.

"What has he done with it, Brother Rector?"

"He left it in place, and intends to inform the Holy Father of its existence and whereabouts."

Their faces darkened.

"Whether he does so or not is of no importance: Nil will go through Breczinsky to get to the Pope. The twelfth apostle has the Pole under his thumb – isn't that so, Brother?"

Antonio nodded gravely, in silence.

"As soon as Breczinsky has been informed by Nil – probably tomorrow – we will swing into action. The Pole is at our mercy, and will lead us to the letter. In two days, Brothers, the letter will take up its rightful place in front of us, safeguarded by our fidelity as by this crucifix. And in the months and years to come, we will use it to obtain the means we need to accomplish our mission: to crush the serpents who are bruising Christ's heel, to stifle the voice of those opposed to his reign, to restore Christianity in all its grandeur, so that the West may regain its lost dignity."

As he left the room, he silently handed Antonio an envelope: it contained a summons to see him in Castel Sant'Angelo two days later, in the morning. This would give Nil time to talk to Breczinsky.

And enable him to keep his mind completely free for to-morrow's evening session with Sonia, a session from which he was expecting a great deal. Things could not have turned out any better. Thanks to her, he would be imbued with the strength he would be needing. The inner strength that a Christian receives when he identifies with every fibre of his being with Christ crucified on his cross.

Antonio slipped the letter into his pocket. But instead of heading back to the city centre, he turned off to the Vatican.

The Cardinal Prefect of the Congregation always stayed up very late in his office.

82

Rome lay stretched out in the morning sunshine. It was still distinctly nippy, but the approach of Christmas lured the Romans out of doors. Standing at his window, Leeland gazed absent-mindedly at the spectacle in the Via Aurelia. The day before, Nil had informed him of his decision to return to France without delay: what he considered a mission he had been given by Andrei had come to its conclusion with the finding of the epistle.

"Have you ever thought, Remby, that the area of desert situated between Galilee and the Red Sea has given birth to the three monotheistic religions of the planet? It was there that Moses had his vision of the burning bush, there too that Jesus was radically transformed, and there that Muhammad was born and lived. My own desert is going to be on the banks of the Loire."

Nil's departure cast a harsh light on the emptiness of Leeland's life. He knew that he would never reach his friend's level of spiritual experience: Jesus would never fill his inner void. Nor would music: one plays in order to be heard, to share the music's emotion with other people. He had often played for Anselm, who would sit at his side and turn the pages for him. A wonderful communion would grow between them at those times, the violinist's handsome features bent over the keyboard as his hands moved up and down it. Anselm was lost to him for good, and Catzinger had the means to plunge both of them into an ocean of suffering. "Life is over."

He gave a start on hearing a knock at the door. Nil?

It wasn't Nil, but Lev Barjona. Surprised to see him here, Leeland was just about to start asking him questions, but the Israeli placed a finger on his lips and murmured:

"Is there a terrace on top of your apartment block?"

There was indeed, as on most apartment blocks in Rome, and it was deserted. Leeland allowed Lev to lead him to the side furthest from the street.

"Ever since Nil arrived in Rome, your apartment has been bugged. I've just found out. Every least little conversation you have is recorded and immediately transmitted to Mgr Calfo – and to other, far more dangerous people."

"But…"

"Let me have my say, time is pressing. Without knowing it, you and Nil have started to play the 'great game', a game on planetary scale, one you have no idea about, know nothing about – so much the better for you. It's a dirty game played between professionals. You two are like school kids in short pants, leaving your playground to wander slap bang into the yard where the big boys play. And they're not playing marbles. It's a violent struggle, always with the same objective in view: power – or its visible form, money."

"Forgive me for interrupting – do you still play that particular game?"

"I played it for a long while, with Mossad, as you know. You never get out of that game, Remby, even if you'd like to. I won't say any more about it, but Nil and you are in great danger. By warning you like this, I'm playing against my own side, but you're a friend, and Nil is a nice guy. He's found what he was looking for: the game can now carry on without the two of you. If you want to keep on living, you need to disappear, and quickly. Very quickly."

Leeland was staggered.

"Disappear… but how?"

"You're both monks: hide out in a monastery. There's a killer hot on your heels, and he's a professional. Leave – leave today."

"Do you think he'd kill us?"

"I don't think: I know. And he'll do it without delay, while he's got you at his mercy. Listen, I implore you: if you want to stay alive, leave today – by train, plane or car, it doesn't matter – and make yourselves invisible. Warn Nil."

He clasped Leeland in his arms.

"I've taken a risk in coming here: in the great game, they don't like those who don't respect the rules, and I'd like to stay alive to give lots more concerts. Shalom, my friend: in five years, in ten years, we'll meet again. No match in the game lasts for ever."

And the next minute he was gone, leaving Leeland on the terrace, stunned.

83

Mukhtar had granted himself a lie-in: for the first time he didn't need to be at his post at daybreak, headphones on, listening in on the least conversation in the studio above.

So he didn't see Leeland hurrying out of the apartment block on the Via Aurelia, hesitating for a moment and then heading for the stop where he could catch a bus to the Via Salaria. The American stood anxiously waiting for the first vehicle to come along and jumped on board.

Nil pushed back the sheet of paper on the table: trusting to his memory, he had just set down the letter of the thirteenth apostle, which he had memorized without difficulty. Together with the Pope, he would be the only one to know that a tomb containing the remains of Jesus lay somewhere in the desert, between Jerusalem and the Red Sea. He opened his bag and slipped the letter inside.

He would soon have packed, and would keep his bag in his hand. And take the night train for Paris – it was never full at this time of year. Leaving the ghostly monastery of San Girolamo was a real relief for him: once he was back in St Martin's, he would hide the most compromising of his papers and settle into the desert. Like the thirteenth apostle in bygone days.

He still had the most important thing: the person of Jesus, his gestures and his words. In a desert, he would need no other food to survive.

He was amazed to hear a knock at the door of his cell. It was Father John – another person he wouldn't miss. The unstoppable chatterer's eyes were gleaming.

"Father, Mgr Leeland has just arrived and wishes to see you."

Nil rose to greet his friend. The erstwhile playful student was now a hunted man, who hurried into the cell and flopped onto the chair that Nil pushed forwards for him.

"What's up, Remby?"

"My studio on the Via Aurelia has been bugged ever since you arrived, Catzinger and his men know everything we've been saying. And so do others, people who are even more dangerous. For different reasons, they want us put away."

Now it was the turn of Nil, shocked at this news, to drop into an armchair.

"I'm dreaming – or have you succumbed to an attack of paranoia?"

"I've just been paid a visit by Lev Barjona, who brought me up to date very briefly, but without room for doubt. He told me he was acting out of friendship, and I don't doubt him for a moment. We've got ourselves involved in something much bigger than us, Nil. Your life is in danger, and so is mine."

Nil buried his face in his hands. When he looked up again, he stared at Leeland with eyes filled with tremulous tears.

"I knew, Remby. I knew right from the start, as soon as Andrei had warned me. It was in the monastery, in the apparently changeless peace of a cloister protected by its silence. I knew it when I learnt of his death, when I went to identify his dislocated body next to the track of the Rome express. I knew it when history caught up with me, in all its horrible reality, thanks to Breczinsky and certain things he told me in confidence. I never felt afraid because of what I discovered. Is my life in danger? I'm the last in a very long list, one that starts at the moment the thirteenth apostle refused to see the truth being manipulated."

"*The truth!* There's only one truth, the truth that men need to establish and maintain their power. The truth of the very pure love between myself and Anselm is not their truth. The truth that you have discovered in the texts isn't the real truth, since it contradicts their truth."

"Jesus said: 'The truth will make you free'. I am free, Remby."

"You're free only if you disappear, and if your truth disappears with you. The philosophers you like so much teach that truth is a category of being, that it subsists in itself, like the goodness and the beauty of being. Well, it's false, and I've come to tell you so. The love that brought Anselm and myself together was good and beautiful: it was not in conformity with the Church's truth, so it was not true. Your discovery of Jesus's face contradicts the truth of Christianity: so you've got it all wrong, the Church will not tolerate any truth other than its own. Nor will the Jews or the Muslims."

"What can they do against me? What can they do against a free man?"

"Kill you. You need to hide – to leave Rome straight away."

* * *

There was a silence, broken only by the chirruping of the birds in the reeds of the cloister. Nil got to his feet and went over to the window.

"If what you say is true, I can't go back to my monastery, where the desert would be peopled by hyenas. Hide? Where?"

"I've been thinking about that on my way here. Do you remember Father Calati?"

"The superior of the Camaldolese? Of course, we both had him as professor in Rome. A wonderful man."

"Go to Calmaldoli, ask him to take you in. They have hermitages scattered through the Abruzzi, you'll find just the desert you're looking for. Do it quickly. Do it now."

"You're right, the Camaldolese have always been very hospitable. But what about you?"

Leeland closed his eyes for a moment.

"Don't worry about me. My life is over – it's been over ever since I learnt that the love preached by the Church might be just one ideology like any other. Your discoveries, with which I have become associated even though I didn't ask to be, have merely confirmed my feelings: the Church is no longer my mother, she is rejecting the child I have been because I loved in a different way from her. I'm going to stay in Rome; the Abruzzi desert isn't the right place for me. My desert is inside me, as it has been ever since I was forced to leave the United States."

He headed for the door.

"Your suitcase can be packed quickly. I'm going to go downstairs and ask Father John to show me the library, to keep him away from the porter's lodge. In the meantime, you can slip out of the monastery, take a bus for the Stazione Termini and jump into the first train to Arezzo. I trust Calati, he'll keep you safe. Hide away in a hermitage of the Camaldolese and write

318

to me in two or three weeks: I'll tell you if you can come back to Rome."

"What are you going to do?"

"I'm already dead, Nil – they can't hurt me any more. Don't worry: you've got a few minutes to leave San Girolamo without being spotted. See you soon, my friend: truth has made free men of us – you were right."

Father John was surprised at the sudden interest Rembert Leeland seemed to have developed in the library, which was generally considered to be a jumble. While the American asked him questions that proved how totally incompetent he was when it came to historical scholarship, Nil, his suitcase in his right hand, slipped aboard the bus that passes down the Via Salaria and serves Rome's main railway station.

In his left hand, he clutched a bag that seemed to be his most precious treasure.

84

Antonio walked along with a spring in his step. Nestled in a bend of the Tiber, the Castel Sant'Angelo reflected the setting sun from its tawny bricks. Here, papal justice had once been dispensed: it was divine justice that he was going to enforce this evening. A man was preparing to oppose the government of the Church for a cause that he thought was right – but there is no right cause outside the hierarchy. And the man in question was depraved, a Satanic pervert. The Spaniard leant against the guardrail of the Victor Emmanuel II Bridge. Before he took action, he wished to remember the words the Cardinal had uttered the evening before and rekindle his burning sense of indignation: then his hand would not tremble.

* * *

"You say he is going to use the epistle to put pressure on us?"

"He's stated as much on several occasions, Your Eminence, and the Twelve agree. The letter of the thirteenth apostle will give considerable power to anyone who possesses it: making it public would cause such an uproar that our Church – and even certain Western heads of state – will be ready to pay a considerable amount of money for the Society to keep it secret. The Templars did not hesitate to use this means."

"Jesus's tomb… Incredible!" – The Cardinal wiped his brow. "I thought the epistle contented itself with denying Jesus's divinity. It wouldn't have been the first time – the Church has always been able to overcome that particular danger and throttle heresy. But discovering the real tomb containing Jesus's bones! Not just one more theological quarrel, but tangible, undeniable *proof*! It's unthinkable! It's the end of the world!"

Antonio smiled.

"That's just what Mgr Calfo thinks, but he has his own ideas. He thinks the Church is too timorous in the face of a rotten world that's going its own way without us, or against us. He wants money, a lot of money, so that he can influence world opinion."

"*Bastardo!*"

The Prelate quickly got a grip on himself and continued:

"Antonio, when I knew you in Vienna, you were a fugitive from Opus Dei – but you had sworn to serve the Pope and, if his health were to fail, to serve the Papacy, the backbone of the West. Our venerable Holy Father is ill – or at all events he devotes his strength and his attention to the crowds that acclaim him everywhere he goes on his travels. For twenty years, the real governance of the Church has rested on shoulders such as mine, and sometimes the Pope has not even been informed of the dangers we have been forced to face. I have often had to act in his name; I'll do the same again here. Can I count on your help? We need to… neutralize Calfo, and take over control of the Society of St Pius V. Without delay."

"Your Eminence…"

The Cardinal pinched his lips, sucked in his cheeks, and his tone of voice became harsh.

"Remember, my child: when you arrived in Vienna, you were being followed. Nobody leaves Opus Dei, especially not after criticizing it the way you did. You were young, idealistic, unaware! I gave you shelter, protection, and then my trust. It was I who made you a member of the Society of St Pius V, I who paid up so that the Catalans of Escrivá de Balaguer, those fanatics, would keep quiet when Calfo made his inquiries about you. I've come to collect my dividends, Antonio!"

The young man lowered his head. Catzinger realized that, for what he was demanding, a simple command would not be enough: he would need to arouse his indignation, awaken the Andalusian's volcanic temperament. Touch him at his sensitive point: his rigid, intransigent character, his rejection of the body, kept in force by so many years of sexual frustration at the school of Opus Dei. He puckered his lips, and they distilled honey.

"Do you know who your Rector is? Do you know what kind of a man he is, one you respect in spite of his lack of discipline? Do you know what horrors the first of the Twelve is capable of imagining, a hundred feet away from this Holy City and Peter's tomb? A few days ago I heard, in confidence, the story of one of his victims, a young woman as beautiful and pure as a Madonna, whose very soul he humiliates – the soul of a believer – even as he enjoys her body. And she is not the first to have been sullied by him. You don't know? Well, I'm going to tell you what he has done, and what he is planning to do tomorrow."

He whispered for a few moments, as if he wanted to stop the crucifix hanging on the wall behind him hearing what he said.

When he had finished, Antonio looked up: his black eyes were glinting with a harsh, inflexible light. He left the Cardinal's office without uttering a word.

With a sigh, the Andalusian pulled himself away from the parapet of the bridge: it had been a good idea to relive that scene before he started to act. The Church ceaselessly needs to be purified, even by steel. The Cardinal's commands exonerated him from all responsibility: this too had always been the Church's strength. A difficult decision, a moral violence, a gangrenous limb to tear off... The man who wielded the knife, who plunged it deep into living flesh, did not view himself as responsible for the blood shed or the lives destroyed. The responsibility lay with the Church.

85

Alessandro Calfo took a step back, looking satisfied: it was perfect. On the parquet floor of his bedroom, a big cross was laid out, two broad beams of wood that would allow a body to lie at ease. Sonia would be fine there. He would tie her hands with the two soft silk cords he had prepared; her legs must remain free. As he imagined the scene, the blood rushed to his temples and his lower belly: to unite carnally with the young woman lying in the place of the divine crucified one was the most sublime act he would ever accomplish. Divinity finally merged with humanity, the least of his cells experiencing ecstasy in union with Christ's redemptive sacrifice in its most perfect form. No violence: Sonia would be consenting, he knew it, he sensed it. Her horrified reaction the other day was merely the effect of her surprise. She would obey as she always did.

He checked that the Byzantine icon was directly above the cross: in this way, while he was celebrating the cult, she would be able to contemplate, merely by lifting her eyes, this image that would appease her Orthodox soul. He had thought of everything, since everything needed to be exemplary. And tomorrow evening he would place the cursed epistle on the empty shelf which had been awaiting it for so long.

He gave a start when he heard the doorbell ring. Already? Usually, always discreet, she came only after nightfall. Perhaps, today, she was impatient? His smile broadened. He went to open the door.

It was not Sonia.

"An... Antonio! But what are you doing here today? I asked you to call round for tomorrow morning; Nil first needed to see the Pole this afternoon... What is the meaning of this?"

Antonio advanced towards him, forcing him to retreat down the entrance corridor.

"The meaning of this, Brother Rector, is that we need to talk, you and I."

"To talk? But *I* talk to *you,* at times of my choosing! You are the last of the Twelve, in any case..."

Antonio was still advancing, his eyes focused on the face of the Neapolitan, who retreated before him, bumping into the walls as he did so.

"No longer at times of your choosing, but when the God whom you claim to serve chooses."

"Whom I... claim to serve? And who has given you permission to speak to me in that tone of voice?"

The one man pushed the other before him until they reached the bedroom door, which Calfo had left open.

"Who has given me permission? And who has given you permission, you wretch, to betray your vow of chastity? Who has given you permission to humiliate one of God's creatures, hidden behind your episcopal ordination?"

With a jerk of his hips, he forced the pudgy little man to back into the room. Calfo stumbled over the foot of the cross. Antonio looked round at the carefully elaborated setting: the Cardinal had not lied to him.

"And what about this? What you were planning on doing is an abominable blasphemy. You are not worthy to possess the letter of the thirteenth apostle, the Master cannot be protected by a man like you. Only someone pure can keep at bay the filth that is menacing Our Lord."

"But… but…"

Calfo again tripped over the upright of the cross, slipped over and fell on his knees in front of the Andalusian, who stared at him with contempt, his lips pursed with disgust. This was no longer his Rector, the first of the Twelve. It was a human wreck, trembling, drenched in foul sweat. His eyes suddenly dulled over.

"You wanted to stretch out on the cross, didn't you? You wanted to unite your body, transfigured by ecstasy, with the Master transfigured by his love for each one of us? Very well, so you shall. You will never suffer as much as He who died for you."

A quarter of an hour later, Antonio gently closed the apartment door behind him and wiped his hands with a paper handkerchief. It hadn't been difficult. It's never difficult when you obey.

86

Leeland walked like a jerky automaton down the uneven cobbles of the Via Salaria Antica. "Nil loved to take this route when he came to see me... Already I'm thinking of him in the past!"

He had succeeded in keeping Father John busy in the library for a long while, but had declined his invitation to share in the community's lunch.

"Father Nil and I are meeting in the Vatican at the start of the afternoon. He's probably already left without telling me. He'll be coming back... late this evening."

Nil would not be coming back: at this very moment he would be on the platform of the Stazione Termini, ready to get into a train for Arezzo. Or was already gone.

Overwhelmed by anguish, Leeland felt as light as a feather: in fact he was emptied, down to the smallest fibre of his muscles, down to his fingertips. "Life is over." What he had been refusing to accept ever since he had been exiled to the Vatican, the truth that he had been hiding from himself, had just been made absolutely clear to him by Nil's short stay in Rome: his life no longer had any meaning, all zest for living had left him.

He found himself, without knowing how, outside the door of his studio. He pushed open the door with a trembling hand, shut it behind him and sat down with an effort at the piano. Would he still be able to play music? But... for whom?

On the floor below, Mukhtar had again taken up his listening post and set the tape recorders going. Today the American had come home later than usual, and he was alone: so he had left Nil in the Vatican – the Frenchman must be talking to Breczinsky. He settled down comfortably, headphones on.

Nil would be coming back at the end of the afternoon and would talk to Leeland. At nightfall he would head back to San Girolamo, as usual. On foot, through dark and deserted streets. His friend would go part of the way with him.

The American first. Then the other one.

But Nil did not return. Still sitting at the piano, Leeland watched as the shadows filled his studio. He didn't switch the light on: he was trying to struggle against his fear with all the strength at his disposal – struggling against himself. There was only one thing left for him to do. Lev had provided him, unwittingly, with the solution. But would he have the resolve and the courage to go out?

An hour later, night had fallen on Rome. The tapes were turning round and round in silence – what could the Frenchman be up to? Suddenly, Mukhtar heard muffled noises from upstairs, and the studio door opening and shutting. He took off his headphones and went to the window: Leeland, alone, had left the building and was crossing the street. So had they agreed to meet on the way to San Girolamo? In that case it would be even easier.

Mukhtar slipped out. He was armed with a dagger and a steel coil. He had always preferred weapons with blades, or strangulation. Physical contact with the infidel gives death its proper value. Mossad preferred to use its crack sharpshooters, but the God of the Jews is merely a distant abstraction: for a Muslim, God is reached in the reality of direct physical combat. The Prophet had never used arrows, but always his sabre. If possible, he would strangle the American. He would feel his heart stop beating under the pressure of his hands – that heart ready to provide those of his nation with a decisive weapon against Muslims.

326

He followed Leeland, who walked round St Peter's Square without passing under the colonnade, and turned into Borgo Santo Spirito. He was heading for the Castel Sant'Angelo. It was a chilly night and the Romans were all snug at home. If those two had arranged to meet up at the foot of the castle, it was because they knew there wouldn't be a soul there. All the better.

Now Leeland was walking along slowly, and he felt at peace. In the twilight of the studio he had come to his decision, repeating to himself the words that Lev had used: "A killer, a professional. Leave, go and hide away in a monastery…" He would not leave, he would not hide away. On the contrary, he would march towards his destiny, as he was now doing, in full visibility. Suicide is forbidden to Christians, and he would never by himself put an end to this lifeless life that was henceforth the only life he would have. But if someone else assumed responsibility, that was fine. He came out on the left bank of the Tiber, passed in front of the Castel Sant'Angelo, and turned onto the Lungotevere. Cars – few and far between – came down this road overlooking the Tiber, then turned left to the Piazza Cavour. There was nobody about; the damp was rising from the river and it was biting cold.

On arrival at the Umberto I Bridge, he looked round. Under the light from the lamp-posts he spotted someone who was walking the same way as he was, following the parapet. He slowed down, and had the impression that the man did likewise. It was most likely him. Don't run, don't hide, don't flee.

"Life is over." Brother Anselm, his vanished illusions! Church reform, married priests, the end for so many noble-minded men of a long period of torment, the chastity imposed by a Church paralysed by human love… He saw some stone steps leading down to the bank of the Tiber: without hesitating, he walked down them.

The quayside was barely lit and still cobbled in the old style. He walked on, gazing at the black water: the strong current, hemmed in at this point, swept over rocks scattered over the river bed. Clumps of reeds and dense thickets of vegetation covered the steep slope stretching down to the water. Rome has never quite stopped looking like a provincial town.

Behind him, he heard a man walking down the steps; his feet echoed on the flags of the quayside as he approached. Although he had been of the right age, the fact that Leeland was a monk had in days gone by allowed him to avoid being called up for Vietnam. He had often wondered if he would have shown much physical courage out there. When faced with the shadow of an enemy intent on killing him, how would his body have reacted? He smiled: this river bank would be his Vietnam, and his heart was beating no faster than usual.

A killer, a professional. What would he feel? Would he suffer?

The one man followed the other towards the arches of the Cavour Bridge. Just afterwards, a high wall barred the quayside, marking the end of a walk that the Romans much enjoyed when the weather was good. There were no steps along the wall at this point: to get back up to the clearway that runs along the Tiber he would have to retrace his steps. And confront the man following him.

Leeland took a deep breath and closed his eyes for a moment. He felt very calm, but he would not see the man's face. Let death come from behind his back, like a thief in the night.

Without looking round, he stepped resolutely under the dark arch of the bridge.

Behind him, he heard the footsteps of a man running, as if

to gain momentum. Running lightly, with steps that hardly touched the cobbles.

87

Holding his bag in one hand and his suitcase in the other, Nil climbed out of the bus. The village was just as rustic as Father Calati had described it.

"Our bursar is going just now to Aquila, you can get into his car. He'll leave you at the local bus station. In the afternoons, there's a bus service to this out-of-the-way part of the Abruzzi. Get off in the village, then follow the road on foot until you come to a crossing. Turn left, and carry on for about half a mile on an earthen track until you reach an isolated farm. You're bound to meet Beppe, he lives there alone with his mother. Don't be surprised – he doesn't speak but he understands everything. Tell him that you've come from me, and ask him to take you to our hermit's. It will be a long walk through the mountain – Beppe is used to it, he's the only one who goes up to the hermitage to take a little food there from time to time."

Then Calati had raised his hands heavenwards, and silently given Nil his blessing as he kneeled on the icy flagstones of the cloister.

When he had presented himself at Camaldoli, his old professor had hugged him, his bushy beard caressing Nil's cheek. So he needed to settle in the desert, for an indeterminate period? Nobody must know where he had taken refuge? Calati did not ask any questions, was not surprised at his arrival, nor by the way he looked like a fugitive, nor by his unusual request. He would be fine with the old hermit – that was all he had said.

"You'll see, he's rather an odd fellow, who's been living in the mountains for years. But he's never lonely: he is in contact with the whole universe through prayer, and he possesses a gift of divination of the sort sometimes developed by great spiritual masters. We remain in contact thanks to Beppe, who comes down from the mountain every fortnight to sell his cheeses in Aquila. God bless you!"

Nil watched as the bus set off in a cloud of smoke, and turned down the village's only street. It was still day, but the low-roofed houses were draught proof to keep out the night cold.

As he walked down the street, he glanced into a window and smiled at the image it reflected back at him: his close-cropped hair, which had still been grey when he had left St Martin's Abbey, had become completely white ever since he had discovered the epistle.

The suitcase was a weight on his arm by the time he stopped outside the farm. Dressed in a sleeveless sheepskin jacket – the traditional costume of Abruzzi shepherds – a young man was chopping wood in front of the door. On hearing Nil, he looked round and stared at him with disquiet, his brow furrowed under a crown of curly hair.

"Are you Beppe? I've come from Father Calati. Can you take me to the hermit's?"

Beppe carefully set his axe down against the pile of logs, wiped his hands on his jacket lining, and then came up to Nil and examined him more closely. After a while his face relaxed, he gave the ghost of a smile and nodded. He vigorously picked up the suitcase, jutted his chin in the direction of the mountain and motioned him to follow.

The path plunged into the forest and then rose sharply.

Beppe strode along, his gait giving the impression of ease and almost of grace. Nil found it difficult to follow him. Had the boy understood him? He needed to put himself in his hands, and keep his precious bag with him.

They arrived at a point where the path seemed to peter out: a dead end, where one could see the already ageing traces of furrows dug by mechanical contraptions – the tractors of the foresters, who obviously did not come here very often. There was clear water flowing into a ditch: Beppe put the suitcase down, bent forward and took a long drink from his cupped hands. Then, still in silence, the teenager picked up the suitcase again and set off up a path that led into a coomb on the mountain side. Between the treetops, a distant crest could be seen.

Night had just fallen when they reached a tiny esplanade looking out over the dark valley. Nil could make out a lit window level with the rock face. Without hesitating, Beppe went over to it, dropped the suitcase on the ground and knocked on the window pane.

A low door opened, and a shadow filled its frame. Dressed in a sort of smock tied by a belt, a very old man, his head surrounded by white shoulder-length hair, took a step forwards: behind him, Nil could see a hearth in which a faggot of wood was burning, shedding a bright light. Beppe bowed, uttered a grunt and pointed towards Nil. The old man gently touched the boy's curls, then turned to Nil and smiled at him. He showed him the inside of his hermitage, from which a mild heat was emanating, and said simply:

"*Vieni, figlio mio. Ti aspettavo.*"

"Come, my son, I was expecting you!"

88

On that particular morning, the Vatican City was filled with a feverish agitation, at least relatively speaking given the nature of the place: some prelates walked down the marble corridors at a pace slightly less stiff and solemn than usual, a few violet belts fluttered a little higher as people dashed up the stairs four at a time. A car with the SCV registration plate swept through the main gate of the Belvedere court, saluted by a Swiss guard who recognized inside it the Pope's personal doctor, a middle-aged man clutching a black briefcase on his knees.

Anywhere else, these imperceptible signs of agitation would have passed unnoticed. But the Swiss guard, as he witnessed this unusual tenseness in the Holy City, felt cheered: today there would be plenty for his colleagues to talk about.

The SCV car went all the way down the Via della Conciliazione, turned left, passed in front of the Castel Sant'Angelo and parked a little further on, on the pavement of the Lungotevere, behind a van with its roof light flashing. The man with the briefcase hurried down the steps that led to the Tiber bank and walked along the uneven cobbles towards the Cavour Bridge, where a dozen or so Italian policemen were gathered around a dark shape, dripping with water, that they had apparently just pulled out of the reeds at the river's edge.

The doctor examined the corpse, talked to the policemen, snapped his briefcase shut and then went back up to the Lungotevere, where he spoke in a low voice into his mobile phone, taking care to keep his distance from a few curious onlookers. He nodded several times, motioned to his driver to go without him, and hurried back to the foot of the Castel Sant'Angelo. He crossed through, carried on walking for a while and then plunged into a recent apartment block, at the foot of which a young man dressed like a tourist seemed to be waiting for him.

They exchanged a few words, and then the young man took a key from his pocket and motioned the doctor to follow him into the building.

Late that morning, Cardinal Catzinger was standing before the Sovereign Pontiff, who had been placed behind his desk. The Pope's right hand, adorned with the ring of the Second Vatican Council, at which he had participated, trembled as he read a sheet of paper. He was broken by his illness, but under his beetling eyebrows his gaze was bright and sharp.

"Can it be true, Your Eminence? Two Vatican prelates dying within a few hours of each other last night?"

"A painful coincidence, Most Holy Father. Mgr Calfo, who had already had a mild attack a few months ago, succumbed to cardiac arrest last night and did not survive."

Alessandro Calfo had been discovered in his bedroom, lying on the two beams of wood arranged in the shape of a crucifix. His empurpled face was still crumpled into a grimace of pain. His arms were held out, tied to the horizontal beam of the cross by two silken cords; his glassy eyes were staring at a Byzantine icon hung just above the scene, representing the Mother of God in all her virginal purity.

Two nails had been pulled out of the transom of the bed and pushed through the dead man's palms. No blood had flowed: the man had probably already been dead by the time he was crucified.

As the apartment was some distance from St Peter's Square, the affair fell into the jurisdiction of the Italian police. But the violent death of a prelate, a Vatican citizen, always puts the Italian government in an extremely delicate situation.

The police superintendent – a Neapolitan, like the dead man – was highly embarrassed. Was this crucified man part of some Satanic ritual? He didn't like it, and remarked that, after all, as the crow flies, the immaterial frontier of the Holy City was only a hundred or so yards away: so it could be considered that the Pope's personal doctor, who would be arriving any minute now, was perfectly competent to deliver the burial permit.

The worthy practitioner did not bother to open his suitcase: helped by the young man with the strange black eyes who had come with him, he began by carefully buttoning up Calfo's collar, so that the traces of strangulation would no longer be visible. Then he pulled out the nails, called over the police officer, who had discreetly stepped to one side, and told him his diagnosis: cardiac arrest, an excess of pasta combined with lack of exercise. These are things that a Neapolitan understands immediately. The police officer heaved a sigh of relief, and without further delay handed the body over to the Vatican authorities.

"Cardiac arrest," sighed the Pope. "So he won't have suffered? God is kind to his servants, *requiescat in pace*. But what about the other man, Your Eminence? There were two deaths last night, weren't there?"

"Indeed, and this is a much more delicate matter. This was Mgr Leeland, of whom I have already spoken to you."

"Leeland? The Benedictine abbot who had noisily come out in support of married priests? I remember very well, it led to him being given a *promoveatur ut amoveatur* and, ever since then, he'd kept quiet here in Rome."

"Not entirely, Your Holiness. In this very city he met a rebel monk, who communicated to him his senseless theories about the person of Our Lord Jesus Christ. It seems this deeply disturbed him, and doubtless led him to despair: he was found this morning, drowned, among the reeds at the edge of the Tiber, near the Cavour Bridge. It may be a suicide."

The doctor had not wanted to pay any more attention than did the police to the marks of strangulation around Leeland's neck. It was obviously a steel coil that had crushed his glottis. The work of a professional. Strangely enough, the American's face had remained serene, almost smiling.

The old Pontiff raised his head with an effort and stared at the Cardinal.

"Let us pray for that unfortunate Mgr Leeland, who must have suffered greatly in his soul. You will now hand on to me any letters addressed to him that might arrive. And... what about the rebel monk?"

"Yesterday he left San Girolamo, where he had been staying for a few days, and we don't know where he is. But it will be easy to track him down."

The Pope waved his hand.

"Your Eminence, wherever do you think a monk will go to hide if not in a monastery? Anyway, don't do anything for the time being, let's give him time to recover the inner peace that he seems to have lost, from what you tell me."

Once he was back in his office, Catzinger realized that he shared the Pope's sentiments unreservedly. Calfo's death had taken a huge weight off him. Antonio had intervened just in time: the letter of the thirteenth apostle would remain buried away in the secret collection of the Vatican, and there was nowhere it would be safer from prying eyes. Leeland? A mere insect. One of those you brush aside with the back of your hand. And as for Nil, he was dangerous only when he was inside his abbey. Until he returned there, there was no hurry.

That left Breczinsky: his presence within the Vatican walls was an intolerable thorn in the flesh. It reminded him at every instant of a dark episode in Germany's history, and stoked in him a sense of collective guilt which he had been struggling against for ever. His father? He had merely been doing his duty by carrying out his mission bravely: fighting against Communism which threatened the whole world order. Was it his fault, was it the fault of any of them, if Hitler had hijacked so much nobility of spirit to establish the domination of his so-called superior race, even if it meant apocalypse?

The Pole had been broken by his father, but that was the fate of all the vanquished. The Cardinal, without admitting it to himself, felt humiliated by a tragedy in which he had not after all taken part himself. But his father... That feeling of humiliation galvanized him in his permanent combat on behalf of the purity of Catholic doctrine. There lay his mission – he would not be part of the lineage of the vanquished. The only superior race, the only one that could win, was the race of men of faith. The Church was the last rampart against the modern apocalypse.

Breczinsky had become hateful to him, and needed to be got rid of. Catzinger would find no peace as long as he had in front of his eyes that last witness to his own history and that of his father.

For the time being, his energies were mobilized by one dossier, and one alone: the canonization of Escrivá de Balaguer that was to take place in a few months' time. The founder of Opus Dei had managed to consolidate the edifice founded on the divinity of Christ. Thanks to men of his mettle, the Church could carry on resisting.

But he'd still need to make up his mind to perform a miracle. These things can be arranged.

336

89

The desert of the Abruzzi was just as Nil wished – and no doubt just as the thirteenth apostle had experienced it after his flight from Pella, as Jesus had experienced it after his encounter with John the Baptist on the Jordan. The hermit had pointed to a straw mattress in the corner.

"It's the one that Beppe uses when he spends the night here. That boy has grown attached to me as if I were the father he never knew. He doesn't talk, but we manage to communicate all right."

Then he had said no more, and for several days they lived together in complete silence, sharing without a word their meals of cheese, herbs and bread on the terrace, where the mountain spoke its own language to them.

Nil realized that the desert is first and foremost an attitude of mind and soul. One that he could have experienced just as easily at the Abbey, or in the centre of a city. A certain quality of inner asceticism, an abandonment of all the usual landmarks of social life. The extraordinary poverty of the place soon became a matter of indifference to him, to such a point that he soon ceased even to notice it. His contact with the hermit meant that he was soon sensing a very strong, warm presence, of an unsuspected richness. To begin with, he perceived it as coming from outside, from nature, from his companion. Then he realized that it was linked to another presence inside him. And that if he became attentive to it, contenting himself with observing it before welcoming it, nothing else would ever matter again. There would be no more discomfort, nor loneliness, nor fear.

Nor, perhaps, any memory of the past and its wounds.

* * *

One day when Beppe had just left them after replenishing their supplies, the hermit smoothed down his beard and turned to him.

"Why do you still wonder what my words of welcome meant, when I said: 'I was expecting you, my son'?"

This man could read him like an open book.

"But... you didn't know me, you hadn't been informed of my arrival, you don't know anything about me!"

"*I do know you*, my son, and know things about you that you yourself are unaware of. You'll see – living here you will acquire the vision of inner Awakening, the one that Jesus possessed when he left the desert and that enabled him to see Nathanael under the fig tree, even though this was outside his field of vision. I know what you have suffered, and I know why. You are seeking the most precious treasure, the one to which not even the Churches possess the key, and to which they can merely indicate the way – when they don't actually block access to it."

"Do you know who the thirteenth apostle was?"

The hermit gave a silent laugh, and there was a sparkle dancing in his eyes.

"And do you think one always needs to know facts in order to be acquainted with realities?"

He allowed his gaze to wander across the valley where the high-altitude clouds cast moving shadows. Then he spoke as if he were addressing someone other than Nil.

"Everything can be known only from within. Abstract knowledge is merely a rind, you need to get past it to reach the heart, the sapwood of real knowledge. This is true of minerals, plants, living beings – and it is also true of the Gospels. The ancients called this inner knowledge 'gnosis'. Many of them were intoxicated by the excessively rich nourishment they found in it, it went to their heads, and they thought themselves superior to every one else, *catharoi*. The person you meet in the Gospels – the same person you experience in prayer – is neither superior nor inferior to you: he is with you. The real presence of Jesus is so strong that it joins you to everyone but also separates you from everyone. Already you have started to experience this, and here you will not live on anything but that presence. That is why you came.

"I was expecting you, my son…"

90

Rome observed with indifference as the Society of St Pius V was taken in hand by Cardinal Emil Catzinger. In the name of the Pope, he himself appointed the Rector who would succeed the Neapolitan Alessandro Calfo, who had suddenly died at home without having been able to transmit the coffin-shaped ring, which recalled his formidable task as the guardian of the Catholic Church's most precious secret: that of the real tomb in which the bones of the crucified man of Jerusalem still rest.

He chose this rector from among the Eleven, and wanted him to be young, so that he would have the strength to combat the enemies of the man who had become Christ and God. For those enemies would soon be lifting their heads again, just as they had always done, ever since it had been necessary to wipe out the person and especially the memory of the impostor, the so-called thirteenth apostle.

As he slipped the precious jasper onto his ring finger, he smiled at the deep black eyes, as tranquil as a mountain lake. Antonio's only thought was that, now that he was Rector, he was finally safe from Opus Dei and its tentacles. For a second time the son of *Oberstleutnant* Herbert von Catzinger, the ward of the Hitler Youth, was offering him his protection – but he would still be requesting his dividends. In the coffers of the Society, Antonio found a file marked *confidenziale*, in the Cardinal's name. If he had opened it, he would have seen documents concerning his powerful protector, documents bearing a swastika at their heading. Not all of them went back to before May 1945.

But he didn't open it, and handed it over in person to His Eminence, who in his presence fed it into the shredder of his office in the Congregation for the Doctrine of the Faith.

In his severe black cassock, Breczinsky watched the monotonous and gloomy Polish countryside go by. He had been apprehended in his office in the stacks by Antonio in person, and bundled away to the central station in Rome. Since that moment he had been incapable of thinking. After crossing the whole of Europe, the train was now speeding across the plains of his native land: he was surprised to discover that he felt no emotion. Suddenly he sat up, and his round glasses hazed over with tears. He had just raced past a small provincial station: Sobibor, the concentration camp around which the *Anschluss* division had regrouped before embarking on its hasty retreat westwards. Pushing ahead of it one last convoy of Poles, who were to be exterminated in this very spot, just before the Red Army arrived. In this convoy had been all that was left of his family.

A few days earlier, a young priest, Karol Wojtyla by name, scorning the danger, had taken him by his hand and hidden him in his cramped apartment in Cracow, to shelter him from the round-up organized by the German officer who had just succeeded Herbert von Catzinger, killed by Polish partisans.

Breczinsky would be getting off at the next station: it was there, a small Carmelite nunnery far from the world, that he had been placed under house arrest by His Eminence Cardinal Catzinger. The mother superior had been sent a letter bearing the coat of arms of the Vatican: the priest they were sending her must never be allowed any visitors, nor could he correspond with the outside world in any way whatsoever.

He needed care and rest. Probably for a long time.

91

The audience rose to its feet as one: for Lev Barjona's last concert in Rome, the Academy of Santa Cecilia was filled to bursting. The Israeli was going to perform the third concerto for piano and orchestra by Camille Saint-Saëns, and in the first movement he would be showing off his panache, in the second the extraordinary fluidity of his fingers, and in the third his sense of humour.

As usual, the pianist came on stage without deigning to glance at the audience, and went straight over to the piano stool. When the conductor motioned that he was ready, his face suddenly became set, and he played the first solemn, pompous chords that announce the romantic theme, introduced by the orchestral *tutti*. In the second movement, he was dazzling. The acrobatic twists and turns spun magically under his fingers, the notes came rippling out, each of them distinct in spite of the infernal tempo he had adopted right from the start. The contrast between this perilous quicksilver and the total impassivity of his face fascinated the audience, which, after the last chord, gave him one of those standing ovations with which the Romans never fail to acclaim those who have conquered their hearts.

There was a general expectation that, as was his habit, Lev would immediately vanish off into the wings, without granting the audience the traditional encores. So the audience was greatly surprised when he advanced to the edge of the stage and signalled for a microphone. He took it and looked up, dazzled by the footlights. He seemed to be gazing far away, beyond the audience which had suddenly relapsed into silence, beyond even the city of Rome. His face was no longer set, but wore an expression of gravity that was unusual in such a relentless charmer. The scar that vanished into his mop of blond hair heightened the dramatic character of what he was about to say.

It was very brief.

"To thank you for your warm welcome, I am now going to play you the second *Gymnopédie* by Erik Satie, a marvellous French composer. I especially dedicate it this evening to another Frenchman, a pilgrim of the absolute. And to an American pianist who died tragically, but whose memory will never leave me. He himself performed this music from within, since, like Satie, he had believed in love, and he had been betrayed."

While Lev, his eyes closed, seemed to abandon himself to the perfection of this simple melody, a man at the back of the hall watched him with a smile. His muscular body was hunched up, and he rather stuck out among the poised and elegant women around him.

"Those Jews!" Mukhtar Al-Quraysh was thinking. "They're all so sentimental!"

With the death of Alessandro Calfo, his mission was coming to an end. He had had the satisfaction of eliminating the American with his own hands. As for the other man, he had vanished, and Mukhtar had still not picked up his trace. It was just a question of time. The next day he would go back to

Cairo. He would report to the Council of Hamas and receive his instructions. The Frenchman *must* be got rid of: to track him down, Mukhtar needed help, financial and practical. Lev had just publicly declared his admiration for the infidel, he could no longer count on him.

As for Sonia, she was now out of a job. It wouldn't be long before he brought her over to Cairo. Wearing a black veil, her gorgeous shape would do him honour. He'd keep her for himself. After passing through the hands of a perverse prelate from the Vatican, she must know how to do things that the Prophet might well have condemned if he had been aware of them. The Koran merely states: "Women are a field to be ploughed: go up and down that field and plough it as you wish." He would plough Sonia. Completely indifferent to the delicate music that was emerging from Lev's fingers, he felt the blood swelling his virility.

92

Three weeks had gone by since Nil had arrived in the Abruzzi, and he felt as if he had spent his whole life in these solitudes. Little by little he had told the hermit his whole story: his arrival in Rome, Leeland's attitude up until his dramatic confession, the meeting with Lev Barjona, the apostolic letter that had been so hard to track down and its discovery in the secret Vatican collection…

The old man was smiling.

"I know that this changes nothing in your life and the direction it is taking. It's the truth that you have always sought; you have found the rind, you now need to deepen that understanding in prayer. You must never bear a grudge against the Catholic

Church. She does what she has always done, that for which every Church is designed: to win power and then keep it at all costs. A monk of the Middle Ages defined it realistically: *casta simul et meretrix*, the chaste whore. The Church is a necessary evil, my son: its continual abuse of power must not lead you to forget that it is the repository of a treasure, the person of Jesus. And that without the Church you would never have known him."

Nil knew he was right.

Intrigued by this newcomer who so much resembled his adoptive father – including even his white hair – Beppe started coming up to the hermitage a little more frequently than usual. He would sit next to Nil on the dry stone parapet of the terrace, and their eyes would meet just once. Then the Frenchman would perceive nothing more than his breathing, regular and calm. Suddenly he would get up, give a nod, and disappear down the forest path.

One day, Nil said to him:

"Beppe, will you do me a favour? I need to get this letter to Father Calati in Camaldoli. Can you do that for me? You have to give it to him in person."

Beppe nodded and slipped the letter into the inside pocket of his sheepskin jacket. It was addressed to Rembert Leeland, Via Aurelia. Nil told him briefly about his arrival at the hermitage, the life he was leading in it, the happiness that for so long had evaded him and that seemed, here, to have become a reality. Finally, he asked after his news, and whether Nil would need to go back to Rome to meet up with him.

A few days later, the Pope opened this letter and read it out twice in front of Catzinger, who had handed it on to him as instructed.

Wearily, the Pope placed the letter on his knees. Then he looked up at the Cardinal, still standing respectfully in front of him.

"This French monk you have told me about – in what way do you think he is a danger to the Church?"

"He casts doubt on the divinity of Christ, Most Holy Father, and in a particularly pernicious way. He needs to be silenced and sent back to the solitude of his abbey, which he never should have left."

The Pope allowed his chin to drop onto his white cassock. Christ would never be known in all his truth. Christ was ahead of us: we could only set out in search of him. To seek him, St Augustine had said, was already to find him. Ceasing to seek for him was to lose him.

Without raising his head, he muttered a few words, and Catzinger had to prick up his ears to follow them.

"Solitude... I think he possesses solitude, Your Eminence, and I envy him... yes, I envy him. 'Monk', you know, comes from *monos*, meaning one, alone – or unique. He has found the one essential thing, of which Jesus spoke to Martha, the sister of Mary and Lazarus. Leave him to his solitude, Your Eminence. Leave him with Him whom he has found there."

Then he added, in an even more imperceptible voice:

"That is why we are here, is it not? The reason why the Church exists. So that, within it, a few may find what you and I are seeking."

Catzinger raised an eyebrow. What *he* was seeking was to solve one problem after another, ensure the Church endures, protect it from its enemies. *Sono il carabiniere della Chiesa*, I am the policeman of the Church, his predecessor of illustrious memory, Cardinal Ottaviani, had said one day.

The Pope seemed to emerge from his reverie, and made a sign.

"Take me over to that machine in the corner. If you don't mind."

Catzinger pushed the wheelchair towards the little shredder placed in front of a waste-paper bin half-filled with confetti. As the Pope, with his trembling hand, couldn't switch the machine on himself, Catzinger deferentially pressed the button.

"Thank you… No, it's all right, I can do that myself."

The shredder spat out some shreds of confetti that fell into the basket filled with other secrets, which the Pope preserved as mere memories in his still astonishingly perspicacious brain.

"There's only one secret, and that's God's. He's a lucky man, that Father Nil. Yes, a really lucky man."

93

In the middle of the night, Nil was woken by an unusual noise, and lit a candle. Lying on his straw mattress, his eyes closed, the old hermit was uttering a low throaty rattle.

"Father, are you feeling unwell? We need to get Beppe, we need…"

"Don't worry, my son. I just need to leave the shore, to slip into deeper waters – and the moment has come."

He opened his eyes, and enveloped Nil in a gaze of great kindness.

"You will stay on here – it is the place set aside for you since time began. As the beloved disciple did, you will lean your head towards Jesus, so as to listen. Your heart alone will be able to hear him, but every day it is a little more alert. Listen, and do nothing but listen: he will lead you along the path. He is a sure guide, you can place all your trust in him. Men have betrayed you: *he* will never do so."

He made a final effort:

"Beppe... look after him, he's the son that I am entrusting to you. He is as pure as the water that flows down from this mountain."

In the morning, the light struck the crest on the opposite slope. When the sun's flames enveloped the hermitage, the old hermit murmured the name of Jesus and breathed his last.

That same day, Nil and Beppe buried him in a sheer cliff face which perhaps resembled – thought Nil – those overlooking Qumran. In silence they returned to the hermitage.

Once they were on the little terrace, Beppe seized the arm of Nil as he stood there motionless, bowed his head before him and gently placed the monk's hand on his head of thick curly hair.

Days followed days and nights followed nights. Time stopped, and seemed to have assumed another dimension. Nil's memory had not yet healed, but he suffered less and less from the anguish that had oppressed him throughout those terrible days that he had spent trying to track down some illusion of the truth.

Truth did not lie in the letter of the thirteenth apostle, nor in the Fourth Gospel. It was not contained in any text, however sacred it might be. It lay beyond words printed on paper, words uttered by human mouths. It lay in the heart of silence, and silence slowly took possession of Nil.

Beppe had transferred to him all the adoration he had shown to the old hermit while the latter was still alive. When he came, always without warning, they would sit together on the edge of the terrace or in front of the fire in the hearth. Nil gently read him the Gospel and told him the story of Jesus, as the thirteenth apostle had done for Yokhanan in days gone by.

One day he had a sudden inspiration. He traced an im-material cross on the forehead, lips and heart of the young man. Spontaneously, Beppe showed him his tongue, and his fingers lightly grazed that too with the sign of death and life.

The next day, Beppe came very early in the morning. He sat on the straw mattress, gazed at Nil with his tranquil eyes and murmured, in a clumsy whisper:

"Father… Father Nil! I… I want to learn to read. So that I can study the Gospel by myself."

Beppe could speak. From his overflowing heart, the words spilt out.

This led to a slight change in Nil's life. Now Beppe came to see him almost every day. They would sit down at the window, and on the tiny table Nil would open the book. In a few weeks, Beppe was able to read it, only stumbling over the complicated words.

"You can always take St Mark's Gospel," Nil told him. "It's the simplest, the most limpid, and the one closest to what Jesus said and did. One day, later on, I'll teach you Greek. You'll see, it's not so difficult, and if you read it aloud, you'll hear what Jesus's first disciples said about him."

Beppe fixed his grave eyes on him.

"I'll do what you tell me: you are the father of my soul."

Nil smiled. The thirteenth apostle, too, must have been the father of the souls of those Nazoreans who had fled the very first Church.

"There is only one father of your soul, Beppe. The one who has no name, whom nobody can know, of whom we know nothing except the fact that Jesus called him *abba*: father."

94

On this October morning, St Peter's Square was in festive array: the Pope was to proclaim the canonization of the founder of Opus Dei, Escrivá de Balaguer. On the façade of the basilica, the centre of Christianity, a huge portrait of the new saint was displayed in front of the assembled throng. With his mischievous eyes he seemed to be looking down at them ironically.

Standing at the right of the Pope, Cardinal Catzinger was radiant with joy. This canonization had assumed a particular significance for him. To begin with, it marked his personal victory over the members of Opus Dei, whom he had forced to come and eat out of his hands for years while the process of beatification of their hero proceeded. Now they were in his debt, which placed him somewhat further out of reach of their never-ending schemes. Catzinger was pleased at the fine trick he had just played on them and, for a while at least, he now had the upper hand.

In addition, it meant that Antonio was safe from any pressure from Balaguer's Spaniards. It was a matter of importance to him that the Society of St Pius V be governed with a firm hand, to avoid the trials it had undergone while Calfo was rector.

Finally – and this was not the least of the reasons for feeling happy on this particular day – the Pope (who was increasingly incapable of making himself understood) had entrusted to him the task of giving the homily. He would take advantage of this opportunity to set out his programme for governing the Church, in front of the TV cameras of the whole world.

For one day he would indeed govern the ship of Peter. Not surreptitiously, as he had been doing for years. But openly, in broad daylight.

Mechanically, he lifted the hem of the Pope's chasuble: the tremors that shook the Pope kept making it slip off in a far from telegenic way. And to disguise his gesture, he smiled at the camera. His blue eyes, his white hair, cut quite a dash on screen. He straightened: the camera was pointing at him.

The Church was eternal.

Lost in the throng, a young man was gazing mockingly at the spectacle of the Church's pomp. His curly hair gleamed in the sunshine, and his jacket, the type worn by Abruzzi peasants, did not stand out: Catholic delegations from the whole world, in their national costumes, made splashes of colour in St Peter's Square.

His hands were not free: clutched to his chest, they were hugging a round leather bag.

Nil had given it to him the night before. He was worried: in the village, where any stranger was immediately spotted, a man had been seen asking questions. He was definitely not from these mountains, nor even an Italian: too many muscles, not enough of a paunch – and the villagers' eyes were infallible. Given the way things are in a village of the Abruzzi, the rumour had soon reached Beppe's ears. He had mentioned it to Nil, who had sensed all his old anxieties reawakening.

Could it be possible that they were looking for him, even here?

The very next day, he had entrusted Beppe with his bag. It contained the results of years' worth of study. In particular, it contained the copy of the epistle that he had made. From memory, admittedly, but he knew that it was faithful to the text that he had briefly held in his hands in the Vatican's secret collection.

His life had no further importance, his life no longer belonged to him. Like the thirteenth apostle, like many others, perhaps he would die for having preferred Jesus to the Christ-God. He knew this, and accepted it in advance, his heart filled with peace.

His only regret was a sin against the Spirit that he would not be able to confess to any priest: he would have liked, in spite of everything, to see Jesus's real tomb in the desert. He knew that this desire was merely a pernicious illusion, but he could not extinguish it within himself. He would have liked to excavate the vast sandy wastes between Israel and the Red Sea. To discover the tumulus, lost in the midst of an abandoned Essene burial ground unknown to anyone. To go where the thirteenth apostle had expressly stated he wanted nobody to go. Even to think of it was a sin: silence had not accomplished its work of purification within him. He would struggle, with all his strength, to eliminate from his mind this thought that kept him from Jesus's presence, which he encountered every day in prayer.

Between a pile of bones and reality, the choice was easy.

But he needed to be careful. Beppe would go alone to Rome and entrust the bag to someone in whom he had every confidence.

Cardinal Emil Catzinger concluded his homily amid thunderous applause, and modestly sat down again at the Pope's right hand.

Furtively, Beppe lowered his head and respectfully grazed the bag with his lips.

The truth had not been erased from the face of the earth.

The truth would be transmitted. And one day it would resurface.

* * *

Hidden under Bernini's colonnade, Mukhtar Al-Quraysh did not take his eyes off the young man. He had located the village. The infidel must be somewhere hereabouts, in the mountains.

He would just need to follow this peasant from the Abruzzi, with his naive expression.

He would lead him to his prey.

He smiled: Nil had succeeded in escaping from the men in the Vatican, but he would not escape from him. You do not escape the Prophet, blessed be his name.

Just as I was leaving the hermitage, I could not refrain from asking yet another question:

"Father Nil, aren't you afraid of the man who's looking for you?"

He reflected for several moments before replying:

"He's not a Jew. Ever since the Temple was destroyed, they have been torn apart by a deep sense of despair: the promise was in vain, the Messiah will not come. But God remains a living reality for them. However, Muslims know nothing of Him – except that he is unique, greater than everything, and that he judges them. The tenderness and proximity of the God of the prophets of Israel are still foreign to them. Faced with an infinite but infinitely distant Judge, Jewish despair has become transformed, in their case, into an anguish they cannot master. And some of them still need violence to exorcise the fear of a nothingness that God cannot fill. He is probably a Muslim."

With a smile, he added:

"Intimacy with the God of love destroys fear for ever. Perhaps he is indeed hot on my heels? If he wants to drag me down into his own nothingness, he will still never appease the anguish dwelling within him."

He took my two hands in his own.

353

"Seeking to know the person of Jesus means becoming another thirteenth apostle. Anyone can be a successor to that man. Will you be one of them?"

Ever since, in my Picardy of forests, or fertile fields and taciturn men, the sound of Nil's last words has never left me.

When they echo in my ear, I start to feel a longing for the desert.

The Truth Behind
The Thirteenth Apostle

Where does fact end and fiction begin in *The Thirteenth Apostle*?

History is not an exact science, it only manages to achieve increasingly refined *hypotheses*. As time goes on, some of these findings settle down and are sometimes termed "definitive". But in the field of history nothing is established for ever: the discovery of new sources, or simply a new perspective on events, can call into question an almost official historical truth which had been long-accepted by everyone.

The novelist follows his investigation up to the point that history has reached. He then imagines what history would have become, *if...* But he must do so in strict coherence with preceding events. If what he writes is not *real*, it must be *realistic*. Historical fiction does not create an entirely new world, as science fiction does: it imagines what the world could have become, if a minuscule grain of sand had oriented history – as we know it – along a different path. It must be plausible hypothesis, coherent with what we know from other sources.

That is how I constructed *The Thirteenth Apostle*. We know for a fact that this man existed. Did he write an epistle to tell his truth about Jesus the Nazorean? There is no trace of such a letter, but he *could have* written one, which *could have* been transmitted to us, as it was the case for many other works left behind by the founders of Christianity.

What would have been the content of such an epistle? Obviously we can't tell, but a good knowledge of first-century history allows us to imagine it.

Fiction, then, is an extension of history. Like a flower bud opening out and blossoming, the hidden facet of world events is revealed at the novelist's touch. He makes us imagine, but also pushes open new doors, possibly for a new generation of scholars to go through one day. I have attempted to give body, voice, sensitivity to this man whose memory the primitive Church sought to annihilate at all costs. *The shadow of the thirteenth apostle* looms over my novel, and beyond his that of another man, Jesus the Nazorean, whom he had loved more than anyone else, of whom he had been the most intimate and loyal disciple.

At least, that's what he claims.

Twelve Apostles?

The literature we possess on Jesus – the man, his personality and the events which led to his crucifixion – is remarkably vast and detailed. We know a great deal more about him than about most of the great figures of antiquity.[1] His death, for example, is precisely dated 7th April 30 AD,[2] a Friday, at three in the afternoon: such a degree of precision is most rare for this period. We know its official reasons, as well as the true reasons hidden within the texts. The events of the final weeks of his life unfold in front of our eyes as in a film, orchestrated by four more or less scrupulous directors.

This literature – the New Testament – was written in stages, over a period which began around 50 AD and ended around 100

---

1. With the exception of Julius Caesar, Cicero and Marcus Aurelius, who have left us biographical fragments.
2. Or 3rd April 33 – but most scholars tend towards the 30 date.

AD. The New Testament itself is not a historical document, but a *polemical*, even *political* one. It was written during a time when the Church was establishing itself, transforming Jesus into God and inventing a legitimacy for itself in relation to the Judaism it had derived from and the other religions of the Roman Empire.

The choice of twelve men among those who were following him can be traced back to Jesus himself. Why this number? Because it was immediately recognizable for the Jewish crowds of the time: twelve, like the twelve sons of Jacob, ancestors of the twelve tribes of mythical Israel. It is interesting to note that Jesus never once gives them the title of "apostle", nor even that of "disciple".[3] In his lifetime he simply called them "the Twelve",[4] and it is only later that the expression "twelve apostles" starts to appear in texts.[5]

In fact, the title of apostle became a kind of trademark within the Church. Composing his Acts of the Apostles between 80 and 90 AD, Luke describes the choice of the twelfth apostle who will replace Judas, who died in mysterious and tragic circumstances. For the election of the replacement there is only one criterion: he must be chosen from among those "who have been with us the whole time the Lord Jesus went in and out among us, beginning from John's baptism to the time when Jesus was taken up from us".

That is to say from the time of his leaving the desert until his death.

3. All the uses of this term seem to denote, to differing degrees, the hallmark of the primitive Church. See for example Matthew 10:24, 10:42, 13:52, 26:18, Luke 14: 26–27, etc.

4. The expression "the Twelve" in the New Testament can be traced back to Jesus, although the phrase ascribed to him by John 6:70 ("Have I not chosen you, the Twelve?") indicates the fierce hatred the writers of the fourth gospel felt towards the "apostles".

5. Matthew 10:2, voicing here the viewpoint of the Church in the latter half of the first century.

This condition alone is enough to validate the candidacy for the title of apostle and the authority that comes with it.[6] This title is so honorific that Paul of Tarsus – even though he had not known Jesus and therefore not fulfilled the essential condition – would later acquire it by force, in order to feel better equipped in the fierce conflict which would pit him against the legitimate apostles.

But for the barons of the Church, there cannot be more than twelve apostles. Not one more.

A Thirteenth Apostle?

The crucial moment then is when Jesus emerges from his desert solitude, after a long period of meditation. Before this experience he had been a pious Jew among many; afterwards he becomes a different man, filled with a new-found sense of charisma and the promise of a new world. It is at this precise moment that five men meet him. The so-called gospel of St John provides an astonishing account of this meeting:

> The next day John was there again with two of his disciples... they followed Jesus... they went and saw where he was staying, and spent that day with him. It was about the tenth hour. Andrew, Simon Peter's brother, was one of the two who heard what John had said and who had followed Jesus.[7]

One of the two: who is the other disciple, the one who tells the story? He is an apostle, since he has met Jesus as he left the desert, and will follow him to the end. Along with Andrew, he is even the first one to have met him, and will be the last to see him – on the cross. Despite this, he will never appear on the official lists of the

---

6. Matthew 19:28 puts into the mouth of Jesus the following words: "when the Son of Man sits on his glorious throne, you who have followed me will also sit on twelve thrones, judging the twelve tribes of Israel".
7. John 1:35–40.

apostles. Nor in any other New Testament text, except the fourth gospel, of which he is the initiator.

This man who could have – more than anyone else – laid claim to the title of apostle, refers to himself as the *beloved disciple of Jesus*. This is the man whom I refer to as the *thirteenth apostle*, without being able to name him, since even his very name has been cancelled from memory.

He reappears at the beginning of the final week of Jesus's life in Jerusalem and describes the dramatic events of this period so vividly, warmly and precisely that he must have been an eyewitness. But before investigating this account, we must go back and recapitulate what we know about this man.

The Rediscovery of a Suppressed Eyewitness

In the 1980s Raymond E. Brown, a Catholic scholar, officially recognized that the *beloved disciple* was definitely a thirteenth apostle, distinct from St John the Evangelist: "It is evident that the *disciple beloved by Jesus* was a historical figure and a companion of Jesus."[8]

This unknown witness, a kind of "man in the iron mask" of the primitive Church, appears eight times in the text of the fourth gospel, either explicitly or in unequivocal allusions. Chapter 21 for example describes Peter and six other disciples' short stay around the lake of Galilee, where they had fled to after the crucifixion. The author gives us the following names: "Simon Peter, Thomas (called Didymus), Nathanael from Cana in Galilee, the sons of Zebedee, and *two other disciples*".[9] Who are those two other disciples? A bit further in text, one of the two emerges from anonymity: "Peter turned and saw that the disciple whom Jesus loved was following them."[10]

8. *The Community of the Beloved Disciple* (Boston, MA: Pauline Press, 1983).
9. John 21:2.
10. John 21:20.

That's him again: *the thirteenth apostle*, and in this scene he is explicitly distinguished from the apostle John, the son of Zebedee, whom tradition labels "the Evangelist".

When Jesus and the four others leave John the Baptist to return to Galilee, the thirteenth apostle does not join them but goes back to Jerusalem, where he lives. He knows the city well; his descriptions in the fourth gospel are exact, colourful and have been confirmed by archaeological excavations. He possesses a house there, situated not far from that of the high priest Caiaphas and in the wealthy western quarter, heavily protected by the Jewish police.[11] As all the villas in the neighbourhood, his is vast and contains, on the first floor, a large "upper room". This is the room in which Jesus will take his last supper, and where the terrorized disciples will hide after the crucifixion of their master, before leaving for Galilee. Some of them will find refuge there again on their return to Jerusalem several weeks later. And it is also there that the miracle of the Pentecost will occur fifty days after Passover.

The thirteenth apostle therefore takes the risk of housing the accomplices of a crucified man, a huge favour to the apostles, with whom he is still on good terms.

But this mutual understanding was not to last long: as we have seen, his name and his very existence have been erased from the New Testament entirely, apart from his narrative in the fourth gospel. When Paul makes three "official visits" to Jerusalem (in 39, 48 and 52 AD), he provides the details of his meetings with the "columns", i.e. those who matter in the nascent Church: the *beloved disciple* is mentioned nowhere, either directly or by allusion. Has he already disappeared from Jerusalem, has he already taken refuge in the silence that has been imposed on him?

If the apostles have pursued him in their hatred of him to the point of annihilating his legacy, he likewise does not think highly

11. These details have been provided by the team of J. Charlesworth, *Jesus and the Dead Sea Scrolls* (New York: Doubleday, 1992).

of them at all: it has been noted that in the fourth gospel the word *apostolos* is never used to refer to the Twelve. Almost as if he had wanted to deny them their official label of authority, he for whom Jesus is the only *apostolos* of God. He describes himself as *mathetes*, a disciple in the Greek philosophical tradition.

A Respectable Local Figure

He is wealthy and owns a large household: it is one of his servants even who discreetly ushers the *rabbi* and his followers into the western quarter, where their Galilean accent and scrawny appearance would have made them immediately noticeable. Jesus has carefully prepared his clandestine entry into the city; a signal has been agreed upon between himself and his friend, and he warns his disciples:

> Go into the city, and a man carrying a jar of water will meet you. Follow him. Say to the owner of the house he enters, "The Teacher asks: where is my guest room, where I may eat the Passover with my disciples?" He will show you a large upper room, furnished and ready.[12]

The anonymous *owner* is the thirteenth apostle, who is treated here as the stranger he has become for the official Church, when this gospel was written forty years after the fact.

And this short passage is the *only* one in which the shadow of this man briefly appears in the Synoptic Gospels:[13] the apostles overlooked this detail in their bid to cancel him from history – the water carrier, the servant of the *owner* who was one of theirs, their brother, before saving their lives. Forty years later he has become a stranger to them, an enemy to be mentioned fleetingly.

12. Mark 14:13–15.
13. I.e. the three gospels of Matthew, Mark and Luke (as opposed to the fourth gospel).

This detail is authenticated by those who report it – because they cannot do otherwise. It shows that a trusting, friendly, intimate relationship had been established between Jesus and him, which must have incurred fierce jealousy on the part of the Twelve.

He is not only wealthy, but also well connected. He has free access to the palace of his neighbour Caiaphas, the highest authority in Israel. The staff there recognize him immediately and let him come and go as he pleases: a regular visitor, as opposed to Peter, who does not dare to enter and stays outside.

> Simon Peter and another disciple were following Jesus. Because this disciple was known to the high priest, he went with Jesus into the high priest's courtyard, but Peter had to wait outside at the door. The other disciple, who was known to the high priest, came back, spoke to the girl on duty there and brought Peter in.[14]

Still no name: but the "*another disciple*" is him – just as on the banks of the Jordan, as on the shore of the lake of Galilee.

And it is he who will introduce Jesus to the State Councillor Nicodemus, the landowner Lazarus and Joseph of Arimathea, who will provide a temporary tomb for Jesus. All of these notables would not have been part of Jesus's social sphere in Jerusalem and he would not have been able to meet them without his friend as an intermediary. They will all play a crucial role in Jesus's final days and they are mentioned *only* in John's gospel. Another testimony to the privileged link which united the Galilean and the man from Jerusalem.

Essenian or Nazorean?

One thing is certain: the thirteenth apostle is, at the moment he first encounters Jesus, a disciple of John the Baptist, like the

14. John 18:15–16.

four Galileans he seems to be consorting with: only the enthusiasm generated by the Baptist's teaching could have temporarily brought closer men from such different social backgrounds as the rich worthy from Jerusalem and the four poor fishermen.

They are therefore all five of them Baptists.

The Baptist movement was a loose collective born out of rejection of the Temple, its cult, its corrupt hierarchy, its compromises with money, power and the Roman occupier. The Baptists had replaced the Temple's sacrificial ritual by immersions into water, which provided internal purification, and were done more or less frequently. The most famous Baptists were the Essenians, who spread all over Israel. Some scholars believe that St John the Baptist had been a member of an Essenian community – perhaps that of Qumran – before leading the life of a hermit on the banks of the Jordan.

So, was the thirteenth apostle not only a Baptist – because he followed St John – but also an Essenian? One cannot prove it conclusively, but numerous clues in the fourth gospel point towards a strong Essenian influence. When in my novel I make him out to be a non-ordained Essenian I am going beyond the strict facts of history, but without straying from the domain of plausibility.

The Nazoreans were one of the Baptist sects. The thirteenth apostle, in the section of John's gospel written by him, is the only one to insist on the fact that Jesus belonged to them: when he describes Jesus's capture by the Temple police, his narrative makes them repeat, with a quite theatrical insistence, that they are looking for "Jesus *the Nazorean*".[15] Again according to him, the sign attached to the cross of the condemned man bore the inscription "Jesus *the Nazorean*, King of the Jews".[16] However, the Synoptic Gospels are categorical: the inscription, according to Roman custom, only included the official ground for the condemnation of the crucified one: "Jesus, King of the Jews". His

15. John 18:5 and 18:7.
16. John 19:19.

affiliation to one or another Jewish sect was absolutely irrelevant to the occupying forces.

These details allow one to advance the following hypothesis about the thirteenth apostle's background: that he, even though he had been an Essenian at one stage, eventually became a Nazorean like Jesus – hence his insistence on labelling him "the Nazorean". And this adherence to the same movement must have been an additional source of friendship and intimacy.

We know very little about the Nazoreans in first-century Palestine: had Jesus not been part of this movement, it would have probably sunk into oblivion entirely. Quite unexpectedly the Nazoreans' legacy can be found in the Koran, which often mentions them and is influenced by their own particular conception of the identity of Jesus.

In the Synoptic Gospels, "Nazorean" has been transformed into "Nazarene" – i.e. an inhabitant of Nazareth – or even "Nazarite" – a reference to an Israelite who has taken a specific ascetic vow. This is one of the most subtle manipulations undertaken by the evangelists. The Nazorean identity of Jesus must at all costs be prevented from passing into posterity, his Baptist roots be erased from the collective memory. The evangelists therefore made him out to be an inhabitant of Nazareth (Jesus *of Nazareth*), even though archaeological investigations have demonstrated that there is no trace of a village in Nazareth in the first century. Furthermore, the contemporary historian, Flavius Josephus, who described Galilee in minute detail, never speaks of a place called Nazareth as a birthplace of Jesus, of whom he had not even heard.

Jesus *of Nazareth*, as usually translated? No: Jesus *the Nazorean*.

A Legitimate Heir?

Since the Church's inception, three men – Peter, James and Paul – are at the front line of a struggle to appropriate Jesus's heritage. In this conflict, James possesses a considerable advantage: he is the *actual brother* of Jesus, his blood brother,[17] his legitimate successor.

To counter this birthright legitimacy, the disciples of the thirteenth apostle will try after the fact to invent a superior claim to legitimacy for their leader: he was chosen *in person* by Christ at the moment of his death. Similar to Paul's claim, in order to legitimize his status of apostle, even though he had never met Jesus, that he was chosen by God.

The result is a short scene which can only be found in the fourth gospel, and with reason: a scene which has become emblematic, been represented everywhere in Christian art and generated countless commentaries.

Jesus has just been crucified. The Synoptics are categorical: a band of Roman soldiers, led by a centurion, surrounded the site of the execution and saw to it that no one would approach the condemned men. There are many spectators, but all "kept their distance" according to the Gospels. One can find a confirmation of this practice in an enjoyable anecdote in Petronius's *Satyricon*,[18] which recounts the lamentations of a widow being prevented by soldiers from taking her husband's crucified body down from the cross: no spectator was allowed to go near the feet of the crosses and speak to those being executed.

However, the fourth gospel contains the account of a dialogue between Jesus and his mother:

Near the cross of Jesus stood his mother, his mother's sister, Mary the wife of Clopas, and Mary Magdalene. When Jesus saw his mother there, and the disciple whom he loved standing

---

17. The question of Jesus's siblings has been the subject of many discussions. From the second century onwards the Church refused to consider them as anything but cousins or Joseph's offspring from a previous marriage. Uncomfortable with this rigid dogmatic position but impelled by textual evidence, most specialists now admit that they were indeed brothers and sisters by birth.
18. *Satyricon* CXII.

nearby, he said to his mother, "Dear woman, here is your son," and to the disciple, "Here is your mother." From that time on, this disciple took her into his home.[19]

An entirely improbable encounter, and no doubt entirely fabricated. Why? Because it was intended to be read as Jesus's testament, addressed to his friend. "From now on *you are my spiritual brother*, since my mother here present is your mother." Spurred on by the need to affirm itself, the community which claims to follow the thirteenth apostle does not shy from calling him the "brother of Jesus", not by birth as in James's case, but due to the final wish of Jesus himself. Brother and heir to Jesus: this community can therefore – to the same extent as James's – stake its claim on Jesus's legacy.

Yes, the thirteenth apostle was present at the West Gate of Jerusalem, in the heavy and oppressing atmosphere of the crucifixion. But no, he did not advance to the foot of the cross. He saw from afar the compassionate gesture of a legionnaire giving some water to the dying man. He saw the thrust of the spear, and he is the only one to report this historically plausible fact, in emotion-laden words. He saw from afar, and he was the only one present out of all the apostles, the others having fled as soon as Jesus was captured in the Olive Garden.

He saw, but it was his community who invented the dialogue at the foot of the cross.

When they add that "From that time on, this disciple took her into his home", it's a lie. He did take her in, but not right after her son's death: a few weeks later and along with other survivors from Jesus's following. They were to find themselves again in the upper room of his house, "along with the women and Mary the mother of Jesus, and with his brothers".[20]

Did he keep her at his side *from then on*? This is traditionally claimed and is quite possible.

19. John 19:25–27.
20. Acts 1:14.

When, in *The Thirteenth Apostle*, I show Mary having followed our hero all the way to Pella, the first stage on his long itinerary, it is very plausible. We know from a reliable source that some Christians sought refuge for a while in the Transjordanian town, with some members of Jesus's family. But we don't know anything more about this: neither Mary nor the *beloved disciple* are ever mentioned. What I have invented is coherent with the facts in our possession – there is an extension of history.

This claim to power legitimized by spiritual inheritance would later give the fourth gospel considerable clout over the years, because its author became gradually assimilated with one of the twelve apostles, John the Evangelist, who would posthumously reap the rewards.

The Initiator of the Fourth Gospel?

Until recently, *the disciple whom Jesus loved* had been identified by the Church as St John of Zebedee, known as the Evangelist.

Who was this apostle John? We know his occupation, that of labourer and fisherman on the lake of Galilee. He must not have gone to school or synagogue, because several months after the death of Jesus, he was arrested along with Peter by the Jewish authorities, who "realized that they were unschooled, ordinary men".[21]

This is around 31 AD: John is then formally described as uncultured, knowing neither how to read nor write. How could this fisherman, who only spoke Galilean Aramaic, be the author of the gospel ascribed to his name, of which numerous passages were written first of all in Greek, and in a supremely elegant, poetic and beautiful Greek to boot? How could he have then gone on to compose the Apocalypse, which demonstrates a profound knowledge of oriental myths and religions, which is replete with cryptic cultural references that baffle modern specialists to this day?

---

21. Acts 4:13.

How would he know the city of Jerusalem so well, its streets and pools, he who only rarely went there to sacrifice in the Temple? And even more importantly, how could he be on familiar terms with Caiaphas – the Jewish state's premier political figure – how could he enter and leave his palace freely (when his companion Peter had to wait outside)?

And there is more: we know from a reliable source that James of Zebedee, John's brother, was decapitated by King Herod in 44 AD.[22] Father M.E. Boismard, with his customary erudition, demonstrated in 1966 that – most probably – John was killed at the same time as his brother. So if John died in 44 AD, when no gospel had yet been written, how could he have been the author of the one attributed to him, which has been dated by everyone to 100 AD, and perhaps even later? How could he have written the Apocalypse, which was finished between 110 and 120 AD?

No, John never wrote anything: he who had only ever handled fishing nets instead of a quill.

But *who* then is the author of the "Gospel according to St John"?[23]

By following the minute, extremely technical work of scholars, I have been lead to the most probable hypothesis: in the origin of the fourth gospel (the definitive version of which came later than the three others), is what I refer to as "the narrative of the thirteenth apostle". He tells us what he has seen during Jesus's stays in Jerusalem, up until the week ending in his crucifixion.

Whoever reads the fourth gospel will notice that there are great differences in vocabulary, style, expression, doctrine, sometimes from one page, paragraph or even line to another. One has to face facts: this is not the work of *one single author*, but of several. Can we be more specific?

22. Acts 12:2.
23. I am leaving aside the question of the three epistles attributed to him, as well as the Apocalypse: to discuss this would stray too far from the subject at hand.

One of the most immediately noticeable things about the gospel is the proliferation of small passages of extremely vivid, detailed description. For example, seventy-two hours after the death of Jesus, while everyone is hiding out in the upper room of the house in the western quarter:

> Early on the first day of the week, while it was still dark, Mary Magdalene went to the tomb and saw that the stone had been removed from the entrance. So she came running to Simon Peter and the other disciple, the one Jesus loved, and said, "They have taken the Lord out of the tomb, and we don't know where they have put him!"
>
> So Peter and the other disciple started for the tomb. Both were running, but the other disciple outran Peter and reached the tomb first. He bent over and looked in at the strips of linen lying there, but did not go in. Then Simon Peter, who was behind him, arrived and went into the tomb. He saw the strips of linen lying there, as well as the burial cloth that had been around Jesus's head. The cloth was folded up by itself, separate from the linen.[24]

The visual quality of this short passage is remarkable: we are told it is still dark, that they are running together in the dimness of the dawn of this 9th of April, that the *other disciple* has managed to distance himself from his oafish companion. We can almost hear Peter finally arriving, puffing like a blacksmith's forge. The laundry is described with almost professional precision...

This is the hallmark of the thirteenth apostle, the *other disciple*. The gospels of Mark, Luke and Matthew were compiled belatedly, with numerous alterations, with more or less acknowledged intentions. In these passages of the fourth gospel, nothing has been altered: we have here the testimony of the *only eyewitness* of the events he narrates.

He narrates, he does not interpret. He says what he saw.

24. John 20:1–7.

* * *

Such scenes, taken straight from reality, pervade the fourth gospel. Acquaint yourselves with them and you will immediately recognize the hand of the thirteenth apostle: the aforementioned first encounter (John 1:35 ff.) After that, not many continuous occurrences: Jesus lives in Galilee, his friend does not see him again until he comes to Jerusalem for the major Jewish festivals. So he recounts what has made the greatest impact on him: the scene at the Temple (John 2:13–25), the healing of a paralysed man (John 5) and a blind man (John 9), the episode of the adulterous woman (John 8), the resurrection of Lazarus (John 11) and his hospitality (John 12:1–11)... And right at the beginning the scene of the "miracle" of Cana, where his account would later be reinterpreted by one single sentence – which gives it an entirely different meaning.

Then Jesus goes to Jerusalem, where he dies: the thirteenth apostle finds him again in his own city and does not let him escape his gaze until the very end, until his grave is found empty and the subsequent surprise encounter on the shore of the lake of Galilee.

In my novel, I have called all these bits and pieces, this journalistic record of a first-hand eyewitness, "the letter of the thirteenth apostle". It is not a gospel like that of Mark, which claims to be a biography of Jesus and would inspire the two other Synoptics. No, it's the case of a man remembering the most remarkable events of a friendship established two years previously on the banks of the Jordan.

My hypothesis is that this letter constitutes the initial core of the fourth gospel. In order to understand how, by various retouchings spread across time, the letter of the thirteenth apostle has been modified by successive acts of sugar-coating – going as far as completely transforming the person and personality of Jesus – one must investigate the thirteenth apostle's community.

The Community of the Thirteenth Apostle

Minute research has given us the means to establish what the texts do not say at first hand: around the thirteenth apostle a *community* has formed itself, which has met with a complex destiny. And it's the complexity of the *community of the beloved disciple* which alone helps explain the complexity of the fourth gospel and its apparent contradictions.

The primitive Church is not what we imagine now, a uniform group of people, united by a homogenous conception of Jesus. It comprised several communities, gathered around one apostle or another, who would serve as a rallying point and banner. Paul of Tarsus, in one of his authentic letters, describes the situation well:

> My brothers, some from Chloe's household have informed me that there are quarrels among you. What I mean is this: One of you says, "I follow Paul"; another, "I follow Apollos [a collaborator of Paul]"; another, "I follow Cephas [Peter]"; still another, "I follow Christ."[25]

In other words, several apostles had founded their communities, which "belonged" to their founders.

The Acts of the Apostles describe three of these communities, which are opposed to one another in violent skirmishes: that of Peter, a majority which the old ruler controls with an iron fist, up until his final eviction from Palestine. He will then be replaced in Jerusalem by James, Jesus's brother, who little by little takes charge of what will later be called (using a term too general to be exact) the Judaeo-Christians.

Then a newcomer enters the stage in quite a dramatic manner: Paul of Tarsus. He displays his disdain for the official apostles: "As for those who seemed to be important – whatever they were

---

25. 1 Corinthians 1:11–12.

makes no difference to me."[26] Numerous communities under his authority will be born all around the Mediterranean Basin.

A fourth community has been discovered in Palestine,[27] the one that was formed around the thirteenth apostle. This community, just like its founder, has been erased from the Church's memory: a meticulous textual examination does however allow one to get an idea of his tortuous journey.

The first to rally round the *beloved disciple* would be the Jews who had come to Jesus. It is no doubt to this initial group that he will transmit his memories of the man he knew: they constitute what I called his *letter*. His testimony will be integrated into the community's successive and evolving structures. Indeed, the community exists out in the open, in the midst of a general climate of turmoil difficult to imagine today, characteristic of the Jewish context of the period. We see it clashing with all the pressure groups intermingling around it.

The first clash will happen with Peter and his people, who claim to be the sole representatives of the "correct teaching". The opposition between the Twelve and the thirteenth apostle has been violent; we have several accounts of this in the fourth gospel.

Then there is the confrontation with Paul's disciples, Jews of Greek origin. Caught between these two groups, which fought violently during the 48 AD assembly in Jerusalem,[28] the community keeps its distance from their struggles.

I have described this crucial assembly in chapter 28 of *The Thirteenth Apostle*. And when I imagine that it is on this day that a permanent rift occurs between our hero, his community and the rest of the nascent Church, I do not have any historical proof as such – but it is entirely plausible.

Rejected by the Church, the community of the thirteenth

26. Galatians 2:6.
27. See the work of Raymond E. Brown, mentioned above.
28. Acts 15.

apostle clashes with the Jews, who do not make any distinctions between the various Christian factions and subject it to the mistrust, hatred and exclusion which the early Christians fell victim to on Jewish territory.

Finally there is the encounter with the pagans of the Empire, whose philosophy and strange religions would continue to fascinate nascent Christianity.

Under the pressure of these combined influences, the community of the thirteenth apostle will experience very pronounced internal tensions. Around a central question which the Church will take seven centuries to resolve: the *identity of Jesus*, who will be referred to less and less as *the Nazorean* and increasingly as *Christ* (or *Messiah* in Hebrew). However, this term does not yet imply deification of the friend encountered on the banks of the Jordan. Now the Messiah, Jesus is no longer quite an ordinary man, but still belongs to the ordinary circle of humanity.

The community of the thirteenth apostle is then joined by new members from the Greek territories.[29] Under their influence, Jesus will progressively be identified with God the Creator: he leaves the world of men to be placed on a divine orbit. One can imagine the shock felt by those who wanted to stay faithful to the teachings of the thirteenth apostle: this was a pure and simple denaturation of his testimony. The community therefore splits into three groups:

1) Those who accept the deification of Jesus and join the increasingly dominant Church: it will take another generation for them to assimilate Greek popular philosophy. At the end of the first century they use its vocabulary to cast in stone the divine nature of Jesus: this is the prologue to the fourth gospel. Written

---

29. I am leaving out an important step here, namely that of the encounter with the Samaritans. For further details see my essay, *Jésus et ses héritiers, mensonges et vérités* (France: Albin Michel, 2008).

directly in Greek, this text is one of the highlights of ancient poetry. It describes Jesus having become dematerialized, become the Word of God and creator of the universe: we are miles away from the friend encountered once upon a time on the banks of the Jordan!

2) Those who do not want leave Jerusalem: after the eviction of Peter they join the Judaeo-Christians led by James and his successors.

3) Those who have remained loyal to the thirteenth apostle through thick and thin. Around the year 90 AD, the Acts of the Apostles speak already of a "Nazorean sect",[30] which does not yet distinguish itself fully from Christians in general. Soon after, the annals of Christianity mention them as being heretics, sometimes confusing them with the Ebionites, another heretical sect condemned by the Church.

My hypothesis is that the disciples who remained loyal to the thirteenth apostle can be identified with those Nazoreans which appear as an autonomous movement from the second century onwards, persecuted wherever they went. They will write a gospel of the Nazoreans, which came to the attention of the early Christian scholar Origen before it was destroyed by the dominant Church. Perhaps it can be assimilated to the gospel of the Hebrews, of which some lines have survived. History has been rewritten so skilfully by the Church that it is now difficult to be certain on this point.

But the Nazoreans will be granted posterity from an unexpected source: if one reads the Koran in the original Arabic, one can see that our modern translations often mention "Christians", but the word used in the Koran is *naz'ra*, *Nazorean*. And it is from their conception of Jesus that the Koran derives its own particular understanding of Christianity. We are therefore grateful to the

30. Acts 24:5.

Koran for providing relatively broad documentation on how the seventh-century Nazoreans developed the teachings of the thirteenth apostle on Jesus.

In *The Thirteenth Apostle* I have attempted to recreate this troubled and patchy part of history, from the disappearance of the thirteenth apostle until the reappearance of the Nazoreans in the Koran.

The Community's Farewell

The death of the thirteenth apostle was a considerable blow for those who had stayed loyal to him. His community had even hoped that he would not die. It manifests this mixture of despair and mad hope in the final lines of the fourth gospel:

> Peter turned and saw that the disciple whom Jesus loved was following them. (This was the one who had leant back against Jesus at the supper and had said, "Lord, who is going to betray you?") When Peter saw him, he asked, "Lord, what about him?" Jesus answered, "If I want him to remain alive until I return, what is that to you? You must follow me." Because of this, the rumour spread among the brothers that this disciple would not die. But Jesus did not say that he would not die; he only said, "If I want him to remain alive until I return, what is that to you?" [31]

This same community solemnly attests that all that has been preserved of him does correspond to his own testimony, what he has seen with his very eyes:

> This is the disciple who testifies to these things and who wrote them down. We know that his testimony is true. [32]

---

31. John 21:20–23.
32. John 21:24.

By doing so, they are vigorously resisting those who have transformed Jesus first into Christ and then into God: they have managed to insert their own statement into the text of the Bible. It contradicts the previous statement:

> But these are written that you may believe that Jesus is the Christ, the Son of God, and that by believing you may have life in his name.

Several lines apart, these two contradicting proclamations eloquently illustrate the tortuous destiny of a group of people led by *the one who saw*. His account has been preserved in the final text of the fourth gospel: the different strata cover and mingle with one another, but nothing crucial has disappeared. This must be seen as a witness to the thirteenth apostle's exceptional aura of influence. Fiercely committed to his disappearance, his enemies did not dare touch his testimony. By amending it to the point of betrayal, they paid him the best kind of homage: thanks to them we know, like Father Nil (the protagonist of my novel), that truth always resurfaces in the end.

The Legacy of the Thirteenth Apostle

Research into the historical figure of Jesus has made leaps and bounds in the last fifty years. I have contributed to this research by publishing first *Dieu malgré lui, nouvelle enquête sur Jésus*[33] in 2001 and then *Jésus et ses héritiers, mensonges et vérités*[34] in 2008: in the present postface I have had to limit myself to a brief and very incomplete summary of these recent works. The burning question of the betrayal of Jesus and the roles played by Judas and Peter remain unanswered. I refer the reader to those two publications. All the evidence of what he or she has read here can be found there: the plot around Peter and the thirteenth

33. Published by Robert Laffont, 358 pages.
34. Published by Albin Michel, 150 pages.

apostle, the assassination of Judas by Peter… This is not fiction, but the result of a hypothesis founded on meticulous research. The outcome of this research will surprise more than one: I vouch for its historical pertinence.

However, making the epistle of the thirteenth apostle the treasure of the Templar Knights is pure invention on my part, and this idea has entertained me greatly. As for the events happening in the corridors of the Vatican, my experience of the Holy City permits me to say that my depiction actually tones down reality.

* * *

For nineteen centuries, an *official version* of events has been imposed on Western Christianity, based on a skewed reading of the texts. State-sanctioned lies have enabled a civilization – our civilization – to evolve and endure to this day.

At a time when traditional Churches appear to be entering a prolonged state of agony, plunging this civilization into deep uncertainty about its own founding values, scholars are freeing themselves of the weight of official history and gaining a new and refreshing perspective on Jesus. I would like to see in this more than simple coincidence: the promise for the West of a new hope, which has been sorely lacking of late.

Prisoner of God
Michel Benoît

ISBN 978-1-84688-052-0 • 384 pp • £8.99

A brilliant student with a promising career ahead of him as a biologist under the guidance of Nobel Prize-winner Jacques Monod, Michel Benoît decided at the age of twenty-two to follow the path of God and take on monastic orders as Brother Irénée. But after over twenty years of self-sacrifice and a fraught quest for God, Michel was "discharged" by the Church. What happened? What led to the Catholic hierarchy rejecting one of its own?

Prisoner of God is a revolutionary testimony against the Church and its methods, against the brainwashing to which many members are submitted, and the power and influence it exerts across a broad spectrum of society. It is also an account of the mysterious world of the abbeys: the monks' everyday life and the way they deal with solitude, silence and sexuality.

I'm twenty-two, with two university degrees, a profession. I do not know it yet, but I have chosen death... In my suitcase, two shirts, such was my conviction that I would not stay more than eight days. It lasted twenty-two years.